W9-BZH-656

SOMEBODY ELSE'S MUSIC

The Gregor Demarkian Books by Jane Haddam

Not a Creature Was Stirring
Precious Blood
Act of Darkness
Quoth the Raven
A Great Day for the Deadly
Feast of Murder
A Stillness in Bethlehem
Murder Superior
Dead Old Dead
Festival of Deaths
Bleeding Hearts
Fountain of Death
And One to Die On
Baptism in Blood
Deadly Beloved
Skeleton Key
True Believers
Somebody Else's Music

SOMEBODY ELSE'S MUSIC

Jane Haddam

ST. MARTIN'S MINOTAUR
NEW YORK

This book is for

Joan Gaffney Burke

Id quot circumiret, circumveniat—

and sometimes we win.

For information, address St. Martin's Press, 175 Fifth Avenue, New York, N.Y. 10010.

www.minotaurbooks.com

Library of Congress Cataloging-in-Publication Data

Haddam, Jane.

Somebody else's music : A Gregor Demarkian Novel / Jane Haddam.—1st ed.

p. cm.

ISBN 0-312-27186-7

1. Women authors—Fiction. I. Title.

PS3566.A613 S66 2002

813'.54—dc21

2001058899

First Edition: June 2002

10 9 8 7 6 5 4 3 2 1

ACKNOWLEDGMENTS

This is the longest book I've ever written, and both the easiest—and the hardest—to write. I'd like to thank my sons for putting up with me during a year when I often woke up having dreams in my characters' heads, and spent dinner discoursing nonstop on Why Americans Are Obsessional About High School. I'd like to thank Joanne McGahagan for her invaluable help getting me information about the area to which I'd transposed a very real town from another state, complete with weather details I'd never have been able to discover on my own without actually going up there and camping out for a winter.

I'd like to thank Don Maass, my agent; and Keith Kahla, my editor; and Teresa Theophano, the world's greatest editorial assistant, for all the help and encouragement it took to write this—and for not fainting dead away when the manuscript arrived looking like a first draft of the *Oxford English Dictionary*.

And finally, I'd like not to thank—I'm not that much of a masochist—but to acknowledge RH, MC, EK, PC, and NW. I've found myself thinking about them, and what they're doing now, at the oddest times. I hope they will take some satisfaction, or something, in knowing they were the inspiration for this book.

"Easily"

—RED HOT CHILI PEPPERS

In the very early hours of that morning, it rained. The water came down in a steady hissing stream, so that, lying in the too-large bed under too many blankets, Liz Toliver was sure she must be hearing snakes. Later, she would wonder what she had been thinking of. It made no sense to buy a king-size bed for just one person. It was like sleeping in the middle of the ocean, too open and free, too abandoned and lost. The water brushed against her fingertips. She jerked away from it. The snakes slid silently through the folds in the sheets. All of a sudden, she felt suffocated.

Slit his throat. Slit his throat. Slit his throat. The words bounced back and forth across the walls, the wooden walls, much too close to her. The snakes were coiled against her skin. Everything was dark. *Slit his throat. Slit his throat. Slit his throat.* Somebody was singing it. The blood was everywhere on the ground. It seemed to be soaking up the dirt. *Slit his throat*, she thought she heard again, but this time the voice was high-pitched and eager, the voice of a woman who can't wait a moment longer to consummate an act of sex.

Slit his throat, something sang again—but then she knew what she was hearing. It was the phone. She sat up in the gray half dark.

"Liz?" Jimmy's voice came through the answering machine. "Liz? Are you there? I thought you were having a nightmare."

Liz reached over to the night table and picked up. "I was having a nightmare. How do you always know when I'm having a nightmare?"

"I don't know. I just do. Are you all right?"

Liz leaned over a little farther and turned on the lamp. She saw the book on the night table—the Hollman High School *Wildcat*, 1969—and looked away from it. The walls of her bedroom were plaster. There were pictures in frames hung in a line across one wall, the original paintings for the covers of all her books.

"Liz?"

"I'm fine. I was thinking of the paintings. Does it make any sense for me to keep the paintings? It seems so—conceited somehow."

"Jesus Christ."

This was the point where, ten years ago, Liz would have lit a cigarette. Instead, she sat up farther and stretched. This week's copy of the *National Enquirer* was lying across the seat of the stuffed chair she kept next to the fireplace. She could see her own face on the cover of it. Her face and the picture of a snake.

"Liz?"

"I'm fine. I'm just not all the way awake yet. I think it's a really bad idea to try to do color on newsprint."

"What?"

"The *Enquirer*."

"What are you *talking* about?"

"Never mind. Like I said, I'm not all the way awake yet. And I've got a headache. And I've got to go into the city to teach this morning. What time is it?"

"Six-fifteen."

"Maybe we're having a snowstorm."

"If you're coming into the city, we could have lunch. At the apartment."

"Good idea. Never mind the fact that there are probably twenty tabloid reporters outside the front door of the building right this minute."

"Not that many. And they know we screw."

"What a delicate way of putting it."

"We'd be married if you'd have me. Listen, Liz, let me ask one more time. Let me send the lawyers down to take care of your mother, okay? There's no point in your doing this."

"She's my mother."

"She also hates you. She always has. And the rest of that town isn't much better, and you know it. And you're worried about the tabloids? Watch what they do when you get down there."

"Watch what they do if I *don't* go down there. Elizabeth Toliver abandons sick mother. I can see it all now."

"Liz? *Listen* to me. Those stories aren't an accident. Somebody's doing that on purpose. Somebody's feeding the *Enquirer* all kinds of—"

"I don't want to have this conversation again."

"Jesus Christ," Jimmy said.

Liz threw off the covers and swung her legs off the bed. "I'll meet you at the apartment at one," she said. "I'm fine. Let me go check on the boys. I know you don't get along with Maris. You don't have to see her if you don't want to. I'm all right."

"I think of you as a saint," Jimmy said. "Sort of the Mother Teresa of public intellectuals. No matter what the provocation, your faith in human nature will never waver—"

"I'm not Mother Teresa, and I'm not a public intellectual. Get off the phone. I'll talk to you this afternoon."

"Somebody *is* planting those stories, Liz."

Liz hung up. Outside, the sky was getting a little lighter. It looked like the gray muslin curtain that hung across the wooden cells in Carmelite monasteries in France. Once, when she and Jimmy were first seeing each other, before she got used to the fact that anything he did showed up on *Entertainment Tonight* as soon as anybody got wind he'd done it, she'd taken him to visit a friend of hers who'd left Vassar their junior year to become a nun. The resulting headlines had been ridiculous—*Jimmy Card Converting to Catholicism!*—but the day had been a good one. That had been the first time she'd realized, deep down, that he was in love with her. Before that, she had tried not to think about what he might be feeling. That had been the first time, too, when she had known that he could hear her thinking, even when they were not in the same room. The monastery where her friend lived was in a little town on the Normandy coast. When the visit was over, Jimmy rented a hotel room overlooking the water, and they fell into bed together, wordlessly, as if they'd thought of nothing else in all their time together. They started at four o'clock in the afternoon and lasted past midnight. They left the window open so that they could hear the sea pounding against the rocks as a storm moved in across the channel. They came to at one, hungry and out of luck. Everything in town was closed. The wind was so strong, it broke the glass in the window they'd left open and sucked a discarded bedspread into the street.

Once, when she was just seventeen, she had beaten her hands bloody against the locked door of an outhouse latrine, beaten and beaten them until her pain and her fear had become so loud in her ears that all she could hear was her own wailing. Above her head, the wind had become a shrieking howl—or maybe it hadn't. Maybe that was just her own head, too, maybe it was all inside her, just herself, trapped where she was in the dark with the snakes covering the floor under the latrine seat and moving, moving steadily, in and among and between each other, trying to climb up to where she was. Out there, though, there was something: that woman's voice singing "*slit his throat slit his throat slit his throat*" and then laughing as the blood poured out on the ground and over the water of the river and into the mouths of snakes, into the mouths of snakes, because the snakes were everywhere then, on the floor, on the seat, on her arms, crawling up into her clothes, crawling inside of her, until she felt full of snakes writhing and jamming and making her bleed.

She was standing next to the chair with the *Enquirer* on it. She had no idea how long she'd been there. Her mouth was very dry.

"I ought to go check on the boys," she said to the air. Then she looked down at the *Enquirer* and made a face.

Shocking Secret Never Before Revealed! the headline said, *Did Elizabeth Toliver* GET AWAY WITH MURDER?

In the picture under the headline, her hair looked the color of spilled ink.

PROLOGUE

"Pinch Me"

—BARENAKED LADIES

"Be True to Your School"

—BEACH BOYS

"Broadway"

—GOO GOO DOLLS

1

Stopping at the newsstand on the corner of West Fourteenth Street and Broadway, Maris Coleman told herself that she was only buying this copy of the *National Enquirer* because she bought everything she saw with Betsy's picture on it. Then she laid two dollar bills down on the newsstand counter and wished that it was not so very bright. It was ten o'clock on the morning of May second, and she was feeling guilty. It was much too late to tell Debra, once again, that she had slept in, and yet she had no other excuse she could give. She had been sleeping in more and more often lately. She had even bought a new alarm clock, a loud one, when it became clear that the old one wasn't going to do her any good. The new one hadn't done her any good either. It rang so loudly that the neighbors complained, later, when they met her in the narrow front hall of the building, everybody trying to squeeze by everybody else to get their mail out of the slotlike metal boxes set into the wall. If they'd come and complained to her at the time, they would have done her some good—but then, nobody in that building ever came to anybody else's door, if they could help it. Or maybe they did, and they just didn't come to Maris's. For some odd reason Maris could never quite determine, the residents of her building were still exactly what they had been on the day she first moved into it, in 1974: young men with jobs on left-wing radical newspapers; young women with jobs in restaurants and dreams of ending up on a soap opera; middle-aged men who taught at the New School; middle-aged women who—what? Maris could see her hand in the hard light from the sun. The skin on the fingers sagged, loose and too soft. Lines ran from between her knuckles to her wrist. Liver spots dotted the surface like freckles. Nobody ever knew what the middle-aged women in the building did. They seemed to be dissolving, like sugar cubes in hot tea.

I should have moved out years ago, Maris thought, taking the paper and folding it, meticulously, into her Coach Legacy small tote. That was, after all, what the people who had been living in that building when she moved in had mostly done. The young men had left their radical newspapers for major publishing houses, or *The Nation*, or law school. The young women had won their soap opera roles and moved uptown or married and moved out to Westchester. The middle-aged men had found better living arrangements by moving in with a friend from the sociology department who owned a loft on an iffy street in SoHo. She passed over, without pausing, what it was the middle-aged women had done, because she didn't actually know. All she was sure of was that one morning they were gone. The doors to their apartments stood propped open so that the landlord could send in a team of exterminators. If you stood there and looked through, you saw that their apartments had been much like the others in this building, small, cramped, with high ceilings but peeling paint. Maris did stand there and look through. Once every three years, she painted her apartment by herself, with a careful precision born of both habit and desperation. She didn't want to wake up one morning and find strips coming down off the wall above her head as she lay in the pullout bed, the bed she'd bought at Castro Convertibles her third year in the city, for $5,500 plus tax.

She should take the subway, she knew that. She had already spent most of the money from her paycheck on Friday, and it was only Tuesday. The week stretched ahead of her endlessly, the trips she would have to take to and from the office, the lunches she would have to eat somewhere. She hated the women, like Debra, who brought their lunches in pastel Lord & Taylor bags, a small bottle of Perrier, a tuna sandwich without mayonnaise, and one perfect peach, all laid out across their desks as they tapped away at their computers, much too busy to take time to eat. She hated even more people like Betsy, who didn't seem to notice what they ate, or if they ate it—just the way they didn't notice what they wore, unless there was a reason to notice and three makeup people from the network bothering them about it. Maris was now, as she had always been, obsessed with appearance. If she had had the money, she would have put herself through enough plastic surgery to look respectable again. She didn't understand women, like Betsy, who had the money and didn't want to. For the same reason, she would never live in one of the outer boroughs or in the suburbs, no matter how much more space she could get for how much less money. It said something about you that you could not stay in Manhattan, that you valued a few extra square feet over the chance to be close to art and literature and history. The six tall tumblers in her kitchen cabinet had come from Steuben Glass and cost $345 for the set. The green silk dress she was wearing had come from Brooks Brothers and cost $225 off the rack. Her head hurt, dreadfully, in that pounding, insistent way that told her she had not put enough Gordon's in her coffee when she had first woken up. If she hadn't put enough in the coffee in the thermos bottle she always brought with her to the office, her head would pound all day no matter what she did. It wouldn't matter if she had swallowed a whole bottle of aspirin.

There was a cab a block and a half away, coming toward her. She stepped halfway into the street and flagged it down. When it stopped, she got in and gave the address of Betsy's offices, on the Upper East Side, to a driver who didn't find it necessary to give her a grunt of acknowledgment in return. Living in New York these days, she often got the impression that she had gone deaf to the sound of the human voice. She took her thermos out of her tote bag and poured a little of the coffee in it into the thermos's own plastic cup. She hated drinking out of plastic—things tasted differently when they were drunk out of plastic, except things like soda pop, which didn't matter—but she kept her good traveling cup at the office, and she didn't feel ready to wait. The coffee was good Colombian, bought at a specialty store near Wall Street, ground in her own hand grinder next to her own kitchen sink. If it had been up to her, she would have changed everybody, men as well as women. She would have made them care about the things that really mattered, graciousness and style, uncompromising standards, that innate sense of perfection in art and life that cannot be taught and cannot be bought. Since that was not possible, she sometimes wished them all dead, machine-gunned into pulp, laid out in the streets like so many rag dolls for the few real people among them to use as a carpet. Her head really was very bad, insane, pounding. When she got like this, she forgot that there was only one person she had ever truly hated.

Somewhere around West Fortieth Street, they hit bad traffic. She could have gotten out and walked from here—it was only twenty blocks, a single mile, plus the crosstown, she'd done it before—but she was afraid the headache would come back. She took her cell phone out of the black leather carrying case she kept it in and dialed. Her hands were shaking. She had to make them stop before Debra saw them, because Debra would know what to think.

"Hollman Public Library," Belinda's voice said.

Maris relaxed a little. The phone could have been answered by Belinda's boss. That would not have been good.

"It's me," she said.

"Oh, hi. Where are you? Are you at work?"

"I'm in a cab stuck in traffic," Maris said. "It's official. We're all coming down in two weeks. At least, she and the boys are, and I am, because she says she needs me. What do you think?"

"I think we're all counting on it. It's been in the papers so much. Well, it's been in the *Enquirer*, but you know what I mean. People say they don't read it, but they do. Do you think all those reporters will come down here, too? You know, to take pictures of her?"

"Probably. Mostly to take pictures of Jimmy Card, if he's around."

"Jimmy Card," Belinda said. "Can you imagine, Betsy Wetsy going out with Jimmy Card? It makes me sick. I mean, who does she think she is?"

" 'The freshest new voice in American letters in a generation,' " Maris quoted.

"What?"

"Never mind. It was in a magazine called *The New York Review of Books*. You wouldn't know it."

"I know all about *The New York Times Book Review*," Belinda said. "You don't have to get that way with me. I hope she doesn't think that everything's going to be wonderful when she gets down here. I hope she doesn't think we've changed our minds. I mean, my God, we know her for what she really is."

Maris closed her eyes. Her old headache was not coming back—it wasn't that bad—but Belinda often gave her another kind of headache, a blunt-edged throbbing that was the strain of trying to get past the fire wall of her stupidity. It had been that way from the first time they had ever met, in the kindergarten that was held in the basement of Center School, where they had been the two prettiest and most important girls in the class. There was something odd about the fact that she could remember so much about that year, in such detail. It should have ceased to matter forty-five years ago. Still, she *could* remember, and not only about herself and Belinda.

"You aren't listening to me," Belinda said.

"I was thinking about kindergarten."

"Excuse me?"

"It doesn't matter." Somewhere up ahead, the traffic had begun to clear out. She didn't have much time, and she didn't want to be seen talking into a cell phone on the sidewalk. That was one of those things, like smoking in the street, she would never allow herself to do. "I just wanted to let you know," she said. "For sure. We're coming. She's got the boys in some private school up where she lives in Connecticut. They finish the year at the end of May, and then we're coming."

"Private school. Don't you know she'd think her children were too good to go to public school? God, she's such a snot. She's always been such a snot. She makes me sick."

"You can tell her so when you see her on Grandview Avenue."

"What I'm going to do is call her Betsy, just like I always did," Belinda said. "I don't care what she likes to call herself now. And I'm going to try to talk some sense into you. You should get out of there, Maris, you know you should. You're wasting yourself covering up for her. You're the one who ought to be a big-shot panelist on TV. You're the one who was Phi Beta Kappa in college. She practically flunked out."

"True enough."

"Betsy Wetsy," Belinda said. "Do you remember that? Everybody used to call her that. Betsy Wetsy. Who does she think she *is*?"

The cab was moving across town now. In a second, it would be standing outside the tall, narrow town house where Betsy had her offices on the first two floors. Maris lifted the thermos to make sure there was still enough coffee in it. She could always pop out and get a little extra gin, but she couldn't replace the coffee, and she needed it to stay awake. She got her wallet out of the tote bag's zippered inside side pocket. *Betsy Wetsy*, she thought, and giggled, because of course, in her head, that's the way she thought of Elizabeth Toliver. Elizabeth the Great, sitting on the podium at the press conference that announced the first big fund-raising drive in support of the senate candidacy of Hillary Rodham Clinton. Elizabeth the Great, being introduced to President George W. Bush at a White House press dinner. Elizabeth the Great, caught walking hand in hand with Jimmy Card on the beach at his private estate in the Bahamas. Elizabeth the fucking Great. Jimmy the fucking Card. Sometimes, she thought that something had come to her in the middle of the night and drained all the blood out of her veins and replaced it with poison.

"You never listen to me," Belinda said. "I've been trying to tell you that nobody down here is fooled. We know she must have planted those stories herself. The ones in the supermarket papers. She's just trying to get herself a lot of attention."

"By accusing herself of murder?"

"Everybody knows she had nothing to do with Michael's murder. God, Maris, who does she think she is? I mean, really. She isn't anybody. Somebody should tell Jimmy Card that she wasn't even invited to her own senior prom."

"I've got to go," Maris said. The cab had pulled to a stop at the curb. The spindly trees all seemed to be full of green and caterpillars. "I'll talk to you later. I'm late as it is. Maybe we can all get together and have a drink at the White Horse when I get down here."

"Maybe we could do it again," Belinda said. "Do you remember? The time we told her to meet us at the White Horse and then we went out to the Blue Note in Johnstown instead, and she had to walk all the way back on the highway on her own."

"I've got to go," Maris said again. She came up with a twenty-dollar bill—she only had it and a ten and maybe another hundred in her checking account—and passed it over into the front seat. She left a two-dollar tip and got out onto the pavement with her tote bag held carefully on the tips of the three middle fingers of her right hand. She had been in New York long enough to know that image mattered more than substance did, and in the matter of image, she was something of a genius.

Up in the big window that looked out over the town house's entrance, Debra was standing with a pen in her teeth, watching. If Maris could have taken out the thermos and poured herself a cup of coffee right that minute, she would have done it—but of course she couldn't, and she had the copy of the *National Enquirer* to worry about, too, since none of them was supposed to bring the tabloids anywhere Betsy Wetsy would be able to see them. The wind coming down the street was unexpectedly cold. Her dress felt too thin for the weather. Debra looked murderous. It didn't help to remember that it didn't matter, because Debra was no more able to fire her than she was able to sprout wings.

She went up the front steps as slowly as she could, counting them as she went, not looking at Debra at all, and as she went she thought about what it would be like to be back at home, where everything belonged to her. It didn't seem possible that she was really fifty years old. It hardly seemed possible that she was older than twenty-eight. God only knew, she wasn't ready for her own personal story to be over.

2

Belinda Hart Grantling knew with certainty that she was a very stupid person. She had known it since her very first week in school, which had begun as a great adventure (new children to play with, a *good* thing) and ended in a confusion so deep, it was something like terror. Even now, she could see Mrs. Thompson standing in front of the class, smacking her rubber-tipped wooden pointer along the long row of letters that hung over the blackboard. She knew the alphabet song from home, but it had never occurred to her that it was anything other than nonsense. She knew a lot of nonsense songs. Maybe they all meant something, and as the days went by she would be expected to know what that was, and to stand up in front of everybody else and say so. The worst thing was that she seemed to be the only one who did not know. When Mrs. Thompson wrote a letter on the board, all the rest of the class would call it out. Only Belinda would sit silently with her hands folded on her lap under the table, only pretending to let sounds come out of her. Some of the others knew it all so well, they were restlessly bored. One of the others could read the cover on the big hard-edged book Mrs. Thompson kept on the corner of her desk. "Teacher's Manual," Betsy Toliver said it said. Belinda wondered what "manual" meant, and then why Mrs. Thompson never opened it, if it was something for teachers.

By the end of Belinda's first month at school, she had developed a deep-seated resentment that would never leave her, a bone-crushing conviction that there was something truly evil, truly hateful, about all smart people. Another child would have acted out—and some of them did—but Belinda had a single gift, and that was the ability to know where the advantage lay. It didn't take her long to realize that most people didn't really like smart people. She wasn't the only one who hated Betsy Toliver. Even Mrs. Thompson grew stiff and offended when Betsy jumped in with the answer to every question, or read a notice put up on the bulletin board for grown-ups only, or spent recess working out math problems from worksheets she'd found discarded in the wastebasket. What people really liked in other people was something Belinda had in abundance. They liked prettiness. Betsy Toliver wasn't ugly, but her pale-faced, wide-eyed darkness couldn't begin to compete with Belinda's own blond porcelain fragility. Belinda was everything little girls were supposed to be, and older ones too, when they grew up to become Claudia Schiffer or Christie Brinkley. Her hair was as blond as possible without becoming that odd hard whiteness that makes some people look like bleached rabbits. Her eyes were large and round and blue. Her features were so regular they could have been used as an illustration in a textbook lesson on proportion. In a room full of children, older people looked at Belinda first, and the children themselves gravitated to her, fighting among themselves to get her attention. Like a lot of stupid people, Belinda was also very shrewd. She knew power when she saw it. She was also sure of her own righteousness. It was just not *fair* that there were people like Betsy Toliver in the world. It was just not *fair* that so much of the school day should be taken up with classes, where she was always at a disadvantage, and where she never seemed to know the answer, when the teacher called on her even though she hadn't raised her hand. It was not an accident, she thought, that so many of the women teachers were so plain, or that the women writers they studied in English and the women scientists whose pictures lined the margins of the enrichment booklets in General Science and the women everybody rhapsodized over in World History were all so downright ugly. Some women seemed to be able to get away with being intelligent—Maris Coleman, for instance—but for most of them, it was the kiss of death. Their intelligence sucked away whatever looks they'd had to begin with. They ended up deformed, in a way gnarled. Thinking seemed to be a disease that grew unsightly knobs of flesh, like warts.

Age was also a disease that grew unsightly knobs of flesh, but not warts. Belinda was far too careful of herself ever to get really fat—even during her three pregnancies, she had followed a Weight Watchers diet she had modified just for herself—but being careful was not quite the same thing as being disciplined, and the result was that she had become sort of . . . lumpy. The effect had not been helped by an early menopause, or by the fact that she truly hated any kind of vigorous physical exercise. By the time she was forty-two, she had stopped menstruating, and her waist had thickened so much she'd had to throw away all her old belts. Her calves had thickened, too, she had no idea why. She'd bought a StairMaster and used it only twice. The first time she had stopped after three minutes, because her ankles hurt. The second time, she had stopped after one. Then her hair had begun to thin, just as her mother's had at the same age. In no time at all, she began to look predictably middle-aged.

That, Belinda thought now, was when the trouble had started—or maybe the trouble had started a long time before that, but she'd been so busy with her own life, and so happy to be who and what she was, she had never noticed. It made her uneasy to think she might have been all wrong all the time, and she didn't think it was possible. Obviously, something had changed, in the sixties, maybe, when everything changed, so that the girls she knew who went off to college didn't join sororities when they got there, because that wasn't cool anymore. She, herself, had only gone for two years to a junior college three towns away, to get an associate's degree in Business Management. It was a glorified secretarial course, but it had accomplished the two things she'd wanted it to accomplish. She'd met a man to marry there, and she'd learned enough about typing and bookkeeping to make herself feel that she'd always be able to get a job if anything should ever happen to her marriage. That was in 1975, and she was sure nobody could blame her for not expecting the computer to come along and make everything she'd ever learned completely obsolete.

"I should have done things differently," she said to the air. Then she stared down at the phone she had just hung up and thought that Maris *had* done things differently, and it hadn't done her any good. Belinda was a sincere believer in all things supernatural. She had a fevered relationship with God, but she also put her trust in other things: astrology, Tarot cards, palm reading, *The Celestine Prophecy*. Belinda knew the world to be a place full of dark, obscure, occult, and powerful forces, pushing mere human beings around at will. Only forces like that could account for the fact that things had worked out the way they had, that she was an aide in her own hometown library and divorced and living in an apartment the size of a matchbook, that Maris had been fired from three badly paid jobs in two years and would probably be living on the street if Betsy hadn't hired her, that Betsy was living in a 6,000-square-foot house in the Connecticut suburbs and getting ready to marry a pop star. Other people might have seen the irony in it, or a lesson about life, but Belinda saw the hand of the devil himself.

The library telephone was in the library office, which was a big loft room overlooking the main floor of books and periodicals. Belinda went to the balcony railing and found Laurel Haynes, the head librarian, busy with an elderly woman in a paunchy denim jumper and black cotton tights. Here was something else that was different, a piece of the same conspiracy. When Belinda was growing up in Hollman, the librarian was a local spinster with no better than a normal school education, whose qualifications were that she was unlikely ever to marry and very likely to be vigilant about keeping things like pornography and James Joyce out of the stacks. Now they had Laurel, who had a doctorate in library science and wrote long essays for literary magazines on the relationship between the writings of Aphra Behn and the emergent lesbian-feminist aesthetic consensus. Needless to say, she kept both Joyce and pornography in the stacks, and even put on special exhibits to celebrate Beat poets and Deconstructionism.

Belinda went back to the table where the telephone was and sat down. If she stayed up here too long, Laurel might complain—but then, she might not. Laurel didn't seem to notice what most of her staff was doing most of the time. As long as the work got done and done more or less on time, she didn't lecture. Belinda picked up the receiver and dialed the number she knew better than any in the world. She had, after all, been dialing it for over forty years.

"Country Crafts," Emma's voice said, picking up.

"It's Belinda," Belinda said. "Did I get you at a bad time?"

"Not at all. There hasn't been a soul in here all day. What's up with you? Aren't you at work?"

"I just talked to Maris."

"Ah. And?"

"Well," Belinda said, "it's true. She is coming, at the end of May, and bringing her children. Betsy, I mean. Not Maris. Maris is coming too, though. That could be good."

"You'd think she'd have come before this," Emma said. "I mean, for God's sake. Her mother wanders away from her nurse at least twice a week, and last Friday she went to the parking lot of the Grand Union and took off all her clothes. If she had any sense of family feeling, she'd have come right that minute. You've got to wonder what's wrong with her."

"Have you thought of it?" Belinda asked. "About having her here? About what it would be like."

"I don't think it's going to be like anything. I don't intend to see her. Why would I? Would you?"

"Laurel wants her to come and speak at the library. She says other libraries have writers in, but we never do because we don't have the budget to pay their traveling expenses, and Betsy wouldn't have to travel. She'd be right here."

There was a pause on the other end of the line. "Nobody would come," Emma said finally. "We all remember her. We know what she really is. Nobody's going to come to the library to listen to Betsy Wetsy lecture."

"We don't all know what she's like," Belinda said stubbornly. "There are lots of new people in town. And people younger than us. And there's been all that stuff. In the papers. Saying she killed Michael. And Maris says she's writing something. About that night. That she heard more than she's ever said and now she's going to name names. It might be just about the outhouse. But it might not."

"Horseshit. Betsy spent that whole night locked in an outhouse stall. I should know. I locked it. And I helped nail it shut."

"I know that. And you know that. But not everybody knows it. And there have been all those newspaper stories. And other people might come because she was nominated for that prize that Laurel thinks is so important—"

"The Pulitzer."

"Whatever it was. It could get to be a pretty big deal, is all I'm saying. And what if she wants to write about it. About us. About the—the—"

"Murder?"

"I don't like to think of it as murder," Belinda said. "Maybe it really wasn't one. They never did catch any murderer."

Belinda felt the silence descend between them like a curtain. It always did, when they got on this subject. For a split second, she had one of those visions she could not repress: all of them standing in a semicircle around

Michael's body at the edge of the river. She was the one who had knelt down into the mud and put her hand in the dark puddle next to Michael's head, so that when her cupped hand had come up to the air again it had been filled with blood. Then it had started to rain. She was wearing a halter top over cutoff jeans, their uniform for that summer, their declaration of independence from the prissy constraints of high school dress codes. The rain had come down so hard and so fast, she had been soaked through in an instant, and the blood had disappeared from her hand as if it had never been there at all. She had had the feeling, at the time, that she had been imagining the whole thing.

There was the little matter of the fact that his throat had been slit straight across, Emma could have said—Belinda knew it was what she was thinking—but of course Emma didn't say it. She never said it. Nobody did.

"Well," Belinda said. "I just wanted you to know. That it was for certain. Maris says she's got her children in some private school that gets out at the end of May, and as soon as it does they're all coming down here."

"Fine," Emma said. "I hope she has a good time. I hope the town gets a little good publicity instead of the kind it's been getting. I hope she doesn't expect us all to fall all over her and tell her how wrong we were, because I for one don't think we were wrong. God, she's still a frump. Did you see that? In *People* magazine. She still wears T-shirts over turtlenecks, except they're not turtlenecks anymore, they're these crew-neck sack things—"

"It's not fair," Belinda said virtuously.

"Nothing is ever fair," Emma said. "I've got to help a customer. I don't know what we were thinking when we opened this place. Nobody ever shops in town anymore. They go out to Wal-Mart. I go out to Wal-Mart. We must have been on drugs."

"Okay," Belinda said. She was sure she was supposed to say something else, but she wasn't sure what, so she let it go. *It's not fair* was all that was really stuck in her brain, and she had no idea how to expand on that, or how to interpret the strained undertone that always came into Emma's voice when she said it.

"Well," she said instead. "I'd better let you go."

"Right," Emma said. "Drop in after work. I'm going to be here all night. George's gone over to Harrisburg to pick up some things."

"All right," Belinda said. Then the phone began to buzz in her ear, and she felt an electric jolt of resentment go through her, as if she'd stuck her finger in a light socket. Except, she thought, it wasn't like that, because a light socket could kill you, and she wasn't dead.

Belinda hung up and went back to the railing to see what Laurel was doing now, but Laurel was still talking to the elderly woman, and the library was still mostly empty. Far too often lately, it felt to her as if nothing ever happened in Hollman at all.

3

No matter what Belinda thought, Emma Kenyon Bligh did not go silent every time anyone brought up The Incident, except in the sense that she was struck dumb by boredom, which was not what Belinda meant. Unlike the others, Emma had never really been able to think of The Incident as significant. Yes, Michael Houseman had died, but a lot of people they'd gone to school with had died over the years, some of them even younger than Michael had been. Carolanne Verelli, for instance, had died of leukemia when they were all only eight, and Mitch Wazinski and Tom Kolchek had killed themselves junior year, trying to drive the complete length of Clapboard Ridge at 105 miles an hour in a Volkswagen bug. Emma found something morbid about this constant picking at an incident that had been finished years ago—decades ago, by now. It didn't seem to her to matter that they had been out in the same park on the same night, boarding Betsy up in that damned outhouse with those silly little snakes. It was the kind of thing you did in those days. Every school class had a target. It was just the way the world worked. Looked at rationally, from a perspective without sentimentality, it was more the target's fault than anybody else's, and Emma had been very careful to make sure neither of her own daughters was in any danger. What she would have done if one or the other of them had been like Betsy, with that queer turn of mind and the need to be carrying a book around every place she went, she didn't know. At any rate, it hadn't come up. Both her girls had been models of sanity and popularity. Both of them had been cheerleaders, and Tiffany had been both a prom princess and the student council president her senior year. Now they were safely out of the house and settled with husbands, not too far away. They had both gone to UP-Johnstown. They had both gotten degrees in education. They had both quit work for three years after their first children were born. All in all, it had turned out very well, and Emma had not had to worry for a moment that one of them would suddenly develop a desire to move to California or go to medical school. She hesitated to admit it—people always took it the wrong way—but she had been far more worried that the girls would be too intellectual than she had that they would be too ugly. You could always get ugly fixed with plastic surgery.

She looked down at the pile of things on the counter that she had stacked neatly to place into a brown paper bag, and realized she had been paying no attention to her customer the entire time she had been ringing up. The customer was not anybody she knew, but she wasn't a tourist, either. Tourists bought yarn dolls on polished wood stands or handmade wooden spinning wheels that could really spin if they ever wanted to learn how to use them.

This woman had bought supplies: thirty yards of yarn; six packets of multi-colored pipe cleaners; a wire wreath frame; a bag of cotton flannel scraps that could be stitched together to make the shell of a quilt or a comforter cover. Emma looked up at her and smiled, uncertainly. Her lined elderly face did not smile back.

"It should come to sixteen dollars and forty-six cents, with tax," the woman said.

Emma took the woman's twenty-dollar bill and started to make change. What gave her pause, what really made her silent when she and Belinda had these conversations, was the fact that she knew something Belinda did not know, and that she had not been able to explain no matter how often she had tried. Unlike Belinda, she had actually seen Betsy once since they all graduated from high school. Maris had gone away to Vassar and come back every summer for vacation, but Betsy had never come back, and Maris had never had that much to say about her.

"She's Betsy Wetsy," Maris would tell them when they asked. "She has practically no friends. She's not important. She sinks into the woodwork. She isn't an academic star. The college is probably sorry they ever took her."

From Maris's reports, Emma had expected Betsy to go on looking the same, a little frumpy, a little heavy without being heavy enough to be called fat, her hair hanging limp and her clothes always mismatched and one or two sizes too big. It had occurred to her, once or twice, in high school, that Betsy just didn't *care* about the way she looked—but that had seemed so fantastic, she had never been able to maintain the thought for more than a minute and a half. She, like most girls, spent at least an hour a day making sure she looked the way she was supposed to look. She slept every night on rollers the size of beer cans so that her hair would curl up at the ends in exactly the right way at exactly the right place, and if she couldn't find the knee socks that matched the Bobbie Brooks skirt and sweater set she had intended to wear to school, she found something else to put on. Shoes were Bass Weejuns. Pocketbooks were hard leather shoulder bags in British tan that could only be had at Elsa-Edna's right in the middle of town. Betsy's father had been the richest man in the entire county, a lawyer with a state-wide reputation, but Nancy Quayde had seen it with her own eyes that Betsy bought her school clothes off the rack at Bradlee's bargain store.

The woman in Fortnum & Mason's that morning in July had been nothing at all like a frump, and her clothes hadn't come from some bargain knockoff place where all the seams gapped while the clothes still hung on their hangers. That was why it had taken Emma as long as it had to believe she was seeing what she was seeing. She was in Fortnum & Mason's with a tour group. She and her husband—George Bligh, from the class ahead of theirs at school—had joined it to celebrate their fifteenth wedding anniversary. Neither of them had been to Europe before, and the idea of having a guide and an itinerary to protect them had seemed like the only sensible choice. Emma remembered staying up all night the morning before they were supposed to leave, worrying about everything that could go wrong. What if something happened to the plane? What if they weren't able to make the right connections at JFK in New York? What if they got mugged? What if they got robbed? What if they got lost? Emma did not like to travel, not really. It was too unsettling on too many different levels, and there was always the danger that she would come back somehow changed, so that her own real life wouldn't feel real to her anymore. It was the same problem she would have had if one of the girls had wanted to go somewhere fancy for college. That sort of thing changed you—it had even changed Maris—and Emma had never really believed that a change could be for the better.

It was their last morning in London before moving on to Wales. The tour guides thought that Fortnum & Mason's would be a good place to go for novelties and souvenirs. Emma had already decided that it was not, because it was far too expensive, and the things it carried were far too odd. One whole aisle was taken up with food she could have bought anytime she wanted to, at home, but at prices so exorbitant they made her breathless even before she did the currency conversion from pounds into dollars. Kraft macaroni and cheese, Miracle Whip, Skippy peanut butter, Niblets brand corn, Twinkies—women in plain cotton shirtwaist dresses and thick cawing British accents snapped them up, telling each other how it was much less expensive when they got a package sent to them from their married daughter in New York, but she was pregnant now and not able to get around as easily as she used to, so they had to pay the prices here. Other aisles contained things Emma didn't know if she believed: eels in gelatin, tins of pate made out of lamb brains and strip bacon and butter. The worst thing was the big glass case with the candy in it. Emma loved candy. It was why she weighed nearly 250 pounds by the time she'd had her second daughter, and had probably weighed 50 pounds more than that on that day in London. No matter how expensive it was, she would have bought candy if she could have found any she liked, but the glass case was full of abominations. Candied violets turned out to be candied violets. They had a bright purple flower hardened by sugar on top of a chocolate shell, and when people bit into them they oozed a bright purple creme. Candied ginger turned out to be candied ginger, too. When you bit into *that*, it burned your mouth.

When the woman in the yellow dress walked through the door, Emma's first thought was: *Oh, my God. That's Betsy Wetsy*. Then she backtracked, because she couldn't quite figure out how she knew. Most probably she *didn't* know, she told herself. What would Betsy Wetsy be doing in London, and how could she have transformed herself into this, this—what? It wasn't that this woman was good-looking, although she was, in an odd way that had nothing to do with what Emma had always called "cute." It was the aura, if there was any such thing, the easy grace that came from a radiating confidence so complete it drew attention from half the people in the room. It was a big room, and crowded, and noisy, and the woman in the yellow dress wasn't speaking much above the level you'd use to talk to a good friend in a quiet corner over tea—but people were looking at her anyway, as if she were royalty or a movie star, somebody they felt they ought to know.

Emma pinched George on the elbow and said, "George. Listen. Isn't that Betsy Wetsy?"

"Who?"

"Betsy Toliver. From Hollman."

"There's nobody like that in Hollman," George said confidently. "I'd have noticed."

"I don't mean from Hollman now," Emma said. Sometimes George made her so frustrated, she wanted to break his neck. "From when we were in high school. Betsy Toliver. You know. The girl who was locked in the outhouse at the park the night Michael Houseman died."

George squinted, as if that could make him see better. He'd run to fat, just as Emma herself had, and for most of the time they had been on this tour he had been uncomfortable. Everything the Europeans made—chairs, sofas, beds, the aisles in theaters and fancy stores—was just so small, he couldn't fit into it. Once, at a restaurant in Scotland, he'd had to have a chair brought especially from the manager's office so that he could sit down at all.

"You know," he said. "I think it is. I think it is Betsy Toliver."

She was standing at the side of the candy counter, attended by a deferential man with a clipboard, her head bent, listening. There was, really, no mistaking it. It had to be Betsy Toliver. It could be no one else. What Emma had thought was the one conclusive proof she was not—she was too tall—turned out to be a pair of two-and-half-inch-stacked high heels. The man with the clipboard was nodding, pointing to things on the paper in front of him. Betsy was pushing one long-fingered hand through the thick permed cloud of her hair, and as she did the large diamond on her fourth finger glinted in the uncertain illumination of the display lights.

"Yes, madam, everything is very much in order," the man with the clipboard was saying. "The package will be delivered to Hollman, Pennsylvania, USA, no later than noon on July twenty-fourth. It's all arranged. Once it reaches New York by international carrier, it will be carried inside the United States by the United Parcel Service."

Emma was standing so close, she could have touched Betsy on the cheek. Some part of her was signaling that she should do just that. Wasn't there something odd about running into an old . . . acquaintance . . . thousands of miles from home, and not even making yourself known to her? If she went back and told Belinda and Nancy and Chris just how this had happened, they would think she was off her head. It didn't make any sense to run into Betsy Wetsy in Fortnum & Mason's and not even find out what she was doing with her life. Still, Emma made no move in Betsy's direction, and George didn't either, because he recognized exactly what she did: there was something about Betsy, something that put her totally beyond their reach, so that either one of them would have been ashamed to have her see them the way they looked now.

The man with the clipboard held it out to Betsy. She took it, took the pen off the metal clasp, and signed. When she handed it back, the man had a candied violet to offer her, and she laughed.

"Thank you," she said. "Thank you for everything. I'm going to go eat this on the sidewalk so I don't get the urge to buy a pound and take them home. Have a good afternoon, Terence. I'm sorry I put you through so much trouble."

"It was no trouble at all, madam. I hope very much we can be of service to you again."

"Twice a year, Christmas and her birthday. You've been wonderful. Thank you, again."

Betsy turned around and went across the large open front section between the candy case and the front door, and then she was gone. For a moment, Emma could still see her through the windows, striding out onto the sidewalk. In no time at all, though, she had disappeared, and Emma found herself counting it all up in her head: the yellow dress, real silk, and fully lined; the shoes; the handbag; the hair; the diamond engagement ring, backed as it was by a thick gold band more like the ones men wore than the ones women did. Emma looked down at her own shoes, good sensible canvas ones so that her feet wouldn't hurt if she walked too much in the city. She looked at her own diamond engagement ring, which George had bought her when she had only been out of high school a year. She looked at the canvas tote bag she was carrying instead of a real purse, because she thought it would be better for carrying the things they bought when they went to the kind of places that really interested her, like the Tower of London.

"Well," George said. "*She's* changed a lot, hasn't she?"

"You've given me ten cents too much change," the old woman said, tapping her knuckles against the counter next to her brown paper bags. "I don't think you're paying attention. I don't think you've heard a single word I've said the whole time I've been in here."

"Sorry," Emma said. "I've been a little distracted today."

"You can't expect to keep customers if you don't listen to what they say," the old woman said. "You take me, for instance. I won't be back here again. You've got good stock, but I won't go where I'm not being listened to. I'm a customer with money to spend. I have a right to be listened to."

"Yes," Emma said. "Of course."

"You're only saying 'of course' because you're trying to humor me," the old woman said. "I won't be humored. I'm not some senile old cat."

"Yes," Emma said. Then she stopped. She had been about to say "of course." "I hope you enjoy your things," she said, instead.

The old woman looked ready to start up again, but instead she just gathered up her bags, and looked Emma over—*fat cow*, Emma could almost hear her say—and left, making her feet hit the floor with particular emphasis, and slamming the door as she went out.

Emma took a chamois cloth and gave the counter a quick rub, just to give herself something to do. What bothered her about her talks with Belinda was that endless complaint: *it isn't fair*. What frightened her, ever since she had first started hearing Betsy's name on television, was that it might be very fair, there might be something about Betsy that really deserved to be famous, if only in a minor way, something about her that the rest of them, even Maris, did not have. It was not something that Emma herself wanted, but it was something that the rest of the world might easily judge to be better than what she had, and she hated the thought of that, much in the same way she had once hated the sight of Betsy in the hall at school with the top button of her blouse buttoned tight, even though everybody knew that when you wore a blouse that way you looked like a jerk. Now Betsy was coming home, moving back into that big brick house in Stony Hill, and everything would be ruined.

4

It had been a bad day, one of the worst Peggy Smith Kennedy could remember in at least six months, and that, she told herself, was why it bothered her so much that nobody had thought to call and tell her the news about Betsy Toliver. Of course, there *wasn't* much news about Betsy Toliver. There wasn't anything she didn't know. Unlike most of the others, she didn't try to hide her interest in what Betsy was doing by buying *People* or the tabloids up in Johnstown or out at the mall. She could even remember the first time she had realized that Betsy was becoming Something Important, and it had burned into her brain the way such incidents do, the ones you think later were the billboards that announced your life had changed. Peggy had a lot of those incidents emblazoned on her brain, but not quite enough of them. She tried to remember the first time Stu had hit her—really hit her, so that she came right up off the floor and slammed into something—but she always came up blank. It seemed to her that he had always hit her, even when they were children together, even back in high school. She knew that wasn't true. She had pictures of herself—homecoming queen, prom princess, president of the student council—and in those days her eyes had been as clear and unclouded as the water in one of those Japanese pools, those oases of serenity. She did remember the first time she had ended up in the emergency ward, with Stu pacing the corridor and her left arm held away from her body at an odd angle, broken in one place, dislocated in another. The doctor who had seen to her had had eyes as flat as the eyes of an android in the science fiction movies Stu liked to see when he wasn't loaded. When he was loaded, he came home with porn, slick black videotapes that looked as if they had been rubbed all over with linseed oil. He made her sit with him and watch women do things she didn't have words for, that he said she wanted her to do to him, but that they never did together, ever, for some reason that seemed to be clear to him but that she couldn't figure out. What bothered her was that she was sure the doctor knew exactly what had happened. When he looked at Stu, his eyes became even flatter than they had been at the beginning. He looked almost two-dimensional. She suddenly realized *everyone* knew, everyone in this emergency room, everyone (maybe) in town, so that all the energy she had spent trying to keep this secret had had no purpose at all. *That* was one of those moments that was emblazoned on her brain, because ever afterward—this morning, for instance—when she went into town and walked down Grandview Avenue, or when she left her classroom to go to the teachers' lounge at school, she was sure that people could look straight at her and know her for exactly what she was. Not a homecoming queen. Not a prom princess. Not a student council president. Not even one of the girls who had gone up to UP-Johnstown to get her teaching certificate, unlike the others who had had to stay home and settle for junior college, or worse. What she really was, was one of those people who are nothing, not a thing, without any value whatsoever, so that it didn't matter if they were beaten bloody twice a month or if the one baby they had ever managed to conceive had died in a miscarriage brought on when their husbands kicked them senseless on their own kitchen floors—it didn't matter because they deserved it, they *deserved* it, God marked some people out from birth to be the ones who *deserved* it, and it was only an accident that she had been able to hide the truth about herself for so long.

"I couldn't let you have a fucking baby," Stu had said, when she came back from the hospital after the miscarriage. In the hospital, he had been different, not only sober but reasonable, so reasonable that the doctors had finally had to stop asking the questions that danced around the whole issue of what had made her lose the child. Once they got home again, he had started drinking. To give himself a bigger kick, he had done four lines of cocaine from her tortoiseshell hand mirror while she was in the bathroom. When they were both in college, after her junior year at UP-Johnstown, he had wanted her to try cocaine, too. He had even laid out the lines for her so that she wouldn't have to struggle with them herself, in the back of his van, out in the parking lot of the little supermarket across from the Sycamore. Later, that would seem significant, too, that they had stopped going to the Sycamore, where all their friends went, even then. If she had really been what she thought she was, if she had really been somebody to be proud of, Stu would have wanted to go on showing off their relationship in front of all the boys who rightly should have envied him.

"I can't let you have a fucking baby," Stu had said, lying on the couch while she sat huddled in an armchair that had springs poking out all over it. One of them was digging into the soft skin of her right arm, but she liked it. She kept rubbing her arm back and forth across it, trying to make it hurt more than it did. Stu had a six-pack of beer cans on the floor and his nose was running. "If I let you have a fucking baby, you'd kill it."

The teachers' lounge was full of potted plants. That had been true when she was a student at Hollman High School, and it was true thirty years later, when she was a teacher. She had no idea who brought the plants or who watered them. She never did either. The first time she'd realized that Betsy Toliver was becoming Something Important was on one of those weekends when Stu went off hunting—if anybody wanted to know how truly awful she was, she'd only have to tell them how often she wished that Stu would come back dead from hunting, Stu, whom she had known all her life, whom she had fallen desperately, hopelessly in love with at the age of six. She had had the house to herself, and she had pulled all the blinds down tight and locked all the doors and turned on the answering machine. She had wanted to be safe, just that once, not only from Stu but from everybody and everything she knew. She had a little stack of romance novels from Silhouette and Second Chance at Love that she had been keeping hidden in her work bag under the textbooks and assignment sheets she needed from school. Stu really hated it when she read romance novels. He said it made her stupid, and she couldn't afford to get any stupider than she already was. Actually, he called her a stupid c_____, but she couldn't say that word even in her own mind, and she didn't really hear it when Stu said it. Instead, let out into the air, it turned into something physical, the bouncing ball in those old Merrie Melodies cartoons, follow it and you don't have to have memorized the words.

She turned on the television just to have noise in the house. She liked music, but there was no point buying CDs of Mozart or Bach. If it wasn't what Stu liked, he broke it, at the first opportunity, and there was always opportunity. She thought vaguely that she would turn on PBS, or Bravo, where there were often orchestras on Saturday afternoons. She flicked clumsily at the remote and went through channels, channel after channel, the Sci Fi Channel, Comedy Central, Nickelodeon, TV Land, MTV, and then, on her second run-through—how could they possibly have all three tiers, HBO, Showtime, everything, and still have nothing to watch?—it had suddenly occurred to her that the woman on the CNN panel show was vaguely familiar. She settled down to watch, a copy of a book called *Reckless Desire* held in one hand, idly, so that she would have something to fiddle with while her stomach dropped out of her body and her brain froze tight. It wasn't that the woman was vaguely familiar. She'd known who it was at first glance. It was almost impossible to mistake that dramatic, high-cheekboned face—although, in spite of the fact that it looked the same, for some reason it now seemed handsome instead of ugly. Peggy had a line of bruises going up her arm from her wrist to her shoulder, dots of black and blue where Stu had held his fist against her so that his high school ring cut into her flesh. All of a sudden, all the bruises started to hurt, and all her muscles lost control. She was as cold as if she'd been locked into a butcher's walk-in freezer. The people on the panel show talked, but she didn't understand a word they said. She caught the fact that the host called Betsy "Liz," and that was it. Then she was utterly, irrevocably sick, so sick she didn't have time to get out of her chair and run for the bathroom. She leaned over and put her head between her legs and vomited, right there on the floor, vomited and vomited. So much stuff poured out of her, she thought she was vomiting up her own intestines. When she was able to sit up again, the show was rolling credits. *Regular Correspondents*, one category said, *Michael Kinsley, Ramesh Ponnuru, Laura Ingraham, Elizabeth Toliver.* Oh, she thought, Betsy must be some kind of liberal. Then she was vomiting again, and it had begun to occur to her that there was no way she was going to be able to clean it all up before tomorrow evening, to get it so clean that Stu would never notice what it was she had done. She could not have explained it to him, any more than she could have explained it to anybody else, this idea she had that a judgment had been passed, not only on her or on Betsy but on all of them.

Now she realized that she had been staring at the plants for what seemed like forever, and that her free period was going to come to an end sometime, and maybe it already had. She looked up at the clock on the wall—she didn't understand why they had to have the same kind of clock in here that they had in all the classrooms; it made her feel as if she were still sixteen years old and waiting for the bell like she would wait for a governor's pardon—and saw with some relief that she'd only been zoning out for maybe fifteen minutes. Her head hurt, badly. She thought she might have another mild concussion, but she had decided, years ago, never to go to the emergency room for anything minor. Never mind the fact that she would have to pay for any treatment she had herself. The system had gone to an HMO a little while back, and now if she wanted her insurance to pay for her trips to the ER, she had to get permission from her primary care physician. He was not, thankfully, one of the boys she had grown up with, but she still hated to see him for every little thing. He had flat eyes, too, when he wanted to.

The door to the teachers' lounge opened and Shelley Brancowski came in, closing the door behind her with a snap, so that none of the students would be able to look in and see what went on when the teachers weren't working. Why that would be important, Peggy didn't know. It wasn't like any of them smoked anymore, and if any of them did they had to go outside the building just like the students did. Shelley threw her pocketbook into one of the chairs and went to get herself coffee from the big spigoted pot that was kept hot all day long. By the time the final bell rang at three-thirty, the coffee inside it was a thick mud sludge like the mud pies they used to make in the sandbox at Central School after a good hard rain.

"So," Shelley said. "You okay? You've been looking a little distracted all day."

"I'm fine. I'm just a little tired." Shelley's eyebrows shot up. Peggy ignored them. "I've been talking to an old friend of mine, sort of by accident. Elizabeth Toliver really is coming to stay here for a month."

"I know," Shelley said. "It's been everywhere, really. It's exciting, don't you think? I mean, it's not like she's a movie star, or somebody the kids would understand, but it's still exciting. It's not every day we get somebody who's been to dinner at the White House in Hollman."

"Mmmm," Peggy said.

Shelley cocked her head. "So, what's wrong? She was a friend of yours, right, or somebody you knew? She was in the same graduating class. I looked it up in the old yearbooks. She was really remarkable-looking even then."

"We thought she was ugly," Peggy said. "And maybe she was. For high school. Your tastes change when you get older."

"So, what is it? I mean, I know there's all that about the murder, but I can't see that it matters. It doesn't have anything to do with anything, no matter what the tabloids say. I looked that up, too. Were you there, the night that boy died in the park?"

"Everybody was there, really. Wandering around. We used to go to the park on Saturday nights and neck. There was a pine forest there and you could lie down on the dead needles and it was soft. That was one of the few times I ever wished I'd gone away to college. It would have been much easier if we'd had a bed in a dorm room to use for what we were trying to do."

"Were you and Stu already going out then?"

"Stu and I started going out in kindergarten. Or something like it. Well, I wanted to go out with him, and I just sort of hung around until he got the idea himself. I think he finally made it when we were freshmen in high school."

"Were you one of the people who locked Elizabeth Toliver into the outhouse?"

"No," Peggy said, and that was true. Whatever else she had been in those days, she had not been one of those girls—like Maris and Belinda and Emma—who had felt the need to make Betsy's life as miserable as it was possible to make it. She had only wanted to keep her distance, because she knew that guilt by association really worked. On the other hand, it was also true that she had known what they were going to do, and had listened to Betsy screaming just before she'd run off to look for Stu, and that she hadn't done anything to stop what was happening.

Now she glanced back up at the clock and began to gather up her things. If Emma hadn't called here looking for Nancy and if she hadn't answered the phone accidentally, she would never have heard the news about Betsy Toliver, except thirdhand, from newspapers, the way Shelley had. Guilt by association still worked, she understood that. It was just that, now, she was the one they were all afraid to be associated with. She didn't even blame them. If it had been one of them in her position, she would have done the same thing. *Things*. When they saw her in the mall, they pretended not to, and if they were walking toward her they turned around abruptly, or crossed the corridor to the other side to pretend to look at window displays of electronics or candy canes. When they saw her in town, they smiled and said they couldn't understand why they never saw anything of her anymore, even though they did understand, completely, and so did she.

"It *will* be exciting, don't you think so?" Shelley said. "Old Hacker has been talking about asking her to come and speak, and so has Dina Wade. I guess Dina was her English teacher, one year. It's so, I don't know, stultifying out here. Nobody ever goes anywhere. Nobody ever does anything. It's like, if you're born in Hollman, you're destined to stay here, do you know what I mean?"

"Yes."

"It will be good for the students to be able to see somebody who got out and did something with her life. Maybe it will give a few of them ideas. I can't get most of my students to even consider going away to a college somewhere out of state, never mind applying to somewhere good. Is she nice, do you think? Was she nice in high school?"

"I don't really know what she was like in high school," Peggy said, and that was true, too, since she had made such a point of not knowing. She made sure her papers were in an orderly stack. She had meant to correct a few of them, but she hadn't gotten around to it. She put them back into her big work bag and rummaged through her small purse for a comb. She really did have a mild concussion. Her head throbbed. She kept going in and out of dizziness. Maybe Stu *would* come back dead someday from hunting, but if he did, what would she do without him?

"So," Shelley said. "Take it easy."

Peggy went out without answering her, because that was a statement in code, and she couldn't handle statements in code on this particular afternoon.

5

For Nancy Quayde, anger was a familiar feeling, so familiar, she no longer recognized it for what it was. Still, *this* particular anger had made her jumpy, and as she walked down the wide corridors of Hollman High School with her sharp high heels clicking against the vinyl tiles of the east wing first floor—*noise control undersystem my foot*—she found herself running through the reasons that Hollman ought to find a way to fire Peggy Smith. It wasn't the first time, and, Nancy thought, it probably wasn't going to be the last. Peggy had tenure and sympathy. Most of the other women on staff thought she was heroic for putting up with Stu all these years, and even if they didn't they would have resisted firing Peggy, who would need the job if she ever did leave the jerk. The problem, for Nancy, was that she saw Peggy's troubles with Stu to be practically a matter of will. Peggy's will was to dither and refuse to make decisions, just as it had been Peggy's will to dither and refuse to make decisions all those years ago in high school, when people like Maris and Belinda and Emma were torturing the hell out of stupid Betsy Toliver. The past always came back to bite you on the ass. Nancy could have told them that when they were all only fourteen years old, but she had known, even at the time, that the effort would be futile. Belinda was the next best thing to mentally retarded. Emma was not much better. Maris was—

Nancy had come to the fire doors that separated the East Wing from the main body of the school. She pushed through, strode across the little breezeway where the stairwells were—*damned fool janitors must have forgotten to turn off the heat*—and wondered what Betsy Toliver was actually like these days. In high school, she hadn't been much better than Peggy, and she'd been clueless on top of it. All those shirtwaist dresses a little too long at the knee, and the hair bands, and the knee socks that didn't actually match her sweaters. Somebody had taught her to dress in the years since she'd left Hollman, although that could be the result of television stylists and network publicists, so that, left on her own for the weekend, Betsy might look just as odd now as she had then. What Nancy couldn't believe was that Betsy still had the attitude she'd had back then, that cringing fear, that wounded vulnerability that practically asks to be hit again, and again, and again. All things considered, Nancy had never been able to blame Maris and Belinda and Emma for the things they'd done. If she'd been a less careful person, she might have done the same things herself. Lord only knew, she had wanted to, over and over again, whenever she ran across Betsy in the halls or in the lavatories, because Betsy really had seemed to be coming right out and asking for it. There was something about that kind of fear that made Nancy Quayde want to explode, and she had exploded, time and time again, over the years. Lab partners, sorority sisters, boyfriends, best girlfriends, classmates, all the people who wanted to break down and cry, who felt hurt, who felt scared, who let you know that if you tapped them on the shoulder they would fall apart and fall down—they worked on her like a trigger, so that all she wanted to do was swat them down, make them move, get some sense in them. *She* had had sense all her life, for as far back as she could remember. That was why, in the end, she hadn't hit the same wall all the rest of them had. Even Maris had hit that wall, she'd just waited to hit it when she graduated from college. Nancy graduated from college with her first job tucked neatly under her belt and with a record anybody who wanted a career in education would have found enviable. *She* hadn't ended up at Johnstown just because it was only half a mile away and easy to commute to. *She* hadn't dropped out sophomore year, or gotten married senior year, or hooked up with some damned idiot boy who would end up resenting the hell out of her competence and ambition. It was all a matter of planning, and none of them had ever wanted to plan, not even Maris, so of course, they had ended up, at fifty, not knowing what had happened to their lives. She wondered if Betsy had planned, if not in high school, then later. Maybe some sea change had come over her at Vassar and the quivering vulnerability had dropped off her like leaves off a tree at the beginning of November. Nancy was sure that nobody could end up on CNN, or nominated for a Pulitzer Prize, or teaching at Columbia University, without having planned it all down to the last smear of eye makeup. At the very least, she must have had drive, and drive was what Nancy admired in people more than anything else.

In the foyer at the center of the main corridor, Nancy stopped to review the exhibits in the glass cases. One was full of trophies for the football and basketball teams. In her day, Hollman had had terrible sports teams, so that it was embarrassing to be a cheerleader, although she had been one. That was planning, too, because even then she'd known that cheerleading would look good to the sororities she wanted to check out when she got to college, and the sororities would be important to her later, when she was looking for a job or a change or a promotion. By some miracle, though, the last few years had been good for Hollman sports. They had a lot of trophies, and some banners, and the display case did not look barren. The other display case did not look barren, either, but Nancy liked it less. It was one of those cheery pastel and primary colors booster projects the language clubs were so fond of, and like all such projects it had created a stir in "the community." *Citizens of the World!* the felt letters across the top of the display case shrieked, and then, across the bottom: *Hollman High Celebrates Fifty Years of the United Nations!* Dickie Baird and his little crowd of true believers had come out of the woodwork at the last board of education meeting, cackling away about how Hollman High was in league with the Satanic Freemason Popish global conspiracy to impose a one-world government under the rule of the Antichrist and destroy the United States and all the Christians in it. Really, Nancy thought, if she hadn't already decided she wanted the superintendent's job when it became vacant next year, she would have stood right up and told that idiot off. She hadn't been able to stop herself from telling the language clubs that the U.N.'s fiftieth anniversary had been over a year ago, and their celebration was somewhat out of time.

She got to her office door—NANCY QUAYDE, PRINCIPAL—and went through to the anteroom where her secretary was tapping away at a computer keyboard. She actually liked her secretary, this time, and it hadn't been easy to find somebody she could live with. She'd been through three in the last two years. Lisa Bentkoop had come to her from a secretarial school in Pittsburgh and would probably go back to Pittsburgh as soon as her husband got transferred out of whatever job had brought him here, or so sick of the country that he was willing to quit, and then she would be back to square one again, saddled with some teenager who thought the most important thing in life was her emotional atmosphere. Nancy was sure that she, herself, didn't have an emotional atmosphere. Her mood was steady at all times, and if she needed to express herself or wallow in the maudlin and ridiculous, she went to the kind of movie that made her cry. Needless to say, it wasn't the kind of movie that made other people cry. When she was in college, she'd gone to see *Love Story* in a packed theater where every seat was taken, and right at the crucial moment—right at that point where Oliver climbs into his dying wife's hospital bed to give her one last kiss—Nancy had burst out laughing.

On the walls of her inner office, she had everything that defined herself: her bachelor's degree from Penn State, her master's degree from Penn State, her doctorate, in education, also from Penn State. She had exactly one photograph, and that was of her with the Alpha Chi Omega pledge class in the fall of 1972, her senior year, when she had been pledge chairman. She had not kept pictures of herself from high school or from her earliest days at college, because they had seemed unnecessary to her. You came through a phase and then it was over. What was the point of reminding yourself, again and again, that you had once been much stupider than you were now? Sometimes she told herself that she wished she had taken time out to have a husband and children, but she knew it wasn't true. Men drove her to distraction. They wanted too much not only of her attention but also of her "inner self," and she had never seen the point of allowing anyone to have anything of her inner self. That got you what Peggy had, and what was the point of that? Children she simply hated, the way other people hated field mice that had managed to gain entry to the house. She had not even liked herself very much as a child, and by the time she was ten years old, she had found herself looking at her parents in puzzlement, wondering why they had bothered to do it. Neither she nor her brother seemed to give them much satisfaction, and in the end, when Nancy was a senior in college, they had taken off to Florida to live among people they didn't even know. Nancy saw them now and again the way she saw her brother. They were always uncomfortable when she was around, and she was impatient.

She sat down behind her desk and buzzed for Lisa. The buzz was unnecessary. She had left the inner door open, and Lisa would have been able to hear her if she called. She rubbed her forehead while she waited for Lisa to come in and went over, one more time, what the issues were. There were a lot of issues. There was, especially, the issue of what Betsy would think about all this, because there was nothing to say that Betsy would be flattered to be asked to speak at her old high school, if indeed they did ask her to speak. There was something else Nancy didn't understand, and that was the way so many people harbored grudges, as if they wanted desperately to hold on to any emotion at all, even a bad one. Nancy thought she was incapable of that kind of emotional confusion, but the truth was that she had only one emotion that she really enjoyed, and it never left her. At any rate, she would never allow it to interfere with anything she wanted to do, and maybe Betsy wouldn't either. It was just more than possible that the Betsy Toliver of CNN and Columbia University would not much want to do something bush league like speak at a high school.

Lisa came in carrying her steno pad, although she didn't take shorthand. Nobody did, anymore. Nancy waved her into a seat.

"Have you checked the papers the way I asked you to?"

"Absolutely," Lisa said. "It's still only the tabloid press. The only mentions of it in the regular papers have been along the lines of 'who could be planting these rumors after all these years.' Do you think somebody is planting rumors?"

"I've got an old friend who apparently thinks Ms. Toliver is planting the rumors herself, but she's not a very intelligent old friend. I suppose somebody could be, or maybe it's just opportunism. The case is there, after all, and she's been in the public eye a lot lately because of her relationship to Jimmy Card. Maybe it's just serendipity. Or another friend of mine could be right, and she could be writing something about that night in the park. And that friend ought to know."

"Do you think Jimmy Card will come here if she does?" Lisa asked. "That would be interesting. Jimmy Card on Grandview Avenue."

"I have no idea. You'll get a chance to find out, though. I just got word that she definitely will be coming, at the end of May. The question is, what are we going to do about her coming?"

"I think we'd be silly not to ask her here to speak. Or even to spend the day. When I was in high school, they used to bring in artists from the local community every year, and they'd spend the day, they'd teach a couple of classes, they'd give a talk, they'd eat in the cafeteria, that kind of thing. Think about all the kids in Honors English."

"Just in Honors English? We'd get a rash of complaints from the rest of the parents."

"All the kids, then. What was she like, do you remember? Was she nice? I suppose people don't stay the same as they grow older and, you know, as they get more successful, but if she was nice I guess there's always a chance. I'm dying to see what she looks like in person. On television, I always see her sitting down."

Nancy shook her head. "The thing with the murder still bothers me. Not that I think she had anything to do with it, mind you. In fact, I know she couldn't have. But all the publicity has not been good, even if it has been restricted to the tabloids. That's the problem with an unsolved crime, really. It hangs around to haunt you. So to speak. I'm not thinking clearly today."

"Maybe she wouldn't want to speak because she'd be afraid somebody would ask her about the murder," Lisa said. "There's always that. We could, you know, guarantee that that wouldn't happen."

"However would we guarantee that?"

"We'd forbid it."

Nancy laughed. "I can think of three students we have right this minute who would come armed and ready to ask if we *did* forbid it. Lord, I think it's so annoying that they never caught whoever it was—oh, they probably did, in Indiana or Ohio or someplace, and we just don't know about it, or he didn't confess to Michael's murder along with whatever others he'd done. It happens like that all the time. But it does cause a great deal of difficulty for those of us who have to live with the uncertainty. And the utterly rank stupidity of the general population."

"Right," Lisa said.

"I think we ought to at least assume we're going to invite her," Nancy said. "I know Laurel at the library is going to invite her there, murder or no murder, because of course she doesn't have to worry about Dickie Baird having the vapors or some deputation of Full Gospel Christian Mothers marching down the sidewalk accusing her of trying to destroy their children by exposing them to a Satanist and a murderer. God, it's ridiculous. People can't keep two ideas in their heads at the same time. They can't keep even one in their heads. And if we don't invite her, someone might think—"

"Someone might think what? That you thought she was a murderer?"

"No," Nancy said. "Don't be stupid. Why don't you try drafting a letter for me. Something suitably general, that we'd like to talk to her about the possibility of doing something at Hollman High School. Just 'doing something.' Nothing more specific than that. We'll send it to her mother's house and see what she answers."

"All right," Lisa said.

"Fine," Nancy said.

Lisa hesitated, as if she were not sure if their conversation was over, and Nancy nearly bit her head off—what could the confusion possibly be? Then she went out and left the door open behind her, but Nancy didn't mind. She could use the air. She seemed to be having some kind of mild hot flash, and with it that odd feeling of uneasiness that made her think she had forgotten to do something very important, something that was going to change her entire life, or maybe had changed it already. At the very core of her, there was something that wished she could avoid this whole thing, just forget about it, just go on doing what she did every day as if Betsy had not come back to town at all, or as if she had, but hadn't been anybody Nancy needed to pay attention to.

She picked up her phone and accessed her private line. The light would go on on Lisa's phone as well as her own, but Lisa would never pick up to listen in.

If they didn't ask her to speak at the high school, the papers would pick up on that, too, but it would be the good papers this time, or the entertainment press, which everybody read, instead of things like the *Enquirer* that sensible people dismissed out of hand. Then there really would be a lot of publicity—there might even be another interview on *60 Minutes*—and in the end she would be lumped in with the rest of them, with Maris and Belinda and Emma and Peggy, just the way she was lumped in with them in the minds of half the people in town. *Damn*, she thought. *Chris, for God's sake, pick up.*

Then she looked at the back of her hands, and for a moment she thought she saw blood on them again, just like Lady Macbeth.

6

The trouble with Nancy Quayde, Chris Inglerod Barr thought, snapping off the powder-blue McGrath cell phone her husband had given her for Christmas—the problem with Nancy was that she took things too seriously, as if everything that happened were part of a vast plot, and the plot existed only to determine whether or not Nancy Quayde would get what she wanted out of life. Chris had always known exactly what *she* wanted out of life, and as she looked around her big custom-fitted kitchen, with the Jenn-Air grill in the long center island and the breakfast nook that bumped out into a peninsula of windows to keep it chastely separate from the vaulted-ceilinged family room beyond, she thought she had it. Sometimes, on days when she was home alone, she walked through this house room by room just to experience it. She'd been planning it for a long time, longer than anybody knew. Daniel, her husband, thought that her mania for it had begun when he was doing his residency, but that was only when she had started to tell him about it, and when she had started drawing floor plans and room sketches on a spiral-bound pad of thick white paper she'd bought at a pharmacy on her way home from work. The truth was, she'd been thinking about it all the way back in high school. That was why she had been so careful to be nice enough—not quite nice, that could have ruined her—to the boys with pimples and badly fitting jeans who sat in the front of the room in chemistry and biology, getting straight As. She knew that they talked about her when she was out of the room: of all "that crowd," Chris Inglerod was "the nice one." Every year, her yearbook had more signatures in it than anybody else's, and she signed more yearbooks than anybody else did, too. Shy, plain girls who only seemed to blossom in home ec, frightened math whizzes who had somehow reached the tenth grade at the age of nine, people she'd grown up with all her life and still didn't know the names of, all of them counted her as their friend, or something close to it, and in spite of the rude things she had heard from Belinda and Emma, Chris had always known it would pay off. It *had* paid off. She'd met Daniel at Penn State instead of in high school biology—and she'd thought he was after Nancy, at first, because it was Nancy he'd spent all his time with at the first big mixer they'd gone to at Zeta Beta Tau—but they had come back to Hollman to live, and she had been able to present him with a patient list, on a platter, made up of all those people she had known forever who wanted to go on knowing her now. Sometimes, these days, she would catch sight of her reflection in the plate-glass windows of the little grocery store across the street from the Sycamore, this perfect woman in a golf skirt and pastel polo shirt, this vision in a three-quarter-length black cashmere coat and high-heeled boots, and be so happy she was barely able to breathe. She even kept clippings, from the Hollman *Home News*. It only came out once a week—if you wanted a real newspaper, you had to buy the one published in Kennanburg—but it had the news she loved most in it, and it had her picture almost every week: chairwoman of the Heart Fund Drive; organizer of the Friends of the Library lecture series; secretary of the Center School PTA; parent-adviser to the Hollman High School varsity and junior varsity cheerleading squads. Underneath all the pretentious nonsense, Chris Inglerod was a ferociously competent woman. If she'd been born ten years later than she had been, she would have picked up a good MBA as a matter of course. Having been born when she was, and where she was, she had ended up as Mrs. Dr. Barr, and that suited her as perfectly as anything ever would. She had told her mother, when she was small, that she would have a maid when she grew up, and she did. She had promised herself, in those days when all her friends cared about was having exactly the right kind of Bass Weejuns, that she would someday buy all her clothes at Saks Fifth Avenue and Peck and Peck, and the only compromise she'd had to make was to change Peck and Peck for Talbot's, because Peck and Peck had gone out of business when she was barely out of college. If there were drawbacks to her situation—if she sometimes lay in bed in the dark with Daniel hunched and pumping over her, counting the seconds before she could start her ritual moaning to signal to him that he could safely finish, wondering how other women managed to do this night after night without throwing up—in the clear light of day, looking at the Volvo station wagon in the driveway and the Royal Doulton china stacked behind the glass doors in the butler's pantry, they seemed too minor to really worry about.

Now she tapped her fingernails against the back of the phone—short fingernails, colored with an almost-transparent polish, to distinguish her from her husband's receptionist and the cashiers at the supermarket with their curving, three-inch, glitter-painted spikes—and decided there was nothing to do about it, she would have to call Dan. She made a face at the air, because she truly hated calling Dan, and it had nothing to do with the fact that he'd be impatient about her for worrying about high school. Chris swiveled around and looked at the clock on the wall. It was just after one, which meant that Dan would be taking his lunch hour, which he did by locking himself in a back room at the office and eating tuna-fish sandwiches while listening to the Grateful Dead cranked up so high it would split open a normal person's skull. That meant he would have the ear phones on, and that meant that Chris would have to go through the receptionist, even when she used the private line, because Dan listening to the Grateful Dead was Dan dead to the world. Chris didn't understand the attraction. She had gone to a Grateful Dead concert at Penn State with a boy she had had her doubts about, and the band had looked to her like the kind of men you see begging booze money on the side streets of Philadelphia when you got lost trying to remember where you parked your car when you got to the Art Museum. The boy she had had her doubts about had ended up going to New York and getting a job at some publishing company. Maybe he knew Betsy Wetsy himself these days. She tapped her fingernails against the phone again, and looked at the clock again, and promised herself not to let Dan get her all worked up again. Then she made herself dial.

The receptionist, Maura, picked up and sounded vague. Chris counted the minutes—Maura would have to go down the hall and shake Dan out of his reverie; Chris had done it herself from time to time; she knew what it took—and then, when the line was picked up again, heard Uncle John's Band hammering along in the background.

"Jesus Christ," she said before Dan had had a chance to say anything. "What would your patients think if they could hear that stuff you listen to?"

"They probably listen to it themselves. I'd have it playing in the offices while we worked, but I couldn't make it loud enough. People tend to dislike loud noises when they're sick. Is there a point to this call, Chris, or are you just having your monthly nervous breakdown about how the hell I really blew it by not getting a better paying specialty?"

Chris bit her lip. It was true, Dan could have had a better specialty. She would have liked to marry a man who was doing something more impressive than primary care physician, but no matter how often she had talked to Dan about cardiology and cancer, he had put her off.

"Look," she said, "I just got a call from Nancy. Betsy Wetsy is coming back to town at the end of May. For a month."

"Ah," Dan said. "The conquering hero returns. Or heroine. This ought to be interesting. Has Belinda had apoplexy on Grandview Avenue yet, or is she going to wait until Betsy actually gets here?"

"This is serious," Chris said. "God, I don't know how you can make jokes about things that are serious. She's coming here. For a month. And you know she won't be alone, either. She'll have reporters with her."

"As part of her entourage?"

"Don't be ridiculous."

"Relax, Chris. There will only be reporters here if Jimmy Card comes with her, and I don't think he's going to agree to come down here for a month while she straightens out her mother's affairs no matter how much he's in love with her."

"She's famous all on her own, you know, even without Jimmy Card."

"She's not the right kind of famous. Women who appear on panels on CNN and get nominated for Pulitzers for writing books on the crisis of liberalism in America do not attract tabloid journalists and representatives of gossip magazines. The only reason she's been getting the kind of press she's been getting over the last year is because of Jimmy Card. If it wasn't for that, Belinda wouldn't even know she was famous. God only knows, Belinda doesn't watch CNN unless she's forced at gunpoint."

"She would have known because of Maris," Chris said.

"Possibly. I still think you're getting all worked up for nothing. So she's coming for a month. So what? Ignore her if you want to. You were never great friends with her in the past. Act like she isn't here."

"I can't do that. She'll get asked places. Nancy's thinking of asking her to talk at the high school, and Laurel what's-her-name at the library is going to ask her to talk there. She'll be everywhere."

"One more time, Chris. So what?"

Sometimes, Chris used the cell phone as if it were attached to a wall. She forgot she could take it with her when she walked. She went into the breakfast nook and sat down in the chair closest to the long wall of windows looking out on the deck.

"I was in the park that night, you know, the night Michael died."

"You've told me."

"I had blood on my clothes."

Chris could hear Dan clearing his throat in the background. "Chris, be serious. We've been all through this a dozen times. It was, what, thirty years ago—"

"I had blood on my clothes," Chris insisted.

"Yes. Yes," Dan said. "You've told me. You all had blood on your clothes. Belinda and Emma had it all over them. The rain washed it off. Or nearly off. But the last I heard from you, you were actually—"

"Nailing Betsy Wetsy in the outhouse with a bunch of black snakes."

"Was it a bunch? I thought Belinda always said it was only two."

"There were twenty-two of them," Chris said. "I know. I helped collect them. It took us all morning and most of the afternoon. And Betsy doesn't know who it was. If she did, she'd never have hired Maris and kept her on all this time."

"I'll admit the whole thing with your friend Maris sounds odd as hell to me," Dan said.

"She's a drunk." Chris propped one leg up on a chair on the other side of the table. "I don't know why you're having such a hard time getting this into your head, but having Betsy here for a month could turn out to be a major league disaster, for you as well as for me. I don't mean about Michael. Of course that's stupid. Of course it was a coincidence, and even if it wasn't, there's nothing anybody can find now that wasn't found out at the time, more or less. But it's just the kind of story, what we did to Betsy, it's just the kind of story—"

"I didn't do it," Dan said.

"What?"

"I didn't do it," Dan said, again. "If you're worried about her finding out after all this time who did it to her, that's your problem. I was growing up in Radnor at the time. And from what I've seen of that pack of wolves you had for high school best buddies, I fervently believe they've got it coming to them."

"It'll affect you, too," Chris said, frightening herself by the high shrill voice that came out of her. "If she comes down here and does some smear job on the town, makes all the members of our class look like psycho killers, it will affect you, too. We're *married*."

"No," Dan said. "I don't think it will. My tuna fish is getting soggy, Chris, and my Dead album is almost finished. I'm going to get off."

"It'll affect you, too," Chris said, and this time it came out in a shriek, high-pitched and wild, that reminded her of nothing so much as Betsy screaming that night in the outhouse while the rain started and the thunder began to pound overhead.

Dan had hung up. Chris clicked off herself and stayed where she was. The deck was wide and long and ended in a half hexameter. The trees beyond it were tall pines and maples, meticulously kept up by a lawn service she hired to come all the way out from Johnstown. Her hair felt damp. She had been sweating. Of course, it would figure, the one time she had broken her rule for herself, the one time she had not tried to be at least minimally nice, that one time would be the most important one, and now here it was, thirty some odd years later, coming back to haunt her. It bothered her even more because she had known, at the time, that she shouldn't have had a part in it. She had almost tried to talk the others out of it, while they had been stumbling through the forest growth that morning finding the snakes, finding them one after the other, carefully, because if they heard you coming they slithered out of sight. She knew snakes were dry and not slimy wet, but they felt slimy wet to her, so that she could only touch them with two fingers right behind their heads, and she could only hold on to them by keeping her eyes closed while they struggled against her on their long way to the bucket. Twenty-two. Would it have mattered if they had had fewer of them? Would Betsy have screamed like that if there had been only the two snakes Belinda liked to say there were? They had all stood in the trees just out of sight of the clearing and listened as Betsy began to panic. They had stayed just long enough to be sure that she was losing it completely, going out of her mind—what had they expected her to do, exactly? She could have been locked up there for days, if it hadn't been for the police in the park after Michael was murdered.

It wasn't true that Michael being murdered was just a coincidence, Chris thought. It was something more like fate.

7

There were no bells at the ends of class periods at Columbia—Liz didn't know why she had expected there to be. There had been none at Vassar, and none at the University of Michigan where she had done her graduate work—and for some reason this always left her feeling a little off balance, as if she had mistimed her day and everything would now be out of schedule. The truth was, her classes were timed down to the moment. She was legendary, from one end of the campus to the other, for both starting and stopping exactly on time, just as she was legendary for following the syllabus, to the letter, as if it were a television script. It was odd, the things that stayed with you and the things that did not. If you had asked her, when her first husband had died, what she expected to retain of the habits she had picked up in his last illness, that ferocious dedication to organization would not have been one of them, and yet here she was, five years later, more reliable than the atomic clock that determined Greenwich Mean Time. She looked out over the big, amphitheaterlike lecture hall as it emptied. She was always glad they had given her a room like this, in one of the old buildings. It satisfied her long-held aesthetic fantasies about what colleges ought to look like, which came down to thinking that all schools should be either Oxford or Yale. The last of the students were filing out, unaesthetically costumed in ragged jeans and T-shirts with *Abercrombie & Fitch* printed across the chest. Light was coming in through the great arched windows at the back, letting her know that the day had turned out to be a good one. The clouds hadn't turned to rain. She packed her books into her black leather tote bag and thought that there was only next week, two more class meetings, before this course would be finished, and she would have to sit down and give her students grades, which she hated to do, because she always felt it was so counterproductive. The ringer on her cell phone went off, and the little caller-identification window on the side of it let her know it was her office on the line. She considered not answering it, and then decided that that was ridiculous. It wasn't necessarily the call she had been dreading. It could be a call about her mother, or about Jimmy Card, or about a last-minute appointment that she absolutely had to make somewhere in midtown before she even thought about getting herself some lunch. She had a sudden, violent wish that she could go back five years to just after her husband's funeral and do what she'd done then, turn off the ringers on all the phones and not care, for weeks, if anybody could reach her.

Asinine, she thought, picking up. "I'm here," she said.

"It's Debra," Debra said. "I'm making this phone call from the guest bathroom off the conference room. I'd have made it from the sidewalk, except the way things are, I'd be afraid she'd see me. Assuming she can see anything. If you know what I mean."

"Crap." It *was* the phone call she'd been dreading. "What happened?"

"For one thing, she didn't show up until nearly ten-thirty. For another, she'd already been drinking."

"Okay."

"I think she spikes that coffee she brings in a thermos every day. In fact, I'm sure of it. It's the only thing that makes sense. Only, today, when she'd been in for about an hour, she went out again, up the street to get some tampons, she said, although why she needs tampons at her age—"

"Some of us do."

"She doesn't. Don't you remember? It was on her health form when she first came to work for us. I remarked on it at the time. She went through menopause at forty."

"Yes. Okay. I remember." Liz sighed. "Just tell me what happened. Did she go out and never come back again? It hasn't really been that long. It's only, what, twelve-thirty?"

"I wish she'd gone out and never come back," Debra said. "She came back in less than ten minutes and locked herself into the bathroom for another fifteen. When she came out she was, quite frankly, potted. And I do mean potted. There was no mistaking it."

"Crap, crap, crap. *Then* what?"

"Then she sat down at her desk, spread the copy of the speech for the Armonk library talk all over it, started to giggle like a lunatic, and threw up. On the speech. All over the speech. And then she looked at it and started giggling again, and then she threw up again, on the carpet. The new carpet. The one you had installed two months ago after she threw up on the old one for the fifth or sixth time. There's vomit everywhere in that office. The other girls have had to get out. They didn't have any choice and I wouldn't have tried to make them sit still. We're not getting any work done. It's going to be one o'clock before the cleaning guy gets here to mop it all up, and in the meantime we're all milling around as if we're at a cocktail party. And that's just for starters."

"Marvelous," Liz said. "I can't wait to hear the rest of it."

Debra hesitated. "You don't have to hear the rest of it," she said finally. "There's no point. I've got the speech on the computer and I've got a backup on diskette. It's not lost. I can rescue your appointment diary from the computer, too—did I tell you she took your appointment diary when she locked herself in the bathroom?"

"No."

"She did. It doesn't matter. But this does matter, Liz, and I mean it. This is an ultimatum. Either she goes or I do. We've been together for what, fifteen years? I stuck with you when your finances collapsed after Jay died and you couldn't pay me. I stuck with you when you seemed determined to go to hell in a handbasket and end up dead yourself. I think I've been more of a friend than a secretary most of this time and I know you've made it worth my while financially in the long run, but I can't handle this. I appreciate your loyalty to your old friends, I really do. It's a wonderful quality in somebody in your position. I love it that we kept Celia Frank on the payroll right up until the day she died from breast cancer because you didn't think it was right to let her go and make her lose her insurance. Your generosity is something I would not like to see you lose, but, Liz, there's a limit, and this is it. This was it, months ago, and you know it. Pension her off, if you have to. Set up some kind of trust that will keep her from ending up homeless and on the street, pay for her apartment yourself so she doesn't spend the rent money on booze, have food shipped in from grocery stores that deliver, do whatever you have to, but get her out of here. Someday, she's going to pull one of these stunts in front of Dan Rather or the president of AOL-Time Warner and it's going to make a difference. And you know it."

"I keep hoping she'll decide to get her act together and change."

"She doesn't want to change. Trust me. My father was an alcoholic for thirty years. Some of them want to change and they do, but none of them changes with an attitude like that."

"Okay," Liz said. "Let me think."

"There's nothing to think about. Fire her. Or let me fire her. Do it now. Tell Jimmy when you meet him for lunch and he'll buy you a bottle of champagne to celebrate. Remind him to save a glass for me."

"Let me think," Liz insisted. "I can't just fire her right this second, don't you realize that? We're supposed to be going down to Pennsylvania in two weeks."

"So?"

"So she's expecting to come with me. It's her hometown, too. That's all been set up in advance. She's probably told people she's coming, people we've both known forever. We wouldn't want to embarrass her—"

"Like hell."

"*Listen*," Liz insisted. "I've got it all worked out, all right? You won't ever have to deal with her again, I promise. Does that work?"

"It might."

"Don't be facetious. When you get her awake again, do that however you want, tell her that she's obviously sick and needs to go home. Insist on it. Say you've talked to me and I said to send her home and make her stay there for the rest of the week until she's over whatever she's got, stomach flu, think of something—"

"I will not call a gin binge a stomach flu."

"Then don't call it anything. Just get her home and make sure she understands that I said she was to stay there and not come into the office for at least a week. I'll call her later this evening and talk to her—"

"If she's sober."

"If she isn't, I'll talk to her in the morning. Okay? She's not a reeling drunk all the time, Debra, and you know it. I'll talk to her. I'll tell her I need her to go out to Hollman early and do some advance work for me, and then I'll send her off and give her some make work to do. She'll know it's make work, of course, but we can't be picky at the moment. Anyway, then, when I get down to Hollman myself, I can have a talk with her. Between now and then, I ought to be able to figure out another arrangement that will keep her out of your hair—"

"What are you going to do to keep her out of *your* hair?" Debra said. "Liz, I hate to sound like a broken record, but I don't think she even likes you, and I don't think it's all envy, either, although she's got enough of that. I think she hates you."

"She doesn't hate me," Liz said automatically.

"Right. Okay. Whatever. Look, I'll do what I have to do, and all I want from you is the promise that I never have to put up with her in the office again. Fair enough?"

"Yes, fair enough. I'm sorry, Debra. I know this hasn't been easy for you."

"I wouldn't mind if I thought there was any point to it. You going to go meet Jimmy for lunch?"

"I was intending to."

"Good. Go. Give me a little time to get this stuff straightened out. Don't come back until I'm likely to have got her off the premises and on her way home, at least. You don't need this today."

"Right," Liz said. "Thanks again."

Then she flicked the phone off—you couldn't say "hang up," could you, when there was nothing to hang the receiver up *on*—and shoved the phone back into the little leather pocket in her tote bag. Jimmy had bought her the tote bag, at some leather store on Fifth Avenue, on a kind of whim, because he said she didn't understand how to spend money on herself. She thought for a moment of all those things in Maris's apartment—the Steuben glass tumblers, the one-of-a-kind handmade king-sized down-filled quilts, the shoes from Brooks Brothers and Coach—but that, of course, was because Maris had never had children. She had nothing to spend her money on but herself, and besides, she was used to having that kind of thing in her life. If she were ever forced to go without it, she'd be too depressed to function.

Liz checked, one more time, to make sure that she had everything she'd brought with her packed up and ready to go. Then she hoisted the tote bag over her shoulder and went out the door at the side of the podium, out the wide corridor with its twenty-foot-high ceiling, into the sun and light and spring of Morningside Heights. Students at Columbia liked to tell their friends back home that they were going to school "in Harlem," but although it was technically true, it was fundamentally a lie. On an afternoon like this, Columbia could have been set in the middle of a field in Vermont or on the edge of an English village, it had so little in common with the raw violent ugliness of so much of the city around it.

And not just Harlem, Liz thought, flagging an empty cab on its way downtown. She settled herself in the back and gave the driver the address of Jimmy's apartment. She put the tote bag on the floor at her feet and her head back on the curved top of the seat. Jimmy's apartment was in the Dakota. His neighbors had approved mightily when they had first taken up together—they liked to think of themselves as cultivated and intellectual—but approved less so now, when her picture was on the cover of every tabloid in the supermarket. Sometimes, she wondered what it would take for her to stop feeling so guilty, because guilty was what she felt, all the time, about everything, and especially about Maris. It seemed to her that the things that had happened for her had been entirely a matter of chance and circumstance. A lot of people who were better writers than she would ever be had not been given spot after spot on CNN. A lot of people who had had more promise and more talent than she could ever have imagined in herself had ended up flat on their faces, like Maris, through no fault of their own. Of course Maris drank, Liz thought. She would drink herself, if she were Maris, if she had started out with all of Maris's brilliance and talent and promise and watched it come to dust in her hands. Liz knew what they said about her, at home: that she had somehow caused Maris to fail; that she had no right to succeed when Maris had failed so badly; that it wasn't *fair*. She knew, too, that this was the kind of thing people did as they reached middle age and found that their lives had not worked out the way they wanted them to. What she couldn't shake was the feeling that, in her case, they were absolutely right. It wasn't fair, and she had no right to any of it. What had happened to her was not like working hard and getting ahead, but more like winning the lottery. One day, the numbers on her particular ticket had been drawn, and forever afterward—

What?

The cab had pulled up to the curb in front of the Dakota, on Central Park West, not around the corner at the gate where John Lennon had died, because Liz truly hated that gate. She remembered taking a friend from out of town up there on the morning after it happened, when she was still an editorial assistant and her friend was still in graduate school. They had been lovers once, but her move to New York had been too much for whatever they'd seen in each other. He was the kind of man she'd gotten used to in college, with family money and the disdain for routine work that went with it, and by the time she had been working and on her own for a month, she was already disappointed in him. What bothered her about the Dakota now, of course, was Jimmy Card. All she needed in her life was some guy who wanted to be the second one to gun down a rock star at that damned metal gate.

Actually, Liz thought, that wasn't what she'd been thinking about at all. What she'd been thinking about was that high keening wail in the wind and the rain and the words that sounded like music in the claustrophobic bubble that covered her head.

slit his throat slit his throat slit his throat

PART ONE

"At Seventeen"

—JANIS IAN

"The Boho Dance"

—JONI MITCHELL

"A.M. Radio"

—EVERCLEAR

ONE

1

In the beginning, the problem of the body of Anne Marie Hannaford had not been as simple as it should have been. The Commonwealth of Pennsylvania had seemed reluctant to give it back, as if they were afraid she had become an icon, like Jeffrey Dahmer, and that people would make a shrine out of her grave. When they finally did give it back—three days late, and not embalmed—Bennis had decided that there was nothing she could do. In spite of the Hannaford tradition of being buried in the big family plot in the cemetery behind the Episcopal Church in Ardmore, where Hannafords had gone to rest since 1762, Anne Marie would have to be cremated. Bennis tried to consult her brothers about this decision, but it was hopeless. Christopher didn't care. Bobby had other things on his mind. Teddy didn't want to talk to her. It felt, she sometimes told Gregor, as if they were all still children growing up in Bryn Mawr, where boys were the ones that mattered and girls were supposed to fend for themselves as much as possible, unless they were debutantes, when they deserved the kind of attention that would make it possible for them to marry well.

After Anne Marie was cremated, her body was put into a small brass urn with handles that looked like a bowling trophy and then—because nobody could decide what was going to happen with that, either—left on the top of Bennis's low dresser in her own bedroom in her apartment on the second floor of the brownstone house on Cavanaugh Street. It would have been a morbid thing, except that Bennis never slept in that bedroom anymore. She rarely even went to that apartment, except to work, and these days she had her work station set up in the living room on a big table pushed up against the plate-glass window that looked down to the street. She said she never thought about it, but Gregor did. He thought about it all the time, and once a day, when he knew Bennis would be out at the Ararat or at Donna Moradanyan's, he went down to look at it for himself, just to make sure it was still there. He had no idea why he thought it might be gone. She couldn't very well bury it, or place it in a vault, without a good deal of formality.

The people who ran cemeteries were sticklers for paperwork. Dead bodies could be dangerous, even if they had been burned to ashes. That was why the Commonwealth insisted that anyone who wanted to scatter ashes within its precincts get permission. Maybe, Gregor thought, he was afraid that she'd open the urn and scatter the ashes on her own, without permission. He just didn't understand where she would scatter them. God only knew, she didn't want them on Cavanaugh Street. She said that often enough, and vehemently, when Tibor brought up the possibility that the ashes could be placed at Holy Trinity Church. Maybe she would take them out to Ardmore herself, or take them with her to one of those "events" she was always being invited to but never agreeing to attend, like the Philadelphia Assemblies. Maybe she would *eat* them. The whole thing had become a matter of annoyance, because Gregor didn't really know what he thought of it, but he couldn't stop obsessing about it. He felt like Lida, or Hannah, whenever it looked as if someone new would be moving onto the street. They obsessed, too, and also to no good purpose. Eventually whoever it was moved in and got settled, and they knew no more about it than when they had started staying up nights to speculate to each other on the phone. Sheila Kashinian would have stayed up with them, but Howard couldn't stand it when Sheila talked on the phone in bed.

Actually, somebody was moving onto Cavanaugh Street this morning. That was why the building was nearly deserted, and why Gregor felt completely easy about looking in on the urn for the first time in weeks. Bennis, like the rest of them, was out in the street, watching the moving men bring what looked like a small, oddly shaped piano up to the fourth floor of their own brownstone, into the apartment that had been Donna Moradanyan's before she married Russ and moved into a town house on the other side of the Ararat. It was a rental, at least for the moment, that was all that anybody knew. Bennis had been out the door before the Ararat opened this morning, to hear what Donna had to say about the new tenant one more time—although, Gregor thought, she couldn't really believe that Donna, or Russ, would turn the apartment over to somebody who wouldn't be good for Cavanaugh Street. It was just that this was the first time an apartment here had been advertised in the classifieds, the way apartments were when they were anywhere else. Usually, apartments on Cavanaugh Street were passed from tenant to tenant by way of family connections, church connections, and a tenuous network of refugee contacts that Tibor kept up as part of his attempt to make it possible for every single Armenian who wanted to be resettled in Philadelphia. This time, Russ had insisted—there were antidiscrimination laws, after all, and he was not only a lawyer with a reputation to maintain, but he approved of the laws to begin with.

"It's a woman, that's all I know," Donna had said, a couple of weeks ago, in Gregor's kitchen, as she stacked her books for her Literature of the English Renaissance course into a pile. The books were huge, and the pile was not little. Bennis sat drinking coffee and reading the titles on the spine: *Imagery and Iconography in Tudor Poetry; The Figure of the Virgin in the Work of Edmund Spenser*. Gregor thought it looked like one of the piles in Tibor's apartment, except that there was nothing out of place in it. Donna needed a copy of *I, the Jury* or *Passionate Remembrance*, or both.

"Anyway, that's all he'll tell me," Donna said, "except that she's some kind of a musician. A classical musician. She plays in some orchestra—"

"The Philadelphia Philharmonic?" Bennis suggested.

"No," Donna said. "It had an odd name, and then when I asked him to tell me again, he wouldn't. He says we all worry too much about stuff like this, and I suppose he's right, but it's Cavanaugh Street, for God's sake. What does he expect us to do? Anyway, I'm sure it'll be fine. Russ likes her a lot, whoever she is, and he says she's met Gregor sometime or the other, although I don't suppose that's much of a recommendation. A lot of mass murderers have met Gregor at some time or the other."

"Thank you very much," Gregor said.

"Well, it's true. She's moving in on Wednesday, for whatever that's worth, and we can all find out then. Lida is threatening to throw a reception for her. Wouldn't that be something? One poor defenseless woman and those Medusas on the warpath. Mrs. Valerian grilling her about birth control."

"They might like her just as much as Russ does," Bennis said, reasonably.

"Ha! That would be worse. Then they'd try to marry her off, if she isn't married already, and if she is they'll try to find out why she isn't with her husband and if he hasn't been beating her into a pulp on a regular basis for years, they'll try to get them back together. And they'll bring food day and night until she's gained at least twenty extra pounds, and then she'll probably be too fat to play in that orchestra she's in and she'll get fired, and she won't pay her rent, but Russ won't be able to evict her, either, because they'll kill him if he tries, and then she'll get a job at the Armenian Christian school because Father Tibor will feel sorry for her, and that won't be enough to cover the rent either, but that won't matter because we won't be charging her any by then, because how could we do that with a woman who'd lost her job just because her employers thought it was okay to discriminate against fat people?"

The urn was still on the dresser, sitting on top of a copy of Janson's *History of Art*, exactly where Gregor had seen it yesterday. There was still a thick coat of dust on the top of it, so thick that if he ran his finger through it he would make a deep-sided groove, gritty and jagged. Bennis was telling at least this much of the truth. She was not tending this urn, the way she might tend the grave of somebody she had cared deeply about, or somebody she felt so guilty about that she was forced to make reparations and atonement on a daily basis. It was just here, as neglected as Janson's book and the scattered pages of old newspapers that covered the rest of the dresser's surface. Gregor would have felt better if the old newspapers hadn't all contained stories announcing the execution of Bennis Hannaford's oldest sister.

"It would be a lot easier to handle this," Bennis said at the time, "if I hadn't always disliked her so much."

Gregor went over to the urn and put his finger on the dust. He took his finger off and wiped it on the white handkerchief he still kept in the front vest pocket of his good suit jacket, as if, even in this small way, he was stuck in the time warp Bennis always accused him of inhabiting whenever she was angry with him. Then he went out of the bedroom and down the hall to Bennis's living room, which no longer had much in the way of furniture in it. He went over to the worktable and looked out over the computer, through the window, and the moving men still struggling with whatever it was. They were trying to hoist it up to the fourth floor and bring it through the living-room window. There was probably no other way to get it upstairs at all. Bennis and Donna and Lida and Hannah and Sheila were all sitting across the street on the steps to Lida's town house. The very old ladies were not in evidence at all, but they would be somewhere, at one of their windows, taking notes in Armenian. Tibor would be in his own apartment, posting messages to rec.arts.mystery, having forgotten the time. Old George Tekemanian would be sitting on the sidewalk under the umbrella at the outdoor table-and-chair set his nephew Martin had ordered for him at L. L. Bean. Gregor checked his hip pocket—it wouldn't be the first time he'd forgotten his wallet—and then left Bennis's apartment and headed down the stairs to the street. There had never been a chance that he would be able to leave today without passing through crowds like a movie star on her way in to the Oscars. Except, Gregor thought, that the movie star would probably be pleased with the crowds, and she'd never have to see anybody in them again.

When he left the building, the whatever-it-was was in the air, just about level with Bennis's living-room window, where he had been standing only moments before. He crossed the street to Lida's and stopped in front of Bennis.

"How do I look? Is my tie on straight?"

"When have you ever cared about your ties?" Bennis asked, straightening anyway, because she always did. "You look very nice. You went to more trouble than you needed to. Jimmy never notices what he wears."

"When you do business, it's good to be businesslike. Are you sure you won't come with me? I doubt if he'd mind, no matter what you say. After all, he called you. And I could use the support."

"You don't need any support," Bennis said. "You're a lot alike, actually. Big ethnic guys with unwavering moral compasses. The *same* unwavering moral compass. If anything, I'd say he was far less sophisticated than you, even now. But no, I would not like to come along. His lady friend might object."

"She's not going to be there."

"This meeting is going to be in the *National Enquirer*, and don't you think it won't. There's no real way for people like Jimmy to keep things secret. I should know. I was once one of his not very well kept secrets."

"That was a long time ago."

"Agreed. It was. But it's not like she doesn't know. The lady friend, I mean. And I don't care how intellectual she is, she wouldn't like it. Just go and listen to what he has to say. You'll be fine."

Gregor looked around. The whatever-it-was was now level with his own living-room window, which did have furniture in it, mostly Bennis's. She had put the stuff he'd had when she moved in into storage, and would have done worse than that (*this stuff deserves to be ritually burned*) if he'd let her.

"What is that thing?" he asked. "It's not a piano."

"It's a Peter Redstone harpsichord. That's what the moving men said. Donna asked. She's got Peter Redstone virginals, too. Mother and child virginals. They're still in the van. It's all musical instruments, everything that's been moved in so far this morning. I don't think there's even been a bed."

"Why isn't she coming with him?" Gregor asked. "The lady friend, I mean. This is supposed to concern her, isn't it?"

Bennis sighed. "Go ask him," she said. "I don't know anything but what I told you and that stuff I showed you from the *Enquirer* and the *Star*, and I wouldn't have known that if he hadn't brought it up. Just be glad it's Elizabeth Toliver who's got the problem and not that idiot he was married to before. The supermodel, you know. She's congenitally brain dead. I don't understand why men like that always do that sort of thing. I mean, can't they count? Those women reach forty like the rest of us, and then what do you have? Nothing at all in the head and not much left in the body. You'd think—"

"That's a cab," Gregor said.

He leaned over and pecked her on the cheek, eliciting a loud "bravo!" from Donna Moradanyan. There was indeed a cab turning onto Cavanaugh Street, and not just going through but pulling up to the curb right in front of where he was. He hurried down Lida's steps to the sidewalk and got there just as a small, dark-haired, painfully thin young woman got out, fumbling with a purse almost half her size.

"Oh," she said, seeing him come toward her. "It's Mr. Demarkian. Good morning."

"Good morning," Gregor said, and then the next thing he knew he was in the cab and the cab was moving, and he still couldn't remember who that young woman was or where he had seen her before. That he did know who she was and that he had met her before was not in doubt, but when he turned around to get another look at her from the cab's rear window, she had disappeared into a huddle of Cavanaugh Street women. He turned back around again. They'd know her shoe size, her favorite dessert, and her blood type by the time he got home, and they'd either be for her or against her.

Then he wished, for the fortieth time since Thursday, that he had not let Bennis talk him into meeting with Jimmy Card and listening to his problem.

2

It wasn't true, as Bennis liked to claim, that Gregor Demarkian had a prejudice against celebrities. For almost twenty years of his life, he had worked with them more often than not, although they had been the high-government-official type of celebrity rather than the been-seen-on-TV-a-lot kind. There was less of a difference than he had expected there to be. All of the ones he could remember, including the presidents of the United States, had been vain, in that anxious, uncertain, panicky way that indicated that, deep down, they didn't much like what they really looked like. They were people who had placed their trust in the illusions they were able to create. If they were really good at it, like Bill Clinton, they could do anything they wanted to do and get away with it. If they were really bad at it, like Richard Nixon, they might as well never have gotten out of bed. Gregor had been a fairly senior agent in the FBI during Richard Nixon's last year in office. He could remember watching the man on TV, the jerky movements, the paranoia so palpable it glistened on his skin like sweat. Gregor had never been able to understand it. Usually, a man that badly fitted for celebrity never got near to public office, except maybe on the most local level, where it was possible for personal loyalties to outweigh appearances. The miracle of Richard Nixon was that he'd managed to last as long as he had in national office. Gregor didn't think it could be done anymore, when everything was television, and the only people who got their news from newspapers were fussy academics in the more progressive colleges who thought even PBS was dangerous to the mental health of our nation's youth. Except, Gregor thought vaguely, as he got out of the cab in front of Le Cirque Blanc, they wouldn't say "our nation's youth" these days. They'd say "young people" or "the young" or maybe even "teenagers." It was like Hillary Clinton's vast right-wing conspiracy. It was everywhere, and it changed the words on you, just when you thought you knew what to say.

Le Cirque Blanc was the closest thing Philadelphia had to a "celebrity" restaurant, and Gregor had not been surprised when Jimmy Card had asked to meet him there. It was not Philadelphia's best restaurant, or the one most famous for its food, but like certain places in New York it had a couple of curtained-off back rooms that could be reached by a side entrance and a staff that understood what privacy did—and did not—mean. In New York, such a place would be full of people like Madonna and Harrison Ford, people so famous that they really had had enough of having their privacy invaded every time they went out for a drink or a little light dinner. In Philadelphia, Gregor got the impression that the place was full of members of the city government who didn't want their dinner meetings to show up on the six o'clock news and Main Line society women who wanted to have flings that wouldn't do them credit with their friends. Most of the time, both these groups of people tried to be as public as possible, on the theory that well-known people were more important than the less well-known kind. Some of the Main Line society women must have known this wasn't true, since they were probably married to men so important that their entire lives revolved around staying strictly out of sight.

Le Cirque Blanc had an awning that reminded Gregor of the ones on Manhattan apartment buildings, and a doorman who reminded him of Manhattan apartment buildings, too. The doorman wore a uniform and a cap, like a chauffeur. What really bothered Gregor about "celebrities" was that they reminded him, so much, of the serial killers he had spent the last half of his career chasing. The Ted Bundys, the Jeffrey Dahmers, the John Wayne Gacys, all had that hard streak of vanity and that desperation, as if in some way they weren't really alive unless other people said they were. When the Bureau had first been putting together the composite psychological profile that later became the basis for the entire Behavioral Sciences Unit, Gregor had wanted to put that in, but none of them could think of a way to phrase it so that somebody who had never encountered it could understand it. Gregor had always thought that the most obvious case of it had been—still was—Charles Manson, a man who lived entirely by the effect he had on other people, so much so that he hadn't even had to do his own serial killing. It was an open question as to whether or not that quirk of personality, and the charisma that went with it, had survived all the years in prison. Gregor made it a point to watch Manson's parole hearings when they were shown on Court TV, but it was hard to tell. He was cleaned up now, and subdued, but that could be for the benefit of the parole board, which wasn't going to release him in any case. It was too bad that monsters didn't stay monsters in real life, that growing old meant growing weak for even the most dedicated of them. For some reason, watching a Charles Manson turn into an old man made Gregor far more aware of his own mortality than the death of someone like Princess Diana did. Maybe that was because he had never been able to think of Princess Diana as really being real.

"Mr. Demarkian," the man on the front desk said. He was dressed in a white tie and tails, in spite of the fact that it was barely noon. The restaurant lobby and the restaurant behind him were both dark, as if nobody could eat unless it was the middle of the night. The man himself was just slightly overweight, in that smug, self-satisfied way that some people equated with high social status, even though these days, everybody who really did have high social status was bone thin. Gregor decided he must have been hired for effect, like a stock actor hired to play a stock character, the point being that nothing mattered except keeping the ambiance unbroken, whatever the ambiance was supposed to be.

"If you follow me, I'll take you back myself," the man said.

Gregor nodded toward him, half afraid to speak. *That* would break the ambiance soon enough. Part of him wanted to jump up and down or shout or do something equally ridiculous, because this place was so false, so uncomfortable, so strained, that even the air felt oddly synthetic. He looked from left to right as they walked through the large main dining room, empty except for two elderly women in a booth along the west wall, drinking cocktails with paper umbrellas in them. You could buy those little paper umbrellas in party stores for $6.95 a hundred.

At the back of the main dining room, the man in the tails paused and felt along the wall. The door that opened there had been papered to look as if it wasn't a door at all, and it didn't, unless you knew what to look for. Then the outline was painfully obvious and—like so much about this place—completely unnecessary.

"Normally, I'd take you around to the back," the man in the tails said, "but under the circumstances . . ." He nodded toward the two elderly women, who were paying no attention to them at all. "They wouldn't notice if a train went through here, once they'd had their third round. If we begin to fill up while you're at lunch, I'll take you out the other way. We do try to accommodate our patrons' need for discretion."

Gregor didn't comment on the man's use of the word "discretion"—which, in its obviousness, was even worse than the "secret" door. He just went through into the back room and let the man come in behind him. The room was smaller than the dining room outside and had nothing in it but booths, each fitted into the wall behind heavy velvet curtains that could be drawn on shiny corded ropes. All of these curtains were now open, and all the booths but one were empty. A tall man, not Jimmy Card, stood up in the one occupied booth and then slid out into the room. A second later, Jimmy Card followed him, as if he'd been waiting for the signal that would tell him nobody was coming in he didn't want to see.

"Very good," the man in the tails said. "I'll send your waiter in a moment. I hope you have an enjoyable meal, gentlemen."

They all murmured incoherent things, and the man in tails bobbed solemnly and "withdrew," walking backward all the way until he reached the "secret" door, as if he were dealing with royalty and in a distinctly outdated fashion.

Gregor waited until the door was firmly shut and they were alone and then said, "When I was in the army, I went to a place like this in New Orleans. Rich men would bring high-class call girls there for dinner, and they'd have the curtains so that they'd be safely out of sight if their wives came looking for them."

"Ha," Jimmy Card said.

"Why didn't the wives just draw back the curtains?" the tall man said.

"Maybe they did. Or maybe they just had sense enough to stay home. I never saw a run-in with a wife." Gregor looked Jimmy Card up and down, but he looked no different in person than he did on television: a short, dark, trim man just beginning to flesh out with middle age, the kind of man who worked out to stay in shape, but didn't work out enough to stay in perfect shape. For some reason, Gregor found that comforting.

"I'm Gregor Demarkian," he said.

"We recognized you from *People*," the tall man said. "Or at least, I did—"

"Of course I recognized him," Jimmy Card said. "What do you take me for?"

"You say you never read *People*," the tall man said.

"I watch the news. I read the papers. Give me a break."

"I'm Bob Haverton," the tall man said. "I'm Jimmy's lawyer. It used to be a full-time job."

"Used to be?" Gregor said.

"Bob's of the opinion that Liz has mellowed me out," Jimmy Card said. "I keep telling him he's got it backward. It's not that Liz mellowed me out. It's that I mellowed out and that got me together with Liz."

"At least she isn't likely to try to use the divorce courts to turn you into a financial basket case. Jimmy used to have that short ethnic guy's insecurity thing with women. He could only marry tall upper-middle-class WASP blondes. He just couldn't get it through his head that they always marry for money."

"Oh," Gregor said.

"You're going to make Mr. Demarkian think you're a bigot," Jimmy said.

"I'm a realist," Bob Haverton said. "My own sister is a tall upper-middle-class WASP blonde, although hardly in the same league with either of Jimmy's wives. One of the perks of being a pop star is that you get to marry the kind of women who show up on the cover of the *Sports Illustrated* swimsuit edition. And Jimmy did. Twice."

"Right now, I'd like to marry a short brunette," Jimmy said, "except that she keeps saying no and now she's trying to go off and commit suicide, which is why we're here. We do have a reason why we're here. Maybe we should all sit down and discuss it."

"Maybe we should find another restaurant," Bob said. "You know the food in this place is going to be god-awful."

"If we find another restaurant, we'll be photographed," Jimmy said. He looked around. The room really was awful. The food really would probably be worse. "At least let's sit down and discuss this and see if we can come to some kind of arrangement. It will all come out eventually. I'm just hoping to give Mr. Demarkian a head start. Sit."

"The only way you could give me a head start is to put me in a time machine and send me back thirty-two years," Gregor said, sliding into the booth anyway. "Before we do anything at all, Mr. Card, I need to stress that. The possibility that you can actually solve a case that's over thirty years in the past is virtually nil. It's been done, but it takes luck, and you can't plan for luck."

"I know," Jimmy Card said. He looked at the ceiling, and at the table, and at the palms of his hands. The light around him seemed to shift, and for a moment he looked like what he would look like in another twenty years, when the hope was gone. The effect was faintly shocking, and it made Gregor far more sympathetic to him than any appeal he might make could have done. Most "celebrities" managed to keep from looking old, not only through diet and exercise and plastic surgery, but through arrogance as well. You didn't get old when you still believed that you would live forever.

"So," Gregor said. "If you still want to go through with this, even if you know it's probably going to fail, I'll be happy to help you out, for Bennis's sake, if for no other reason. But I feel dishonest doing it."

Jimmy Card and Bob Haverton looked at each other. Bob Haverton drew in a deep breath and said, "There are other considerations here, besides finding out who killed Michael Houseman. If you manage to find out who committed the murder, we'll be ecstatic. But what we really need for you to do is to find out something else—"

"Not find out," Jimmy said. "We already know."

"Find the proof of something else," Bob amended. "So, if you wouldn't mind, I'd like to lay this whole thing out for you from the beginning, and then you can tell us what you think."

3

They waited until they could order, and they each seemed to be intent on ordering as little as possible. The menu was a horror of pretentiousness that included things like "sea bass en croute" and "crepes Madeleine," both described in flourishes that made the restaurant critic for *Gourmet* magazine sound like Ernest Hemingway. It was, Gregor thought at one point, the Banana Republic catalogue of restaurant menus. Every offering had a story, and every story had a wry, whimsical, pixie-sophisticated tone to it, like the brightest kid without ambition in an Ivy League freshman class. He asked for something he hoped would turn out to be a steak, and Perrier, because it was obviously going to be impossible to get something as simple as a glass of ginger ale. They did have Diet Coke on the menu, but Gregor never drank Diet Coke. He couldn't imagine asking for a Café Creme Virginite, which seemed to be a Kahlua and cream made without Kahlua. The other two men asked for salads, with dressing on the side, probably the safest thing, under the circumstances. If they couldn't cook it, they couldn't ruin it.

They all waited, talking about nothing, until the food was served. Gregor's lunch turned out to have something to do with steak, but only vaguely, as it was covered in grapes and a thick brown sauce that reminded him of the stuff that came with Egg Foo Yung. He ignored it in favor of the green beans, which had nothing more complicated on them than almond slivers and melted butter.

"I warned you," Jimmy Card said.

"I'm not in the habit of eating at restaurants in central Philadelphia," Gregor told him.

Bob Haverton picked up his attaché case, laid it on the clear end of the table, and snapped it open. He had his initials on it in polished brass, and the brass sparkled in the light.

"I've had our people put together as complete a dossier on this case as it's possible to get," he said. "It is, as you've pointed out, over thirty years in the past, but the records are still available, not only police records but newspaper files, the file from the Parks and Recreation Service, a couple of articles that ran in the true crime magazines. It's not as good as being there at the time, I admit, but it's something to go on. Would you like to see?"

Gregor took the thick stack of papers Haverton was handing out to him and put it down next to his plate. "I can keep these?"

"If you take the case, yes. I've got copies."

"Have you read them?"

"We both have," Jimmy Card said. "I've read them over and over again. I think, from what Liz told me, well, I hadn't expected—"

Bob Haverton cleared his throat. "Liz told him they locked her in an outhouse with some snakes. She didn't tell him that she'd had a phobic reaction and beaten herself bloody on the outhouse door, trying to get out."

"Beat herself bloody and practically unconscious," Jimmy said. He gestured at the papers. "It's all in there. When they found her, the skin was flailed off her arms and the sides of her hands and she just fell out onto the ground at this police officer's feet. There were still snakes in the outhouse, two or three. She—"

"She really is phobic," Bob Haverton said. "Genuinely. She can't be in the room with a picture of one, and we found school records going back to kindergarten of her panicking when there was one on the playground, having complete screaming fits—"

"So," Gregor said. "All the people she knew, knew she was afraid of snakes? And one of these people locked her into an outhouse and put snakes in there with her?"

"Right," Jimmy said. "A lot of them, according to Liz. But the thing is, with Liz and snakes, a lot could mean only three. And she really doesn't know how many."

"What was the point?" Gregor asked. "Were they trying to kill her? People have died of shock from phobic reactions."

"I doubt they were actually trying to kill her," Jimmy said. "They were all, what? Eighteen. Seventeen. And this was 1969. And it wasn't the first time."

"It wasn't the first time they'd locked her in an outhouse with a lot of snakes?" Gregor's eyebrows raised.

"Liz," Bob Haverton said carefully, "was not exactly popular in high school. Or in elementary school. As far as we can make out, she was one of those kids who's sort of like a target, the one all the other kids pick on.

It had been going on for years. And some of the incidents were pretty damned nasty. They took all her clothes while she was showering after gym once. They told her they wanted to meet her at this place they all went to—"

"The White Horse," Jimmy said. "It was a bar. The kind of place you could go drinking and not get carded."

"Right." Bob nodded. "Anyway, they told her they wanted to meet her there and then they took off for a different place in a different town and left her stranded so that she had to walk home, in the dark, or call her parents and tell them where she was. She walked home. Jimmied her locker and took all her books. Spray-painted 'big wet turd' in red on the back of her best black sweater during an assembly and then laughed at it all day—"

"And this was everybody in the whole school?" Gregor asked. "Nobody told her about the spray paint?"

"A teacher did, eventually," Jimmy said. "But you know, I've seen it happen, mostly with girls. Boys get cut a lot more slack. But some girls are just—I mean, even the teachers can't stand them, they're just—"

"Targets," said Bob Haverton wryly. "I've had a better education than Jimmy did. I actually went to college, instead of just hauling ass to New York City to make my fortune. You can tell by our bank accounts who made the wiser choice."

"It was only Adelphi," Jimmy said.

"It was Yale Law. My point, however, is that I've read *Lord of the Flies* a few times. And that's what this was, as far as I can make out. *Lord of the Flies* on a somewhat attenuated scale. Although, considering the thing with the outhouse and the snakes, it's probably just as well that she was getting out for college the following fall."

"I think that's part of what did it," Jimmy said. "Drew them over the edge, I mean, into doing something that could have been dangerous. Because she got into a good college and that just made them madder."

"Back up," Gregor said. "This was when—the day it happened?"

"July twenty-third, 1969," Bob Haverton said.

"And what time of day?"

"Early evening," Jimmy said. "A lot of them worked, you know, and when they got off work they'd go to this park where there was a lake for swimming and a lifeguard. And the park had woods around it and this set of outhouses—"

"Set?"

"I think it said four stalls in a row," Bob Haverton said.

"Okay," Gregor said. "It was early evening, and people went to this park, including Ms. Toliver. Was she getting off work, too?"

"No," Jimmy said. "Her father was this hotshot lawyer. She was taking the summer off. She used to go to the park in the daytime when pretty much everybody she knew was working, and then she'd leave as they started to drift in."

"But this evening she stayed?" Gregor asked.

"I don't think so," Jimmy said. "I think she was going to leave the same as always, but then things happened. One of them called her over and told her they needed her to see something, and I suppose she should have known better by then, I mean, for God's sake, it had been going on long enough, but she went to look. And that's when they pushed her into the outhouse and locked the door."

"To be specific," Bob Haverton said, "they nailed it shut."

"What?" Gregor said, bolt upright. "They *nailed* it shut?"

"That's what I said." For the first time, Haverton looked thoroughly disgusted. "I know adolescents can be evil, but this was a bunch of sociopaths, if you ask me. They gathered a bunch of snakes, granted small black snakes, perfectly harmless—"

"—except to somebody like Liz," Jimmy said.

"Except to somebody like Liz," Haverton agreed. "Anyway, they put them in there, and then one of them, Maris Coleman, called her over and asked her to look inside, I don't remember what the pretext was—"

"He can ask Liz himself when he gets to Hollman," Jimmy said.

"—and when she looked in the rest of them rushed up from out of the bushes where they'd been hiding and pushed her in. Then they slammed the door and nailed it shut. She says she was screaming the whole time, and I believe her. I've seen her around snakes."

Gregor considered all this. "Most of them were hiding. How many of them is most of them?

"Six," Jimmy said. "Maris Coleman, Belinda Hart, Emma Kenyon, Nancy Quayde, Chris Inglerod, and Peggy Smith."

"We don't actually know that all of them were there, or that all of them were involved," Haverton said, "but that was the group of them and they were together later, when the body was found, along with a couple of other people who were not ordinarily part of their circle. Liz says she heard them laughing while they nailed up the door."

"And Ms. Toliver was screaming all the time?" Gregor said. "Why didn't somebody else hear her?"

"There may not have been anybody to hear her," Haverton said. "The lifeguards go off at five. They left promptly. This might have been fifteen or twenty minutes later."

"What about the other people in the park?" Gregor said. "Surely, there were other people in the park. This boy, the one who died, Michael Houseman—"

"He was sort of part of the same crowd," Jimmy said. "He dated one of the girls, or something like that. I'm not exactly clear on that. And yes, later, there were a few other people in the park. When the body was found there were maybe fifteen people present, at the bank of a small river that runs through the place—"

"And those people should have been able to hear Elizabeth Toliver scream?" Gregor asked.

"Yes," Jimmy said.

"And they didn't investigate what was happening? They didn't try to help her? Or did they? Did somebody go try to release her?"

"The cops released her when they came to look at the body," Jimmy said. "They heard her screaming and they went to see what was up. It's in the police reports."

"So you're saying that she stayed in this outhouse, screaming her head off, for—how long?"

"At least an hour," Bob Haverton said.

"An hour. While screaming her head off within hearing range of two dozen people. And nobody went to help her. Nobody went to see what was wrong with her. Nobody paid any attention at all."

"I told you it was like *Lord of the Flies*," Haverton said.

"It's more like *Ripley's Believe It or Not*. Hasn't it occurred to any of you, hasn't it occurred to her, that this makes absolutely no sense? People don't behave this way, not even in groups. *Lord of the Flies* had a hero. Put that many people into one place and at least one of them should go see what's wrong and try to do something about it. Instead, they did what? Wandered around the park? Had a campfire? What?"

"Chris Inglerod and Peggy Smith said they went swimming," Jimmy said. "Maris Coleman says—said—whatever."

"She told the police that she went with Belinda Hart to the lake to sit by the water. She says now that she and Belinda took a walk by the river."

"You've talked to her recently," Gregor said.

"I talk to her every day," Jimmy said. "Much as I'd prefer not to. She works for Liz."

"Works for her?" Gregor blinked.

"She's some kind of personal assistant," Jimmy said. "Liz hired her when she got fired a few years ago. When Maris got fired, that is. For the third time. In two years. Don't get me started. She's going down to Hollman with Liz. You'll meet her yourself, if you decide to do this for us."

"That's what we meant about there being something else to this than finding the person who murdered Michael Houseman," Bob Haverton said. "We're both—Jimmy and I are both—convinced that it's Maris Coleman who's been feeding those stories to the supermarket tabloids. In fact, we don't see who else it could be. We just need you to prove it."

"Liz," Jimmy Card said, angry now, "refuses to believe it."

TWO

1

Somehow, when Liz Toliver had dreamed of coming back to Hollman, what she had imagined was a kind of triumphal march: she would arrive, not only famous but impossibly rich, sitting in the back of a pitch-black superstretch limousine, driven by a driver in livery with her initials on his jacket. Well, she thought now, as she turned off the two-lane blacktop onto the first of the narrow country roads that lay between her and Hollman like a tangled mess of capillaries, that probably wasn't how she had really imagined it, at least not since she was seven or eight years old. Maybe the problem was that she had not imagined coming back at all. There was, Liz thought, no point to it. It had been so long since she had lived in this place, so long since she had even visited it, that it sometimes seemed to her to be one of those mythic archetypes they had studied about in Dr. Weedin's course in Shakespeare. This was not her life. This was a universal expressive form, meant to mirror the reality of all people everywhere: the ugly duckling emerging from a pond of prettier ducklings, with the pond inexplicably populated by snakes. Liz liked that idea better than she liked the one that had been nagging at her since they left Connecticut this morning, and that was that she was fundamentally a coward. She had not come back because she was afraid to come back, and because she knew—as well as she had ever known anything—that she had not really changed at all. The more familiar the roads got, the stronger the feeling got. She didn't have to dig through her tote bag for the copy of the Hollman High School *Wildcat*, 1969, to know what she was really like. She looked at the backs of her hands on the steering wheel and half expected the nails on them to split and go ragged, the way nails do when you bite them, day after day. She found herself expecting the car to change, too, so that instead of this ridiculous Mercedes—$140,000 before sales tax, right off the showroom floor—she would be driving the little blue Ford Escort wagon she had had the year after Jay died, when everything was falling apart, and they had had no money at all. *That*, God help her, didn't make *any* sense, because there hadn't even been any Ford Escorts when she was living in Hollman, and it didn't matter what there had been, because she hadn't had a car at all. Besides, she'd actually liked the Ford Escort. It had been the one thing in her life that year that had gone more right than wrong, and when she had walked back to it across the parking lot at the supermarket or the mall, she had always been relieved to see how shiny and new it looked. It was a kind of camouflage. Her life that year, *their* lives that year, had been anything but shiny and new. They had been living in a rented cabin out at Lake Candlewood, because they'd lost the house, and there were cracks and leaks in every room. When it rained, water came in through the roof and soaked the living room. When anyone took a bath, the water leaked out of the bathtub and turned the bathroom floor into a lake. The only dry space in the whole cabin had been in the little corner of the kitchen where she had set up her computer. After a while, that space had become holy. They had all worshiped at the altar of it. If their lives were ever going to change, if they had a hope in hell of getting back to being the way they were before Jay got sick, then the change was going to come from that corner. That was why Geoff was not allowed to touch the computer keyboard, ever, and Mark was only allowed to touch it when he had an important report for school, the kind that needed illustrations and charts that had to be taken off the Net. God, Liz thought, she ought to remember that better than she did. She ought to have nightmares about the foreclosure or the Christmas they'd spent with two candles, no tree, and presents that consisted of exactly one small box of Russell Stover candy for each of the boys, wrapped in aluminum foil. Instead, she woke up not only obsessed by snakes, but obsessed by trivialities. She had nervous breakdowns remembering the way Emma Kenyon—who'd always had expensive things mail-ordered from Philadelphia, even though the Tolivers had far more money than the Kenyons ever would—laughed at her clothes.

They were passing a road called Watler Marsh, with an empty field on the corner that looked as if it had sunk in the middle. That used to be a pond, Liz thought, and the school bus stopped on that very corner to let off a girl named Penny Steele, who was fifteen and going out with a boy in the army. The next year, the boy came back from the army and decided to marry her. Penny stayed in school right up through the week before the wedding, bringing Polaroid pictures of her wedding dress onto the bus to show all the other girls what she would look like when the day came. The wedding was held on a Saturday afternoon in late April at St. Mary's Roman Catholic Church in town. The honeymoon was a week at a resort in South Carolina. Liz had no idea what had happened to Penny after that. She did know that if she took this turn to the right and went to the end of that road, she would come to Belinda Hart's old house, where, one afternoon when they were all eight years old, Belinda and Emma had pushed her headfirst into a rain barrel full of bugs and slime and rotting fall leaves that had stuck to her skin like face paint.

Mark stirred in the passenger seat beside her, moving his copy of *Metamorphosis* from one leg to another. He was only fourteen, but he was as big as most grown men—nearly six feet tall, and massive, the way Jay had been, but without the tendency to go to fat. Geoff was in the back, secured in a seat belt and a safety harness, fast asleep. Liz found herself wishing that she still smoked cigarettes. It would give her something to do with her hands, and something to distract her, so that she wouldn't still be thinking about the rain barrel and about Belinda trying to seal it shut with the side of a big cardboard box she'd found lying against the garbage cans along the back of the house.

"Are you intending to drive this car, or do you mean for Scotty to beam us up the rest of the way?" Mark said. He had put his book down. It was dog-eared and half destroyed. Liz thought of the set direction at the beginning of *A Long Day's Journey Into Night.* You knew the people in that house really read books, because the books did not look new.

"Earth to Elizabeth. Earth to Elizabeth. Are you okay?"

Geoff stirred in the backseat. He always woke up when the car stopped.

"Are we there?" He was going to say "are we there yet?" but stopped himself just in time. He had heard enough, from his mother and his brother, to know that was something you *never* said. It was worse than saying "shit."

"Not exactly," Mark said. "What about you?" he asked Liz. "*Are* you all right? You're looking a little green. You could always change your mind, you know. We could always turn around and go right back to Connecticut—"

"I'm *hungry*," Geoff said.

"We could eat on the road. We could get a motel room for the night. We could use that nifty cell phone you've got and call Jimmy to come and get us—"

"Cell phones don't work up here," she said. "The mountains are too high."

Liz took her foot off the brake and let them roll slowly forward. She hadn't realized, until Mark had pointed it out, that they had stopped. The field that had once had a pond in the middle of it glided past them, along with the side road it bordered and the side road's destination, a big white ranch house with green shutters and the first three-car garage Hollman had ever seen. Liz had a distinct memory of Belinda talking about it at school while it was being built, and the girls talking behind her back about it in the lavatory, because she never mentioned the real reason it was going up: Belinda's father was an undertaker, and Belinda's mother couldn't stand it one more minute, living in the same house as the funeral home, with the dead and embalmed bodies in the basement.

"Driving usually requires you to put your foot on the gas after you've taken it off the brake," Mark said.

Liz put her foot on the gas, but not very hard. "I was thinking about this girl I knew in school. Belinda Hart—"

"Is this one of the vampire nation?"

"What a way to put it. Anyway, yes. The thing is, her father was an undertaker. Funeral director, she said, and we all had to say it, too, you know, because she was powerful as hell, even more powerful than Maris, and we were all afraid of her. But I was thinking, in most places, that would have gotten her killed. Having a father who was a funeral director, I mean, and living in a house with dead bodies in the basement—"

"They did? Cool."

Liz sighed. "They moved. Down that road." She tossed her head in the direction of the side road they were rolling away from. "That's why I was thinking of it. Are you like this all the time? Are you like this in school?"

"Yep."

"That must have an interesting effect on your social life."

"My social life is fine. It's incredible how much mileage you can get out of just not giving a—damn. I wasn't kidding at all about going back. I think you're nuts to be here. I don't get what you think you're doing at all."

"I'm taking care of your grandmother."

"My grandmother is senile. You could send Batman in a cape and she wouldn't know the difference."

Liz picked up the pace a little. "I was thinking about that year we spent in New Milford, do you remember? About how we had tuna-fish sandwiches on toast, and I felt like a fool, like I'd ruined Christmas for you and Geoff because I was just so damned arrogant, so—I don't know—prideful . . ."

"You have the pride of a sea slug."

"Be serious."

"I am serious. I don't know how I'm ever going to get this through to you, but I loved that Christmas. Okay, we didn't have a turkey and we didn't have a tree and we didn't have much in the way of presents—although I still love Russell Stover, let me tell you, if my soccer coach would let me eat chocolate—"

"Mark."

"I really am serious. I loved that Christmas. I loved the way we were with each other. Before that, you know, we were all kind of numbed out, because of Dad dying, and I'd been thinking that maybe we wouldn't ever be really together again. And that Christmas came and we were *us*, together, not three separate people. That was the first time from when Dad first got sick that I knew I was going to be happy again and—you know, you can't drive too well if you're crying your eyes out, either."

"I'm not crying my eyes out."

"That's Niagara Falls I see falling down the front of your face."

"Is it really?" Geoff said. "Can I see it, too?"

"Sit down and keep your seat belt on," Mark said.

They had reached another intersection—it was incredible how many small roads there were, crisscrossing each other back and forth under this thick cover of trees—and Liz turned automatically to the right. At the top of the road's steep embankment, there was a long Cape Cod–style house that she had admired as a child. When she passed it on the bus going to sports games or "special events," she found herself wishing she lived in it. Now it looked impossibly small, and worse than small, dated. She knew, even though she had never been in it, that the ceilings would be no more than eight feet high and the kitchen would be fitted with the kind of laminated cabinets that peeled in the corners after a year or two.

"You know," Mark said, "I don't think you're being stupid, feeling the way you feel. I mean, from some of the stories I've heard—"

"From whom? Has Maris been telling you things?"

"Ms. Coleman barely speaks to me. She thinks I'm cow dung. Okay. I've been reading a few of those stories in those papers, you know the ones—"

"Where are you getting the *National Enquirer*?"

"At the drugstore. And don't say it. Nobody cares what I read in the drugstore, and I'm not buying them. Except that I did buy the *Weekly World News*. You're not ever in that one. To get into that one, you've got to meet with a space alien. George Bush did."

"What?"

"Not this George Bush. The other one. George Herbert Walker Bush. The principal reason why I'm not applying to Andover."

"Right. Mark, where the hell is this going?"

Mark picked up his copy of *Metamorphosis* and ruffled the edges of the pages with the pad of his thumb. This was why his books all disintegrated. He not only read them, he abused them. Liz had grown up treating books as icons, or maybe as incarnations of God. She was no more capable of dog-earring a book than she was of lighting one on fire. The two acts had some strange connection with each other in her mind.

"I don't want to see you get hurt," Mark said. "I'm not stupid. I know why we never came here to visit Grandmother when Dad was alive. I don't need the tabloids or Jimmy Card to tell me that this place sucks for you, it leeches something out of you, and you get, I don't know, odd. Not yourself. Not you the way I know you. So far, all the signs have been all bad, except the car—"

"Jesus Christ."

"—and you can't take credit for the car, because Jimmy nearly browbeat you into it, and you know it. If it had been up to you, we'd have come out here in the Volvo—"

"A Volvo is a prestige car."

"Our Volvo looks like you've been using it to haul horse manure. Literally. I mean, I'm glad we bought the Mercedes. It's neat as hell. I've always wanted cream leather seats, just to see how long it takes to get them dirty. But I can just see you sitting there feeling you don't deserve it. Feeling *guilty* about it. Because that's what this place does to you. It makes you feel guilty about everything good that's ever happened to you."

They were at Plumtrees School. Back in the days when Pennsylvania had still been a colony, and for years afterward, this had been Hollman's one-room schoolhouse. Back in the early sixties, when the town had begun to bulge with the never-ending baby boom, this had been painted barn-red and used as a kindergarten for the children of the people who lived in Plumtrees and Stony Hill. Now, Liz checked the sign on its side, it was some kind of office for the Health Department.

"It's so odd," Liz said. "I can't imagine Hollman having its own Health Department."

"I give up," Mark said. He opened *Metamorphosis* and flattened it out against his leg. That was another reason why all his books fell apart. He had no respect for spines. "Someday, you ought to sit down and figure out what it is you want to do when you grow up. Try to get that done before I leave for prep school, so I don't have to worry about you stranded in the house on your own with nobody but Geoff to take care of you."

I thought you were counting on Jimmy to take care of me, Liz almost said, but didn't, because that was another whole can of worms and she had no intention of going there. They'd reached that odd T-intersection where going to the left led to some kind of industrial plant Liz had never actually understood. It called itself a sand company. She had no idea what a sand company did. She looked in its direction and saw that the big square funnels were still up. She had no way to know if they were running. When they were all growing up together, the girls who lived down that road were the ones they all officially labeled "Poor," and then ignored, because everybody on earth knew that poor people were not as important as rich ones.

She turned to the right, past the houses with the low white rail fences that made her think of horses, although nobody had ever owned horses this close to town, at least since the advent of the automobile. The road sloped upward to yet another intersection. On both sides, there were large frame buildings painted white and gray, with blank windows, like college dormitories in New England. Surely there had to be changes here, somewhere. The old high school was being used for something else now, and a new high school had been built as part of an educational park back there in Plumtrees. The library was supposed to have a new wing. The problem was that it all *looked* exactly as she remembered it. She felt she could get out of the car right now and walk on out to Mullaney's on Grandview Avenue or to the Sycamore farther down the road, and never miss a step or be confused by an uncertain landmark. This was Hollman as Brigadoon. It only woke up and came back to life when she was ready to visit it.

In the passenger seat, Mark put down his book again and reached out to take her hand. He flattened her fingers against his palm and pointed to them, silently, as if they were characters in a movie by a foreign director who believed in moments of significant pause.

Liz looked down at her own hand and saw that, somewhere between Plumtrees and here, she had bitten her fingernails so far down that the skin on her fingertips was split and bleeding.

2

Maris Coleman had been very careful about liquor since that day in New York that had ended so badly, and she was being especially careful about it now, in Hollman, because of the problem of the cars. Like most teenagers—and unlike Betsy—Maris had gotten her driver's license as soon as she turned sixteen, but unlike people like Belinda and Emma and Chris, she hadn't used it much in the years since. Vassar had been very picky about undergraduates with cars when she was there. It made more sense to stick close to campus when she wanted to go "out," and cross the street to Pizza Town, where the drinks were larger and more impressive than any she'd ever seen since. Harvey Wallbangers. White Lightnings. They came in tall ice cream soda glasses, and there was some kind of contest going on that only the boys entered. Drink three and get the fourth one free, or maybe it was four and get the fifth one free—whatever it was, it was dangerous, because those drinks had three or four shots of liquor in them. One White Lightning made her head spin. Of course, she was better than Betsy, who, when she went to Pizza Town at all, nursed along a single rum and Coke or 7UP and Seven, all night, and looked as if she were hating even that. Maris had never understood what it was about Betsy and liquor. Even later, when they had met up together in New York and Betsy had been drinking a fair amount in the evenings, she had never seemed to like it, and she'd treated hangovers as catastrophes. Maris had always thought there was something—prissy—about somebody who pretended not to like liquor, something sour and stuck-up, and she had never believed that bit about how Betsy couldn't stand to be hungover. A hangover was nothing. You could get rid of it in sixty seconds flat by spiking your morning coffee.

The other problem with cars was the years since Vassar, when Maris had been living in New York, where she neither kept a car nor wanted to. She hated to drive, and hated everything that went along with driving. She had never been very good at it, and was probably even worse now. She hadn't been behind the wheel for longer than fifteen minutes in ten years. She didn't have any automobile insurance. There was also the problem of the laws against "drunk driving," which didn't really mean driving drunk, but only driving when you'd had anything to drink at all. Maris knew that much from the public service announcements that played late into the night when she was watching PBS or MTV because she couldn't sleep. In some places, police checked people who didn't look drunk at all. It wouldn't matter that Maris never showed her liquor, or even felt it, most of the time. She had been careful since that day in New York, but not because she believed for an instant that Debra knew what was going on. Debra thought she'd had food poisoning. It had been the talk of the office for days afterward, according to the reports she'd heard—she'd been at home, where Debra insisted she stay, "recuperating"—and the women from the office had trekked down to Greenwich Village every afternoon to bring her boxes of pastry and take-out specialty salads from the little hole-in-the-wall gourmet delicatessen where they always got their lunches. Maris had thought, more than once during that period, that that was as good as life could get. She had never had to go out except to go to the liquor store, and that was only at the end of her own block. The only thing she could think of that might have made it better was a change in location, say to somewhere in the Caribbean, but she wouldn't have been able to afford that. It bothered her no end that Betsy got to go to the Caribbean all the time these days, even though she didn't like the beach.

It was because of the way she felt about cars that Maris was staying with Belinda Hart, and it was because she was staying with Belinda Hart that she saw Betsy get out of the big green Mercedes parked at the curb in front of English Drugs. Obviously, Maris thought, Betsy didn't realize that English now had a parking lot out in back. Maris heard a rustle in the apartment behind her. Belinda was coming out of the bathroom at the back of the kitchen. This apartment was worse than the one Maris had in New York. It had more square footage in absolute terms, but it was much more cramped, and its claustrophobic airlessness was not helped by Belinda's mania for knickknacks. The walls were covered with fake needlework samplers, trumpeting inanities. *He prayeth best who loveth best/All creatures great and small*, one of them said in ornate script made of navy-blue thread to contrast with the faux-natural linen background. The verse was surrounded by kittens, puppies, and birds, frolicking in fields of tiny flowers. The tables were full of fake Limoges porcelain and knockoffs of Hummel figurines: white boxes trimmed in gold and scattered with painted purple violets; three-inch-tall goat girls wearing dirndls and carrying pails. The only thing that was missing was a statue of the Virgin in a grotto—but of course that would have to be missing, since Belinda was a Methodist.

"Look," Maris said, pointing toward the window next to the only dining table in the place. Of course, Maris thought, her own apartment had no room for a table of any kind, but that didn't really count, because it was in Manhattan.

Belinda went to the window and looked out. "Is that Betsy Wetsy?" She sounded startled. "She's so incredibly thin."

"She works out nine hours a week. We've even got a room full of exercise equipment in the office so that she can work out there when she doesn't have time to do it in Connecticut. She hates gyms."

"God, she was bad at gym in high school. Do you remember?" Belinda pressed her face closer to the glass. "Still," she said.

"Still what?"

"I don't know. I guess I thought she'd look more like herself."

"Meaning what?" Maris said.

Belinda backed away from the window and sat down in one of the other two chairs. Down on Grandview Avenue, there was no longer any sign of Betsy or the two boys. Belinda bit her lip.

"I've seen pictures of her, of course," she said, "and I've seen her on television, but somehow I thought that when I saw her in person, she'd look more like herself. You know. Sort of lumpy and . . . whatever. Sort of gray."

"She doesn't look gray. She can manage to look pretty damned spectacular when she wants to make the effort, which she usually doesn't."

"Oh," Belinda said. She tapped her fingers against the tabletop. The top was peeling along the edges, much the way Belinda's nail polish was peeling along the sides of her nails.

"Well?" Maris said.

"Emma said the same thing. That she didn't look like you'd think she would, when you saw her in person. Emma and George saw her somewhere, in England, I don't remember. Emma didn't even tell me about it until last week. I don't understand people sometimes. The only thing is, well—"

"What?"

"Well," Belinda went on, looking stubborn. "It might not work. This thing. I mean, if she's like that, and not like we remember her, then it might not work. So maybe we shouldn't try it. Because she's different."

Maris looked into her cup of coffee, the pale coffee she had made from freeze-dried stuff out of a jar that was all Belinda kept for coffee. She would have to find a way out to a decent grocery store to pick up some beans and a grinder. Made like this, the coffee tasted too much like gin, which wasn't supposed to have a taste, but did. She was not surprised at Belinda's wavering. She had expected something of the kind, from all of them, because they really had no idea what they were dealing with. They all thought they could go back to 1969 and behave as if nothing had ever happened.

"Listen," she told Belinda. "She hasn't really changed. Not the way you think. It's all an act."

"It can't all be an act," Belinda said seriously. "She really does look like that. She can't be doing it with mirrors."

"But she is doing it with mirrors," Maris said. "That whole attitude, that thing she's got of not giving a damn what anybody thinks, it's all an act. She cares just as much now as she ever did. She cares so much, it makes her sick."

"Well," Belinda said dubiously, looking out the window at the Mercedes again. "Maybe she cares about people like Jimmy Card and, you know, those people she's with on CNN. George Stephanopolous. Like that. That doesn't mean she's going to care about us."

"You've got it backward," Maris said. "She can take George Stephanopolous or leave him, it's us who still get to her. And that gives us our chance. If things go on the way they've been going on, something will happen. You know it will. And it won't be good for us."

"Maybe it won't be good for her, either."

"Don't bet on it. She's got Jimmy Card to run interference for her. Christ, Belinda, aren't you sick of it? All those stories in the magazines, making it seem like we were all a bunch of brain-dead hoodlums, torturing the poor genius throughout her whole blameless childhood. That last story in *People* damn near made me throw up. And now she's here, and you know what? Within twenty-four hours, at least two reporters are going to be here, too—"

"I don't understand all this about the reporters," Belinda said querulously. "It's not like she's Julia Roberts. She's not a movie star. She's just on all those news shows and you know nobody pays any attention to the people on those news shows. Why do they pay attention to her?"

"Because they think she's going to marry Jimmy Card," Maris said patiently, "and because she's got a hot-selling book and looks like she's going to have another. Everybody gets fifteen minutes of fame. This is Betsy's fifteen minutes. Does it matter why?"

"I never got fifteen minutes of fame," Belinda said.

Maris considered the possibility that Belinda had never heard the phrase before, or even that she had never heard of Andy Warhol, and dismissed it. Belinda read *Vogue* the way fundamentalists read the Bible, and had, for forty years. The problem with Belinda was that she never remembered anything. Maris knew enough to realize she had only a small window of opportunity. If they started to doubt, it would all fall apart, and in the end nothing would happen but a dull month's visit, with Betsy speaking at the library and the high school and going back to New York to write an essay for *Dissent* on the death of small-town America.

Maris looked up and out the window again, and all of a sudden, there she was: Betsy, coming out of English Drugs' front door, holding Geoff's hand while Mark followed close behind, carrying an enormous brown bag. Belinda moved closer to the window to get a better look, and as she did, old Mrs. Cardovan stopped at the side of the Mercedes to talk. Maris couldn't hear, but she could see what was going on. Betsy and Mrs. Cardovan were exchanging greetings and introductions. The boys were being made to prove that they had been well brought up, and knew how to shake hands and say the right things to older women. Mrs. Cardovan was very, very old. When they were all children, she had been the chief salesgirl at Noe's Dry Goods, which is what Hollman had had for a basic clothing store until the big discount places opened up in the new shopping center out on Route 6. She was as tiny as a dwarf, and hunchbacked. All the girls had wondered how she'd ever been able to get somebody to marry her. Now her gnarled olive-skinned face was beaming under her Darth Vader helmet of white hair.

Betsy was shooing the small boy into the back of the car. Then she turned and shook Mrs. Cardovan's hand, and Mark shook it, too, as if they had all just met in some big crush of a cocktail party. Betsy got in behind the wheel. Mrs. Cardovan waved a little and started to walk again along the sidewalk. The Mercedes kicked into life and edged out onto the road. There were other Mercedes in Hollman these days—no place was as provincial as it had been in 1969—but this particular Mercedes looked bigger than the others, or shinier, or more intimidating.

"Well," Belinda said when the Mercedes was out of view.

"Exactly," Maris said. "You've got to see what I mean, right? We can't just let it go."

"Maybe," Belinda said.

Maris drank down the last of what was in her coffee cup. It was nearly straight gin. She bit her bottom lip to keep herself from heaving. The muscles in her arms started to twitch. She could see the green glint of the car's roof far up on Grandview Avenue, past the place where Noe's had been, past reality. Belinda was staring in the same direction.

"Well," Belinda said again, still sounding uncertain.

"We've got to do something," Maris said, getting up to go back to Belinda's kitchen counter. She put her cup down next to a ceramic spoon holder with "Home Sweet Home" painted on it in yet more ornate purple script, next to yet more ornate purple violets. She wanted to pick the silly thing up and smash it into shards.

"We've got to do something," she said again, instead. "If we don't do something, this whole situation is going to jump right up and bite us on the ass."

3

Chris Inglerod had no intention of doing anything at all about the fact that Betsy Toliver was coming back to town today. In spite of at least three long phone calls with Emma, and one even longer one with Maris, she had her mind made up. As soon as she could, she filled her schedule book with the kind of Things To Do she had always loved best. It was Monday, so she had Literacy Volunteers of America first thing. She had to drive out to a tiny roadside restaurant on Route 47 and tutor a girl named Natalya in the rudiments of English, spoken as well as written. The restaurant smelled of all the food she had learned to despise in the years since high school. It served deep-fried pasties full of meat and beets and heavy soups made with sour cream. Natalya was not only slow and fat, but she wasn't an American. Chris had imagined herself playing Enlightening Angel to one of Hollman's own downtrodden poor—a member of one of the black families who lived in shacks near the edge of the river on the south side of town, or one of the waitresses at JayMar's diner. Volunteering, Chris had learned, was much like anything else. You needed to do it if you wanted to be put on the kind of committees that really mattered to you—the invitation committee at the Club, for instance, or the ball committee at the American Heart Association chapter—but it wasn't what everybody said it was, and it wasn't fun. Still, Chris was nothing if she wasn't somebody who played by the rules. If there was scut work to be done, she did it. She tutored Natalya in the same spirit she had once pushed the magazine tray around the hospital as a candy striper or picked up garbage from the side of the road as a pledge for Alpha Chi Omega. If she hated the work, she could always get it done by being *determined* to get it done. If she was *determined* to get it done, she could excel at it, and in her way, she excelled at tutoring Natalya. They'd been at it for six weeks, and Natalya could already read the front page of the Philadelphia *Inquirer* without a hitch and explain what she'd read in English that was still halting, but no longer incomprehensible. If she was also much shyer, more frightened, and more depressed than when the lessons started, Chris didn't notice it.

The tutoring lesson only lasted an hour. When it was over, Chris drove back to her own house by a side road, avoiding the center of town, and parked in her driveway, nonplussed. She had a date for tennis and lunch at the Club, but that wasn't for hours yet. If she showed up this early, people would talk about it, and if they talked about it, they would probably make all the wrong inferences. At least one of the things Maris and Belinda had been saying was true: there had been a lot of ink spilled on the subject of poor Betsy Toliver's terrible days in high school, persecuted by the evil witches of the Popular Crowd. It had become The Story whenever Betsy was mentioned in the popular press, and that was often, these days, now that she was connected to Jimmy Card. It didn't help that the women Chris knew at the Club weren't Hollman women, but transplants from other places whose husbands worked in research at one of the new tech companies with buildings on the interstate, or the kind of local girl Chris would never have known while she was growing up, because their parents had the money—and the sense—to send them away to boarding school. It sometimes seemed as if she had spent the whole of the last two weeks explaining herself, over and over and over again. She had the car's radio turned to the classical music station. The only other automatic find on her scan function was for NPR, which she almost never listened to anymore, because Betsy was on it so much. She thought about getting out of the car and going into her house. She thought about picking up the phone to call Dan in the middle of the morning and being told by the receptionist that Dan was busy, or by Dan himself that it wasn't Dan's problem, not any of it, and she would have to fend for herself. If she hadn't already had breakfast, she could go out somewhere and eat that. If it wasn't so early, she could go out to the mall and shop—although she never shopped much at their local mall. It didn't have the right kinds of stores. You had to go into Pittsburgh or Philadelphia for those, or buy from a catalogue.

She looked at the rings on her hands. She looked at the green grass on her broad front lawn. She looked at the peaks and gables on her house that let even strangers going past on the road know that several of the rooms inside had cathedral ceilings. She put the car into reverse and backed out onto the road again. Was it really possible she had lived in this place for fifteen years and not managed to make a single real friend? If she thought about it honestly, she would have to say she had never in her life made a single real friend. People were volatile commodities. One day they were good for you. The next day, they dragged you down.

She went straight through town—if she ran into Betsy, she didn't have to stop, and she didn't think she'd run into Betsy. It was still very early—and only when she got out the other side of it did she start to slow down. Her parents' house had been out this way when she was growing up, but she rarely came here anymore. Her parents hadn't been poor, but they hadn't been prominent, either, and this was what she had looked forward to leaving behind. Some of the houses were of a kind that would fetch serious money in a college town or major city: tall Victorians with round towers and gingerbread framing their broad front porches; Craftsman "cottages" with more square footage in their foyers than most of the newer houses had in their living rooms. Her parents, of course, had had one of the newer houses. Like a lot of people in their era, they had equated new with luxury and old with deprivation. They'd had a rec room in the basement, too, not a big family room built above grade on a lower level, like Chris had now, but a low-ceilinged space carved out underground for the kids to put their toys in. Chris had always hated her parents' house. When she was in college, she'd been very careful never to ask her friends home to see it.

Past the houses, there were long patches of green, some of it belonging to houses built far enough off the road to be invisible, some of it belonging to the few small farms that still ran in this part of the state. Chris went past them all without paying attention to any of them, and then up a small hill whose road was entirely lined with tall pine trees. What she wanted was at the end of that—the wrought-iron gate to Meldone Park. Just outside the gate, there were places to park, slots left open in a big unpaved field where the grass had already shriveled into shards of paper brown.

Chris pulled to a stop as close to the entrance to the park as she could and got out of her car. She locked all her doors. The wrought-iron gates looked as if they had been well cared for. The grass at the edges of the park looked as if it had been mowed. As soon as she came through the little stand of trees, she could see the sandy beach and the small lake it circled, man-made by the town in 1967 so that the children of Hollman would have someplace to go that wasn't a concrete public swimming pool. Chris took off her shoes and tucked them into the top of her tote bag. Thank God she wasn't wearing panty hose. She looked across at the few people sitting on blankets near the edge of the water and counted three she knew. All three had been in high school with her, two in her class and one in the class behind. None of them had been important at the time, and all of them were now thick with middle age and ugly with bad hair coloring. It just went to show, Chris thought, that you couldn't be too careful about keeping yourself up.

She skirted the lake and the back of the lifeguard's seat—there was nobody in it at the moment, which for some reason figured—and went into the woods on the hill above it. The path she remembered was still there. A few feet down the path, there *was* something new: a pair of signs, wooden blocks with one end carved into a point to turn them into arrows, announcing that men should go in one direction and women should go in another. Chris turned toward the "women's" outhouses—the old outhouses—and climbed through the pines to the clearing where the outhouses were. They had not changed, except that they'd been painted. They looked exactly as rickety as she remembered them, so that she wondered, yet again, what Betsy had been so frightened of the night when she had been locked in. It wasn't as if she would have been entirely in the dark. There were enough cracks in the walls and doors to let in all the light in the Western Hemisphere.

She turned away from the outhouses and started climbing again, off the path now, through the pines. As she went, she began to feel that she'd made a mistake. She hadn't been out here—all the way out here—since the night of the catastrophe. There couldn't be anything left to see. She wasn't going to stand still in the clearing near the river and hear that voice floating up over her head again, keening and wild. She wasn't going to hear the rushing of the water, either. That night there had been too much water in the river because there had been too much rain over too many weeks. Now the river would be nearly dry. They hadn't had a drop of rain in weeks. Ghosts did not haunt the places where they had become separated from their bodies. Auras did not cling forever to those places where murder had been done.

The real problem with the clearing was that it was so dark. The pine trees around it were too high. They blotted out the sun. If it wasn't for the glint of sunlight that shimmered on the face of the water, she would have thought it was the middle of the night. Her throat was very dry, and tight. She felt dizzy. No, there wasn't anything out here, nothing but pine needles on the ground and the whisper of the wind, like a voice, that was always just a little too far away for her to be able to catch individual words. The river was not dry, but close to it. A trickle of water slithered along the bottom of the bed, leaving the rocks above it dirty and untouched. If blood had soaked into this ground thirty-two years ago, it had soaked away by now, stolen by rain storms and snowstorms and small animals. Small animals would eat dead bodies if they were left to rot in wooded areas. She had read that in the newspaper, once, she didn't know when. She really *was* dizzy. She was going to throw up.

She had no idea when she left the clearing, or when she started running. It wasn't really running. In her bare feet, the best she could do was stumble and make a mess of things. She reached the outhouses and went right past them. They had never meant anything to her. She went down the narrow path and came out at the sanded clearing around the lake. Nobody new had come while she was gone. The lifeguard's chair was still empty. She went quickly along the very highest edge of the sand to the small path that led to the wrought-iron gate. She went through the trees and through the gate and got to her car just as she heard the sound of crows in the air above her head. Weren't crows supposed to be bad luck? She was tugging at her car door. It was locked. She'd forgotten about locking it. She hadn't even taken out her keys. She got them out and let herself in behind the wheel and just *stopped.*

Somebody new drove into the parking lot. Chris sat right up. She wasn't going to let anybody see her like this. The last thing she wanted was for some stranger to tap at her car window to ask if she was all right. The car was hot. It got hot early in Hollman in May. It wasn't safe to put on the air conditioner if the car wasn't running. People overheated their engines that way.

She watched a woman and two small children make their way from the newly parked car toward the pines and the wrought-iron gate. The children were too small to be in school and carried bright plastic buckets, one blue and one red. Chris started her engine and eased out into the openness of the field. What was this place like when it got really busy, when it mattered that it had no clearly marked parking spaces and no corridors partitioned off for people to drive through? Out on the road, the green of the grass looked fake, as if somebody had come along and dyed it with that stuff you colored Easter eggs with.

She decided not to go through the middle of town this time at all. She didn't want to look at it. She went around by the side roads instead, in a big circle that would bring her through Plumtrees and Stony Hill, and that was why she ended up seeing Betsy Toliver after all. She'd forgotten that Betsy's mother lived in Aunt Hack's Ridge, or that Betsy had grown up there, in one of those enormous ranch houses with the three-car garages and the fieldstone walks that led to the fieldstone steps that led to the fieldstone-framed double front doors. *Fifties nouveau riche chic*, Chris thought, and then Betsy was right there, in the big open drive, getting out of a green Mercedes and talking to a woman in a nurse's uniform at the same time. Chris had no idea why she was so certain that this was Betsy Toliver. The woman was a good ways away from her, and the car was moving, and this was neither the Betsy she remembered from high school nor the Betsy she remembered from television. Still, she knew. Other people were getting out of Betsy's car, two boys, probably her sons. Betsy was wearing one of those loose-fitting tunic-y things that women in their fifties wore when they were being "casual" or "artistic" in the city. She had a thick clutch of gold bracelets on her left arm, supple and bright.

Damn, Chris thought. She had slowed to a crawl, and she was gaping. None of the people around the Mercedes seemed to have noticed it. Betsy had her back to the road. The two boys were unpacking the trunk, piling one black leather suitcase onto another. Chris stepped on the gas. A few seconds later she couldn't see them anymore. They couldn't see her.

It was only then that she realized she was still shaking. Her muscles were still twitching. She pulled over onto the side of the road, at the edge of a property that belonged to no one she knew. She put her head down on the steering wheel and told herself to breathe. It didn't work. She pushed the seat back as far as it would go and tried to put her head between her knees. That didn't work, either. She kept thinking of the dark of that night and the whole bunch of them standing in a circle and the blood on the ground and, in the background, like a sound track, Betsy Toliver screaming.

Chris pushed open the door at her side, leaned out over the road, and threw up.

THREE

1

Her name was Grace Feinmann. Bennis found that out and then wrote it down on a three-by-five card along with the five or six other things she thought Gregor should remember while he was away: Tibor's e-mail address and new cell phone number; the hotel she would be staying at in Los Angeles for all of the coming week; the name of the brand of coffee bags he was supposed to buy in case he was in danger of having to make his own; the title of Elizabeth Toliver's last book (*Conspiracy: The Rise of Paranoia and the Death of Politics*).

"She says she met you in Connecticut," Bennis told him, packing his white shirts into the big suitcase he always took when he was traveling, "that time when Kayla Anson died. She had something to do with the case. But I don't remember her."

Gregor didn't remember her, either. The sight of Bennis packing his shirts was oddly unsettling. It wasn't the kind of thing Bennis did, and for a moment—obviously, he wasn't getting enough sleep—he had that gut-twisting reaction that people are supposed to have when they realize they are confronted by a shape-shifter. Maybe he hadn't moved in with Bennis at all, but with Lida, in a body she had put on the way she put on her three-quarter-length chinchilla coat to go to church in the winter.

"Gregor?" Bennis said.

"I'm here."

"Barely."

"Why does she have the harpsichord?"

Bennis pulled the clothing guard down over the shirts and tied it tightly to the suitcase's side with ribbons. "It's what she does. Plays the harpischord, I mean, and the—what. Virginals. That's something else that looks like a piano. She got a job with the Philadelphia Early Music Ensemble."

"And she moved in here?"

"She says she saw the ad and thought she remembered the name of the street and that you lived here, so she figured it must be a nice street. Or something. You really ought to ask Tibor and Lida about this. Ask Lida. I think what Tibor mostly did was get her to tell him what books he should read on early Renaissance polyphonic song."

"I'm surprised there was an ad. I take it that was Russ's idea."

"Probably. I don't know where the ad appeared, though, so don't jump to conclusions."

"Is she buying or renting?"

"Oh, renting," Bennis said. "Donna says she hasn't got any money. Apparently, you don't make much playing early instruments. Didn't I tell you all this before? Whatever. From what Russ is hinting, I think that if they like her and really want her on the street they'll make some arrangement so that she'll be able to buy. You know what it's like around here. Even Howard Kashinian behaves himself when it comes to apartments and town houses. Are you sure you want to take all these suits? It's practically summer and you're going to the country."

"I'm supposed to be working."

"Sometimes I think you think it's still 1965 and you can't get dinner in a good restaurant unless you wear a tie."

"There aren't any restaurants where I'm going," Gregor said. "From what I understand, there isn't even a place to stay in town."

Bennis hung his suit bag on the high arm of his silent valet and unzipped it all the way around. "There's one more thing," she said. "Tibor's absolutely insisting that we all have to go see Grace play when she plays, so he's buying season tickets to their shows, the Ensemble's shows, for when they play here in Philadelphia. They play in a church, but they travel some, so it's a little confusing. At any rate, Lida's buying some, too, and so are Donna and Russ, and they're getting extras. I don't know how many sets there will be in the end, but—"

"You said you'd buy some for us."

"It seemed like the least I could do. And I like early music, or at least some of it. I mean, I don't like chant, but I don't suppose they can be doing chant, not if they have a harpsichord. Anyway, they don't even start playing until September. This summer, they've got rehearsals and some Renaissance fairs and then they're going to make a CD, which is why they needed Grace so early. Their old harpsichordist quit. Grace says—"

"Bennis."

"Right," Bennis said. She took a deep breath. "I'm acting like an idiot. I always seem to. I'm going to go put on a pot of coffee."

Gregor thought about saying *Bennis* again, but didn't. He watched her leave the bedroom and head down the hall instead, wishing that the hall weren't so dark. It was a bright day outside, so bright that the bedroom looked as if it were about to become the landing area for the Second Coming. Sunlight streamed in in those hard-edged rays artists used to represent the gaze of God. If he went to the window and looked down to the street, he could see old George Tekemanian sitting under a huge umbrella at a round table his nephew Martin had sent to him from L. L. Bean. Lately, old George had not been looking as well as he might, and Bennis had begun to look formidable, the way women did when they entered middle age with both confidence and resources. It didn't bother him to think of Bennis reaching middle age, although he doubted she'd look it in quite the same way Lida or Hannah had. He was middle-aged himself, and one of the things that had stopped him for so long from realizing what he felt for her had been the simple fact that he'd thought she was too young for him. His wife—another Elizabeth; he was surrounded by them—had been almost exactly his own age, and they had grown up together, so that by the time they'd been married half a dozen years, they'd no longer really needed to direct whole sentences at each other. He almost went to the drawer where he kept Elizabeth's picture under his socks. When he'd first moved back to Cavanaugh Street, he couldn't remember how many years ago now, he'd kept it out where he could see it at all times. Even after he'd finally made himself put it away, he'd taken it out to look at it almost daily. Now he thought it must have been weeks since he'd seen it, and that part of him that had been able to hear her voice all around him when he was alone had apparently died. Things changed. That was reality. It scared him to death.

He got off the bed and went out into the hall himself. He could hear Bennis in the kitchen, banging around, as if she were doing much more than making coffee. Sometimes she washed a few of the dishes, but not often. One of the first changes she'd made in his life when they'd finally begun to be together was to hire the kind of cleaning lady who came in every weekday and did the dishes and laundry as a matter of course. Some changes, he conceded, were good ones. He had found that he truly loved having his things taken care of so thoroughly that he never had to think of them. His wife had done that for him once, but in the years since her death he had gotten used to always missing things. Suit jackets disappeared and then reappeared under the bed. Clean white shirts became balls of sweat and dust in the bathroom hamper. He went through the living room and stopped long enough to look at the street from the wide picture window there. Then he turned around and looked through the pass-through to the kitchen at Bennis doing something unnecessary at the stove.

"Hey," he said. "Do you want to tell me what's wrong with you?"

"Nothing's wrong with me. I'm not all that happy about our spending a month apart, that's all. If not longer."

"It won't be longer."

Bennis cocked her head. "Why do you think that? You're going off to solve a murder that's thirty years old or more. Why do you think you can get it done in four weeks? I mean, for God's sake, they had an investigation once, didn't they? And they didn't come up with anything. Why do you think you will?'

Gregor went all the way into the kitchen and sat down at the kitchen table. "I don't think I will. Nobody wants me to solve that murder. I told you that. They only want me—"

"To prove beyond a shadow of a doubt that Maris Coleman is planting those stories in the tabloid newspapers. I thought you said that wasn't even a question. I mean, that it was obvious."

"It's obvious if you're looking, yes, but according to Mr. Card, Ms. Toliver refuses to believe it."

"Well, people get like that, don't they, about friends?" Bennis said. "And about family. Look at the way I was about Anne Marie, right up to the end. The way I still am about Anne Marie, really. What good does Jimmy think this is going to do?"

Gregor shrugged. "I'd be the same way, if I thought somebody was exploiting you. I was the same way with what's-her-name—"

"Edith."

"Edith. Except that in that case you realized it perfectly well and I couldn't get you to do anything about it. But Mr. Card's emotions are completely natural. I don't know if Ms. Toliver will actually believe anything I manage to find, but I can at least find it. She sounded like a nice woman, when I talked to her on the phone. From what I've heard of her, she's the kind of nice woman it's fairly easy to take advantage of, and Maris Coleman has been taking a lot of advantage. Let's call it a moral imperative."

"You're going to go spend a month in some godforsaken town in north central Pennsylvania because of a moral imperative?"

"Well," Gregor said judiciously, "there's always the obvious."

"Which is what?"

"Which is that it bugs the hell out of me that nobody seems to give a damn that this boy was murdered. And I do mean nobody. Jimmy Card wouldn't. That doesn't matter. But even the police officer I talked to in Hollman seemed to think that the dead body was secondary to the question of who locked Elizabeth Toliver into an outhouse stall with a bunch of black snakes, and the tabloids—"

"You've been reading the tabloids?"

"I do, every once in a while." Gregor looked around. Surely, he had heard Bennis doing something about coffee, but nothing actually seemed to have been done. There was no kettle boiling on the stove. There were no coffee cups set out on the counter next to the sink. "Well, the tabloids give the details—found in a clearing near a small river, his throat cut straight across; weapon never discovered; motive never discovered—but they treat him like a cartoon—"

"They treat everybody like a cartoon, Gregor. I've been in them."

"I know. My point is that they don't report the story as if it were the story of a murder. The murder is secondary to Elizabeth Toliver. Or maybe

I should say secondary to Jimmy Card's girlfriend. It's the oddest thing. It's not that it's hard to get information. I can get all the information I want. It's that nobody can seem to understand why I'd want it."

"Well," Bennis said, "maybe it's like Lizzie Borden. You know, maybe everybody in town already knows who killed him, and they've got some kind of tacit agreement going not to do anything about it—"

"About an eighteen-year-old boy getting his throat slit from ear to ear during the summer after his high school graduation?"

"You're the one who told me that stuff about Lizzie Borden," Bennis said. "I don't know. I admit, in a small town like that, you'd think this would be an enormous deal, even after all this time. Are the police who did the investigation still around?"

"One of them is, retired and living in town and more than happy to talk to me, or at least he says he is." Gregor shrugged. "The chief of police at the time is dead. He was sixty-six in 1969 and had a heart condition even then. He died about ten years later. There was one other officer on the force that summer and he moved to California a couple of years after it happened. Nobody knows how to find him."

"I can see it right now. He's the real murderer, and his friends on the police force have covered up his crime and given him a chance to escape and make a new life, because the dead boy was really a vampire—"

"*Bennis.*"

"Well, it was a thought. You didn't really want coffee, did you?"

"I thought I did. But all kidding aside, there's something very nasty about the way they treat that murder. I don't care if the kid was on crack and in a gang—"

"In 1969?"

"—he still would deserve to be taken seriously. I find myself wondering if this was the attitude they had at the time, or if it's just what's developed because Elizabeth Toliver got 'famous,' so to speak. It's something worse than annoying. It nags at me. So, I thought I'd go help your friend out and see what the problem was at the same time, and I may be kidding myself. Maybe I'll get there and it will turn out that there's a perfectly good reason why nobody pays any attention to Michael Houseman and how he died."

"I think you're bored," Bennis said.

"I think you're going to Los Angeles," Gregor said.

"I think you've got an hour before you leave, and we ought to go somewhere and neck."

2

It was early evening by the time Gregor Demarkian reached Hollman, Pennsylvania, and when he did he was as rattled as he had been the one time he took a train in the Alps. He had not, this time, taken a train. There might once have been trains that stopped in Hollman or somewhere nearby, but these days the nearest station was fifty miles away and on the other side of what he could only call mountains. He spent a moment thinking how odd it was that the mountains should be covered with vegetation all the way to their tops—sometimes he caught sight of pine trees sticking up like cowlicks, far above him—and then the landscape closer to the ground started to capture him, and he began to feel uneasy. Gregor Demarkian was not a small-town boy. He had never had any part in the great American story, the one that Elizabeth Toliver now seemed to be the public expression of: you start in an obscure small town somewhere, born to unimportant people; you work very hard and get to go away to a good college on the East or West Coast; you leave college for a wretched apartment in a shabby but Bohemian section of New York or San Francisco; you Make Good. This was the part that was left out of Thomas Wolfe's story, Gregor thought. It wasn't that you couldn't ever go home again, it was that you didn't want to. Gregor had grown up in Philadelphia, on the very street on which he now lived, and he had spent all his life in cities except for his obligatory stint in the armed services. That wasn't the kind of memory that would make anybody fond of small towns, if he wasn't used to them—godforsaken backwaters in Mississippi and Alabama, bad weather, bad insects, bad feelings all around, the local cops just itching to get to you the first time you did anything out of line or even before, if you happened to be one of the few black soldiers in that newly integrated army. Still, it hadn't been the hostility to all things military that had bothered him, even at the time. It had been the claustrophobia. It was incredible how airless these small places could get, when they were effectively cut off from the outside world—and they *were*, that was the odd thing, in spite of MTV and CNN and the Internet. It was almost as if they didn't believe the things they saw and read, as if they thought all that was fiction and that in reality everybody on the planet lived exactly the way they did. Or ought to. Gregor was coming in by car, with a driver. It wasn't a limousine—"you don't want to be too conspicuous," Jimmy Card had said, and Gregor had agreed with him. He really hated limousines—but it still had a chauffeur, and although that solved the problem of the fact that Gregor never drove except in an emergency, like maybe the end of the world, it still made him a little uncomfortable. Jimmy Card was not the most formidable man Gregor had ever met. During his years with the FBI, he had met both presidents of the United States and presidents of multinational corporations, the kind of men who got done what they needed to get done, no matter what it was. Still, Jimmy Card had the makings of men like that, even if success in entertainment would never give him the same kind of authority. If it had been up to Gregor, he would have come to town in some neutral way and then hired a car and a driver here, or hooked up with a local private detective—did they *have* private detectives in places like Hollman?—but Jimmy Card had insisted, and Gregor had been unable to resist. Now here he was, in a black sedan with New York plates, driven by a man who was both obviously Hispanic and entirely uncommunicative. He could have gotten more conversation out of a robot. He was also tired. It was a long way up from Philadelphia, and on the Penn Turnpike, too, which Gregor personally regarded as a state-sanctioned instrument of torture. He was also hungry. The Penn Turnpike didn't have rest stops with fast-food places in them every thirty miles or so. It didn't even have rest areas that he could tell. His back creaked. His stomach rumbled. The sight of Hollman beginning to spin out around him made him tense.

"Listen," he said, leaning forward to make sure the driver could hear him. "Maybe we could stop along the way here for a minute. I'd like to get some breath mints."

"There's a parking place at the curb ahead," the driver said, looking straight through the windshield, as if he were talking to a voice on the radio. "There's a place called English Drugs."

"Good," Gregor said. "A drugstore. That will be perfect."

The driver didn't say anything. Gregor sat back and looked out the side window at the narrow streets edged with stores and churches. The stores were made of clapboard and had false fronts, so that they seemed to go up a story higher than they really did. The churches were very old, and looked it. The Methodist one had a square bell tower that looked to be the tallest structure in town. Gregor felt his sense of claustrophobia increasing. He had never been able to understand how people managed to stay in places like this.

The driver pulled the car up next to the curb and cut the engine. He looked up into the rearview mirror—*victory,* Gregor thought, *he knows I'm here*—and said, "What kind of breath mints would you like, sir?"

"Oh," Gregor said. "I don't know. You don't have to go get them for me. I'd like to get out and walk around." He almost added "if you don't mind," but didn't, because it was absurd. You didn't apologize to a man being paid to drive you because you wanted to get out and walk around.

The driver was no longer looking into the rearview mirror. He was looking straight out the windshield, but he didn't seem to be paying attention to the other people on the street or the other cars parked at the curb. Gregor didn't think he had brought a book. What would he do while Gregor was walking around, stretching his legs, looking at the scenery? He didn't even have the job of opening Gregor's door and closing it for him. They'd discussed all that at the outset, and agreed that it—like a limousine—would only be conspicuous. Actually, Gregor thought, they hadn't agreed on anything. Gregor had just given directions, and the driver had acted as if he hadn't heard a thing.

"Right," Gregor said now. He popped his door open. "I won't be long. I just want to walk around a little."

The driver said nothing. Gregor tried to remember his name and couldn't. Then he got out onto the sidewalk and stretched his legs a little.

If he'd been expecting a revelation of some sort, he didn't get it. It was quite possible—in fact it was likely—that Hollman had exhibited a few tense oddnesses in the days after Michael Houseman had died, but that was more than thirty years ago. Now it looked exactly like a hundred other places of the same type, from Maine to Nebraska and maybe even beyond. The men who passed him were wearing either stiff-collared polo shirts with little animals embroidered over their breast pockets (but not Izod alligators) or the kind of suits you bought in Sears when you weren't used to wearing them. The women were not so much fat as lumpy in the way women got when they were neither particularly athletic nor committed to working out. Everybody looked tired. Gregor looked up and down this side of the street. Elsa-Edna's was a dress shop with pretensions to sophistication. JayMar's was a restaurant that would have been called a diner anywhere else. English Drugs was a drugstore and the biggest enterprise on the block, except that it wasn't really a block. It went on for far too long in both directions, broken only by driveways.

Midway up from where he stood now, back the way they had come, the flat faces of the false-fronted windows were broken by the existence of a small Victorian house, painted red. Gregor stepped back a little so that he could get a better look at it. It had a sign hanging over the four small steps of its entryway, the way a bed and breakfast would. The sign said: COUNTRY CRAFTS. Gregor moved up the street a little to get a better look. It was not an unusual or particularly interesting place, on its own. Like the town, it was surely one of thousands of identical places all across the country. The porch made it impossible to see anything that might have been sitting in its windows. Gregor had the idea that that must be a very bad thing for a store. He walked up the slight incline of Grandview Avenue until he was right in front of the place and stopped. There was another sign besides the one over the front porch entry. This sign was bolted into the porch rail next to the steps, and it said more than just COUNTRY CRAFTS. It said: PROPRIETORS GEORGE AND EMMA BLIGH.

Gregor reached into the inside breast pocket of his jacket—Bennis had been absolutely right, as usual. He shouldn't have come here with nothing but suits—and took out the notebook he'd been using to organize his notes on the Hollman trip. Bennis had given him a Palm Pilot last Christmas, but he'd left it in the top drawer of his dresser, the way he always did. He could not get the hang of using it. What he kept in his breast pocket was a simple stenographer's pad. He flipped through it and found want he wanted: *Emma Kenyon. Now Emma Kenyon Bligh. Runs Country Crafts.*

Sometimes, Tibor always said, God is trying to tell you something. Gregor figured this must be one of those times. He put his notebook back in his pocket and climbed the short flight of steps to Country Crafts' front porch. Once he was up on it, he realized that there was one of those ubiquitous driveways running along the side of the building. That meant there had to be a parking lot out back. He stopped on the porch and looked at what was in the windows, which wasn't much: a doll made out of "pulled" yarn in an old-fashioned dress; a little set of bright blue clay pots; a swath of hard red velvet that seemed to have drifts of dust across its surface. He pushed through the front door and heard a bell tinkle above his head. It sounded like a brass cowbell.

The big front room of the house was empty except for a woman standing behind a counter, chewing on a Mars bar and looking through a copy of *Us* magazine. She was, Gregor thought, the single fattest human being he had ever seen outside a hospital. If she went on eating Mars bars, she was going to end up in a hospital. He wondered if she made her dresses herself. He couldn't imagine a store that would sell a size like that. He wondered if she did her hair herself, too. It wasn't just blond. It was a bright egg-yolk yellow.

The woman looked up from her magazine and said, "Hello, there. Can I help you?"

"I don't know." Gregor walked up to the counter. "I'm supposed to be spending the week with a friend. I thought it might be a good idea to take some kind of house gift."

"And you just thought of that this minute?"

"What?"

The woman put her copy of *Us* down on the counter. "I said I can't believe you thought of that just this minute," she said patiently. "I mean, I'll help you out if I can, but let's face it, you'd probably have had a larger selection of house gifts wherever it was you came from."

"Philadelphia," Gregor said politely.

She looked him up and down. "Yeah. I figured it had to be at least Philadelphia. You staying here in Hollman?"

"Yes."

"Anybody who lives in Hollman will have seen everything I've got a hundred times and hated all of it. Unless they're into crafts, of course, and then they come in to buy the material they need. Yarn. Material. Pipe cleaners. Do you smoke a pipe?"

"No. Are you Mrs. Bligh?"

"What?" The woman looked startled. "Oh," she said finally. "The sign. Yes, I'm Mrs. Bligh. Emma Bligh. Emma *Kenyon* Bligh, as they put it in the newspaper when they write me up for being on some committee at the high school. Kenyon was my maiden name. Who are you?"

"Somebody who needs a knickknack to present to a friend of mine before I'm unconscionably late arriving."

The cowbell rang again, and they both looked up at the front door at the woman coming in. To Gregor, she seemed less alarming than Emma Kenyon Bligh—not fat, and with ordinary brownish hair instead of yellow—but there was also something out of key about her, as if, if you scratched the surface, you would get something you didn't expect to see. The surface was ordinary enough, though. She had on a short-sleeved shirtwaist dress of the kind once favored by the women called in Gregor's youth "old-maid schoolteachers," and if it hadn't been for the thin gold wedding band on the fourth finger of her left hand, that was what Gregor would have thought she was.

"Peggy," Emma said. "What are you doing downtown so late?"

Peggy looked at her feet. She seemed not only unwilling, but incapable of looking anyone in the eye. "I had to work late. We had chess club. I—" She looked confused.

"Shit," Emma said, under her breath.

Peggy looked up at the ceiling. There was a fan there, turning slowly, not doing much good. "I had to talk to you," she said.

"Shit," Emma said again.

Peggy seemed not to have noticed.

Gregor grabbed the first thing at hand—a little wooden plaque with a ceramic inset with the words "The Kitchen Is the Heart of the Home" printed across the top of it and a poem underneath, probably a bad one. Emma had come out from behind the counter and was moving through the shelves full of inanities toward the front door, where Peggy was still standing almost still, as if she had just come in. Gregor hadn't realized how many shelves and knickknacks there were. He hadn't been paying attention. Now the place seemed to be stuffed full of them.

"I'll just leave you twenty dollars for this," he said, taking out his wallet.

Emma had reached Peggy and grabbed her by the arm. They were, Gregor realized, the same age. Emma only looked younger at first glance because the heavy folds of fat left her without the kind of wrinkles Peggy had. He had, he was sure, a Peggy in his notebook, but he didn't want to check it here.

Emma had started to drag Peggy through the aisles between the shelves. She had to drag, because Peggy didn't seem to be moving her legs or her feet. She was moving her head, but that was more disconcerting than if she had been holding herself absolutely still. Her head bobbed back and forth on the top of her neck, as if they weren't securely connected.

"Jesus *Christ*," Emma said. "I can't believe you came in here at this time of day. Does he know where you are?"

"I'll just leave this twenty-dollar bill," Gregor said again.

The plaque cost $14.95. He didn't really care. Emma continued to drag Peggy toward the back of the store, and in no time at all, they were out of sight. They were not, however, out of earshot. Peggy had the kind of clear-bell voice that carries for yards, even though it isn't loud, and Emma was hissing.

"He knows I had to work late," she was saying. "You know what he's like. He understands when I have to stay at school to do the chess club."

It was, Gregor thought, like listening to someone talking during an episode of sleepwalking. The voice had no affect.

He anchored the twenty-dollar bill firmly under a small vase of silk flowers. The vase was made of bubble glass. At the last minute, he left the plaque there, too. He couldn't imagine what he'd do with it. Then he headed out the door and across the porch and down the steps back to the sidewalk, having no idea at all why he should feel so much in a hurry.

When he got back to the car and slid into the backseat and gave the robot-driver directions to go straight to Betsey Toliver's house, he reached into his jacket again and looked up the entry on "Peggy."

3

Fifteen minutes later, after some confusion about the difference between Meadow Farm Road and Meadow Farm Lane, the car pulled into the long driveway leading to a low ranch house that stretched out across its property like a ruler made of Silly Putty. It was a fifties ranch, not a modern one, but it had been kept up. The flagstone walk that led from the front door to the street—the one that nobody would ever walk on, because nobody would ever park on the street, out here—was well set and swept clean. The flagstone walk that led from the driveway to the side door was positively new. There were no cracks in the driveway's asphalt paving. The front door had been freshly painted a glossy metallic red. Gregor could easily see how this might have been the biggest and most expensive house in town thirty years ago, especially since Hollman was hardly a bastion of the rich and famous, or even of the rich and bored. He popped open his door, swung his feet out of the car, and vaulted out into the air. At the end of May, it was warm out here, although not as warm as Philadelphia would have been. There was a slight breeze brushing through his hair. The grass smelled as if it had just been mowed. The house looked so quiet, and so deserted, he thought he might have come at the wrong time. Maybe Elizabeth Toliver had taken her mother to a restaurant. Maybe nobody was home.

Gregor was just turning to watch the robot-driver take his suitcases out of the trunk—ever since Bennis had bought him luggage, he looked like a software billionaire when he traveled, or maybe like Steven Spielberg—when there were sounds from the back of the house, and then the clear tap and crack of hard heels on a stone surface. A moment later, a small woman came into view from the backyard. She was small in every way, not only short but very slight, with a fine-boned, high-cheekboned face with edges so sharp they looked as if they'd been drawn with a fountain pen. Gregor recognized her by her eyes, and her hair. Her eyes were enormous. Her hair had that overpuffed look it got when the people it belonged to were interviewed too often on television.

"Shit," she said.

"Excuse me?" Gregor said.

"I'm sorry," she said, running her right hand through her hair and making it puff all the higher. Then she walked up to him and stuck out her hand. "I *am* sorry. I didn't mean to sound as if—oh, I don't know. It's Gregor Demarkian, isn't it?"

"That's right."

"I'm Liz Toliver. And I really am sorry. I know I'm saying it over and over again. I'm not making any sense. But if that nurse quits, we're all up shit creek without a paddle, and the fool woman is totally losing it. I mean, for God's sake—"

"She's changed her mind," a tall man called, coming around the house from the same direction Liz Toliver had. A moment later, Gregor saw that it wasn't a man at all, but a boy, and a fairly young boy—no more than fourteen, he was sure, in spite of the height and the stubble of a beard just beginning to grow at the edges of his jaw. Still, Gregor thought, it would take another man not to be fooled. He'd bet anything that that boy got away with telling girls he was at least seventeen.

The boy came up to them and stopped. "She's changed her mind," he said again. "She's calmed down and she's going to stay, which is a good thing because Grandma is not going to be calmed down until that sedative kicks in. You're Mr. Demarkian, aren't you? Cool."

"How do you do?" Gregor said.

The boy had grabbed his hand and started pumping it. "I'm Mark De-Avecca. Liz is my mother. Jay DeAvecca was my father. He was—"

"*Mark.*"

"Well, whatever. It's complicated to figure out. I've got this whole monologue I use on new people from school. You know how conventional people are. Any sign of the cops?"

"You called the police?" Gregor said.

"We had to," Liz Toliver said.

"Come on back and I'll show you," Mark DeAvecca said. "It's in the garage. It's a detached garage. That's why we didn't hear. But it couldn't have been too long ago. I mean, it was still bleeding when Mrs. Vernon saw it—"

"Who's Mrs. Vernon?" Gregor said.

"Grandma's nurse," Mark said.

"And you only know she said it was bleeding," Liz Toliver said. "Considering the way she was behaving, God only knows what she actually saw—"

"I saw it bleeding," Mark said confidently. "Not much and not for very long, but the blood was definitely liquid. I was the first one out there after Mrs. Vernon had her fit, and it was oozing—"

"*Mark.*"

"She's got that sound programmed on a chip inside her skull," Mark said. "She doesn't have to make any effort to say it anymore. It just comes out automatically, every time I—"

"Mark," Liz Toliver said, more calmly, but not much more. "If you don't start behaving like a human being—"

"I *am* behaving like a human being," Mark said. "I am behaving like a very upset and frightened human being, and also like a very angry human being, because I *told* you so, I *told* you that this was a bad idea. And it's a good damned thing—don't you dare tell me not to say 'damn'—it's a good damned thing that Geoff didn't see it, because if he had he'd be up with nightmares for weeks."

"Wait," Liz said. "Geoff—"

"I've got the garage barricaded off. I didn't want to touch anything, so I piled up a bunch of stuff at the end of the drive so he can't get over it. And as soon as the police get here, I'm going to call Jimmy and tell him about this whole thing, and after that I hope you're going to listen to reason, because this is fucking stupid. And don't you dare tell me not to say 'fuck.' "

"What?" Liz said. "We're in some kind of crisis so it doesn't matter what you say? I don't get that. Since when—"

Mark turned his head to Gregor. "You want to come out back and see before the police get here? It's really lovely. There's blood all over everything. We're never going to get it out of the cement floor. If the real estate agents know about it, we're never going to sell the place. It's unbelievable."

"All right," Liz said. "It's unbelievable. I'll give you that."

Somewhere in the distance, there was the sound of a police siren. Gregor wondered if Liz and Mark had been as incoherent with the police as they had been with him, or if they'd sounded this panicked. That would be enough to bring a siren. Of course, so would boredom, cops with nothing else to do in a small town on a Monday night. He cocked his head at Mark.

"What is it?" he asked. "I take it nobody is dead."

"Not somebody," Mark said. "Some thing."

"It hardly seems right to call it a thing," Liz said.

"A dog," Mark said. "Grandma's dog. She's had it forever. That's one of the things we were supposed to do up here this vacation. Find someplace to put the dog. Except the dog looks as decrepit as Grandma. Although that could just be me. I can't really tell you how good my perceptions are in a situation like this, because I've never been in a situation like this, and I never intend to be in one again. If we can't talk my mother into packing up and going back to New York, I may just tie her up and throw her in the trunk and take her back myself."

"You can't drive," Liz said.

"Don't bet on it," Mark said.

The sirens were much closer now. It was, Gregor was sure, only a single police car, but he had the noise on as high and fast as it would go.

"So," Gregor said. "There's a dead dog on the floor of your garage. Somehow, that doesn't seem to be the whole story."

"It's not just dead," Mark said flatly. "It's been killed. It's been eviscerated, to be exact. Slit right down the stomach with something sharp and the guts are all the hell over the garage floor, intestines that look like intestines, everywhere—"

"Mark."

"That's the cops," Mark said as a white and blue car pulled into the drive, "and what I just told Mr. Demarkian here is the truth and you goddamned know it. Somebody slit that dog open while it was still alive and dumped its guts all over our garage floor and that didn't happen by accident, Ma, that happened on purpose, and you know it as well as I do. And I am going to call Jimmy, I really am, because if you can't get your act together, somebody has to. I want to leave. I want to leave tomorrow morning. Let's take Grandma and the goddamned nurse with us if we have to, but let's go. Somebody who did that to a dog could do that to Geoff. Got it?" He swung around to Gregor again. "You know how I know it was alive? Because it was alive when I saw it. It was in pain but it was conscious and it made eye contact with me and you know I'm not making that up, either. Jesus Christ. I'm going to go talk to the cops."

"Cop," Liz said automatically, because only one man had gotten out of the blue and white car. "It's incredible, the kind of language they learn in very expensive private schools."

Gregor looked up the drive. The garage was a small detached building at the very end of it—maybe at the very end of the property—that had been built to hold three cars, in a style meant to match that of the house. At the moment, there was a huge pile of debris in front of the doors, which were the kind that opened out, like barn doors, rather than the kind that folded up. Behind the garage, there were trees, tall pines that lined the property like a gate.

"What's back there?" Gregor asked. "Behind those trees, I mean?"

"More trees," Liz said. "I don't know. I never was one for going outdoors when I was a child. Do you think the person came from there, from the trees?"

"I don't know. I was really wondering if there was another house back there, but that we couldn't see it except for the trees."

"I don't think so," Liz said. "But you're asking the wrong person. This is the first time I've been back in decades."

"I know."

The cop had finished talking to Mark, or Mark had finished talking to the cop. They were both walking down the driveway toward Gregor and Liz, and Gregor suddenly realized that the warm breeze had come back, or that his awareness of it had. For the first time, he was fully cognizant of just how isolated this house was. This was not a subdivision, or a suburban street. It was a country road, with not too much of anything else on it except this house. The nearest neighbor was a good trek away. The way things sounded around them, the entire landscape might be uninhabited. Gregor did a 360-degree turn, checking things out. It was still light. There were still birds.

Mark and the cop came up to them and stopped. The cop stuck his hand out and grabbed Gregor's. "I'm Kyle Borden," he said, shaking vigorously. "You must be the Armenian-American Hercule Poirot."

FOUR

1

Peggy Smith Kennedy knew her old friends didn't take her seriously anymore. She was kept as carefully out of things as the unpopular people had been when they were all back in high school, and sometimes, these days, some of the unpopular people were let in. It was worse than it seemed, because Peggy knew she wasn't just shut out. It was more like she had ceased to exist. Belinda and Emma and Nancy and Chris had whole conversations around her that they wouldn't explain. If she tried to ask questions, they acted as if she weren't there. They even talked right over her sentences. She could have been a television set, white noise for the background, or a dog, except that they would have petted a dog. They would have made a positive fuss about a cat. She still went to lunch with them because she couldn't imagine not doing it—she'd been going to lunch with them at least once a week since she was twelve years old—but more and more she felt as if they wouldn't miss her if she were gone.

Now she went into the master bedroom of her small house and looked at Stu asleep on the bed. As always, he slept above the covers and in nothing but his underwear. The underwear was stained yellow in a little line at the back. When they were first married, she had tried to insist that he change every day, for the sake of hygiene, and he had often agreed. That was back when there were still times when he acted as if it mattered what she thought of him. He would change clothes, or try to go three or four days without a beer, or bring her flowers after one of their fights. She found it hard to credit, after all this time, that one of the reasons she had been so eager to marry him was that she had been so sure he would worship her for the rest of his life. After all, she was the one who had been popular in high school, when he had been negligible, if that. He hadn't even played a sport, and he certainly hadn't had the kind of cachet boys like Lowell Tomlin and Chet Jabonowitz had, when they finished up senior year clutching their early acceptances to Caltech and MIT. Now, he had even less cachet than he had ever had. The drugs had kept him from getting fat—he was always telling her that if she wanted to keep her weight down, she should get more familiar with cocaine—but his skin sagged horribly all over his body. His stomach hung down like an apron, the way the stomachs of very thin women do right after they've given birth. His face looked pitted and marred. Once, coming up behind him while he was standing at the counter at English Drugs, she had caught sight of his face in the overhead mirror. He had looked like one of the pictures on the FBI's most wanted poster at the post office. He had looked like Johnny Cash. His face was scarred the way the faces of men in prison were, even though he had never been in prison. He'd never even been arrested except once or twice for drunk driving, and those were the worst times of all. He felt caged up when he couldn't drive. He ended up rampaging through the house, and breaking things. Once, when he'd lost his license for six straight weeks after having been caught doing ninety-five on Clapboard Ridge at two o'clock in the morning, he'd gone at the walls of their little basement recreation room with a ball peen hammer and his fists, smashing away until he'd reduced all the drywall to dust and slivers. Then he'd smashed the picture tube of the little television set they kept on top of a small wheeled table so that Stu could watch wrestling when Peggy was asleep. Neither one of them had ever gone back into the recreation room again. Peggy had unplugged the television set, because she was worried it might cause a fire. Stu had moved his base of operations to the living room, where he spent most afternoons and evenings sprawled out along their battered couch, dressed or not, as the fancy took him. Even if he hadn't reacted the way he did when Peggy brought people home, she still wouldn't have been able to entertain. She never knew when he'd be there in his underwear and when he'd be there in a pair of jeans. She did know that he'd be hostile. He'd been hostile for years, especially to the girls they had both known when they were growing up. When Nancy Quayde was made principal of the high school, he had cut her picture out of the Hollman *Home News* and urinated on it.

Peggy made sure, one last time, that Stu was asleep and likely to stay asleep. Then she walked down the short hall to their tiny living room, filthy and dark. There was enough dirt on the carpet to plant in. If she ran her finger across the top of the mantel, she would find not only dust but grime, slick as kitchen grease, half an inch thick.

She went out the other end of the living room, into the dining room, where they never ate. She went into the kitchen and felt a little better. It was much cleaner here, because Stu never came into the kitchen except to get beer from the refrigerator, and he never did even that if she was at home to get it for him. When he was watching wrestling and getting coked up, she could come in here and get rid of her nervousness by scrubbing everything down. She only wished they could do something about the inevitable wear and tear. There were at least two holes in the linoleum floor, both deep enough so that she could see the plywood underneath. Two-thirds of the cabinets had lost their door handles. She went to the refrigerator and got out the little brown bag she'd packed with a Swiss cheese sandwich and a tangerine. She always took a brown bag lunch to school, even when she was eating out, so that Stu would think she wasn't wasting money on what he considered inessentials—although he did less of that now than he had. He bought his stuff once a week, right after she cashed her paycheck, and from that point on it was just a matter of staying out of his way until he got high enough.

Peggy went to the back door and looked out. Nancy Quayde picked her up every morning—Stu absolutely refused to let Peggy have a car, or to drive his unless he was in it, too—but she wouldn't come to the door and knock. She wouldn't even beep her horn. If Peggy wanted the ride, she had to be ready and waiting. Peggy let herself out onto the back porch. She was early. She just wished she knew what she should do about her anger, which had been spilling up inside her since she left Emma's place last evening and come to full fruition while she'd been getting dressed for school. It was one thing to treat her like something less than a human being. It was another to treat her as if she were stupid. There were times these days when they all got her so mad, Peggy thought her head was going to split open. Whenever she thought that, she had a vision of it lying on the sidewalk smashed to pieces, like a dropped watermelon.

There was the sound of a car in the street and then Nancy Quayde's four-door Saab came rolling into Peggy's driveway, but not very far in. Nancy liked to make quick getaways, especially from here. Peggy tried the door behind her to make sure it was locked. Then she walked down the drive to where Nancy was waiting. She really hated that damned Saab. It was so stuck-up and pretentious. Nancy no more needed a four-door car than she needed a pogo stick. She'd only bought this one to let everyone know that she made more money than they did. If she ever got the superintendent's job, she'd probably go out and buy a Mercedes.

"I've got to tell you something," Nancy said, backing out without waiting to make sure Peggy had her seat belt on.

"I've got to tell *you* something," Peggy said. "Gregor Demarkian was in Emma's store last night. I saw him."

The car slid backward into the street. At this time of the morning, there was no real worry about traffic. Nancy looked her over. "How did you know that?" she said.

"Because I saw him," Peggy repeated. "I tried to tell Emma who he was, but she wouldn't listen to me. I'm getting damned sick and tired of the bunch of you treating me as if I'd had all my brain cells removed by laser surgery. I knew who he was as soon as I saw him. He's been in *People*. Emma didn't have a clue."

"Well," Nancy said. Then she fluttered her hands in the air. "Why didn't you tell anybody else? Or was Stu refusing to let you make phone calls last night?"

Peggy let that one pass. "It wouldn't have been much use telling anybody else, would it? You'd all have just acted like Emma. What was the point?"

"Do you happen to know what he's doing here?"

"I'd expect he was doing something with Betsy Toliver. About Betsy Toliver. About Michael Houseman. That's the only murder mystery we've got around here, isn't it?"

The car was going forward again. Nancy leaned over the steering wheel and frowned. "He's staying out at Betsy's mother's place. Nobody knows for how long. Apparently, she asked him to stay with her."

"Are they supposed to be friends?"

"How am I supposed to know?"

"Obviously," Peggy said judiciously, "you know more than I do. You must have been on the phone all night with one or the other of them. Except not with me. Never with me anymore, right? We use Stu as an excuse to avoid talking about why it is none of you are my friends anymore, even though we've all known each other since kindergarten."

"You know what it's like with Stu. If he's in the wrong mood, he goes berserk. None of us wanted to—"

"Talk to me," Peggy said.

"We don't really know why he's here. We just think he's here because of Michael. And the stories in the supermarket newspapers. What else could it be, right? What other reason would he have to be down here? We don't think it's a very good situation, under the circumstances."

"Why don't you ask her about it?" Peggy said. "We're all supposed to be grown-ups these days, right? We're all practically fifty. None of that high school stuff should matter anymore. Why don't you just pick up the phone and call her house and ask her—"

"Listen," Nancy said. "There was an incident. Last night. Somebody got into the garage out there and left a dead dog in it."

"In Betsy Toliver's garage?"

"Right. Exactly. I don't know the details. It was Kyle Borden who took the call, and you know what he's like. Chris couldn't get a thing out of him, even though she tried, except that it was deliberate. I mean, the dog was killed, it didn't just die of something. If you could think of anybody doing anything stupider—"

"It doesn't have to be connected to us," Peggy said. "It could be somebody else, doing it for some other reason."

"What?"

"Kids. Bugging the famous person."

"Don't be asinine," Nancy said. "Why would kids put a dead dog in Betsy Toliver's garage? Even your standard sociopathic adolescent has to have some reason for what he does. No, I'm with Chris. I think somebody meant it as a warning."

"A warning of what?"

"A warning for her to get out of town," Nancy said. "For Betsy to get out of town. Chris thinks it came from one of us, and I'm with her—"

Peggy snorted. "Could you just see Belinda dragging a dead dog out there where the Tolivers live? You must be joking."

"I'm not joking, and you shouldn't be joking, either. The situation would have been mucky enough if she were just down here on her own, but with Demarkian here with her it could get very nasty. So Chris and I decided. We're going to invite her to things."

"What?"

"We're going to invite her to things," Nancy said. "Chris is going to have her to dinner. I'm going to invite her to lunch. We're going to invite her to things. Just like we do when Maris comes down from New York."

"Are you crazy? Whatever makes you think she would come?"

"Oh, she'll come," Nancy said confidently. "People like that always do. I've had enough ed psych to know that, and so have you. It doesn't matter if she lives to be a hundred and five, she'll still be trying to make up for what happened to her when she was fourteen. Why do you think she puts up with Maris?"

"I thought she and Maris had become friends in college."

Nancy smirked. "If Maris is Betsy's friend, I'm Hillary Clinton's hairdresser. Maris can't stand Betsy Toliver now any more than she ever could, and you know how Maris was about Betsy. Worse than Belinda. She'll come, Peggy, trust me."

They were driving through the gates onto the long drive that led to the new high school. Peggy cleared her throat. "Remember that night when we invited her to the White Horse?"

"Yes. It won't matter. She won't believe we'd do something like that again, not at our ages. And we have to make it clear to that Demarkian person that none of us has anything against Betsy Toliver anymore. You got that?"

They were at the end of the drive and into the faculty parking lot. Peggy picked her purse up from the floor and watched a thin line of students climbing their way up from the lower level lot. They carried book bags instead of just books. Peggy couldn't remember when that had started, but she did remember that none of them would have been caught dead with a book bag when she was in high school. Of course, none of them would have been caught dead in jeans, either, at least not on a school day, and now nobody seemed to wear anything else.

"So," Nancy said. "What do you think? You going to help us out?"

"How?"

"Chris is going to have a lunch on Saturday, with Betsy as the guest of honor. Do you think you could manage to be there?"

Saturday was the day after payday. Stu would be unconscious by ten in the morning. "Yes," Peggy said.

"Good," Nancy said. "Chris is going to call her this morning to firm things up. After that, we should know something about times. I think Chris is going to have it catered. All you've got to do is show up and behave yourself. No commenting on how she still has really awful taste in clothes."

"Well," Peggy said, "they're no longer cheap."

Nancy pulled into a parking space and shut off the engine. "No, they're not, and nothing else about her is either. I just hope you take the point. Chris is right. It's been bad enough with those stupid newspaper stories, but it's going to get a lot worse if we don't do something about it. Show up. Make polite conversation. Pretend that you're really impressed with what she's done with her life. That's all I ask."

But I am really impressed with what she's done with her life, Peggy thought, struggling with the door handle and her pocketbook and the brown paper bag all at once. Then she stepped out of the car and looked around, bewildered. There were times when she woke up in the middle of the night and thought she was still fourteen years old. She still lived in the same place and knew the same people. She still went to the same school she'd gone to then, even if it was in a different building.

She turned to say something to Nancy, but Nancy was gone, striding out across the parking lot with her briefcase swinging on the tips of the fingers of her right hand.

If I were Betsy, I wouldn't come, Peggy thought, and then she changed her mind, quickly, because she had to. She was going to come herself. That was just as bad. If she'd had any self-respect left, she would have refused outright.

2

For Belinda Hart Grantling, it was better this morning than it had been for a long time, in spite of all that nonsense about the dog in Betsy Toliver's garage. Part of that was that she had someplace to go, and therefore some reason to stay away from Maris. Always before, when Maris had come home, she'd gone to stay with her own parents in their house out in Stony Hill. Now Maris's parents were both dead, and there was nowhere for her to stay except in one of those motels out on the highway, which weren't feasible, since Maris wouldn't drive. It made Belinda insane. She'd rented that bright yellow Volkswagen at the airport, and driven it out here, and now it was sitting abandoned in the English Drugs parking lot while Maris cadged rides from whoever would give them to her. Belinda wondered, vaguely, if Maris had inherited whatever money her parents had. She had a brother with a wife and a child somewhere in Ohio, but surely that wouldn't mean she'd been cut out of the will entirely. Maybe there was nothing to inherit. Maris never seemed to have any money, and although Belinda knew that was

Betsy's fault—didn't it figure that Betsy was not only stuck-up, but a miser?—it was still odd that Maris could have the things she had and live the way she lived and not have enough pocket money to buy magazines when she went to English Drugs. Maris had been in residence less than forty-eight hours, and Belinda was ready to kill her. If it wasn't for that meeting the night before, Belinda would have kicked her out, first thing, as soon as she woke up.

She stopped in the living room right before she left the apartment, and stared at the television screen Maris had left glowing the night before. Maris never turned anything off. Lights, television, faucets—Belinda found herself wandering from one room to the next, shutting things. Belinda found the remote half under the couch and punched the channel changer. She passed Cartoon Network and Lifetime and the Sci Fi Channel and hunkered down with the news shows: CNN, MSNBC, C-Span. Betsy didn't seem to be on any of them at the moment. Maybe it was the wrong time of day. Maybe they were done live, and Betsy wouldn't be on television at all the whole month she was in Hollman. The idea gave Belinda a little rush of satisfaction. It wasn't, Belinda thought, as if Betsy were somebody *really* famous. She wasn't a movie star or a rock singer or a model or anybody else important. She was just an intellectual, the way she'd always been. The only difference now was that there were a lot of intellectuals on television for other intellectuals to watch. Belinda couldn't imagine who else would watch them. She hated those screaming matches over fiscal policy she sometimes stumbled into looking for a movie or a rerun of *Designing Women*. The shows where they didn't scream were even worse. Four people in four modern chairs on a gray platform on a black set, talking so reasonably you could barely hear them—and about what? The Bush tax cut. The Clinton legacy. The Laffer curve. Belinda truly hated Hillary Clinton, more than she hated anybody on the planet except for Betsy Toliver herself. You could see what Hillary was all about just by looking at her, another stuck-up smart girl who thought people should elect her God just because she listened to classical music. It was disgusting. It was *unfeminine*, too. Belinda didn't understand why all these women didn't come right out and say they were lesbians. What was the point of the pretense, the husband they didn't like sleeping with, the children they kept as pets to drag out in front of the cameras when the holidays rolled around and they needed to take a family portrait? Belinda snapped the television off and put the remote where it belonged, on the coffee table. Then she went to the back of the apartment and looked in on Maris, asleep across the daybed in the back room with her clothes from last night still on, including shoes. Belinda went out again and picked up her purse from the counter next to the sink. She took out her wallet and counted the money in it—$17 in bills, $1.26 in change—and put the wallet back and zipped up the bag. There was just something wrong about the whole thing, something so fundamentally unfair. It was as if all those women—Betsy, and Hillary Clinton, and all the rest of them on the news talk shows—

it was as if they were all cheating, breaking the rules, going behind the backs of everybody else and stealing things that rightfully belonged to others. The worst thing was, men never seemed to catch on. Men *married* them for it.

She was out on the street before she knew it. The day was very bright. She blinked a few times in the sun. She stayed on her own side of the street, because that's where the library was. She went around to the side of the library's new addition and let herself in the back door. It was ten minutes to nine. She had just enough time to put away her things and get her hair brushed before the doors opened. If business was slow, as it always was on Tuesday mornings, she would be able to run across the street to JayMar's to take out a cup of coffee, or over to Mullaney's, near the railroad tracks, for a package of crackers and peanut butter to eat.

She put her handbag behind the take out desk. The lights were all on, meaning that Laurel was already here. She took out her brush and ran it vigorously through what hair she had left. She was balding badly, but she didn't know what to do about it. She thought about trying Rogaine, but that seemed to be for men. She looked at her reflection in the security mirror above the main desk, put her brush back in her bag, and started walking toward the front.

"Laurel?"

"I'm up here." The sound came from the front foyer of the addition. Nobody went into the front foyer of the main building anymore. Once the addition had been fully up and running, the main building had been turned into a museum of things nobody wanted to see. Who cared how people had lived in Hollman in 1865?

"What are you doing?" Belinda asked. She was coming up between the stacks. Laurel was there, at the very front, pinning something on the cork bulletin board.

"I'm putting up a notice. Did I tell you? I couldn't have. You haven't been here. Anyway, she came in late yesterday afternoon, to return some overdue books she found on a shelf somewhere and ask me if her mother had anything else out that I might be looking for. God, she looked great. Do you know if she's had plastic surgery or not? I mean, no crow's-feet at all. Of course, her mother doesn't have them, either, so maybe it's genetics. Wouldn't that be lucky genetics to get? I already look like a road map in the top half of my face."

"So, what did she say? Just that about the overdue books?"

"Oh, no," Laurel said. "We talked about her coming here and doing a program, and she said yes right away. On Saturday, at our regular meeting of the Friends. I've been frantic ever since. I had to call the *Home News* and put in a notice, and I had to make this sign." Laurel gestured at the paper she was tacking to the corkboard. "It's not a very good one, but the letters are big. And I ran off a whole bunch of them to pass out. I mean, of course the Friends will all be there, but I'll be embarrassed beyond belief if we can't get a bigger crowd than that. She's going to talk about covering a political campaign. Did you know she covered the campaign in Connecticut the last time Rosa DeLauro ran for Congress?"

Belinda had never heard of Rosa DeLauro, but she had an instinct not to say so. Obviously, she was somebody Laurel recognized, and that other people would, too. The sign was just an ordinary piece of legal-sized paper printed in red capital letters, boldface and in italics: ***ELIZABETH TOLIVER IS HERE.*** Underneath, there was smaller lettering, giving the day and time and location and a brief sentence about the subject of the talk.

"Do you think a lot of people are going to be interested in an election in Connecticut?" she asked, because she couldn't help herself.

Laurel waved this away. "It's not an election in Connecticut. It's campaign finance reform and celebrity perks and the way the media treats women running for Congress. Especially somebody like Rosa DeLauro, who's so feminist. Oh, and you've got to remember. She likes to be called Liz, not Betsy. She's really adamant about it. It *upsets* her to be called Betsy."

"Betsy Wetsy," Belinda said.

"What?" Laurel blinked.

"Betsy Wetsy," Belinda said. "That's why she hates to be called Betsy. It was a doll when we were all children, a baby doll that you fed with a bottle and then the water came out the other side and you had to change its diaper. So we called her Betsy Wetsy."

"In high school?"

"In kindergarten and all the time after. It was just one of those things."

"What an awful thing to do to somebody."

"I don't see why. It was just a nickname. Lots of people have nicknames when they're children. I had a nickname."

"What?"

"Lindy."

"Not quite the same, is it?" Laurel made a face. "I've read things about how awful she was treated here as a child. I never really thought about the particulars. I think it's a miracle she's willing to be here at all. She must be incredibly close to her mother. And now doing a program for the library, too. You're making me think she's some kind of saint."

"It would have been different if it really fit," Belinda said. "But she didn't really wet herself. It was just a nickname."

"Right," Laurel said. She had finished putting up the folder. With its red lettering, it would be hard to miss. She stepped back and rubbed the palms of her hands against her sky-blue linen Talbots pants. "Pay attention to me. You will *not* call her Betsy while she's here. In the library, I mean. I don't care how natural it feels. If people had called me a name like that when I was growing up, I'd have gotten away as soon as I could and never gone back. It's unbelievable how children treat each other, it really is. No wonder there are school shootings every spring. I've got to clean up the files on late returns this morning. Do you think you can handle things yourself?"

"I don't see why not."

"Good." Laurel looked her poster up and down. "God," she said again. "You'd think people would learn, but they never do. And it always comes out the same. Incredible. You can open up now. It's five after nine."

Laurel strode off through the big main room. Belinda watched her for a while and then did what she'd been asked to do. Laurel, obviously, hadn't heard about the dog. Either she didn't watch the local news in the morning, or the story hadn't appeared there. It wouldn't have appeared in the paper, because that only came out once a week. Belinda looked at JayMar's, and English Drugs, and the railroad tracks, and Mullaney's. She couldn't imagine putting her hands in a dog's intestines. She didn't even like to handle raw chicken. Besides, this was the kind of thing that would appear in the news somewhere, and when it did it would make all of them look like—

—losers.

There were people on the street now, although not many of them. Belinda checked them out to see if she knew them—she didn't—and went back inside and closed the door after her. For the first time, she considered the possibility that *Betsy* might take the dog seriously. Maybe, to Betsy, the dog would be a warning she needed to heed. Then she'd give this up as a bad job, and pack her children into her fancy expensive car, and go back to Connecticut.

For the first time, Belinda truly hoped that Betsy Toliver was scared to death.

FIVE

1

The first thing Gregor Demarkian did when he woke up that morning, before he'd taken a shower, was to get his notebook from the pocket of the jacket he was wearing the night before and make sure he had written down the name and address of the police officer he had talked to about the dog. He'd been dreaming all night that he'd lost both. Either he'd forgotten to write them down, or the ink had paled so much it was illegible, or the page was ripped from the notebook when he went to find it. Even during the first dream, he had been aware that he was dreaming. During the second dream and all the ones afterward, some part of his brain stood outside the action, analyzing. This was a kind of panic attack. He'd been prone to them when he was first in training at Quantico, which was odd, because he hadn't been the least prone to them in the army, and he'd always been half afraid that the army would get him killed. He had no idea why he should suddenly be prone to them again, now, when—at least as far as he could tell—he had nothing at stake at all. It wasn't the dog, although the dog still bothered the hell out of him. Mark had not been exaggerating. Somebody *had* cut that dog straight up the middle, with some kind of a sharp knife or a razor, while it was still alive. The intestines *had* been spilling out all over the garage's cement floor, slippery and wet. Gregor could have understood it if he'd had dreams about that, the way he used to have dreams about the bodies they got pictures of when he was with the Behavioral Sciences Unit. The dog, though, had been worse. He couldn't put his finger on why. Maybe there was some part of him that felt that it made sense for people to kill other people, even if the other people were children. There was something natural about human beings wanting to slaughter each other. Slaughtering a dog was not natural. He was making no sense at all.

Once he found the notebook—Kyle Borden; 555-2627—he put it on the rickety night table by the bed he was sleeping in and thought that it didn't matter. This was a small town. If he'd lost the name and address, he only had to call the police department and ask a few questions to be put in touch with the officer again. For all he knew, Kyle Borden was the *only* officer. He looked around the small bedroom. It was the "spare bedroom" at the back of the ranch. In some places, it wouldn't "count" as a bedroom at all, because it had no closet. For a fifties ranch, this was a fairly nice house, but it couldn't escape *being* a fifties ranch. The ceilings were lowish. Gregor was used to the high ones in the turn-of-the-century town house in which he lived, or the equally high ones in new houses that specialized in tray and cathedral ceilings. The floor was wall-to-wall carpet, fortunately in a neutral navy-blue. Gregor imagined it had once been a fashionable color, like turquoise or black. That was what Gregor remembered best about fifties ranches in the fifties. There was all that turquoise, and all those bathrooms tiled in pink halfway up the wall and papered in black with metallic outlines of pink flamingoes on top of that. Just to make sure, he got his robe and went into the bathroom that was just outside his door, but it was an ordinary bathroom, tiled in white, with a tub-shower combination that you had to step into as if you were stepping over a runner's hurdle.

He got his clothes off and got into the shower. He ran the water as hot as he could make it without squealing and stood under the stream for a good five minutes, only wondering, a little guiltily, at the end, if this house got its water supply from a well. Sometimes, showers helped him think. If he stood under them long enough, ideas came to him that would come to him no other way. Today, nothing like that happened. He only thought more about the dog. That had been an ugly scene out there. He would have thought it was ugly even if it had been a mob operation, where he could have excused it to some extent because the issues would have been serious: the division of several million dollars earned from the sale of a couple of kilos of heroin; the control of vice and gambling on the South Side. This looked like nothing but spite. Who did something like that to an animal out of spite, and who did it so openly, in the still light of a late afternoon, when there were people in the house? Water beat down on his head, making him aware of how thick his hair was. The whole incident stank. What was worse, it had too much in common with that story of what had happened to Elizabeth Toliver on the night Michael Houseman died, except that the intensity had been ratcheted up a notch. If he'd been a younger man, he'd have beat his head against the wall.

He got out of the shower and toweled off. He went back to his bedroom and put on clean clothes, all folded into his suitcase with the precision that only a true fanatic would employ. If Bennis had been with him the night before, she would have insisted that he unpack his suitcases and hang his clothes from the curtain rods over the windows, or she would have done it for him. The idea that he might be too tired would not have occurred to her. Bennis was a woman who had never been tired in her life. Gregor knotted his tie without checking it out in a mirror—there wasn't one in the room; he didn't feel up to digging out the one in the Mark Cross travel set Bennis had given him—and sat down on the edge of the rumpled bed to use the phone. Bennis would have made the bed. Gregor only noticed that the phone was a princess style, and pink.

He dialed his own number first. The phone rang and rang but was not picked up, not even by an answering machine. He must have forgotten to turn it on. He tried Bennis's number next. Bennis was never in her own apartment anymore except when she made those papier-mâché models of Zed and Zedalia she used to help her plot her fantasy novels, and it was the wrong time of year for that. He hung up again and picked up again and dialed the number for Tibor's apartment. There was always a chance that Tibor was home, because Tibor often forgot to go to appointments. Bennis or Lida or Donna Moradanyan had to run down and pull him out of his easy chair to do whatever it was he was supposed to do. If they didn't get him in the mornings, he forgot to go to breakfast. Once, Donna had had to rouse him out and stuff him into his robes because he'd forgotten to go to the church and celebrate a wedding.

Tibor's phone rang four times and was picked up, but not by Tibor. The answering machine whirred into life. Tibor's voice said, "This is Father Kasparian at Holy Trinity Armenian Christian Church. I am unable to come to the phone right now. If you leave your name, the time that you called, and a number where I can reach you, I will call you back as soon as possible."

"Tibor?" Gregor said. Tibor never called anybody back. He forgot to check the answering machine, sometimes for weeks. Of course, sometimes he forgot to pick up the phone, too, so there was no way of knowing if he was in the apartment or not. "Tibor?" Gregor said again. "It's Gregor. Pick up."

Nobody picked up. The tape whirred some more.

"Okay, Tibor," he said. "This is Gregor, calling from Hollman. I'll try to call you back. Or Bennis. I hope you're at the Ararat, remembering to eat."

Gregor put the phone down. He took his comb off the night table and ran it through his hair, not using a mirror for that, either, which meant he had no idea how it had come out. He could look like those old newspaper drawings of Jack the Ripper on the prowl. Tibor not only forgot appointments, and his answering machine, he forgot everything, if he got into a book or involved in that Internet newsgroup he'd become addicted to. RAM. Rec.arts.mystery. Gregor had no idea why he remembered it. He had no idea how a man like Tibor could forget to eat, either. You'd think that after decades of being half starved to death in Soviet prison camps, he'd be eating nonstop for the rest of his life.

Gregor put his comb and his wallet in his pocket and went out into the hall. The house was very quiet. He walked to the edge of the hall and found the living room. He went through the living room and found another hall. "Rambling," that's what they would have called this house in real estate ads at the time it was built. This next hall was very short. He went through it and found the dining room.

"Is anybody home?" he called out.

"Back here," Mark called back. "Go through the dining room."

Gregor went through the dining room. On the far side of it was a door. Through the door was the kitchen with its corner breakfast nook. Mark was sitting at the small round kitchen table, a large-sized paperback book opened and lying down in front of him, a glass of orange juice the size of a small pitcher in his hand.

"Kafka," Gregor said. "I'm surprised. I'd think he was a little too depressing for you."

"He is," Mark said. "But if you think about it, he's better than people like J. D. Salinger. In the depressing department, I mean. At least he's got an imagination. Giant cockroaches. Lots of violence. With people like Salinger, everybody sits around having a nervous breakdown about you don't know what and the world sucks."

"Right," Gregor said.

"There's juice in the refrigerator and Mom had Ms. Vernon get those coffee bags before we came. I'll put on some water if you want."

"Please."

"Luis took your car up the road to Andy's to get something done to it. Gas. I don't know. I've got the number. When you want him, you're supposed to call and he'll come and get you."

"Luis?"

"Your driver. If you're going into town, will you drop me at the library? Mom said I could meet her there if I wanted, and God knows I'm bored out here. Mom took Geoff and Grandma out to do some stuff, see the physical therapist and the doctor, like that. They've got that stupid woman with them, too. Ms. Vernon."

"Are you always this awake first thing in the morning?"

"I've been up since six. It's almost ten o'clock. You going to tell me what's going on here or am I going to have to listen at doors when you talk to my mother?"

Mark was on his feet and moving. Gregor sat down at the little table and let him put a tumbler full of orange juice in front of him—hadn't the boy ever heard of juice glasses?—and then a thick ceramic mug with a coffee bag in it. The kettle was already on the stove. Mark would have been bustling, except that he was too enormous to manage it.

"So," Mark said. "What about it? I know I'm only fourteen, but I'm not stupid."

No, Gregor thought, *you're certainly not stupid.* The kettle whistled. He sat back while Mark poured water over the coffee bag. "You said yesterday that you were going to call Jimmy Card," Gregor said when the water was safely in the cup. "Did you?"

"Yeah. He's coming out as soon as he can get here. Probably not before tomorrow, or else really late today. He was not happy."

"I can imagine."

Mark sat down again. "The thing is," he said, "this is totally nuts. Mom doesn't have to be here. Jimmy could have sent people to clear up the details and make sure Grandma ended up in a decent nursing home in Connecticut. It's not like Grandma even likes her, because she doesn't. And all that stuff about the publicity is crap. So what's she doing here?"

"Maybe she wanted to come back and see how it felt, now that she's successful. Maybe she wanted to let her old friends see how successful she'd become."

"She doesn't have any old friends. You know that book, *Carrie*? Maybe you saw the movie. Mom was Carrie. Except her family wasn't poor and she was smart. But she was like that. Everybody hated her."

"All the more reason to come back for a few weeks and let everybody see how well she's done."

"You don't think showing up in *People* walking into the Oscars on Jimmy Card's arm is enough for that?"

"She can't see their faces when they react."

"Yeah. Okay. Maybe." Mark slumped, stretching his long legs straight out in front of him. He scratched the side of his face. It was still a smooth face, in most places, but there were patches of beard here and there. In a couple of years, the beard would be full, and he'd have that ticket to teenage popularity, a face that looked old enough not to get carded in liquor stores.

"You met Maris Coleman yet?" he asked.

Gregor shook his head. "That's the woman that Mr. Card, ah—"

"Thinks is planting the stories in the tabloids. It's not a secret. Mom knows he thinks that. I think it, too. You met her yet?"

"No."

"She was here. She came from Hollman. And Mom and Maris both went to Vassar for college, so they were together in college, and from what I can see, Maris was a bitch to Mom there, too. But that isn't the point. The point is, it's really weird."

"What's weird?"

"It's like she never grew up," Mark said carefully. "Maris, I mean. She's, what, practically fifty. And it's like she's still living when she's seventeen. She *harps* on it. When you go out with her, it's all she talks about. Well, not really, you know. She'll talk about the ballet or the mayor or whatever. But she always brings it up. She brings it into every conversation."

"And?"

"And I was wondering if they were all like that. That whole group that Maris was part of. It has to do with the dog, somehow, because the dog was—it was an angry thing, you know? Whoever did it was right in the middle of a world-class piss-off. It wasn't something someone considered and did. It was a kind of explosion. I sound like a moron. God."

"No," Gregor said, pushing his chair back from the table. "You're right. That's what was bothering me."

"What was bothering you?"

"The dog," Gregor said. "And the snakes. And Michael Houseman. Do you know what happened to Michael Houseman?"

"The guy the tabloids say my mother killed? Somebody slit his throat. From ear to ear, as the *National Enquirer* is always putting it."

"Exactly," Gregor said. He stood up and looked around. There was a note tacked to the refrigerator door with a magnet. When he looked more closely at it, it had the number for "Andy's Garage" printed across it in thick black letters.

There was a phone on the wall next to the refrigerator.

Like the one in his room, it was pink.

2

Luis the robot-driver—Gregor was beginning to think of it as a Greek epigram—came to fetch him in no time at all, and seemed to get him into town even quicker, although that might have been an illusion caused by the fact that Gregor had now traveled that road at least once. It helped that Mark talked, on and off, about everything from Kafka to Isaac Asimov. It was a relief to find a teenaged boy who cared about books the way most of the rest of his tribe cared about video games and Arnold Schwarzenegger movies. On the other hand, Mark also seemed to care about Arnold Schwarzenegger movies. Gregor was sorry when they came to the library and had to drop him off. Driving down Grandview Avenue, Gregor felt, as he had the night before, that there was something small-minded and suffocating about this place. Too many of the people he saw were too conventional. He never thought he'd be pining for teenaged boys in rainbow Mohawks and double nose rings, but after a few minutes of Hollman that was exactly what he needed. He could have used a little rock and roll, or whatever they called it these days, too. The few times since coming here that he had heard music coming out of a radio, it had either been "oldies"—meaning the Beatles and the Beach Boys—or Britney Spears. If there were people in Hollman who liked jazz, or classical, or Ozzy Osbourne, he hadn't found them yet. The Hollman Police Department was in a small brick building on Grand Street, way up toward the far end of Grandview Avenue and just around the corner from a small Catholic church. The street was lined with tall old trees and meticulously kept up. The police department parking lot was free of grass and twigs. Its walls looked as if they had been hosed down sometime recently. That was when something else hit him: he hadn't seen any black people, either. He hadn't even seen any darkish people, of any kind, not even anybody he could pin down as definitely Italian. He didn't think he'd ever been in such a homogeneous place in his life.

Gregor got out of the car and walked around to the front of the building automatically. There was an entrance from the parking lot, but he wasn't sure who was allowed to use it. The front of the building faced the side of the Catholic church. The rest of the side street seemed to be made up of small frame houses, some of them being used for doctors' and dentists' offices, some of them cut up into multifamily dwellings. He tried to imagine the kind of person who would live in a multifamily dwelling in Hollman, but his mind balked. He let himself in the department's heavy front door. He found himself in a wide room with a counter across one end of it, like a registrar's office in a very small college.

The girl behind the counter looked up. Her name tag said "Sharon Morobito." She was blond, blue-eyed, and as fair-skinned as a Swede. "Can I help you?" she said.

Gregor gave his name and explained his business. Sharon Morobito nodded and bustled to a small door at the back of the room. Presumably, that was where the real police department was, if there was a real police department here at all. Gregor wondered where the criminals were. Was it really possible that, first thing on a Tuesday morning, the Hollman Police Department wouldn't have anything at all to do?

Sharon Morobito came back to the counter where Gregor was waiting. "Come on through," she said. "He's back in his office. We had a bad night last night. *Three* drunk driving arrests. I don't know what's gotten into people around here lately."

"Mmm," Gregor said. Philadelphia would probably be overjoyed if it could clock only three assaults with intent to commit bodily harm in any single night.

They were at the door to the office in the back. Gregor saw Kyle Borden get quickly to his feet.

"Mr. Demarkian," he said.

Gregor edged into Kyle Borden's very small office and found a chair. The chair was very small, too, but then, Kyle Borden was also very small. Gregor doubted if he was five feet four.

Kyle gestured to the mess on his desk. "You've come to talk about the dog. Or maybe about Michael Houseman. That's what you said you were here for, wasn't it?"

"Here right this minute, or here in Hollman?"

"Whatever."

"Well, it's like I told you last night. Jimmy Card asked me to come down here and find out something about the death of Michael Houseman. I think he's really less interested in solving an old crime—"

"It would be damned near impossible."

"—than in stopping the tabloid stories that keep accusing Ms. Toliver of having committed the crime. But the dog puts an interesting spin on things, don't you think? It's not the kind of thing you'd do just because you hated somebody in high school and now you're really upset because she grew up to be famous. Or at least it's not the kind of thing I would do in those circumstances. Would you?"

If Gregor had expected a quick denial, he didn't get it. Instead, Kyle Borden looked at him long and hard, and then turned away to shuffle through the mess of papers on his desk again.

"Look," he said finally. "This may be a little hard to explain. How long have you lived in Philadelphia?"

"This time?"

"In your life. How long have you lived in cities? Philadelphia. Wherever."

"I've always lived in cities, except for when I was in the army. I grew up in Philadelphia."

"Okay." Kyle sighed. "This is going to be *very* hard to explain. This is not a city. It's not even close. Maybe about half of all the people who grow up here stay here. It was more than that for my high school graduating class—did I tell you I graduated in the same class as Betsy Toliver?"

"Liz," Gregor said automatically. "No, you didn't."

"Liz, right. I'll try to be careful. I had a nickname I didn't like much myself. I didn't get rid of it until I had a gun to threaten people with. Guns. Shit. I was thinking last night after I left the Toliver place that these days she wouldn't have gone to Vassar and gotten to thumb her nose at all of them. She'd have just gotten a handgun out of her daddy's bedside table and laid 'em all to rest. A couple of them deserved it."

"She doesn't seem like the violent type. I think she's on some committee that works to ban handguns."

"Yeah," Kyle said. "The thing is, what you've got to understand, is that for people in a place like this, high school is a *big* deal. Most of them think it was the best time of their lives. Most of them never did anything afterward but work, except go to the junior college down the road or maybe, if they were really bright, to UP-Johnstown. There were one hundred and twelve people in my graduating class and only six of them went away to any college more impressive than that, and two of them went to Penn State. High school is the be all and end all of everything in a place like this. High school football games attract hundreds of people. Homecoming saturates the whole town. All the businesses on Grandview Avenue decorate. There's a big parade. The Homecoming Queen and her court get their pictures on the front page of the town paper. And forever afterward, if they stay in town, they keep *nurturing* it. Does that make any sense to you? Go into Emma and George Bligh's place sometime and look on the walls. Emma was captain of the varsity cheerleaders our senior year. She's got a picture of herself in her uniform, blown up to eight and a half by eleven, right behind the cash register. Sheila Sedding over at JayMar's can tell you who was Homecoming Queen every year back to 1948."

"Liz Toliver's son Mark said that what bothered him about Maris Coleman here was that it was like the years between then and now had never happened."

"Yeah, well. Mark DeAvecca spent the first seven years of his life in London and he's got a mother who's on TV all the time. He's probably going to have Jimmy Card as a stepfather. He can afford to think high school is stupid."

"What are you saying, exactly?" Gregor stretched out his legs. "That somebody might have—done that—to Mrs. Toliver's dog in her own garage just because they were mad at Liz Toliver for getting to be successful when she wasn't particularly successful in high school?"

"No, not exactly. I'm just saying that you maybe don't want to make assumptions about what's an overreaction to all that stuff about high school. I think the dog is too much myself, but I could see something close to it. I keep expecting to get a phone call that somebody's taken the sharp end of a can opener to that car."

Gregor shook his head. "I don't get it. She seems like a perfectly nice woman. Does she turn into a vampire when the moon gets full? Why all this—emotion?"

"It's werewolves who come out when the moon is full," Kyle said. "And I don't know why all this emotion. I didn't understand even back then, although I know why they thought she was so odd. Everybody thought she was odd. She used to walk around with all these really strange books. Jean-Paul Sartre. I remember that one. That's how I found out who Sartre was. I asked her."

"Seems a little thin to cause the kind of reaction she got. Gets."

"I agree. I don't pretend to be able to explain it. She did get a reaction, though. Some of them—well, anyway. That was it. I wanted to warn you. You wanted to know something about the death of Michael Houseman."

Gregor nodded. "Doesn't it ever bother you that nobody talks about that? We wander around here talking about how people hated Liz Toliver in high school, and somebody is dead. I've been thinking of it all the way up from Philadelphia."

"Now you can do something about it." Kyle stood up, took a thick manila folder off the top of the debris, and handed it over. "That's a copy of the complete file on the death of Michael Robert Houseman. You can look through the originals in the office if you want. Everything is in there, the stuff from the time, but other stuff that's come up over the years. His mother's still in town. She's seventy-two. Not in too bad shape. She wants to talk to you one of these days. Most of the other people involved that night are still here, too, except that a couple of them have died. Some of them may not want to talk to you, and some of them may know they don't have to. He was sort of a friend of mine. I wouldn't mind if you *did* find out who killed him."

"Do you have any idea who might have killed him?"

"Not a clue. The official but unstated premise around here is that he was killed by a tramp or a drifter who was out of the area before anybody started looking for a murderer. But the story is weirder than you know. It's even weirder than the tabloids know. Whoever is giving them their information isn't giving all the information there is to give. You want to go out to the park and look over the area?"

"You mean the area where he was killed?"

"Right," Kyle said. "Also the area where Ms. Toliver got nailed into that outhouse. It's all in the same general place. It's hard to describe unless you see it. Let's drive out there and I'll walk you around."

"All right." Gregor stood up. Kyle Borden's office window faced the parking lot. Gregor could see Luis the robot-driver standing idly by the car he was supposed to drive Gregor in. He wasn't even reading the newspaper. "Maybe I'll just give my driver the morning off," he said as they both headed out the door.

3

When Jimmy Card, and Liz Toliver, and Kyle Borden had said "park," Gregor had imagined something very large and open-ended, like Yellowstone, except not so large as that. It was the outhouses in the woods that had engendered that image. Gregor didn't think he had ever been in a park with outhouses except the one time he *was* in Yellowstone, on kidnapping detail in his early years with the Bureau, and that might have been the only time he'd seen "woods," too. In the one other case he'd consulted on since his retirement that had had a park in it, the park had been like Central Park, large but cultivated, with paved walkways through every part of it. When Kyle Borden pulled into the parking lot at Meldane Park, Gregor was disoriented. The parking lot was minuscule. It wasn't even paved. The one other car pulling into it at the same time contained a young mother and two children with plastic buckets and shovels. Up ahead, there was what looked like an arched entryway to nothing. It had gates that could be shut, but it was not connected to anything on either side. "Meldane Park" was cut into the curve of the arch, all the way through, as if somebody had been trying to make a stencil. At the arch's side was a sign with dates and times on it, announcing when the park was officially open.

"That can't help much," Gregor said as Kyle Borden switched his engine off. "All anybody would have to do was go around to one side of the arch, and they'd be in."

"It's to tell people when the lifeguard will be on duty," Kyle said.

Kyle got out of the car, and Gregor got out after him. The day was getting hot. Kyle headed toward the archway and Gregor followed, looking from one side to the other. He truly hated the country. He would far and away prefer to deal with a serial killer in a gang-infested ghetto than with anything at all that lived in harmony with insects and trees. The ground around the archway was sandy and dry. The plants that grew on it were anemic and scraggly. The trees in the immediate vicinity were pines. Gregor didn't know what kind of pines.

"Michael Houseman," Kyle said as Gregor went on following him. "Michael had just graduated from high school about a month before. We all had. Like most of us, he wasn't doing much of anything. He was going on to college—"

"Where?"

"UP-Johnstown. We send a fair number of kids up there. It's close, and it's relatively cheap if you're a state resident. And if you're one of those people who don't really know what you want to do, and don't really care much about education. If you know what I mean. Betsy wrote this column once I read in the newspaper about education—"

"Liz," Gregor said automatically. "I know. Education as an intrinsic good. In *Paris Review*. When I was trying to find out something about her, a friend of mine showed it to me."

"I didn't read it in a review. I read it in a newspaper. Never mind. Michael was one of those guys. He did okay in school without doing really well. He got, maybe, Bs and Cs. He played a little football without being a star on the team. He played a little baseball in the spring, same deal. He wasn't particularly popular, but he wasn't particularly not. Are you getting the picture?"

"It's like a hole in the atmosphere," Gregor said dryly.

Kyle Borden laughed. They had come to the end of a short path that meandered through the trees. A few feet away, Gregor saw a narrow beach that ended in a smallish lake. There was a tall lifeguard's seat near the edge of the beach. There was a raft out in the middle of the water. The little beach was full of sunbathing mothers on terry-cloth towels and children throwing sand at each other.

"It's like a public swimming pool," Gregor said. "Not what I expected."

"It *is* a public swimming pool," Kyle agreed, "except instead of building a pool we built a lake. This is man-made. The town put it together back in 1964 because the people on the board didn't like the idea of our kids going over to Kennanburg to swim there. There was getting to be an 'element,' if you know what I mean."

"Not exactly."

Kyle's eyes slid sideways, cynical. "An African-American element. Welcome to Hollman in the sixties. Welcome to Hollman now, for that matter. Anyway, that's why we built it. I was thirteen years old when it opened and I remember the first day. Dozens of people showed up, with folding lawn chairs and inflatable water toys. I even remember the first lifeguard. Bobby Resnick. It was the summer before his senior year in high school, and he went on to be the biggest damned deal in the history of Hollman. Captain of the football team. Homecoming King. He's got a garage out on Route 15 these days."

"Does everybody in this place know what everybody else has been doing for the last forty years?"

"Well, hell, Mr. Demarkian. There are some women in this town who could tell you whose great-grandmother slept with which traveling moonshiner in 1892 and how that ended up with three kindergarteners having red-haired eyebrows in 1957."

Actually, Gregor thought, that sounded familiar. It sounded just like the Very Old Ladies on Cavanaugh Street. Kyle had steered them onto a path that skirted the sandy beach and went around in a half circle. "What does this have to do with Michael Houseman?" he asked.

"Well," Kyle said, "that summer, Michael Houseman was the regular lifeguard here. There was a relief lifeguard for weekends, but Michael had the job Bobby Resnick baptized. So, unlike everybody else in this story, when that evening started, he was already here."

"He was working?" Gregor asked.

"No. He had been working. He'd worked all day since ten o'clock. By the time the nonsense started, the park was officially closed. That doesn't mean nobody was here, or that nobody was supposed to be here. All that the park being closed ever means is that there's supposed to be no swimming allowed, and some of the teenagers don't pay attention to that. But it's not like the park was deserted. There are always people here in the early evening in the summer."

"All right," Gregor said. "So, what time are we talking about?"

"Good question. Michael would have gotten off at five. With the rest of them, though, it's hard to tell. I included all the paper on the incident with Betsy Toliver with what I gave you. Liz. It's part of the story of Michael dying, or at least it was for the police at the time. From what I remember, she had been in the park before it closed, too, sitting on the beach or reading a book or something. But she wasn't going to leave just because the park was officially closed."

"How did she get here?"

"I don't know, but I'd suspect she drove. Her father gave her a nice little car for graduation, I forget what kind. Two-door. Like that."

"Do you remember if it was parked in the parking lot? And is that the same parking lot?"

"It's the same parking lot. As to whether Bet—Liz's car was parked there, like I said, I'd have to check. But as long as you're going on about cars, Michael *didn't* have a car parked there. His car was in for repairs. Chris Inglerod had dropped him off in the morning. Chris Inglerod was supposed to pick him up."

"Chris Inglerod." Gregor stopped on the path and took out his notebook. "She's one of these people, isn't she, one of the ones—"

"Who spent most of their childhoods torturing Betsy Toliver? Absolutely. She went up to Penn State and found herself a medical student. Now he practices here in town and Chris has a big house out by the golf course. Good luck getting to talk to her. She'll know she doesn't have to let you in the front door."

"Was she Michael Houseman's girlfriend?"

"No. The girls in that group didn't go out with boys their own age, except for Peggy Smith, and that didn't count, because she'd been after Stu when they were both in diapers. When the rest of them got to senior year, they dated guys at UP-Johnstown. The guys in our class dated the girls in the classes behind us."

"You've said that Michael Houseman wasn't important," Gregor prompted.

"Not very important." They had stopped walking to talk. Kyle started heading up the path to an opening in the pine trees. "He dated a sophomore our senior year. By summer it was over. He and Chris Inglerod had known each other for years. They lived next door to each other in these two little ranch houses that were built side by side in this neighborhood full of old people, so maybe for the first five years or so they had nobody else to talk to. And they were still living in the same places, so Chris took him places when his car messed up. According to her, she got to the park at five-fifteen. She was with Nancy Quayde at Nancy's house and they forgot the time. And when she got here, the other girls were collecting the snakes."

"How do you collect snakes?" Gregor asked. "That's one of the things I haven't been able to figure out about this."

"It's not hard to collect snakes," Kyle said. "Especially not those little black snakes the girls had that evening. I think a couple of them—Belinda and Emma, maybe Maris—had been at it most of the day. They had a lot of snakes. Belinda said later that it was twenty-two. I figure she should know."

"This took all day?"

"A good part of it."

"And then what?"

"Well," Kyle said. "That's a good question. Because you're now talking about maybe five-thirty, right?" He stopped walking and looked around. Gregor looked around with him. They were in the middle of a very small clearing, to one side of which was a low wooden shed with two outhouse stalls in it.

"These are the famous outhouses?" Gregor said.

"That's right. Betsy was on the beach. The girls—Belinda, Emma, Maris, Chris, Nancy Quayde, Peggy Smith—had the snakes, and Maris went down to the clearing to call Betsy up from the beach. Betsy came up from the beach, and Maris started having this panic about how Emma was sick to her stomach in the latrine and Maris was on her own and couldn't help Emma by herself, so would Betsy come, and as soon as they got near the outhouses a bunch of the girls jumped out of the trees, rushed Betsy into the one on the right, dumped the snakes right on her legs, and slammed the door shut. Then they *nailed* it shut. So how long do you figure that took?"

"I don't know," Gregor said. "Maybe another half hour?"

"Fine. Now we're up to six. Where do you think Michael Houseman was?"

"I don't know," Gregor said.

"Good." Kyle nodded. "Nobody else does, either. Chris said at the time that when she got to the beach, he was nowhere in sight. She thought he'd gone to the latrine—there are other latrines, for men, up that way a little—but then she met the girls and forgot about him temporarily. According to the rest of the girls, all they did after they nailed Betsy in was to go back into those trees"—Kyle gestured behind them—"and sit still and listen. Then it started to rain, thunder, lightning, and they thought they'd better get out of there and go home. So they got up and got moving, and a few of them went this way. Come with me."

Gregor came. Kyle made his way up the hill next to the outhouses, through the pines and across a thick carpet of needles. They came out on another small clearing, this one next to a small river. Gregor didn't know if "river" was the right word. It didn't have much water in it.

"Here," Kyle said. "Right here. Maybe another ten or fifteen feet up that way. What Belinda said was that when they found Michael Houseman's body, they just stood around it for a while, and they were all covered with blood."

"What?"

"Covered with blood," Kyle said. "And then it started to get crazy, because people were screaming, Betsy was screaming, there was thunder. Maris said in her interview at the time that if it hadn't been raining so hard they would still have it all over them, over their arms, over their legs. The rain washed it off. And Belinda was there, on her knees, laughing her head off and screaming, and Peggy Smith was screaming, too, and they were all screaming, 'slit his throat, slit his throat.' "

"Jesus," Gregor said.

"I told you it was weird," Kyle said.

Gregor walked up and down by the side of the river. They were not very far from the little beach. Gregor guessed they weren't even a full tenth of a mile. The trees around him were tall and straight, so tall they blocked off some of the light from the sun. It was a dark and quiet place.

"And that was it?" he said finally. "Nobody was ever charged with this crime? Even though a whole group of girls was found with the body and they were covered with blood, literally or metaphorically, nobody was ever charged with this crime?"

"There was nobody to charge," Kyle said. "They were all together most of the time. When would any of them have had the time to do it? And there was no murder weapon. The police searched the park. They brought in state police. They tore this place up. There was no sign of it. And it wasn't on the girls, trust me. They kept the girls in the town jail overnight until they could get a matron in to search them. This town went crazy over the next couple of weeks, but nobody ever figured out what happened, and nobody ever got arrested for killing Michael Houseman."

"Crap," Gregor said.

He walked back and forth along the river, counting steps, thinking hard. It wasn't the alibis that were the problem. With people wandering around in the dark like that, it was foolish to believe they all had their eyes on each other all the time.

The problem was going to be the weapon.

SIX

1

For Liz Toliver, the oddest thing about being back in Hollman wasn't being back in Hollman, or even that damned dog—although she had dreamed about the dog, as well as the snakes, and had ended up taking a call from Jimmy at three o'clock in the morning—but the fact that she was completely without a schedule. All that morning during breakfast, she'd kept looking up, expecting Debra to call to tell her what was on her book for the day. Then she'd had to walk around the kitchen a few times, feeling dizzy, because there was nothing at all on her book for the day, or for the day after, or for the day after that. On Friday, she had a phone interview with a woman writing an article for the *Vassar Quarterly*, and strewn in and out of the next two weeks she had appointments with her mother's lawyers and doctors and acupuncturist. The appointments were all fluid. She could cancel any of them she wanted to cancel, at will. She could write or not write. She had cleared her deadline schedule to keep the month free. Even the one idea she'd been able to come up with—somebody ought to do a skeptical update on New Age medicine—fell flat. She didn't much approve of New Age medicine, and she certainly didn't believe it worked, but lots of people took comfort in it, and there didn't seem to be much harm as long as they didn't ditch their insulin and chemotherapy.

"I think I'm going to go insane," she had told Debra, right after breakfast, when she'd checked in to the office. "I know I don't need to call you, but I had to hear a businesslike voice."

"Thanks a lot."

"You know what I mean. I'm dropping my mother and her nurse off at the physical therapist's. Then I'm meeting Maris for lunch. Then I'm picking my mother up and taking her to her gynecologist's. Anyway, that's my day. How do people retire?"

"Have you told Maris yet that we're firing her?"

"I haven't even seen her."

"You're seeing her at lunch. Tell her. I'm serious, Liz. If you don't tell her, I will, and you don't want the news coming from me."

"I know. I know. It's okay. It's just—well, never mind. I'm not in a very good mood this morning. You're sure there aren't any urgent telephone calls?"

"Nothing I can't handle."

"Right."

Now, pulling into the parking lot at the Sycamore, it hit her: she hadn't told Debra about the dog, and Debra hadn't asked, which meant Debra didn't know. She shut down the engine and looked at Geoff through the rearview mirror, safely strapped into a backseat.

"You ready?"

"I want to go to McDonald's."

"There isn't a McDonald's in Hollman, as far as I know. This is where we used to go out for hamburgers when I was a kid. I'll buy you an ice cream soda."

"Can we sit at a different table from Maris?"

Liz made a face at herself in the mirror and got out to get Geoff out. The Sycamore looked the way it had always looked: a low, white building surrounded by trees, with a wide window on one side that had been built for the days when there had been "car service." She couldn't imagine that whoever owned the Sycamore now still sent girls racing out to cars with trays of food that could be hooked to a rolled-down window. The street—still Grandview Avenue—curved around the edge of the Sycamore's lot. Across the curve to the front was a small grocery store. Across the curve to the side was something that called itself the Hollman Adult Theater. Liz blinked.

"What's the matter?" Geoff said.

"Oh, nothing. I was just surprised at how some things have changed since the last time I was here."

She locked up. Then she took Geoff by the hand and took him in through the Sycamore's front door. It was more like a house than a restaurant.

Inside, in the dim cool put together from shaded windows and ceiling fans, Liz looked up and down among the tables and the booths, fully expecting to find no sign of Maris. Maris was always late. Maris turned out to be taking up the big booth in the back corner, and for just a second, looking at her, Liz went cold. She remembered all about that corner booth. By the time they'd all been seniors, it had been an unspoken but vigorously enforced social law: *nobody* sat in that corner booth but Maris and Emma and the girls they were friends with. Students who came in to the Sycamore when it was packed to the gills refused to sit in that booth if it was empty. Students who broke the law found their lives uncomfortable for weeks to come, especially if they were girls. Even the greaser boys didn't take that booth, and they did everything they were supposed not to do.

"Crap," Liz said, under her breath.

"You should say 'carp,' " Geoff said automatically.

Liz tugged him along to the back. The Sycamore was probably the one thing almost everybody who had gone to Hollman High School since 1950 had a memory of, but Liz's memory of it was faint. She'd only been in it half a dozen times. When she was in high school, coming here had been like volunteering for abuse. No matter what Jimmy thought, she didn't volunteer for abuse.

"Don't you think this booth is a little big for the three of us?" she asked Maris as she slid Geoff in between them. "Or are you ambushing me with a bunch of people I have no intention of talking to?"

"It was just force of habit," Maris said. She looked around the big room, at the empty tables and booths, at the empty stools at the fountain counter. "Nobody is in here anyway. It won't matter. This place doesn't start to get crowded until after school."

"Is school still in session?"

"Until June fifteenth."

"God, I don't remember going that late. Did we? Sometimes it seems like the whole school year changed sometime while I was in graduate school. Do they start in August here, now? I think I would have killed somebody if I'd had to go back to school before Labor Day."

The waitress came up, with her pad and a Bic pen, a tired-looking fortyish woman with deep lines on either side of her mouth and streaks of gray in her hair. Liz ordered Geoff a vanilla ice cream soda and a plate of french fries. She ordered herself a salad and a Diet Coke. Around the corner on the other side of the booth, Maris ordered a club sandwich and a regular Coke. She only ordered regular Coke when she was spiking her drinks. Diet Coke tasted awful when you combined it with gin.

"Well," Liz said. "Here we are. I don't know why, but here we are."

"It seemed like a place to go. And it's quiet this time of day. I don't understand what you're all worked up about, Betsy. Nobody is locking you in the utility closet these days."

"I'm not worked up. I'm just—I don't know. Maybe Jimmy was right. Maybe I should have sent the lawyers. And there was the dog."

"Just kids thinking they're cute," Maris said. She had that deep, contemplative look in her eyes that said she'd been drinking, seriously, for hours. When Maris got drunk, she did not get sloppy, or slurred, or uncoordinated. She got serious, so serious she seemed to be looking into a crystal ball where she could see all the secrets of time—until it got to be too much, and she threw up. She shifted on the booth's seat. "Chris is putting together a cocktail party for you, out by the golf course. Or maybe it's a lunch. I don't remember. She's going to call you this afternoon."

"I won't be home this afternoon."

"Be reasonable," Maris said. "You know, you just might be wrong. People are impressed with what you've done with your life. They really are. They just want to get a chance to catch up with you again—"

"About what? Maris, for God's sake, what's the point? It would be one thing if we'd all been friends, but the last real memory I have of Belinda Hart is from when she backed me up against the sinks in the west wing girls' room and told me that I was nothing but a worm who made everybody I talked to sick. Why don't we all just let it be? They do what they do. I take care of my mother. You have a vacation and come in here to eat twice a day. Then you and I go back to New York and back to work and—"

"You can't let Debra fire me," Maris said.

"What?"

The waitress was back, with the food. Liz looked up as she put down the plates one by one, her face impassive and marred, her body stiff. Geoff looked impressed with the ice cream soda, which came in one of those tall old-fashioned glasses that looked like a champagne flute on steroids.

"Cool," Geoff said.

The waitress disappeared. Maris put her purse on the table, opened it up, and took out a Chanel Number 5 bottle, a big one, the kind that people gave their mothers for Christmas presents. She took a long suck on the straw that was stuck into her Coke. Then she uncorked the Chanel bottle and dumped about a quarter of the liquid in it into her glass.

"I can't believe you just did that," Liz said.

"Don't worry," Maris said. "I'm not drinking perfume. I cleaned the bottle very thoroughly ages ago."

"I know what's in the bottle. I can't believe you did that. What are you trying to do to yourself?"

Maris put the Chanel bottle back in her purse. "You can't let Debra fire me," she said again. She was very calm. Liz thought she might even be depressed—except that with Maris, it was hard to tell. "If Debra fires me, I'll have absolutely no place to go, and you know it. I was fired from my last three jobs before this one. It's like a curse. Image is everything."

"Image?"

"After a while, you start getting fired for things nobody else would ever get fired for. It's like getting a reputation when you're in high school. It doesn't matter if you're a lily-white virgin. Once you've got the reputation, you'll get blamed for everything. If you let Debra fire me, I'll kill myself. I'm not bluffing. I've got two months of prescription tranquilizers saved and I always carry them with me. I'll down them all with straight gin and do it right in your own living room, here or in Connecticut, or I'll do it in the office in New York."

Liz looked swiftly at Geoff, who did not seem to be paying attention. "Maris, for Christ's sake," she said.

"I'll do it where the papers will be sure to connect it to you. I'll send my suicide note to Matt Drudge. I'll go out with a bang. Just watch me."

"Maris," Liz said again. "What do you think you're doing?"

What Maris was doing was almost finishing her Coke, and getting the Chanel bottle out, and spiking it some more. By now, Liz thought, it had to be not much more than caramel-colored gin. She had never seen Maris drink with this much determination, or subterfuge. It was always at parties, or in real restaurants with wine lists, so that—until just this second—it had seemed to Liz that the stories of Maris's drinking were mostly exaggerated. She drank at home. She drank when she went out to eat. People did that. It was only the getting sick that was really a problem.

Maris sucked up gin and Coke through her straw. She had begun to sweat. A thin line of beaded wet snaked across her forehead just above her eyebrows. Her fair hair glinted and darkened in the uncertain light coming through the window above the booth. The polish on her nails was much too red. For just a single, surreal moment, Liz didn't recognize her. She was not the girl Liz had seen for the first time in kindergarten and watched, with envy and frustration, for sixteen years afterward. She was not the girl who had always been everything Liz had ever wanted to be, the girl who had achieved what Liz only fell short of, the girl who really was what Liz only fooled people into thinking she was. She was just a middle-aged woman with a drinking problem and a chip on her shoulder, too expensively dressed, too out of shape, and too drunk—at noon—to think straight about what she was doing.

The air around them seemed to warp and snap. The fans whirred above their heads. Maris put her mouth around the straw and sucked down everything in her glass except the ice.

"You can't let Debra fire me," she said for the third time. "It would put an end to me. It would be everywhere. In all the papers. I wouldn't even be able to come back to Hollman. Do you think it's easy, even the way it is, coming back here when you're Queen of the goddamned May and I'm, what, your secretary?"

Geoff was paying attention now. He'd gone absolutely still, the way children did when they wanted to listen to the conversations of adults and not be noticed doing it. The surreal moment was over. Maris looked like—Maris. "I don't know what you want me to do," Liz said. "I don't know what I'm supposed to say to all this."

"Say you won't let Debra fire me."

"I would never let Debra fire you," Liz said carefully.

Maris shot her a quick, calculating, amused look. "My, my. Aren't we being Jesuitical this afternoon." She zipped her bag shut and slid out of the booth, into the narrow aisle between it and the first row of freestanding tables. "I'm going to go. I had to walk down here from Belinda's place. You know as well as I do that I don't drive if I don't have to. I've got a long walk back up the hill."

"I'll drop you off," Liz said.

"Don't bother. Pay for lunch. You've got the money. And cheer up. Today, you achieved a lifelong ambition. You got to sit in the corner booth."

Maris turned her back to them and walked off. She was not weaving. Liz watched her go all the way to the door and out of it. Less than a minute later, she came into view through the window, crossing the parking lot toward the sidewalk that edged Grandview Avenue. It was a long walk to Belinda's, at least half a mile, but maybe that would help.

"Mom?" Geoff said.

"What?" Liz wasn't really listening. She hadn't eaten any of her salad. She didn't want to. She was feeling a little sick to her stomach herself. It hit her, suddenly, that she truly hated this place: the Sycamore, the corner booth, the tables where little knots of girls had sat in triumphant exclusivity from which she had once been systematically and brutally shut out. Geoff was right. They should have gone to McDonald's, even if it meant getting into the car and driving back out to the Interstate to do it. If there was one thing she had earned, in thirty years of a very eventful life, it was the right not to be here, now, or ever to be here again. The waitress had left the check on the table. Liz picked it up.

"Tell you what," she said. "You haven't eaten a single french fry. Why don't we get out of here and drive out to McDonald's and get you a Happy Meal? We could pick Mark up that chicken sandwich thing he likes and bring it back."

"I only drank half my ice cream soda," Geoff said solemnly. "Are you going to let me ask you something?"

"Ask away." Liz got out her wallet.

"If Debra fires Maris, does that mean we don't have to see Maris anymore?"

Liz took out two ten-dollar bills. Lunch came to only $13.95. She put the bills down on the table and put the check upside down on top of them.

"Debra can't fire Maris," she said slowly. "Only I can fire Maris. And I wouldn't fire Maris. She's not as lucky as we are. She needs a job just to have food to eat and a place to live."

"She could get a job with somebody else."

"What may happen is that Maris may stop working in the office with Debra and start doing some things just for me. She'd come out to Connecticut when she needed to or I'd meet her at her apartment."

"She shouldn't come out to Connecticut," Geoff said quickly. "I hate it when she comes out to Connecticut. She makes up new rules for everybody and she's always mad at us."

"Well," Liz said lamely, "she's not used to children. She doesn't realize they make a lot of noise."

She ushered Geoff down the long aisle and out the door they'd come in through. In the parking lot, the sun was brighter and the leaves on the trees were heavier than she remembered them having been when they'd arrived. She unlocked the doors to the Mercedes and got Geoff belted in the backseat. She stepped back and looked around her. If you went around the curve and to the left, instead of going back up Grandview Avenue, there was a school called Grassy Plains, a red brick one, just the same as the one called Center School where she had gone to kindergarten, first, and second grades. It was surely closed now, just like Center, since all those grades had been moved to the new complex out at Plumtrees. If you stayed on the curve and veered to the right, there was the house where a girl named Debbie had lived with her mother. She was the only single child Liz had known in those years, and the only one with a single mother, but not the only one who lived in an apartment instead of having a whole house.

Liz slid in behind the wheel. She wanted to cry, but that was not news. She had wanted to cry ever since she first pulled into this parking lot. She couldn't cry in front of Geoff. He associated her crying with his father dying. Still, she thought. It was all wrong. Everything was. She was all hollowed out inside, as if all that was left of her was a great draining pulse of pain and guilt, and she couldn't figure out which one was true. It was the guilt that held her attention. She felt guilty every day, as if she'd stolen her own life and owed it back to somebody. It seemed to her that she was somehow to blame for what had happened to Maris, or had not happened to her. It didn't make any sense, but it wouldn't go away, and as long as it was right here in the front of her mind, she didn't know if she would be able to move. She tried fixing her hair in the rearview mirror. She got Geoff, staring at her, instead.

"Well," she said.

"We should start the car," Geoff said.

"You're right," she agreed. "We should start the car."

She started it, and backed out of her parking space, and headed for Grandview Avenue, but she couldn't help looking back at the Sycamore. Then she was winding up the hill on Grandview, headed for the center of town, and for a moment it seemed as if Maris was headed right back at her, driving that bright yellow Volkswagen she had said she'd rented, but that she wouldn't drive. Then the car passed and Liz realized that she recognized the woman driving it, but that that woman was not Maris.

She was halfway out to the Interstate when she pegged the face as Peggy Smith's.

2

Emma Kenyon Bligh had been restless all day. In fact, she'd been restless since some time the night before, when she'd sat in Chris Inglerod Barr's living room and listened to Chris and Nancy go on at length about image laundering and strategic campaigns. *Image laundering.* That was the first time she had ever heard that one, and she had been almost as annoyed with it as she had been with Chris's tray of perfectly matched china and monogrammed silverware. *Real* silverware, of course. Chris's whole life seemed to come out of an issue of *Better Homes and Gardens*. Years ago, she'd even badgered her mother into getting her *real* engraved wedding invitations—not just thermoplated ones—from Tiffany's in New York, and Emma knew for a fact that the Inglerods couldn't afford it. They'd probably had to put the expense on a credit card and borrow the rest of the money for the wedding, too. Emma had had her own wedding at St. Mary's Roman Catholic Church right here in town, with a reception at the Holiday Inn out on the Interstate.

This morning, her restlessness had had some use. The store needed a good cleaning. She cleaned it. She took all the objects off each of the shelves, one by one, and dusted them, with a damp cloth if appropriate. Then she dusted and polished the shelf itself. Then she put the objects back. It had taken her two hours to get it all done, and when she was finished she had started in on the rest of the woodwork, the counter, even the windowsills. When *that* was done, she'd had a customer, and for half an hour she had been able to lose herself in an elaborate discussion of the differences between crocheting and knitting and the relative merits of needlework and brocade. It was only after that that she felt herself begin to fall apart. She didn't keep a television in the shop, because she thought it looked tacky. She had the radio on to the easy listening station out of Johnstown, but that wasn't enough to keep the brain of a fruit fly occupied. She had one of Betsy's books that she'd taken out of the library—*Making It Out: A Look Into the Real American Dream*—but she'd already tried three times to read it and never managed to make it through more than a page and a half. Betsy still used words so big no normal person could possibly know what they meant. Sometimes, when Emma felt like this, she went through the scrapbooks and picture albums she brought with her every day when she came in to work—pictures of herself as a cheerleader and in Tri-Y; pictures of herself in her formal dresses from every junior and senior prom and junior-senior semiformal from the day she started high school (it paid to go out with older boys); dance bids; prom cards; the certificates she'd received for being voted Cutest Girl and Best Dressed four solid years in a row—but since she'd first heard that Betsy was coming home, she hadn't been able to get into the spirit of them. Even eating didn't help. She sat still next to the cash register in the empty store and felt weighed down and bloated, as if she'd eaten lead.

It was almost one o'clock when Emma went out to the porch to get some air. She looked up one end of Grandview Avenue and down the other. She saw Maris Coleman walking slowly across the railroad tracks near Mullaney's. Maris trudged up past the Opera House. At English Drugs, she stopped, looked at the newspapers in the rack outside, picked one up, and went into the store. She came out barely two minutes later, carrying the newspaper under her arm.

Under most circumstances, Emma would not have volunteered to spend time one on one with Maris Coleman. Maris Coleman *had* changed, at Vassar and in New York, and these days she didn't do much for Emma but make her uncomfortable. This afternoon, though, Emma thought she was going to go crazy, and so she raised her arm and tried to signal at Maris coming up the street.

Maris didn't see her. Emma watched her turn off the sidewalk into the small door that led to the little clutch of apartments where Belinda lived.

There wasn't a single customer in the store. There had only been a single customer since she'd opened up this morning. Emma turned back and went inside again. She switched the OPEN sign to CLOSED and stepped back onto the porch. She locked the front door of the shop and then tried the knob to make sure she hadn't made a mistake. She was sweating. She sweat when she did any sustained movement. Once, worried about her weight, she'd tried a Richard Simmons program, but she'd stopped after only three sessions with the workout tape. Each time, she'd sweat so much there had been big circles of black dampness in the armpits of her T-shirt, and more sweat down its back and on the inside of the thighs of her workout pants. She had been ashamed to look at her clothes in the mirror when she went into the bathroom to take them off. Anything at all, even weighing five hundred pounds, would be better than seeing her clothes all wet like that.

She went down her front porch steps and onto the sidewalk. She went up the sidewalk past the half-dozen little stores. She stopped just past Elsa-Edna's, without bothering to look at the clothes in the display window. It had been a long time since she'd been able to fit into them, and when she had been able to fit into them she hadn't been able to afford them. She suspected that she wouldn't be able to afford them now. She went up the steep flight of steps at the side of the building, moving carefully, stopping every once in a while to take a breath. She didn't want to give herself a heart attack just because she'd run over to Belinda's on a whim.

When she got to the landing, the first thing she noticed was that Belinda's apartment door was standing slightly opened. The next thing she noticed was that Maris was talking, not only out loud, but loudly. Someone thinner than Emma, who had not had to concentrate so hard on getting up the stairs, would have heard Maris from the first-floor entry.

Emma pushed inside and closed the door behind her. Maris was in the living room, her back to the kitchen and the apartment's front door, holding the phone to her ear. It was Belinda's phone, not a cell phone.

". . . that's what I said," Maris was saying. "Her mother's dog. Right. In the garage. Eviscerated. Jimmy's coming down this evening to make sure she's all right. I don't know what to make of it. I just tell you what's going on. She's going to be here until the end of June, unless this drives her out. I expect the usual, of course. If this gets any better, I may need a little more. Yes. Well. Yes. I'll talk to you when I have something."

Maris put down the phone. Emma knocked on one of the kitchen counters. Maris turned around.

"How did you get in here? I thought that door was on automatic lock."

"You left it open," Emma said. "What were you doing?"

Maris cocked her head and smiled. "I was talking," she said, "to a friend of mine at the *National Enquirer*. We have a little arrangement."

"You tell the *National Enquirer* about stuff that happens to Betsy."

"Where do you think they get it?"

"I don't know," Emma said. "I thought they had, you know, reporters. That went and reported things. Dug things up."

"It's much easier to dig things up if you know where to look," Maris said. "Don't worry about it. It's not a secret. Everybody on earth knows all about it."

"Betsy knows all about it?" Emma shook her head. "I don't believe that. I don't think she'd go on giving you a job if she knew you were calling up the *National Enquirer* and saying she murdered Michael Houseman."

"Well, let's just say everybody knows, but nobody can prove it." Maris brushed by Emma and went to the cabinet where the tumblers were kept. She got one down and opened the refrigerator. She got out a big carton of orange juice and poured the tumbler half full. "I think the deal is that Betsy Wetsy's been told, but she just refuses to believe it. In New York I make the calls from pay phones, never anything too close to my apartment or too close to her offices. Do you know she owns a town house on the Upper East Side? She's got an apartment on the top floor of it, but she never uses it anymore. Jimmy's got an apartment of his own and they go there. In the afternoons. To screw."

"What does that have to do with you telling things to the *National Enquirer?*"

"Nothing." Maris went back to the living room and sat down on the sofa. "I tell things to the *National Enquirer* because they pay me for them. And because it gives me a certain amount of satisfaction. She gets *very* upset at those stories. You have no idea. Don't you just love it when you see things like that at the supermarket?"

"Not really." Emma watched as Maris got a huge Chanel No. 5 bottle out of her pocketbook and emptied half its contents into the tumbler. "You're drinking perfume?"

"It's gin," Maris said. "I've got a couple of real bottles around here somewhere, but it's inconvenient to take them out for the afternoon. Places without a liquor license protest when they know you're trying to fortify their soft drinks. I just love it when I see things like that in the supermarkets. And on the newsstands. In New York, we've got these newsstands, these kiosk things, and they hang magazines and papers and things from a clothesline sort of arrangement over their open windows. You can see the headlines for miles."

"Why didn't you use a pay phone here?"

"The only one I know of is in English Drugs. It's the first place Jimmy would check."

"Why wouldn't he check here?"

"How would he ever get Belinda's phone records?" Maris had already finished a third of her tumbler of "fortified" orange juice. She looked much more sober than she had before. "It's not so easy to get hold of private information. The government can get it, but the rest of us have a very hard time, and if Jimmy did manage it Belinda could probably sue him. Not that she'd think of it. Christ. Was Belinda this stupid when we were all in school?"

"You were her best friend. You should know."

"She was this stupid," Maris said. "Never mind. Just don't bother to look shocked, will you? It's depressingly hick of you. I come back here and I just can't believe how god-awful provincial this place really is."

Emma looked away. This apartment was so tiny it would have made her breathless even if she hadn't climbed a steep flight of stairs to get to it, or been so shocked that she could barely defrost her mind enough to think of what she had to do next. Good people, decent people, did not do things like this. If there was one thing she had never questioned, it was that she and all her friends were good and decent people. Of course, there was all that other stuff, about Betsy, not only the outhouse but stuff that had come before, but that was different, somehow. That hadn't been real cruelty, but only kids and the way kids behaved. This was—

Maris had her legs stretched out on top of the coffee table now.

"You *are* going to get all provincial on me," she said. "What the hell. I'm not sorry I did it. I'm really not."

"I've got to get back to the store," Emma said. "We're supposed to be open straight through the day. I've probably missed half a dozen customers."

"Why did you come? Were you looking for Belinda? Belinda works today. Were you looking for me? How did you know I'd be home?"

"I just thought I'd drop by and see how things were going," Emma said. She looked around her, helpless. "I'd better get going," she said. "I really shouldn't be away for long. George has a fit if he finds out."

"Make sure you lock the door when you leave," Maris said.

Emma turned around and shuffled out, past the little dining table, through the kitchen, into the hall. The stairwell was dark. Emma went down half the stairs and then stopped, breathless again.

What struck her, suddenly, was that she did know a way for that dog to have ended up in Betsy Toliver's garage—but that was because she knew the way Michael Houseman had ended up dead.

3

At first, Nancy Quayde thought she would take it easy. It was a nothing much of a day. There wasn't a school board meeting for at least a couple of weeks, and that one would be the end-of-year report, where she spent most of her time listing all the supplies they'd used over the last ten months.

Then she would spend even longer explaining, or *trying* to explain, why they needed at least that much or more for next year: so many cartons of chalk; so many sophomore biology textbooks. Some of the school board members resented the idea that there was any school going on in school at all. Their philosophy of education amounted to the belief, fervently held, that schools should be places where "kids were allowed to be kids." Anything that got in the way of that—say, for instance, the new mandatory state mastery examinations that would retain any student at grade level if she didn't pass—was an obvious evil. Anything that helped that along—like proms, and football games, and the annual class vote for who would be named Most Popular and Cutest Couple for the yearbook—was just as obviously good. Nancy had a fight every year with the mothers who wanted to double the semiformal dance schedule. Aside from the junior and senior proms, they already had a junior-senior semiformal and a Valentine's Day formal and a harvest dance at homecoming in the fall. It wasn't enough for people like Emma, who didn't remember much of anything about high school except the dances, and maybe some of the football games, assuming she ever watched any of the ones she cheered at. Nancy thought it was doubtful. She hated parents, if she were honest about it. They existed only to make her life difficult, and the more involved they got in the school, the worse they were. The rich parents were the worst of all, because it wasn't enough for them if their child was popular. He had to have good grades, too, to make sure he could get into some college whose name their friends would recognize. It was impossible to enforce an honor code. If a student was caught cheating, she couldn't expel him, because if she tried the parents would sue. It was impossible to discipline anybody for anything, except maybe bringing a weapon to school. There had been enough violence that the parents couldn't get away with suing for that. There were days when Nancy Quayde knew exactly why some people got hold of shotguns and strafed their workplaces from one end to the other. There were days when she wanted to do it herself.

Today, it had started out to be all right, except that she was jumpy about the meeting they'd had the night before at Chris's, and still angry with Peggy Smith. She had spent the morning in her office doing the kind of paperwork that she could not avoid, but that required no mental effort whatsoever. A badly made android could have done just as well. Once or twice, she'd tried to call Chris at home, without luck. Chris was probably on the golf course, taking her aggressions out on little white balls. Once, she'd walked down to Peggy Smith's classroom and looked through the big window at the top of the door. Every once in a while, she hatched plans to get Peggy off the faculty, permanently, but they always ran aground on the fact that Peggy ran an excellent classroom. Nancy went back to her office and got her lunch out of the little refrigerator she had had installed her first week as principal. She was working herself into a positively bad mood, complete with tantrum. By the time Lisa buzzed her to tell her the assistant principal wanted to have a word, Nancy nearly had smoke coming out of her ears, and she had begun to tear paper into confetti.

The vice principal was a man named Harvey Grey, who hated her. It was Harvey's opinion that he was the one who should have been made principal of Hollman High the last two times the job had become open, and it was further his opinion that the only reason he hadn't been was that the board had decided they had to give the job to a woman. That he had a master's degree instead of a doctorate in education, and that he'd gotten it at UP-Johnstown instead of Penn State, did not seem relevant to him, any more than it seemed relevant to him that he was a little worm of a man with a high-pitched squeal instead of a voice and the personality of a sex-obsessed, hypochondriacal old maid. He collected resentments the way other people collected stamps.

He came into the office and sat down in the chair in front of her desk, without being asked. Harvey never asked. "It's Diane Asch again," he said. "There was an incident at lunch."

"An incident?"

Harvey looked at the floor, and the ceiling, and his hands. "She's having hysterics in the east wing second-floor girls' room. I'm not sure what started it."

"Has anybody tried to talk to her?"

"Peggy went in and tried for a while. Peggy was lunch monitor today."

"So?"

"Whatever it was started at lunch. She's saying she'll never go back to the cafeteria as long as she lives. Diane Asch is saying it."

"Why?"

"She says they said something to her," Harvey said. "You know. DeeDee Craft and Lynn Mackay and Sharon Peterson. They said something to her."

"What?"

"How am I supposed to know? I couldn't go into the girls' bathroom. Not in this day and age. I'd get arrested. If you ask me, you don't take this situation seriously. Think of Columbine. Think of that place in Kentucky. This is how school shootings get started."

"You think Diane Asch is going to commit a school shooting?"

"Think of *Carrie*," Harvey said darkly.

Nancy stood up. Something at the back of her mind told her that she should not do this. At the very least, she ought to talk herself down from her anger enough so that all her muscles weren't jumping. She ran her right hand through her hair. Her nails were long and sharp enough to serve as a crude kind of comb.

"Did you say the east wing second-floor girls' room?"

"We had a very interesting presentation about situations like this at the last in-service," Harvey said. "It's regrettable you were too busy to attend. There was an educational psychologist down from the University of Pennsylvania—"

Nancy was past him, out her office door, into the anteroom. "Take messages," she told Lisa as she passed. "I'll only be a minute."

She went out into the foyer and down the hall. She got to the stairwell and almost ran up the stairs. Sometimes physical exercise calmed her down. This was not one of those times.

When she reached the east wing second-floor girls' room, there were students in the hall. She pushed past them and went inside.

"Everybody *out*," Peggy's voice nearly screamed at her.

The only other sound in the room was of wracking, shuddering breathing.

"It's me," Nancy told Peggy.

Peggy was leaning against a locked lavatory stall. Nancy pushed her away.

"Diane?" Nancy said.

The breathing stopped, momentarily. Diane did not reply.

"Diane," Nancy said, "listen to me. Come out of there now. Now. If you don't come out of there now, I'll break that door down and drag you out."

"No," Peggy said. "Nancy, what are you doing? You can't—"

"Come out, or I'll break the door down."

There was no sound from inside the stall. Whatever Diane was doing, she was not unbolting the lavatory door. Nancy pushed Peggy away, stood back a little, and raised her foot. She was wearing high heels, but she knew it wouldn't matter.

"One more chance," Nancy said.

"You're crazy," Peggy said, but it was a whisper.

There was still no sound from the other side of the door. Nancy raised her foot even higher and shot it forward, as quickly and with as much force as she could. The tinny bolt that held the lavatory stall door shricked. Nancy lifted her foot again and shot it forward again. This time the door gaped for a moment before it fell back into place. The third hit was all Nancy needed. The door strained against what was left of the bolt fastening. Then it popped open with a bang and shot forward, right into the side of Diane Asch's face. Diane burst into tears.

Nancy reached into the stall, grabbed Diane by the arm, and yanked. Diane stumbled forward. Nancy yanked again and then began to push her toward the sinks.

"What's the matter with you?" she demanded. "What do you think you're doing?"

"They said," Diane started. Then she shook her head. "They said—"

"Sticks and stones can break my bones but names can never hurt me."

"They can if you hear them every *day*," Diane said. "They can if you hear them every hour. I'm not eating lunch in the cafeteria anymore. Not ever. You can't make me. You can't."

"Nancy listen," Peggy said. "Calm down. You're—"

Nancy ran her hand through her hair again. If felt as if she had been doing it without a break since she left her office. Her scalp felt raw. Diane

Asch slid to the floor next to the sink and started to cry. They were not attractive tears.

"God," Nancy said. "Look at yourself. Get up and look in the mirror and really see yourself for once in your life."

"They called me a fat ugly pig," Diane said hysterically. "They said it over and over again. They all did—"

"They chanted it," Peggy said. "That's what I was trying to tell Harvey, but he wouldn't listen. DeeDee and Sharon started it, but then everybody in the cafeteria took it up. Or nearly everybody—"

"It was everybody," Diane said.

"So Diane here bolted," Peggy said. "Nancy, for God's sake."

"For God's sake *what?*" Nancy said. "Look at her. What do you think, it's an accident? She is a fat ugly pig and she won't do anything for herself. You can't blame the rest of them for not liking it. How many people around here have tried to help her get herself fixed up, to wear a little makeup, to stop whining all the time—"

"I don't want to wear makeup," Diane screamed. "Why do I have to wear makeup? I didn't do anything. I'm not the one who calls people names."

"Nobody would call you names if you'd straighten yourself out," Nancy said. "You like to be called names. If you didn't, you'd have done something about yourself years ago. Get your face washed and get back to class. You're holding everybody up."

"Fuck you," Diane said.

"That'll get you a week in detention," Nancy said.

"I won't come." Diane Asch turned her back to them and began to run the water in the sink. She was no longer sobbing, not even silently.

"If you don't come," Nancy said pleasantly, "I'll suspend you. And if you try to break the suspension, I'll have you up before the board of education's disciplinary committee. And if you think they're going to take your side over mine, you'd damned well better think again. You're a mess. Get your act together."

Peggy started to say something. Nancy didn't wait to listen to her. She went out the lavatory door and found the hall still full of students, standing just close enough to hear what was going on with Diane. DeeDee and Sharon and Lynn were standing together in a little knot to one side, looking faintly anxious.

"Go," Nancy said.

A few of the girls hesitated—why was it, Nancy wondered, that boys never hung around in situations like this?—but in the end they drifted off, some of them looking guilty. Nancy went back the way she had come. The tension in her body was gone. She had never been this clearheaded in all her life. Maybe what she needed was to tell the truth more often.

When she got to the front foyer, she had a split second of worry. Maybe this would come back to haunt her when the hearings for the superintendent's job came up. The worry didn't last long. Most of the members of the school board were as exasperated with Diane as she was, and Diane's own mother could barely stand the sight of her. Nobody was going to make an issue of the fact that somebody had finally told Diane what the score was, not even if that somebody was Nancy Quayde.

Nancy passed through the outer office. Lisa called out, "Harvey went back to his office. He had an appointment."

Nancy went into the inner office and shut the door behind her. Her sandwich was on the desk. Her little bottle of Perrier water was still unopened. She pushed them aside and pulled the phone close to her.

After all these years, she still knew the number at Betsy Toliver's house.

SEVEN

1

The last time Gregor Demarkian was in a small town, it was nearly winter, and in New England, so that both the weather and the landscape fit the occasion. Discussions of murder should take place on gray days or in the night. In Hollman, in the spring, Gregor felt as though he were playing a movie scene on the wrong set. It was as if John Sayles had decided to make a movie of Shirley Jackson's "The Lottery," in the bright greens and very early sixties *Happy Days* spotlessness of *Matinee*.

"What are you thinking about?" Kyle Borden asked as he pulled the town's one police car into a parking place on Grandview Avenue.

They were parked right in front of a largish store whose purpose he couldn't decipher—hardware, maybe, or home furnishings. Just across from them, there was a side street split around a small triangular island. On the far side of that from where they were, in a place where the sidewalk curved in a great sweep up the hill, was Hollman's Pizza, where they were headed.

"I was thinking about 'The Lottery,' " Gregor said.

"The Pennsylvania lottery?"

"No. There's a short story, by—"

"Shirley Jackson," Kyle finished. "Yeah, I know it. Small town where they draw lots every year to pick somebody to stone to death. I did two years at the junior college. We had to read it in English. You think Hollman reminds you of Shirley Jackson? That's funny, you know, because she used to say that. Betsy. I mean, Liz. When we were all in high school."

"I can imagine," Gregor said. He got out of the car, looking up and down Grandview one more time. There was really nothing remarkable about it. He just hated it. The last place he had ever truly hated like this was Fort Benning, Georgia, and that didn't count, because what he'd really hated about Fort Benning was the fact that they kept making him make forty-mile forced marches with a fifty-pound pack on his back in ninety-degree heat.

Kyle's idea of crossing the street was to look both ways and run. There was no streetlight on this section of Grandview, and no crosswalk, either. Gregor looked both ways, crossed his fingers, and followed. If Kyle did this all the time, it was a miracle he wasn't dead. Gregor got to the opposite sidewalk just ahead of a green Jeep Cherokee with a very loud horn. Kyle watched the Jeep go up the hill and shrugged.

"This is a famous place," he said, pointing at Hollman's Pizza. "In the story of Betsy Toliver in Hollman, I mean. When we were all freshmen, a bunch of them asked her to have pizza with them one day after school, and then they all snuck out on her one by one and stuck her with the tab. Eight pizzas, they'd ordered. She had to call her mother to pay the bill."

Kyle held open the swinging glass door and ushered Gregor through it, apparently oblivious to the fact that the story he had just told was nasty as hell—that *all* the stories about "Betsy Toliver in Hollman" were nasty as hell, the kind of stories you'd expect to hear about psychopaths. Gregor looked around the small room with its dozen wooden tables and spotted the pay phone on the wall next to the door they'd come in by.

"I want to make a call," he said. "I've got a cell phone with me, but I can't seem to get it to work, and I've been trying to get in touch with someone all day."

"Cell phones don't work up here," Kyle said. "It's the mountains. You go ahead. I'll order us a pizza. Sausage and pepperoni be okay?"

"Fine." Gregor congratulated himself for bringing lots of antacids, and went over to the pay phone to see what he could do. He found his long-distance calling card at the back of his wallet and tried Tibor's first. He got a busy signal. Tibor must be on the Internet. He tried his own number and felt instantly relieved when somebody picked up.

"Hello?" Bennis said in that deep voice of hers that could never quite lose the Main Line debutante, boarding-school accent.

"It's me," Gregor said. "How are you? I miss you."

"I miss you, too. I was just listening to the news. There's a story about a dog found eviscerated in Elizabeth Toliver's garage. Do you know anything about that?"

"Yes, as a matter of fact I do. But don't even begin to think that's the strangest thing about this place. It's insane. It's like living in *Lord of the Flies*."

"Excuse me?"

"Never mind. It's a long story. I wish you were here. I've got no way to judge what people tell me about this place. And they all tell me things. A minute ago it was about a bunch of kids who asked Liz to have pizza with them and then they sneaked out of the restaurant after they'd ordered and stuck her with the bill. Eight pizzas."

"Well, that was sucky of them."

"One story would be sucky. I've heard maybe half a dozen since I got here, and the thing is, when they tell you about them, they act as if it's all perfectly normal. Liz Toliver doesn't, but she was the victim. The rest of them behave as if there's nothing unusual about the stories at all. And what do I know about it? My high school was in an inner city and all I ever did in it was study like a maniac so the University of Pennsylvania would give me a scholarship. If we had a Homecoming Queen, nobody ever told me about it."

"My high school was a rich girls' boarding school where the girls brought their horses and boarded them, too. I'm not really much more of an expert on this sort of thing than you are."

"Maybe," Gregor said, "but I keep feeling that you could tell me what's real and what isn't in this place. You've got to know more about it than I do. Sometimes, I stop in the middle of everything and it all just feels absurd. These are grown people. Most of the ones we're dealing with are fifty or close to it. Can they really still be so—obsessed—with what happened when they were in high school? And I do mean obsessed. It's like they don't have any other frame of reference."

"Well, the murder—"

"Forget the murder. It might as well not have happened. You mention it and people say, 'Oh, I forgot about that.' "

"Well," Bennis said in her "soothing" voice, "they're all stuck out there in the middle of nowhere. Maybe high school was the only interesting thing that ever happened to them."

"I wish you'd come," Gregor told her. "Just get in the car and drive up. If the news about the dog has been on television, it's only a matter of time before we're inundated with reporters. Maybe not the full-court press, but at least a few of them making nuisances of themselves. I could use your point of view, even if you do think I'm crazy."

"I don't think you're crazy. I think you're having a bad case of cultural dissonance. Besides, I can't come up. There's no place for me to stay. We looked it up in the triple-A handbook, don't you remember?"

"The room I'm staying in has a double bed."

"Oh, marvelous. I can just camp on Elizabeth Toliver's doorstep and announce I'm staying. She won't mind. What's the harm of having one of Jimmy Card's old lovers installed in her guest room?"

"Bennis—"

"Be reasonable," Bennis said. "Besides, I'm supposed to go over to Donna's and help her with the flags. Tibor was supposed to help her, but he's having an argument with his friend Vicki about gun control, and it's really heated up, so he spends all his time on the computer posting messages to RAM, and Donna says that if she wants to make the Kashinian's building look like the Armenian flag she's got to order the materials now, and she can't do that until she gets a good picture of what the Armenian flag looks like, and she's hopeless with search engines."

"Wait," Gregor said. "Donna wants to make Howard Kashinian's house look like the Armenian flag?"

"Right. The Kashinians are the Armenian flag, Lida is the American flag, and we're the U.N. I forget what she's doing to her own place, but it's another flag."

"Why?"

"Because June fourteenth is Flag Day," Bennis said reasonably.

On the other side of the room, a middle-aged waitress was putting an enormous pizza down on the table in front of Kyle Borden. Kyle looked up, saw Gregor staring, and waved.

"I'm supposed to eat a sausage and pepperoni pizza the size of a cow," Gregor said. "You know that's bad for me. You could come and make sure I ate right."

"I'll tell you what," Bennis said. "If you don't have this whole thing cleared up by the end of next week, I'll find a hotel someplace within screaming distance and come out and take you to lunch. If we keep this up, Tibor is going to start in again with all that talk about us getting married, probably coupled with how I ought to enter the church. Of course, why he's worrying about me joining the church, I don't know. You're the one who never goes. Are you going to be all right?"

"I'll be fine. We've got an appointment to see Michael Houseman's mother in about an hour and a half. That ought to be some help."

"At least you'll be talking about a murder," Bennis said.

"Right." Gregor thought of saying other things—"I love you," for instance—but he had one of those temporary interior clutches that made him incapable of saying anything, and the next thing he knew the receiver was buzzing in his ear. He hung up and stared at the phone for a moment. They were together so often these days, it no longer seemed natural to him when she was gone.

Kyle Borden waved at him again. Gregor left the phone and went to the table with the pizza spread out across it. It looked even bigger than the large pizzas they sometimes ordered on Cavanaugh Street when they were all playing Monopoly at Tibor's and nobody wanted to deal with the state of Tibor's kitchen.

"Spectacular, isn't it?" Kyle Borden said happily. "Largest pizzas you can buy in the county. They're famous for them."

"Right," Gregor said. He looked Kyle up and down. The man was thin almost to the point of emaciation. So much for the stereotype of the potbellied small-town cop.

The waitress came back to the table with a tray of drinks, both very large on the same scale as the pizza, both dark.

"I ordered you a Coke," Kyle said. "I figured that was safe. Everybody loves Coke. They even love it in China."

Gregor took a single slice of pizza and put it on the plate that had been provided for just that purpose. Except for the size of their largest offerings, this could have been any of hundreds of pizza places from one end to the other of the country, although not in any of the big cities, where real Italians lived. The waitress looked like one more Hollman mayonnaise-and-American-cheese-on-white-bread type, and the woman behind the counter cooking pizza did not look any different.

"You're drifting off again," Kyle Borden said. "If you're tired, we could probably make this appointment for another day. Daisy hasn't got that much to do with her time. She won't be unavailable."

"No, that's all right. I'm not tired. I'm just thinking. Do you always eat this much pizza when you get pizza?"

"Of course not," Kyle said. "I figured you'd have half."

2

Gregor Demarkian wasn't sure what he had expected Daisy Houseman's life to be like, but he knew it wasn't what he got: a neat little brick house on a leafy corner lot on a residential street near the center of town. At first glance, the house seemed to be a story and a half, but as Gregor and Kyle moved up the walk Gregor realized it was an illusion. The roof was steeply pitched, but the house itself was a ranch, probably of the same vintage as the Tolivers', but much smaller. The lot was smaller still. It would be the work of less than a minute to walk out Daisy Houseman's front door and into the front door of the house next door. It would take all of three minutes to make it to the front door of the house on the other side, around the corner. Still, there was nothing crowded about this neighborhood. The lawns were well kept and adequate at the back. The houses were just far enough apart to allow for privacy and fresh air. The trees and grass were lush, and some of the yards already had sprinklers working to keep them watered.

Kyle went up to the front door and started to ring the bell, but his hand was still in the air when the door opened and a neat, trim, well-kept elderly woman came out. Gregor thought she was about seventy or seventy-five, which would make sense, if she had married and had her children young. Kyle said something to her that Gregor couldn't hear, and the woman turned to look him over as if he were a new representative from the gas company.

"I've been telling her all about you," Kyle called, his voice echoing down the quiet, deserted street.

Gregor came up to the little stoop in front of the front door and took the hand Daisy Houseman was holding out to him. "Gregor Demarkian," he said.

"I know." Daisy Houseman nodded. "He *has* been telling me all about you, Mr. Demarkian. And I must admit that I've been looking for somebody to talk to. Although not on my front walk for the whole of the town to hear."

"She thinks I talk too loud," Kyle said.

"Come in," Daisy Houseman said.

She retreated through her front door, and Gregor and Kyle followed her. The door opened directly into the living room, which was high-ceilinged but small and undergirded with wall-to-wall carpeting. The carpeting was relatively new, and it had been vacuumed recently. The furniture had been dusted. Gregor recognized it. It was the "country" set sold by a well-known national chain of discount furniture stores—sofa, love seat, chair and ottoman, all upholstered in the same "country" print, for $799 the set. The coffee table had come from the same source. The television was very old, but very well kept, and encased in a polished wood console that made it look like a piece of furniture itself. On top of it was a doily, and across the doily were a whole set of framed photographs of what looked like high school yearbook pictures, three of boys and one of a girl with her hair held back in a stiff blue headband.

"I have three children besides Michael," Daisy Houseman said, seeing Gregor looking at the pictures. "Two other boys and a girl. They all went to UP-Johnstown and came back to live in town, or near it. My daughter is Caroline Houseman Bray. She teaches at the high school."

"Mrs. Houseman here used to teach at the high school, too," Kyle said. "I had her for sophomore English. She gave me a D."

"You deserved an F," Daisy Houseman said. "I quit the year after Michael died. I hadn't intended to. My other children are all younger, and I'd meant to stay for them. And we needed the money, of course, because we're not wealthy people. My husband was a foreman at the Caravesh plant. They make steel casings, or used to. I guess steel's pretty much dead in this part of Pennsylvania, these days. Can I get you two some coffee? Tea? I know Kyle will take a Coke."

"There's no need to put yourself to any trouble," Gregor said.

"It's no trouble. It's just a matter of putting the kettle on. My daughter bought me a coffee grinder and a percolator for Christmas the year before last, but I still haven't the faintest idea how to work them. I'm a Philistine when it comes to coffee, I'm afraid. I can't taste the difference between fresh ground Colombian and Taster's Choice."

Daisy Houseman left the living room. Gregor walked over to the television set and looked at the pictures on it.

"Is one of these Michael Houseman?" Gregor asked Kyle.

Kyle tapped the one at the very back. "That one. She used to keep it in the front, but maybe the other kids complained. Michael, Steve, Bobby, and Caroline."

Gregor picked up Michael's picture. The boy who stared back at him was nice enough looking, but not particularly handsome. He had regular features and hair that was still more short than not. Gregor put the portrait down.

"Like I said," Kyle told him. "Nice kid. Played decent sports."

"And didn't stand out in any way," Daisy Houseman said, coming back into the living room with a round wooden tray. The tray had a tall glass of

Coke and two coffee cups, plus a sugar bowl, a small cream pitcher, two spoons, and the kettle, which was as small as everything else in this house and still steaming. She put the tray down on the coffee table. "Don't worry," she said. "It won't offend me. He was special to me, of course, but he wasn't the kind of boy who really stood out among his peers. There are always a few of those, even in small towns like this, the ones you know will go on to good colleges and the kinds of careers most of us can only dream of. And then there are the other ones, the ones who have their fifteen minutes of fame at their senior proms. Michael wasn't one of those, either."

"He looks like a very nice boy," Gregor said.

"He was. Nice and steady and reliable. Oh, I know there were things. He drank beer sometimes, not often, but he couldn't really fool me when he did. And that last year before they all went off to college—or didn't—there was a fair amount of marijuana in town. Michael was very disapproving. It upset him. Our principal then was an old fool named Deckart Crabbe. He came close to having a nervous breakdown over that marijuana. These days, they'd probably bring in the state police and send a lot of silly teenagers to prison for five years just for carrying a joint. Excuse me, Mr. Demarkian. I don't much approve of the drug war. You haven't sat down."

"I'm sorry." Gregor sat down.

Kyle reached across the coffee table and took the Coke. "So," he said. "Like I told you, Mr. Demarkian has been asked to come in and look over what happened to Michael, because—"

"Because the supermarket tabloids are making Elizabeth Toliver sound like a murderer, and her famous boyfriend doesn't like it. Yes, Kyle, I know what's going on. Not that I mind, really. If I were in her position, I'd probably do the same thing. Maybe some good will come of it. I've never been in the kind of financial position that would allow me to hire a famous detective to look into Michael's death."

"What about at the time?" Gregor asked her. "Were you satisfied with the extent of the investigation? I keep getting the impression that not very much was done, and yet that makes very little sense. The murder of a teenager in a small town is usually major news."

"And it was major news, for about two months," Daisy told him. "I can't say I was dissatisfied with the investigation. They searched that park backward and forward. It stayed closed for the rest of the summer. They questioned all of those girls, the ones who found the body." Daisy Houseman fluttered her hands in the air. "Maybe I shouldn't start on that. Gene—my husband—Gene was very angry about that. He said they were the ones with blood on them. They were the ones the police ought to keep under observation. He was very bitter when the summer was over and they started going to college and nobody stopped them. But I could see the police point of view. There was no weapon. And unless you thought they were all in it together, they all had alibis. They were all together, you see, not killing Michael in the dark."

"Did anybody ever consider the possibility that they *were* all in it together?" Gregor asked.

Daisy flashed him a smile. "I considered it. Gene did, too. Oh, I did not like that group of girls. Not a bit. I didn't like it when Michael stayed so close to Chris Inglerod, and I didn't like it when he was dating that other one, Emma. Although that came and went the summer between his sophomore and junior years. She dumped him as soon as they got back to school. She didn't think her reputation would survive if anybody knew she was dating a boy in her own class. If it was up to me, the system would be very different. I'd cancel all the proms and all the dances and all the cheerleading squads. I'd make school school. But nobody would listen to that."

"Michael was close to Chris Inglerod all his life, wasn't he?" Gregor said.

"Oh, yes." Daisy nodded. "We bought this house in 1953, and the Inglerods had the one next door around the back on Carter Street. We were the only families in the area who had children. Everybody else in the neighborhood was older. Their children were grown-up and gone. Most new young families in those days bought houses in the subdivisions that had just started going up. They had nobody to play with but each other, when they were very small children, and then later they walked to and from school together. That was why Gene and I bought this house, not so that Michael could walk to school but so that I could, when the children were bigger and I wanted to go back to teaching."

"Excuse me if I'm wrong," Gregor said, "but I keep getting the impression that that was unusual. That in this high school, the groups are pretty much closed off from each other."

Daisy took a long sip of coffee. Gregor hadn't even noticed her making it, but now that he looked down at the tray he saw that she'd made him a cup, too, but hadn't put any milk in it, and probably hadn't added any sugar. She put her cup down again and said, "You've got to understand. Hollman is a small town now, but in those days it was teeny. They all knew each other, all these kids, for most of their lives. In a large school, you can break up into groups and refuse to interact with anybody else, but in a small one you end up having to spend at least some time with almost everybody. There's no practical way to avoid it. And, if you want to know the truth, they probably don't want to avoid it. There's a psychological dynamic there that somebody ought to study. Somebody who isn't a complete fool, that is. I've read some of the literature on 'adolescent status hierarchies,' as they call them. It's completely idiotic."

"Was Michael going out with anybody in particular, that summer?" Gregor asked.

Daisy shook her head. "Nobody. He took the little Haggerty girl to the senior prom, but that was a matter of convenience. They both wanted to go, and neither of them had dates, and they were lab partners in biology. When summer came around, he was just working, just marking time. I'm sure he didn't know what he wanted to do with his life. It seemed to Gene and me that he'd have plenty of time to find out."

The silence in the room lasted for what felt like forever. Gregor tried his coffee and decided it was better, black, than the stuff he made for himself. Kyle, who had never taken a seat, shifted from one leg to the other.

"Well," he said.

Gregor took another sip of coffee. "Do you mind if I ask you about the day in question, the day he died?"

"Of course not."

"He left for work that day, when?"

"Well, he wasn't due at work until ten or eleven o'clock, but he left a long time before that. At eight, I think, or maybe quarter of. Chris picked him up and they went down to the Sycamore for breakfast."

"Was that unusual?"

"Oh, no. They did that maybe twice a week. I think it made them feel adult to sit in a restaurant and order from a menu, even if it was only the Sycamore."

"Do you know if they went by themselves, or if they met people?"

Daisy Houseman shook her head. "I have no idea. The impression I got is that they went by themselves, but the Sycamore is the main teenage hangout in this town. It still is. They might have met a dozen people. They never said so."

"Not even on the day in question?"

"No."

"I don't remember there being anything about them meeting other people that morning," Kyle said. "You know, in the gossip in town after it all happened. Just that they'd gone to breakfast there in the morning."

"Fine," Gregor said. "So. Chris Inglerod took Michael to the park and Michael went to work as a lifeguard. He spent the day sitting on the lifeguard's chair. There's no indication that he was missing from that chair for any significant amount of time, is there?"

"He didn't even take a break for lunch," Daisy Houseman said. "He ate sitting in the chair. I sent a bottle of orange juice and a bologna sandwich with mustard with him, in a brown paper bag. That's what he liked to take to school, too, but at school he had an apple with him, too. You can't send apples with them when they're lifeguarding. They cramp."

"Michael started work in the lifeguard's chair," Gregor said, "and Chris Inglerod did what?"

"Came back to town and met up with Nancy Quayde and went to her house," Kyle said promptly.

"Nonsense," Daisy Houseman said.

"What?" Kyle said.

"I said nonsense. That's not what she did unless she changed her plans that very morning. I heard her talking in this very house before she and Michael left for the Sycamore. She was going to stay in the park and meet with that pack of—well. Those girls. Emma Kenyon and Belinda Hart and Maris Coleman and Peggy Smith. Oh, and Nancy Quayde, too, of course. Always Nancy. I'm glad I left teaching long before she ever got into it."

"Mrs. Houseman," Kyle said patiently, "I've read the reports. And I was here at the time, don't you remember? Chris went to Nancy's house, and the other girls—"

"Nonsense," Daisy Houseman said again. "They'd been planning that operation all summer. Chris told Michael about it, right in my dining room, weeks before it happened. Michael had a fit. He didn't want it happening on his watch. He'd have to go investigate it. They'd put him in a terrible position. I think that's why they waited until after five. So that Michael would be off duty and the park would be closed and he couldn't turn them right in for what they'd done." She wheeled around to look at Gregor Demarkian. "I know you must think we're all a bunch of savages in this town, Mr. Demarkian, but believe me. If Michael hadn't died the same night, those girls would have been in major league trouble for what they did. At the very least, they'd have been hauled in front of juvenile court. Betsy Toliver's father was the most important attorney in this part of the state. He'd have seen to it. And the rest of the town would not have stood behind them. We are not jerks. Did they really tell the police they hadn't thought up that stunt until the day it happened?"

"They told *everybody* that," Kyle said.

"Well, what can I say?" Daisy's hands fluttered again. "I wasn't paying much attention at the time. I had other things to think about. I didn't realize. But if I had, I would have told somebody. Belinda Hart discovered the snakes' nest two weeks before graduation, in June. There were eggs and the eggs would hatch. That's how they were sure of getting enough snakes. Chris sat down at my dining-room table and drew a whole diagram for Michael to show him what it was about. They wanted him to help, but he wouldn't do it. He told me he didn't believe they'd do it. And you know what he was like. He would have turned them in, just the way he always said he'd turn in whoever it was who was selling the marijuana at the high school, if he ever found out. But don't you dare let that pack of bitches tell you that what they did to Betsy Toliver that night was a spur-of-the-moment thing."

3

It was only later, when he was in the car with the robot-driver on his way back to Elizabeth Toliver's house, that Gregor Demarkian thought how odd it was that Daisy Houseman had called that incident at the outhouse an "operation." Of course, television had changed the world, and so had paperback fiction. Lots of people talked like private eyes these days. Even cultivated people—the kind of people who contributed every year to their local affiliate of PBS—thought of Raymond Chandler and Agatha Christie as "classics," as if they were Jane Austen and Henry James. There was also the fact that Mrs. Houseman had ended up calling the girls "bitches," but Gregor put that down to simple honesty. Daisy Houseman had said it, but lots of other people should have. Most of the people Gregor had gone to school with had either been sinking into juvenile delinquency or working their asses off to get the hell out, as Gregor himself had, in the end, with a four-year all-tuition-paid scholarship to the University of Pennsylvania. The Armenian kids tended to stick together. It was safer that way, and they had their own events, on Cavanaugh Street, to compensate for the lack of events at school. Gregor could remember going to dozens of "youth" dances in the basement of Holy Trinity Church, carefully watched over by the Very Old Ladies who had been Very Old even then. Once, he'd kissed Lida—Lida Kazanjian as she was then—right on the mouth in the little niche behind the boiler in the basement's back room. She'd been shocked, and before either of them had had a chance to say a word, Mrs. Varmesian had leaped out of the dark and whacked Gregor in the leg with an umbrella, screeching all the time in Armenian, which by then Gregor no longer understood. Mrs. Varmesian had died the next year, of some "female complaint" Gregor's mother would never specify. Like everybody else on the street, he had gone to her funeral and then followed her casket out of the church and down a long three blocks to the waiting hearse. In Armenia, they would have followed the casket all the way to the cemetery, but Mrs. Varmesian was being taken to an Armenian-American cemetery in Sewickley. That was the same year he had graduated from high school, and his parents had come to the ceremony in their best clothes that even he knew, by then, made them look as if they were just off the boat. That didn't matter too much, because most of the other parents looked as if they were just off the boat, too. Gregor had graduated second in his class—the boy who had graduated first had picked up a Nobel Prize in medicine in 1987—and his mother had carried his diploma around for weeks, showing its gold summa cum laude star to strangers on the street, and discussing Gregor's plans and scholarships with everyone from the men who came around on the garbage truck to the driver of the bus she rode to get to her doctor's appointment. Bennis said she didn't know any more about places like Hollman than Gregor did himself, but it wasn't true. She at least didn't find discussions of things like proms and homecoming queens completely alien. She'd seen all the movies and read all the books, even if she had spent her adolescence at subdebutante dances and champagne teas. Now that he'd spent a day in Hollman, he felt as if he'd landed on another planet.

Gregor looked down at the attaché case he'd put on the seat beside him and wondered if he should be looking through the reports Kyle Borden had given him—but he'd looked those over once, and in spite of the fact that they were filled with the kind of details that were fundamentally necessary to any murder investigation, he already knew he was going to find them unsatisfactory. The more he knew about Michael Houseman, the more the boy bothered him, not because there was something wrong with him, but because there *wasn't.* In Gregor's experience, there were exactly two kinds of murders: the ones committed by psychopaths, for their own reasons, and the ones committed on the sort of people who had more enemies than hair follicles. Michael Houseman hadn't had any enemies. He'd been a nice, upright, conscientiously honest boy with a few bad adolescent tendencies to get high on the weekends, a little too much of a straight arrow, a little too much of an Eagle Scout, but not so much of either that he had been perceived by his classmates as a prig. It was so *trivial.* There was a boy dead, and all the reasons Gregor could think of that somebody might have had to kill him were on the level of the motives in a Hardy Boys' book. No wonder the police had written off the incident as the work of a stray tramp. At least that would make a certain kind of sense. The problem was, the solution didn't quite fit the facts as he had read them so far, and especially the fact that those girls had been so close to that body so soon after Michael Houseman had died, or maybe even before he was all the way dead. Even tramps have to be somewhere, and come from somewhere. Why would one be wandering around a small park in the middle of nowhere instead of hanging around the train station? How would he have found the park to begin with? Gregor had spent ten years of his life tracking serial killers. He knew how they worked, and unless you wanted to say that the one who killed Michael Houseman had been an old resident of Hollman come back to haunt, it made no sense that he would be in that park, prowling around for what he couldn't know would be there. Of course, an old resident wasn't impossible. Hollman must have produced its share of drifters. Every small town did. Gregor was beginning to make himself dizzy. If he followed his instincts and rejected the idea of a tramp or a drifter or a serial killer, he was left with—what? Nothing. Not even something ridiculous, like an argument over who got to be voted Most Popular Boy or who got to date the captain of the cheerleading team.

I'm beginning to sound like a Gidget movie, Gregor thought. Luis was turning the car off the road onto Elizabeth Toliver's driveway, which seemed to be full of vehicles, as if she were having company. The front of the house was dark in the dusk, but as they came around to the big paved area in the back, Gregor could see lights on in the kitchen windows. Mark passed back and forth a few times. The car pulled closer to the garage and Gregor saw Jimmy Card appear suddenly in the window. He was holding a large glass full of something dark. Twenty years ago, it would have been a Manhattan. These days, it was probably a Diet Coke.

"Oh, boy," Gregor said, thinking it wouldn't be long before every celebrity photographer in America knew that Jimmy Card was here and in a house with no security protection whatsoever—and no possibility of providing any, either. The Toliver house was what the Bureau would have called an "undefensible area." It had no fences or gates, and it was surrounded on all sides by open land. Gregor grabbed his attaché case, expecting Luis to pull up to the back door and let him out before parking the car in the garage, but Luis didn't stop. He went straight across the asphalt to the garage and waited while the door pulled up automatically in front of him. If Gregor had been thinking clearly, he would have asked Luis to let him out right then. Instead, he found himself being pulled into the dark garage while security lights flicked on above his head. The garage was half full of things nobody had used for years and nobody would ever use again: an old rotary lawn mower, its long metal handles so thoroughly rusted they looked like sand; a stack of molded plastic garden chairs in black and pink; a pile of boxes marked "Betsy's Books." There were a lot of boxes. Elizabeth Toliver must have been a terrific reader as a child.

Gregor got out of the car. The lights were still on, but the garage door had closed behind them, automatically, the way it had opened. He saw an ordinary door to one side, propped slightly open.

"I'm going this way," he said.

Outside the high windows on the three garage doors, the sky was streaked with bright, hard pink the way it was right before real sunset. The leaves on all the trees nearby were drooping. Gregor let himself out. After the air-conditioned sterility of the car, the air out here was humid and sickly sweet. The house up ahead looked the way houses do in house magazine articles about how to make your house into a home. There was a path that curved around a long, low hedge that had been cropped as closely as it could be and still be left alive. He took that rather than striking out on the lawn, in case the Tolivers cared seriously about the way their grass looked.

He was at the edge of the hedge, right before the lawn itself started, when he realized that something was wrong, and had been wrong, for a while. The sickly sweet smell was getting stronger. All of a sudden, it seemed to envelope him, the way skunk-smell did when a skunk was hit in the road. This was not the smell a skunk made. He knew this smell very well. He had had it around him more times than he liked to remember. He told himself that, in this case, it was most likely to be another dog, or a cat, or a woodchuck, another animal ritually slaughtered at Elizabeth Toliver's altar, another prank.

He looked down at his shoes and saw the snaking curve of something white against them. He was too aware of just how quiet it was. He couldn't even hear Luis in the garage. No sound was coming from the house. He moved slowly to his right, around the end of the hedge, looking at the ground the whole time. He did not want to do any more damage than he had already done.

I need a flashlight, he thought idly. The dark was descending at record speed. The snaking white thing trailed around the end of the hedge and back toward the bushes that flanked that side of the garage. There were dozens of bushes, all evergreen, so densely placed that there was no room for anything between them. *Follow the yellow brick road,* Gregor thought, moving carefully so as not to step on the white thing, not to disturb anything, not to cause any more trouble than he absolutely had to. If he had been one hundred percent certain, he would have gone straight into the house and called Kyle Borden and anybody Kyle could think of to use for reinforcements.

A second later, Gregor *was* certain. The long white thing was an intestine, stretched out by some accident he couldn't begin to determine, and on the end of it was a body, twisted and mauled as if it had been broken in half. *Not Liz Toliver's body,* Gregor thought with relief. Then he wished desperately that cell phones worked in these mountains.

It wasn't Liz Toliver's body, but it was the body of a woman, and she had been as thoroughly eviscerated as yesterday's dog.

PART TWO

"Iris"

—GOO GOO DOLLS

"Mercedes Benz"

—JANIS JOPLIN

"Porcelain"

—RED HOT CHILI PEPPERS

ONE

1

Her name was Christine Allison Inglerod Barr. Liz Toliver recognized her on sight, in that short moment before Gregor realized she'd come up behind him. He'd just had time to push her away and into the arms of Jimmy Card when she vomited, a thick bulk of tan and pink spraying over the front of the man's $2,000 sports jacket. For a moment, everything was totally insane—there was Liz, and Jimmy Card, and Mark, all of whom he knew, but there was also another woman, not the nurse, not the mother, a woman with good jewelry smelling just faintly of alcohol. Gregor's primary thought was of the integrity of the crime scene. He kept trying to herd the whole group back toward the house and as far away from the body as possible. Jimmy Card didn't look as if he'd noticed that he'd been thrown up on. The woman with the jewelry was smoking a cigarette. Cigarettes were a disaster at crime scenes. Around them, dark was falling very fast. It had to be seven o'clock. Only Mark DeAvecca and the woman with the jewelry seemed to be keeping their heads, and Gregor thought the woman with the jewelry might have other reasons for staying calm.

"It's Chris," Liz Toliver kept saying. "I can't believe it. It's Chris."

"What the hell do you think you're doing?" Jimmy Card said. "How could this possibly have happened? I thought you were the great detective."

"Want me to call the police?" Mark said.

"As fast as you can," Gregor said. "Where's your brother?"

"With the bitch nurse and Grandma. Who's a bitch, too. Did I tell you that?"

"Call the police now. Swear like a college student later. Don't let your brother out here to see this."

"Right." Mark turned on his heel and headed back to the house, with the faintly contemptuous air adolescents have when they know they're behaving more like an adult than any of the adults.

Gregor turned his attention back to the group, now in the middle of the lawn, Liz and Jimmy huddled together, the woman with the jewelry just about to light another cigarette.

"Did you drop your cigarette butt on the lawn?" Gregor asked her.

"Oh, for Christ's sake," Jimmy said. "Who cares if she smokes at a time like this? I'd smoke if I still did it."

Gregor tried to explain, patiently: the nature of forensics; the importance at crime scenes of even small things like cigarette butts and stray hairs. Liz and Jimmy looked at him as if he had to be insane. The woman with the jewelry went on smoking.

"Go back to the house," Gregor said finally. "Just go back to the house and sit still until the police get here. You're not doing any good where you are."

"You have to wonder why she didn't come to the door and ring the bell," the woman with the jewelry said.

"Oh, for Christ's sake," Jimmy Card said again.

Liz backed away from him. The vomit on his sports coat had rubbed off onto her sweater. They had been holding themselves against each other without thinking. She blinked at the mess and shook her head. For the first time since Gregor met her, she looked as old as she was supposed to be.

"It wasn't a stupid question," she said carefully. "Maris is right. You do have to wonder why she didn't come to the door and ring the bell."

"She didn't do it because she was out here getting . . . getting . . ." Jimmy gave up.

"It doesn't make any sense that she was out here," Liz insisted. "Why would she be off by the side of the drive? And how did she get here? There's not—"

"There is," the woman with the jewelry said. *Maris*, Gregor told himself. "Her car's down by the third bay. It's hard to see because it's dark. But it's her car. I recognize it."

They all looked toward the other end of the driveway. There were, Gregor realized, several cars now in the parking area—his own, Liz Toliver's Mercedes, a red Jaguar he assumed must belong to Jimmy Card, and the dark car Maris had pointed to, a Volvo station wagon, the sort of car that in most places belonged to doctors' wives. Maris took a long drag on her cigarette and blew a stream of smoke into the air.

"You've got to *assume* she came here to talk to Betsy," Maris said. "So why didn't she just come up and ring the bell? It's just across there. She wasn't very far."

"Whyever would she want to talk to me?" Liz said. "She never did talk to me much when we were growing up. Why would she come here?"

"You were here all by yourself for an hour before any of the rest of us got here," Maris said. "You must have seen her. You must have at least seen the car."

"What the *hell* do you think you're doing?" Jimmy said.

Maris's drag on the cigarette this time was very long, so long it seemed an illusion. "What I'm *doing*," she said, overprecisely, "is injecting a little reality into these proceedings. In another hour, or less, there are going to be hundreds of people here, only some of them from the legitimate news agencies. Some of the others are going to be shilling for the *Enquirer* and the *Star*. And let me tell you what this is going to look like to them. The last time Betsy spent any time in this town, Michael Houseman got murdered. Now that she's come back, Chris Inglerod has been murdered—"

"You came back," Jimmy said. "You're back just as much as she is."

"But not for the first time," Maris shot at him. "I've been back dozens of times before. I've been here to visit my parents. I've been here to visit friends. It's Betsy who took off and never wanted to set foot in this place again. Which is odd in and of itself, if you think about it. Who does that? Everybody comes home from college on vacations."

"You," Jimmy Card said, "are such an unbelievable, unmitigated bitch."

"Don't look at me. I'm not the one who's going to say this stuff. I'm not even the one who's going to think it. But everybody else will. And Betsy knows why Chris would be coming here. Chris was going to invite her to something, a party. I told Betsy all about it at lunch—"

"No," Liz said. "What you said was—"

"And there's the simple fact that all this stuff is happening right in Betsy's garage," Maris said, triumphant. "Swear your head off, it won't matter. This will be in every supermarket tabloid by the end of the week and there's not a damned thing you can do about it."

"What about you?" Jimmy said. "How did you get here? You don't have a car."

"Nancy Quayde dropped me off when she got finished with school. Betsy was already here when we got here. Ask Nancy. Ask Betsy."

"I didn't realize it was Nancy in the car," Liz said.

"She didn't want to come in." Maris looked up over her head. The night was dark enough now so that they should be able to see stars in the sky, but somebody—probably Mark—had turned out the security lights over the garage and the back porch door, and they couldn't see anything but blackness. "You just don't get it," Maris said. "She wasn't locked in an outhouse this time. She wasn't beating herself bloody just because of a few stupid garden snakes. She was right here right now and nobody else was."

"Geoff was," Liz said softly. "My mother was."

"Geoff is a child. Your mother is worse than a child. You'd have had a shot in hell if the nurse had been here, but she didn't get back until after I did. Give it up. And then go back in the house and get clean. You're both disgusting."

Maris turned her back on them and strode across the lawn toward the back door to the house, wobbling a little on city heels. For a while they all watched her go, even Gregor.

"She never came to the door," Liz said finally. "I hadn't seen her in years. I hadn't even thought about seeing her." She looked down at the vomit smeared across the front of her sweater and on her arms. The sweater had short sleeves. She rubbed her hands against the sides of her slacks to clean them off and then rubbed her face, hard, as if she would never be able to rub it enough to wake herself up. "Well," she said finally.

"You need to fire her," Jimmy Card said finally. "You need to do more than that. You need to get her out of your life. I mean, what the hell, Liz, if you don't want to marry me, you don't want to marry me, but there's no point in letting that woman go on screwing you over. You're not doing yourself or anybody else any good."

"She's just—miserable, that's all," Liz said. "She's just upset."

"She just tried to pin a murder on you. And not one that's thirty years old, either."

Somewhere in the distance, there was the sound of sirens, more than one, meaning that Kyle Borden had taken Mark DeAvecca's call seriously. They all looked up and blinked, as if they'd been awakened from a light sleep. Liz put her hand on the mess on Jimmy Card's sports jacket and shook her head.

"Maybe we should go inside and clean up," she said.

"Clean up but leave the clothes intact," Gregor told her. "Take them off, drop them in a plastic bag, put them aside for forensics. Take a shower and do what you have to do to make yourself feel better. A shot of brandy probably wouldn't hurt."

"Jesus," Jimmy said. "You really are going to treat Liz as if she—"

"No," Liz said. "He's going to treat everybody as a suspect. So will the police. That's, what, standard operating procedure."

"You also have to worry about a process of elimination," Gregor said. "If any of . . . that . . . has dropped on the ground, the forensics people may pick it up. It would be necessary to eliminate it. We could do that if we had samples of the—"

"Jesus," Jimmy said again.

Mark DeAvecca came out of the house and walked across the lawn to them. "What did you guys do to Maris? She's smirking."

"Jesus *Christ*," Jimmy Card said.

"It's just *Maris*," Liz said. "It's just the way she is. She panics and she acts like an idiot. She doesn't mean anything by it."

"I think you'd better get cleaned up," Gregor said again, more firmly this time. "Get cleaned up. Have a brandy. Wait until the police want to talk to you. And don't let anybody leave the house. No matter how much you might want to."

"Meaning we're stuck with the bitch of the Western world for the foreseeable future," Mark said cheerfully.

"You go back in the house, too," Gregor told him. "The police will be here any minute, and you don't want to be in the way."

"Yes, I do," Mark said.

"Go."

Mark shrugged. Liz backed up a little and looked in the direction of the body. Gregor didn't think she could possibly have seen much, and she didn't linger to see if she could get a better look. She took Jimmy Card's hand and smiled at Gregor, faintly.

"Well," she said, "I guess we'll go back in the house and get cleaned up. Mark, you come with us."

"Just a second," Mark said.

Liz and Jimmy looked at each other, and then walked off, slowly. Mark stood silently until they were out of hearing range, his boy's face shading in and out of adulthood in the dark and the artificial light. Gregor thought that when he hit twenty Mark was going to be a positive menace to female virtue.

"So," Mark said. "I take it Maris has decided that Mom killed this—person. And she's told you all about it."

"Something like that."

"Well," Mark said, "if she tries to tell you Mom was here alone with Geoff and Grandma, she's wrong. I was here, the whole time. I got back from the library at quarter after three. This woman Mom used to know gave me a lift. You might want to ask her about it."

"Do you remember her name?"

"Emma Bligh. I remember because she reminded me of Captain Bligh. Marlon Brando, you know, in that ancient movie. Except it wasn't Marlon Brando who was Bligh, it was some English guy. She had this other woman with her—Belinda something. Belinda had a daughter."

"Oh?"

"Forget it. IQ in negative numbers, from what I could tell from what she was saying. What Belinda was saying, I mean. *Belinda's* IQ was in negative numbers, if you want to know the truth, and Emma Bligh wasn't much better. Is everybody in this town stupid? Belinda works in the library, by the way. I saw her there. She doesn't know anything about books."

"I know it isn't legal," Gregor said, "but you might want to take a swig of that brandy yourself. You're shaking."

"Yeah," Mark said. "I just—I just want to know what's going on with my mom, you know. I just don't get it. I mean, I've been hearing about these people all my life. They intimidate her, they really do, and I know that she always feels as if she doesn't deserve her own life. The more successful she gets, the more guilty she gets, and I can't figure it out. Now I've met these people and they're stupid, they're shallow, and if they're not that, they're Maris, who's some kind of frigging sociopath. What's the point here? Why does she care so much?"

"I don't know."

"They all care," Mark said. "That's the weird part. They *all* care. You should have heard the two of them driving me home. It was insane. And they hate her for it, you know. They hate her for what she turned out to be."

"They told you that?" Gregor was surprised.

"Not in so many words. But they told me anyway. In the way they talked about her. If I repeated the words, they'd sound like nice things. But they weren't. You know what I mean?"

"Absolutely."

"We shouldn't have come here," Mark said. "Jimmy was right. I was right. Those are the police cars."

The sirens were still blasting, and there were a lot of them: the town police car, a state police car, an ambulance. The vehicles all came careening into the driveway at once.

2

It took Kyle Borden and the state trooper who had shown up to help him exactly thirty seconds to decide they were out of their depth and call for reinforcements. It took the ambulance men less than that to decide they were going to have nothing to do with the body—or the pieces of the body—on the ground in the hedges beside Elizabeth Toliver's garage. Kyle did the intelligent thing and went back to the car to get sick on the floor of the front passenger seat. The state trooper began to pace back and forth along the edge of the lawn, as if the most likely danger was that somebody would drive right up from the street to snatch the body and spirit it away. Gregor went up to the car where Luis was now sitting behind the wheel, staring straight ahead, and asked the man for a flashlight.

Luis rummaged in the glove compartment and came up with a flashlight. He handed it to Gregor and went back to staring out the window.

Gregor flicked the flashlight on and off. The light hiccuped in the darkness. He walked back to the side of the garage and turned it on full blast. Now that he had a chance to really study the scene, instead of just react, he could see that there was more to what had happened to the body than he had originally thought. The cut in the belly was very much like the cut in the belly of the dog the night before, at least as the dog's injuries had been described in Kyle Borden's report and as Gregor himself had been able to see them. There was a slit either up or down the stomach in a single vertical line, or a line that would have been vertical if the victim had been standing. The slit was deep and savage enough to let everything behind it spill out, but it was not the only slit. Gregor let the light from the flashlight roll up the body and stopped at the neck. There was, quite definitely, another slit there, although it was not as easy to see as the one in the belly, and not as dramatic. The line was unmistakable, though, and in at least one place at the front, it gaped. Above it, the face was a jagged white mask, topped with thick dark hair that looked fake. There was no sign of graying at the roots. Either Christine Inglerod was a very lucky woman, or a very careful one.

Gregor snapped off the flashlight and walked back across the lawn to Kyle's police car. Kyle was standing just outside of it, leaning against the side, while the trooper paced by him. The door to the front passenger seat was open. The night was very warm, but very humid.

When Gregor got to the driveway, he stopped, and both Kyle and the trooper moved toward him.

"Well?" Kyle said.

Gregor shrugged. "You need a forensics lab, a good one. This is going to be a little complicated."

"Wonderful," Kyle said. "This isn't Philadelphia, you know. It isn't even Pittsburgh. The state police will help us out—"

"We've got excellent forensic capabilities," the state trooper said stiffly.

"—but the fact of the matter is that when it comes to crime technology, this is hicksville." Kyle sighed.

"In all probability," Gregor said carefully, "she moved after she was cut. She moved herself, I mean."

"She was alive?" Kyle blanched.

The state trooper moved uneasily from one foot to another.

"You need a good forensics lab," Gregor repeated, ignoring Kyle Borden's protestations about "hicksville," "but my guess is, yes, she was alive after she was cut for at least a few minutes. It looked like she tried to drag herself across the ground. That's when the intestines probably spilled out. They're too widely distributed to be the result of gravity alone. She may have tried to call out, too, but it wouldn't have done her much good."

"Why not?" the state trooper said.

"Because she was also cut across the throat," Gregor told him. "Straight across. I think the phrase in the pulp fiction of my childhood was 'from ear to ear.' "

"Christ," the state trooper said. "What was that?"

"He's trying to say she had her throat slit like Michael Houseman did. Michael Houseman was—"

"I know," the state trooper said. "Kid got killed in a park up here, thirty, forty years ago."

"Thirty-two," Kyle Borden said.

"The dog didn't have a slit in his throat, did he?" Gregor asked.

"No," Kyle said.

"It would be interesting to know which cut came first, in this case," Gregor said.

"Why?" Kyle Borden demanded. "And how could anybody know that?"

"A decent forensics lab could make a good guess," Gregor said patiently. "And why is because it would tell us something about the killer, and about the intent here. I remember Mark saying something to me this morning about how killing the dog was an angry thing to do."

"You think this was a mistake?" Kyle said. "You think whoever it really was didn't intend to kill Chris?"

"He or she might not have, at the time it started. Obviously, the intent was there by the time it was over—"

"Thank you for that," the state trooper said.

"But you can't simply assume," Gregor said, "that whoever did this planned it. I'm told that one of the cars in the driveway belonged to the victim—"

"The Volvo," Kyle said.

"—so let's say she got here under her own steam. I'm also told that she was intending to invite Ms. Toliver to some kind of social function, apparently in an effort to make up for what went on here all those years ago."

"Who told you this?" Kyle asked.

"Somebody named Maris," Gregor said. "Maris Coleman, I presume."

"There's only one I know of." Kyle Borden looked toward the house.

"She was just giving us a rundown as to why Ms. Toliver is the most likely person to have murdered Christine—"

"Chris—"

"Inglerod."

The state trooper nodded. "I can see that," he says. "There was a murder here all those years ago, and a bunch of people were involved in it, and most of them have been around the area for years without another murder happening, and then the one that's been away all that time comes back and another murder happens and—"

"And crap," Kyle Borden said. "Betsy Toliver was nailed into an outhouse at the time Michael Houseman was killed. *Nailed.* Literally. They'd taken a hammer and nails and nailed the door shut on her. She was in there screaming her head off when the cops got to the scene and when they did Michael had been dead less than twenty minutes and Betsy had been in that outhouse long enough to have stripped the skin off her arms from pounding on the walls."

"Oh," the state trooper said.

"I think the inference would be unwarranted for a number of reasons," Gregor said. "It's true that anybody might be capable of anything, but it's also true that Liz Toliver doesn't seem to have much of an incentive to commit murder in this case. It's not enough just to have a motive for murder, there has to be an incentive, something to set it off. What's the incentive here? Yes, she and this woman did not seem to be friends in high school, but Elizabeth Toliver and Maris Coleman weren't exactly friends in high school either. If Elizabeth Toliver wanted to kill somebody, or revenge herself on somebody, why not on Maris Coleman?"

"It would have been a better choice anyway," Kyle Borden said. "Chris was part of that crowd, but she wasn't a ringleader. Maris was a ringleader. And a nastier bitch you did not want to meet—"

"I got that impression," Gregor said dryly. "No, my point is, the murder has to be worthwhile for the murderer, or it has to be a spur-of-the-moment, thoughtless thing. That's why I said that it would be good to know in what order the wounds were inflicted. Because if we have here a spur-of-the-moment, sudden burst-of-passion thing, then Liz Toliver might be a credible suspect. But if we have something planned, something thought out, then I don't see it. Jimmy Card is in there, making her tea right this moment. The woman teaches at Columbia. She's got a full-blast public career. What could Chris Inglerod have possibly done to Liz Toliver to be worth the risk of being caught, or even of being definitively suspected, of a brand-new murder?"

"It would make sense if Ms. Toliver had killed the kid," the state trooper said, "and this woman could prove it."

"Absolutely," Gregor agreed. "But that lands us in all kinds of trouble. First being, of course, that one of the few things we know about Michael Houseman's murder is that Liz Toliver didn't commit it. The second being that if Chris Inglerod had had evidence of Liz Toliver's guilt, there's no reason why she wouldn't have said so long ago. These women were not friends. It wasn't a question of one close friend trying to cover up for another. As far as I can tell, Chris Inglerod belonged to a group of girls who would have thrown Liz Toliver to the wolves if they'd been presented with the slightest chance. Since she didn't do that, I'd say she didn't have what she needed to do it. If you see what I mean."

"She might have done it with somebody else," Kyle said slowly. "Chris might have. She might have known something about somebody else. About one of the, you know, uh, popular crowd." He blushed. "She might have kept it quiet if it was somebody she cared about."

The body was already beginning to smell, and it hadn't been long dead when he'd first seen it. Give it another hour, and there would be insects all over it.

The state trooper was looking toward the house. "Did you say Jimmy Card was in there? You mean like Jimmy Card the rock star?"

"It's hard to think of Jimmy Card as a rock star these days," Kyle Borden said. "He does all this classical stuff."

"Whatever," the state trooper said. "That Jimmy Card?"

"Right," Gregor said.

"Jesus," the state trooper said. "This is going to be a zoo. I saw a case in Pittsburgh once, happened in this hotel to some girl seeing somebody in the Rolling Stones. It was insane."

They all turned to look at the back of the house together, but this time nothing could be seen in the lighted windows of the kitchen. They went back to looking at each other. Gregor thought it was always hard to understand motive, because motive often made almost nothing in the way of sense. People killed for money, and for love, but in the end they almost always killed out of either too much heat or too much coldness. Gregor was inclined to go with Mark's assessment and say that this was heat, if only because he could see no other reason for killing in the way it had been done. It would have been so much easier just to stab. It would have been less bloody, although it might not have been as sure. It wasn't just a question of why Chris Inglerod had come here—it might be perfectly true that she'd come to invite Liz Toliver to something, and decided to do it in person because she'd have a better chance of getting Liz to say yes—but of why Chris Inglerod had gone around to that side of the garage. It wasn't the side closest to the house. She hadn't parked in the garage, where she might have been confused as to which door to take and taken that one, just as Gregor had. He hated things like this that seemed to make no sense to begin with, and then made less and less as he tried to straighten them out.

Finally, in the distance, there were more sirens. Gregor supposed they must be coming either from state police headquarters, or from some regional office able to supply not only a crime lab but a real medical examiner. As far as Gregor could tell, Hollman didn't have one of its own.

"Oh, thank God," Kyle said, turning toward the noise. "You have no idea how glad I'm going to be to hand this whole thing over to a real cop."

3

It was after midnight before they were finished, and even then there was a tape up around the place where the body had been found and a single state trooper left to guard it. In the last hour, two unknown young men had shown up and tried to mingle with the police officers, but there was no one to mingle with, and nobody willing to talk to somebody they didn't know with no known reason to be at the scene. Gregor was sure that at least one of the young men was stringing for the tabloids, or hoping to. He not only hung around far too long, but kept walking out to the front of the house and coming back again. Gregor meant to ask Kyle Borden if he knew who the young man was—Kyle seemed to know everybody who lived in town—but he got too involved in talking to one of the newest state troopers. By the time he looked up, the young man was gone. There was no way to cordon off the property. Sawhorses and police guards were all well and good, but they could be sneaked past, and if they could be they would be.

He waited on the back lawn until everybody but the one state trooper delegated to guard the crime area was gone. He said good-bye to Kyle Borden and promised to phone him "in the morning," although he knew it was already morning, and that neither one of them was likely to be worth much until well after ten. He walked back to the tape cordoning off the crime area and looked over it at nothing much. It was far too dark to see anything.

Even the grass looked like a black hole. He turned around and walked back to the house. The air felt heavy and thick, the way it did right before a rain.

Gregor let himself in through the back door of the house and went through the little pantry-cum-mudroom into the kitchen. He'd fully expected to find the place full of people—Liz and Jimmy and Mark and Maris Coleman, at least, and maybe the mother's nurse—but instead, the only person there was Liz herself, sitting at the round breakfast table with a book open in front of her. Bob Dylan's *Blood on the Tracks* was playing somewhere. Liz did not appear to be reading.

Gregor cleared his throat. "Where is everybody?" he asked. "I thought I'd come in here and find a horde of angry civilians, all wanting to know when the police would let them go home."

"We are home," Liz said reasonably. "Except for Maris, of course, and she's passed out on the couch in the living room. My mother is asleep. The night nurse is with her. Geoff is asleep, too, but Mark's in with him reading something or the other. Jimmy's taking a shower."

"It might be best if you got him out of here," Gregor said. "It might be best if you got yourself out of here, too, and your mother, as soon as you can manage it. There's no way to cordon off this house. When the press hits, you're going to be overrun and there isn't going to be much you can do about it."

"I know." Liz got up. "I'm going to make myself some tea. Do you want some?"

"No, thank you."

"Coffee? Wine? Maris has a Chanel No. 5 bottle full of Gordon's gin, if you want me to make you something stronger. One thing you have to say about Maris. She never stoops to cheap liquor."

"She's also a disaster waiting to happen. Mr. Card is probably right about her feeding stories to the tabloids. I'm sure you already know that."

"Oh, absolutely. She's probably getting paid for it, too. It would explain how she could afford to buy some of the things she does. Steuben glass. All those Ann Taylor dresses. Unless she's running up her credit cards again. Which she probably is."

Gregor cocked his head. "Doesn't any of this bother you? You must know she doesn't have your best interests at heart. Why do you put up with her?"

Liz opened the refrigerator door and got out a large glass tray. When she put it down on the table, Gregor saw that it was piled with sandwiches, some ham and cheese, some turkey and Swiss, some tuna fish. The kettle went off on the stove and she took it and poured water into the cup she'd left at her place.

"I've tried to explain it to Jimmy," she said as she put the kettle back and sat down, "and I've tried to explain it to Mark, and I think maybe it's a girl thing. Or maybe it's just that I ran into Maris for the first time in years just after Jay had died."

"Jay was your husband?"

"Exactly. Anyway, I don't know if I can explain it. It's just that, I can remember her, Maris, our first day of school, ever. Kindergarten, Center School, 1956. I remember sitting at this table in the middle of all these other children I didn't know, and Maris walked through the door with her mother and she was—perfect. I don't think I'd had a definition of perfect before then. She was so perfect I wanted to cry, and the more I watched her, the more perfect she got. She was beautiful and smart and—golden. If that makes any sense."

"It makes sense that you felt that way. It makes sense that there are children like that. I don't see how it explains the present situation."

"Yes, well." The sandwiches on the tray were cut into triangular quarters. Liz picked up a triangle of tuna fish on whole wheat and looked it over. "She was like that all through school. Oh, there were other girls who were prettier, really. Belinda Hart was phenomenal when she was young, all huge china-blue eyes and blond hair. But Maris, you see, Maris was smart as well as pretty. Very smart. She could do anything. She was salutatorian of our class. She was president of half a dozen clubs, and not just social nonsense, either. She was a championship debater."

"But you must have been a good student, too," Gregor pointed out.

Liz shook her head. "Not really. For one thing, I was too recalcitrant and contrary. One year they gave us an assignment to write an essay to submit to the Veterans of Foreign Wars for their Memorial Day essay contest. The winner got to read his essay in front of the whole town at the end of the Memorial Day parade. I wrote an essay about how evil war was and how we should never allow the government to draft anybody. If it had been a couple of years later, I might have gotten away with it, but it was 1965."

"Oh, dear."

"Yes, exactly. Anyway, I was always getting myself into that kind of trouble, so my grades were up and down. And my class rank was mediocre. I squeaked into the National Honor Society at the very bottom of the list."

"But Vassar took you," Gregor said.

Liz smiled. "I aced my boards—perfect scores on both aptitude tests and all three achievements. And I got a National Merit scholarship. I actually made the Philadelphia papers for it. So Vassar took me. They were, by the way, the only one. I got turned down at everything from Yale to Tufts. If Vassar hadn't come through, I'd be waiting tables at JayMar's right this minute."

"Somehow, I doubt it."

"I don't," Liz said. "The thing is, I've always been like that. My record at Vassar wasn't all that good, either. I got into graduate school on the strength of my Graduate Record Exam and some recommendations. I wasn't ever like Maris. I didn't shine, you know. I wasn't brilliant. I didn't—earn any of it."

"What?"

"I didn't earn any of it," Liz said. "If you're going to tell me I'm crazy, don't bother. Jimmy's already done it and so has Mark. But it's true. Everything that happened, you know, CNN and Columbia and the doctorate, I didn't earn any of it. They just sort of happened. I can think of a dozen people who are better than I was at all these things who just didn't make it, and there's no sensible reason for why. It's all chance and circumstance and sheer dumb luck. Like Jay getting some weird cancer that nobody had ever heard of and dying at forty-four. Like Maris, really. Chance and circumstance."

"You know," Gregor said slowly, "that's a very dangerous attitude for somebody in your position to have."

"Is it?"

"I'd say so, yes. You leave yourself open to a lot of nastiness that way, and you aren't in a position to protect yourself."

"I don't see that I have anybody to protect myself from."

"Don't you?'

Liz waved a hand in the air. "Oh, Maris. All right. Maris. But none of you understand. She really doesn't mean any harm by it. She's just upset, and depressed, and ashamed, I suppose, and so she lashes out at me because I'm convenient. I don't understand why it is that people can't see that she's in so much pain. It's like watching a child who's been run over by a truck and is taking a very long time to die. That's an image, isn't it?"

"I think it's a faulty analogy. From what I saw, Maris Coleman isn't a child, and she hasn't been run over by a truck. She's a middle-aged alcoholic with a mean streak."

"I know. But she's still a child who's been run over by a truck, and if the world were a just and honorable place, she'd be the one in this position and I'd be the one in hers. I don't know why things don't work out the way they're supposed to. I just know they don't."

"And if things had worked out the way they were supposed to," Gregor said, "what would have happened to you?"

"I'd still be an editorial assistant at Simon and Schuster." Liz laughed. "Except I wouldn't be. I was a terrible editorial assistant. I was disorganized. I was stubborn. I was a mess. Listen, I think that's Jimmy getting out of the shower. I'm going to go check on him. Get yourself whatever you want. Finish the sandwiches. Rummage through the refrigerator. You must be starving."

"I'm all right," Gregor said.

Liz stood up. "And don't worry about Maris," she told him. "Maris is not somebody you have to worry about. She's helpless, really. And harmless, in spite of all that nonsense with the tabloids. I'm just trying to make sure she doesn't disintegrate completely."

Gregor thought about saying that it wasn't Maris Coleman's disintegration he was worried about, but he didn't. A moment later, Liz Toliver was gone, her footsteps almost inaudible on the back hall carpet. Gregor picked up a triangle of ham and Swiss on rye and wished, for the hundredth time since he'd arrived in Hollman, that he had Bennis with him to hold his hand. In some ways, he was even beginning to wish he'd never left Cavanaugh Street. He looked at the ham and Swiss and thought about Chris Inglerod's body lying out on the lawn with the intestines strung out on the grass like ribbons. He put the sandwich back on the tray and stood up.

He would go down to his room and get ready for bed, and then he would call Bennis again to see if she would talk to him until he could go to sleep.

TWO

1

The news got through, even though it wasn't supposed to. Coming downstairs to open the shop, Emma couldn't even remember who'd told her, although there had been enough phoning back and forth during the night, and enough getting up one last time to turn the television on and see if there was just a little more news. Emma had even called the girls, late, to make sure they were all right. It made her cold to think of what went on in the world. She was sure it had not been that way when she was growing up, not even if you took into account what had happened to Michael Houseman. At least Michael hadn't been left with his guts spilling out onto the ground in broad daylight—and it had to be broad daylight, Emma thought, because the man on the news said the body had been found at just about six, and it was still light at six. The details had been dancing through her head all night. She had lain awake next to George for at least two hours, thinking odd things that there was no point to: that she should have gone to the junior-senior semiformal that first year with somebody besides Carl Pittman; that she should have let Tiffany get a second piercing in her ears when she'd first wanted it, when she was fifteen; that Chris had become snobbish and annoying in the years since high school. The images would not go away, no matter how hard she tried to make them. Chris in the Volvo out by the farmer's market stand on Hawleyville Road. Chris in polo shirt and golf skirt buying a paper at the register in JayMar's. Chris checking her eighteen-karat-gold bought-from-the-Tiffany-catalogue watch for the fifteenth time, as much to make sure everybody saw what she was wearing as to check the time.

Somewhere around three, Emma hadn't been able to stand it anymore. She'd gotten out of bed and gone into the living room at the front of the apartment. There wasn't a bar or restaurant open this late anywhere in a hundred miles. Even the Sycamore shut down no later than one on weekends. On weekdays, it closed at eleven.

At five o'clock, Emma took a shower. She had to be very careful to lift and wash under the thick folds of flesh that hung off her torso like garlands on a Christmas tree. If she didn't lift each one and wash under each one, they smelled, the way armpits did, and people in the shop would step back away from her and smile in that odd, strained way that meant they knew something discreditable about her. She got out of the shower without bothering to wrap a towel around herself. The lights were all out in the apartment, except for the one in the bathroom itself. She walked back to her bedroom stark naked and started dressing in clothes she pulled out of a thick oak wardrobe that had belonged to her mother. Her underclothes bit into her flesh and left red welts.

At seven o'clock, restless and with nothing else to do, Emma went down to open the store—well, not to open it, but to get everything ready for the time when she would open it, even if that was a couple of hours away. She set up the cash register and counted the money in the drawer. She spread furniture polish on the counter and wiped it down. She straightened the yarn and muslin dolls on the shelves at the front. She thought about Chris with her guts spilling out across Betsy Toliver's backyard. Years ago, Chris wouldn't have been caught dead in Betsy Toliver's yard, but things changed. It was really disturbing the way things changed.

At seven-twenty, she couldn't stand it anymore. The alarm clock next to the bed upstairs wouldn't go off until eight. George wouldn't be up until then. She couldn't open the store to customers before nine. She checked her wallet and found $6.27. She wondered what it looked like when intestines spilled out of a body. Were they white, the way they looked in the book in biology class? Were they green? In the movies her brother used to watch when she and he were children, guts were always green. Red blood on a green lawn just made her think of Christmas.

She let herself out the front door and locked it behind her. She went down the steep steps to the sidewalk and watched as a garbage truck stopped for a pile of boxes somebody had left out in front of Dan Barr's office. She wondered what Dan would do now that Chris was dead. He was off somewhere, at a convention in Seattle. At least he wouldn't be a suspect.

She went down Grandview Avenue slowly, stopping only once, to look into the window of Emily's Cheese Shop. When she got to JayMar's, she pushed through the glass door and immediately began to shiver. The air-conditioning was turned up full blast. The men at the counter were all people she had known forever. They had copies of the newspapers and cups of coffee. At the very end of one side of the counter, Nancy Quayde was sitting by herself. She had a paper spread out in front of her.

"Hey there," Emma said, sitting down next to her.

Nancy folded her newspaper into quarters. The headline on the page she'd been reading said: *Fatty Food, Stress, Chief Culprits in Heart Disease*. Joyce came down the counter in her white polyester off the rack uniform and said, "Coffee?"

"Yes, thanks," Emma said.

"Oh, God," Joyce said.

Joyce went back on up the counter. Nancy Quayde stared after her, annoyed. "She's been acting like that all morning. Like I'm some kind of a goddamned accident victim. She'll be the same way with you. Was it like this after Michael Houseman died?"

"I don't know," Emma said.

Joyce was back with the coffee. She put the cup and saucer down on the counter in front of Emma and poured. "Isn't it a terrible thing?" she said. "Just terrible. You don't think things like that could happen in a little town."

"It's not like it's the first murder we've ever had in Hollman," Nancy said coldly. "Hollman is not Sunnybrook Farm."

"I don't know where that is," Joyce said. "People have been talking about nothing else since we opened up."

"This is true," Nancy said. "People have been talking about nothing else since I got here, but I haven't been talking with them. I mean, for God's sake. Chris is dead. What's there to talk about?"

"The police are going to have a lot to talk about," Joyce said. "There's going to be an investigation. And state troopers. Kyle Borden can't handle something like this all by himself."

"Kyle Borden has had his head up his ass since kindergarten," Nancy said.

Emma put milk and sugar into her coffee, especially sugar. "I was out there yesterday," she said. "At Betsy's house, I mean. I was out there sort of in the midafternoon. Belinda and I gave the son a ride from the library."

"The son?" Nancy actually looked curious. Joyce looked so eager, she could have been a drug addict in partial withdrawal presented with a packet of unadulterated heroin.

Emma took a long sip of her coffee. "Yes, well. He's only fourteen. The son, I mean. Mark. And he was at the library, and he wanted to go home, but Betsy hadn't come for him yet. So we gave him a ride."

"There are two sons, not just one," Joyce said. "There's one that's fourteen and one that's seven."

"This was the one that's fourteen," Emma said. "Really, he looked sixteen. I was really surprised when I found out he couldn't drive. And he's immensely tall. Betsy isn't. He must take after his father."

"God," Joyce said. "Did you see anything? Was Mrs. Barr there? Did you meet Jimmy Card? I'd absolutely die if I met Jimmy Card."

"I didn't see anybody," Emma said. "There wasn't anybody home, not even old Mrs. Toliver, as far as I know. He said they were bringing his grandmother in to see the doctor."

"It's all over town that he's here," Joyce said. "He went into Mullaney's yesterday and bought a paper and a package of Mentos. Five or six people saw him."

"I forgot to mention," Nancy said. "When they're not talking about poor Chris being cut up like a salami, they're talking about Jimmy Card."

"I'll just go put this coffee away," Joyce said.

Emma's coffee was already cold, but that was probably because she kept putting milk in it. If she were completely honest with herself, she'd have to say she didn't like coffee at all. She only liked having something in her hand and something to sip when she was sitting and talking with people like Nancy, who made her nervous.

"So," Nancy said. "What's he like? Not Jimmy Card. The son."

"Mark," Emma said. Then she shrugged. "He's nice, I guess. Good-looking. And tall, like I said. Very preppy, except, you know, not preppy like around here. Preppy like in those pictures of the Kennedys. Ivy League preppy."

"He probably actually goes to a prep school."

"Not yet. Next year. That's what he said, anyway. Right now he's in some private school near where he lives. Oh, and he reads strange stuff. Like Betsy used to. That's one thing he got from her."

"What's strange stuff?"

Emma concentrated. "The story about the bug. By the German guy. I forget his name, but we had to read it in senior year lit class and it was gross. And *The Color Purple*. I remember that because of the movie. Oprah was in it."

"Right," Nancy said again.

"There's no point in getting snippy," Emma said. "I never did see the point in books. You can get anything interesting on television or go to the movies for it. Do you remember all that stuff Betsy used to read when we were in school? Aristotle. And what's his name, the French guy—"

"Jean-Paul Sartre."

"That one. What good did it do her?"

Nancy looked astonished. "She's about thirty seconds from marrying Jimmy Card, for God's sake. She's on television."

"She's still odd," Emma said. "You can tell, even when she's on television. What's the point of being on television if you're so odd nobody can stand you?"

"Oh, Christ," Nancy said. "You're incredible. Has this situation even penetrated your head yet? Chris is dead."

"I know."

"Chris's husband was out of town. Way out of town. Which means that unless you think he hired a hit man, he's not a suspect. Which means that everybody else in town is. Including all of us."

"I don't see why," Emma said. "It's more likely that he did it. The son. He was there. He must have seen Chris come in."

"Betsy's son Mark killed Chris Inglerod Barr."

"Why not?"

"What for?"

Emma fluttered her hands in the air. "He's odd, I told you. Just like she was. And you know what they do when they're odd these days. Columbine. And that place in California. They kill people. So, you know, maybe he saw Chris come in and there he was with a, well, whatever you need to cut somebody's guts out, and—"

"Jesus," Nancy said.

"You don't have to go all superior on me," Emma said. "He really could have killed her. Or Betsy could have. It's more likely to be one of them than one of us."

"It's more likely to be one of them than one of us because they read Kafka? You're delusional."

Emma drained the last of her coffee. It was stone-cold by now, and almost entirely milk. "It's more likely to be one of them than one of us," she repeated stubbornly. "There's nothing wrong with any of us. We're all normal as the day is long. They're the ones who are odd."

She got her wallet out of her pocketbook and three quarters out of her change purse. She put the money down under the bill and got off her stool. Her ass hurt.

"You ought to make more sense than you do," she told Nancy. "You're the one who's supposed to be the principal."

She went back down the length of JayMar's to the front door and out again onto Grandview Avenue. This was all she ever did: went in and out of buildings, went up and down Grandview. For a split second, the vision was appalling. In the end, it was comforting. It was *normal.* Nothing could be more normal than Grandview at breakfast time with the lights glowing in the deep long recesses of Mullaney's, and the little red signal light blinking at the end of the platform at the train station, and the dresses on mannequins in the window at Elsa-Edna's. This was what people did with their lives. They graduated from high school and got jobs and had families and lived in towns where they knew most everybody and everybody knew them. They gained weight as they got older and took snapshots of their grandchildren to show their women friends when they met them once a month or so for lunch. That was *normalnormalnormal*, and normal people did not take knives to their childhood friends and spew their intestines all over somebody else's backyard.

2

For at least an hour after the news had come on television the night before, things had been all right. They hadn't been great—things were never great when Stu was drinking—but they had been all right, and Peggy had sat by herself on one of the small red chairs at the kitchen table and wondered if he just hadn't heard the news at all. It was one of those nights when everything was very clear to her, not only her marriage, but her house, too, and her face, and her life, as if she were looking at all of them through a magnifying mirror. The west wall in the kitchen was cracked. It had been cracked for at least a year or two. The vinyl on the floor in the entryway was peeling. When she came in after teaching, she tried to come in the back way so that she wouldn't have to see it. In the early days of their marriage, Stu had been good at fixing things. He had a whole wall full of tools in the garage to prove it. Of course, in those days he had also held a job for more than a couple of weeks at a time. He'd come home on Friday nights with two big steaks he'd bought at the Grill Center and a bottle of champagne, and she'd think he was wonderful, so optimistic, so exuberant, so happy with life. Sometimes now she thought about those steaks and wondered what they had cost. The Grill Center was the place where the people who lived out by the golf course went. Peggy had been in there once and seen swordfish selling for fourteen dollars a pound. It was probably a sign of manic depression that Stu bought the steaks there, or a sign of alcoholism, and she knew now that she should have worried once it became clear that he would hit the Grill Center every single Friday night. The problem was that she had wanted steaks from the Grill Center, too, and good china bought in Pittsburgh or Philadelphia, and a house with three bedrooms and a family room with a fireplace where children could hang stockings. That was the kind of thing you aspired to when you grew up in Hollman. Peggy remembered sitting for hours with Emma and Belinda and Maris and Chris, pouring over her mother's old *House Beautiful* magazines and talking about what they would do, what they would have, how they would live once they were married. It was frightening to think of Chris there with them, her legs folded up underneath her, her hair pulled back from her face with clips. Was there some connection between the fact that Chris was the only one of them who had managed to achieve a *House Beautiful* life, and the fact that she was dead? Peggy kept feeling that there had to be some connections somewhere. There had to be reasons for why things happened. She just couldn't think of what they were. It was nearly midnight. The news about Chris had been on at eleven o'clock. Peggy wanted to fall asleep right where she was, sitting up.

It was the crying that started the trouble. Back in the kitchen now, with her dress torn and her eye so painful she knew it had to be black, she had to admit it to herself. It was the crying that started the trouble, and she was to blame for the crying, because it really made no sense for her to cry. Stu was always so rational about everything. Even when he was drunk and crazy, he was rational. He saw situations plain. She was the one who got things confused and made everything wrong and then did the worst possible thing. She was the one who somehow made it impossible for him to *function*. She was a ball-busting bitch—she was—she was—what? *One of those feminists*, Stu said when he really got going. Maybe she was. Maybe she was *one of those feminists*, like Betsy, and she was dangerous to people, she was dangerous to Stu, if she ever had had a child she would have ruined it. *Christine Inglerod Barr was found dead at the home of* . . . Nobody ever called Chris Inglerod "Christine."

She had put her head in her hands and started crying without realizing it. She had been thinking about Chris being dead and the fact that none of the others had called her. Then she'd thought about the phone ringing and realized she didn't want that either. Stu hated to hear the phone ringing. She didn't know what she wanted. It seemed to her that everything she had ever wanted had been wrong.

The punch, when it came, had been a surprise. She hadn't heard Stu come into the kitchen. It hit her in her left eye and knocked her backward in her chair. The chair jumped on the floor and then tilted over backward. Peggy had found herself suspended in midair. The thought that ran through her mind was: *Don't break anything I can't break anything I can't go to the hospital tonight.* It came and went without her conscious mind registering most of the words, and then she hit the floor, hard, with her back against the turned wooden spindles of the chair and the back of her head on the hard linoleum. She was breathless. It reminded her of falling off the side of the slide in Baldren Park when she was a child. You landed on your back and for a moment or two you couldn't breathe, and up above you the sky was bluer than it would ever be again. All that was up above her now was the light fixture. It had started out to be a modest chandelier, but three of the bulbs were out and one of the chandelier cups was broken. She could buy bulbs at the grocery store, if she remembered to bring one with her so that she could check the size. She could take the chandelier cups to the glass place in Johnstown and find out what it would cost to replace them. She might be able to get away with buying them someday when Stu was out of the house, and installing them someday when he was passed out drunk.

She felt the kick in her side as if she'd been hit by a car. Stu was wearing his shit-kicker boots, the heavy ones with cleats that he used in the winter when the driveway got bad. Peggy grabbed at her side and twisted away. The trick was not to cry and not to cry out. He kicked her again, higher, in her rib cage near her breast. She wrapped her arms around her chest and tried to roll away from him. She was stopped by the chair. She was still sitting in the chair, with her legs hanging off the seat, only she was on her back. Over her head, the chandelier swung and shuddered. The whole house was shaking. She had been crying before he ever walked in, and now she couldn't stop. He shot a kick to her pelvis and she cried out. Her voice in the room was oddly animal, too low, too anguished, too everything.

"Fucking *shit*," he said.

And then the boot hit her pelvis again and she did roll. She got off the chair somehow and rolled and rolled until she hit the wall, the cabinets near the sink, somewhere. He was picking his boots up and grinding his feet right down on top of her. The cleats were tearing at her dress and the skin underneath it. She was wet with sweat and blood. She knew that all she had to do was to stay calm, stay calm, not cry out, not get hysterical. It was all her fault when he got crazy because she made him that way. She brought it on with her hysterics and her attempts to manipulate him. She brought it on when she cried.

She had somehow managed to roll in the wrong direction. When his boot came down this time it hit her straight in the gut. It knocked the wind out of her. When she got it back she screamed, and as she did she felt her sphincter releasing, and her bladder, too, everything, she was making a mess of herself and the floor and everything, everything, she was crying and she couldn't stop and he was kicking her so hard she thought she was going to die. She rolled herself up in a ball and turned the right way this time, pressed up against the place where the cabinets met the floor, and from then until she passed out she only cried silently, so that she couldn't even hear herself.

Now it was half past eight in the morning, and except for the black eye—she knew she had a black eye, even though she hadn't looked in the mirror. She never looked in the mirror anymore if she could help it—the house was cleaned up. The kitchen looked normal. The only thing that might have seemed odd was the smell of soap and disinfectant, but kitchens always smelled like that when you cleaned them, and it was better to smell soap and disinfectant than to smell what had been in here before. She was, really, very calm, but she thought she had at least one broken rib, and there was the black eye. If she didn't go in to teach, she would be here in the house with Stu all day. There was always the chance that it would happen again. If she did go in, there would be the black eye, and the fact that she'd had to take a taxi because she hadn't been waiting at the door when Nancy drove into the driveway, and the fact that she was having trouble walking and having trouble breathing, and all the other things. Nancy would be furious. Worse than that, she would tell the rest of them.

Christine Inglerod Barr was found dead at the home of a friend in the Mars Road section of Hollman this evening . . .

She picked up the phone and called the school. She asked for Nancy, and waited. She was not going to stay in this house all day, no matter how much it hurt to walk. She wasn't going to wait in the kitchen with her hands folded until Stu woke up and figured out she had never gone in to work, because that would start him off again. It always did. He was scared to death that she'd lose her job.

"Yes," Nancy said.

"It's Peggy. I'm sorry to call so late. I'm—not feeling very well today. It might be a good idea if you got a substitute."

"It's eight-thirty."

"Yes, I know. I seem to have slept through the alarm. If you'd knocked on the door, I might have heard you, but you must have realized when I wasn't outside and waiting—"

"Realized what? That Prince Charming had been beating you into a pulp again?"

"I'm just sick, Nancy. That's all. I'm just sick. I'm nauseated and I've got a headache. And I'm a little . . . confused . . . about this thing with Chris."

"What's there to be confused about? Somebody took a knife or a razor or something and eviscerated her. Her guts were all over Betsy Toliver's lawn."

Peggy blanched. "Oh," she said.

"Half the town has been on the phone to me, telling me they just know it was one of us," Nancy said.

"Yes," Peggy said, feeling a little desperate now. The students in her homeroom had to be already in their places with nobody to watch over them, and she knew what that meant. "There's homeroom," she said carefully. "Somebody should go down to my homeroom and make sure—"

"Oh, Christ," Nancy said. "All right. I'll send Lisa. She can read announcements as well as the next person. You don't need a teaching certificate for that. I can't believe you did this to me. I really can't. If you have to call in, for Christ's sake, do it at seven, will you please?"

"Yes," Peggy said, yet again. It seemed to be the only word she knew. "Yes, Nancy, I understand that. I slept through the alarm. I didn't do it intentionally."

"You stay with Prince Charming intentionally."

"I'm going to hang up now and lie down," Peggy said.

Nancy hung up instead, and Peggy found herself listening to a dial tone buzzing in her ear. She got up and put the receiver back in its cradle on the wall. Then she sat down again and put her face down on the palms of her hands. She rubbed her eyes with the heels of her palms. She counted to ten. She thought that when she began to feel a little less as if every bone in her torso was broken, she would take a walk to Grandview Avenue and have a coffee and English muffin in JayMar's and just sit there for a while, just *sit*, without thinking about anything, not even about the six of them, that night, gathered around Michael Houseman's body in the rain.

THREE

1

Gregor Demarkian fell asleep in his clothes, and when he woke up—too late, with the sun too high in the sky and the air too warm around him—he saw that he'd mashed his suit jacket into a ball of wrinkles. He checked his watch. It was only eight-thirty, which meant Kyle Borden wouldn't be in the office yet. Gregor was supposed to meet him there at ten. He shook his legs out and eased his shoes off his feet. He took off his suit jacket and dropped it on the floor. He took off his tie. He picked up the phone and heard dead air. Either the service was out, or somebody had cut the phone lines—but that wasn't a very good thought, under the circumstances. It was one thing to watch a butcher work when he was a serial killer who cared not at all about the people he slaughtered. Serial killers were about butchery. They were always looking to take one more step into the surreality of gore. It was another thing to see something like that at least ostensibly committed by a sane person—although, Gregor admitted, he'd always thought that the vast majority of murderers were peculiarly sane. It didn't take madness to kill, although people who were mad sometimes did. It took determination, and a commitment to logic so pure that nothing else was ever allowed to get in its way. What kind of logic would have been required, to rip the guts out of a woman on a bright spring day in the unimpressive setting of a small-town backyard? He tried the phone one last time, because the thing he needed most of all in the world was to talk to Bennis, but the phone was still dead.

I need to take a shower, Gregor told himself. His clothes hung on him the way clothes do when they have been wet with sweat and dried without being washed. The fabric of his shirt was scratchy against his skin. He unbuttoned his shirt cuffs and rolled them back. He unbuttoned his top shirt button and set his neck free. Bennis was right. He was captive to an aesthetic that most people had abandoned decades ago.

He pulled off his socks. He got his second-best robe off the back of the chair near the little window and threw it over his shoulder. He could find the clean clothes he needed when he got back from the shower. It was easier to proceed in a murder case where the murderer was intent on doing odd or outlandish things. It was the ordinary cases, the ones where somebody just shot a gun into somebody else in the middle of a room, that were the hard ones. In another way, though, oddnesses were a headache, because they meant providing the prosecutor with a plausible explanation. Juries were remarkably consistent in finding the odd and outlandish cause for "reasonable doubt" in any case against a white, middle-class defendant. A lot of juries also found it hard to find any doubt at all against a poor black defendant even when he had provably been in another state at the time of the crime. Gregor was eternally grateful that he did not have to worry about that kind of thing on a daily basis anymore. Twenty years in the FBI was enough professional law enforcement for anybody.

Gregor thought about looking out his window and decided against it. He opened the door to his room and went into the little hall. He was halfway to the bathroom—not very far, only a few steps—when he realized there was something going on.

"I heard the door open," he heard Mark say. "I'm not going to wake him up. He already is up."

"Mark?" Gregor said.

Mark appeared in the hall, looking huge, and worried, and even more adult than usual. "Hi. Good morning. I've got to nail your window shut."

"What?"

"He's got to nail your window shut." Liz Toliver appeared in the hall. "It would be even better if we could nail a plank over it, but we don't have any planks in the house, and we can't go out in the driveway. I apologize, Mr. Demarkian. When you said that thing about securing the house, I thought you were crazy."

"I kept telling her," Mark said.

"One of them tried to climb through the bathroom window at the other side of the house. Scared my mother on the toilet. She's had to be sedated."

"I'll be done before you finish with your shower," Mark said, looking at the robe over Gregor's shoulder.

Gregor walked down to the end of the hall instead. Jimmy Card was standing alone in the living room, looking at the flat darkness where the draperies covered the picture window that looked out onto the front lawn and the road. His cell phone lay open on the coffee table in front of the long leather couch. His T-shirt looked as if he had been balling it up in his hands, over and over again, for hours.

"Oh, good," he said when Gregor came in. "I'm glad you're up. We're hoping you can help us out of this."

"Help you out of what? I take it there's press outside?"

Jimmy Card smiled thinly. "The last time I saw press like this, Julie and

I were getting a divorce and Julie had just made the tabloids with pictures of herself sunbathing nude in the south of France. And she wasn't alone. Take a look, if you want. Just be careful how you do it."

Gregor went over to the window and pressed himself against one wall to the side of it. He flicked back the draperies just a little and looked out at what was on the front lawn—and not only on the front lawn, but on the porch of the house itself, everywhere, in the road. There were hundreds of people, all of them with cameras, and beyond them cars, half-abandoned in the road gutters and on other people's lawns. Gregor let the draperies drop.

"My God," he said.

"It's because Jimmy's famous," a little voice piped up. Gregor looked around to find Liz's younger son, Geoff, settled in an enormous armchair with a Game Boy.

"I should have expected it," Jimmy said. "It's not like I don't know the routine. Instead, I didn't even notice until about half an hour ago, and by then it was too late. Everything was nuts."

"Have you called the police?"

"The phone lines are dead," Mark said, coming back from nailing Gregor's window shut. "We think they must have cut the phone lines. And the cell phones don't work."

"The idea is to force us to come out," Jimmy said. "If we can't call out, we're going to have to come out eventually. And they know it."

"We're going to have to come out sooner rather than later," Liz said, "because my mother needs to be taken care of. She's not well in the best of circumstances, and that thing with the window really tore it. She was completely hysterical. She needs to be hospitalized at the least, and if it wasn't for the fact that Chris was found dead in my own backyard, I think I'd pack her up and take her back to Connecticut. I suppose it wouldn't look very good if I tried to duck out of a murder investigation and go back home."

"We'll have her hospitalized," Jimmy said. "That will get her out of the glare for as long as we have to live with it. The trick is to figure out how to get her and us out of here with a minimum of trouble. You drive a car, don't you, Mr. Demarkian?"

Gregor hesitated. "Well," he said, "I have a driver's license."

"You don't drive a car?" Liz Toliver looked appalled.

"I can drive a car," Mark said. "Just let me go and—"

"That's just what we need," Liz said. "Pictures in every paper in the country of Liz Toliver giving her fourteen-year-old son the keys to her car."

"It's been a while since I've driven," Gregor said finally, "but I can surely drive a car far enough to get to a phone. There must be someplace reasonably near here—"

"Go out of the driveway and turn right," Liz said. "It's about half a mile. Some kind of gas station or body shop—"

"They'll follow him," Mark said.

"I wish they would," Jimmy Card said. "I wish they all would. That would be the best possible solution. Unfortunately, they won't follow him. Once they realize who he is, they won't bother him at all."

"Give me a couple of minutes," Gregor said. "I need to throw myself in for a quick shower and get on some clean clothes."

He turned around and went back the way he had come. Now that he knew what to pay attention to, he could hear clear evidence that they were being besieged. The low hissing noise he had noticed and dismissed as wind when he was still lying in bed was talking, frantic overwrought talking, dozens of people who hadn't slept much recently all going on to each other in high gear. Gregor locked himself in the bathroom and dropped the rest of his dirty clothes on the floor as he took them off. The window here had already been nailed shut, and it wasn't much of a window, just a small square high up in the wall. He turned on the water as hard and as hot as he could stand it and stepped under it. He applied soap and shampoo to himself the way bricklayers apply mortar to a wall. He was in and out before he felt as if he had been in at all. He wrapped the robe around himself and went down to his room. He flipped through the things in his suitcase until he found clean socks and underwear. Clothes fell on the floor. If Bennis had been here, she would have picked them up. He wasn't going to take the time.

When he was mostly dressed—complete with tie, although not with suit jacket—he went to the window Mark had just nailed shut and looked through it, standing sideways against the wall again, so that nobody would realize he was there. From this angle, the problem was not so awful. What looked, from the living-room window, like an endless stretch of cars and people, actually ended only about fifteen feet up the road in one direction and maybe six feet up the road in the other. It was the sea of faces looking straight at you that caused the illusion. You looked at them instead of at the landscape. Gregor got on his shoes and took a fresh jacket from his suit bag. Then he went back out into the little hall and down it to the living room.

"Well?" Jimmy Card said.

"I'm ready," Gregor told him.

"I've got everything written down," Liz Toliver said, handing him a three-by-five card with the neatest, smallest printing on it that he had ever seen. "The most important thing right now is to get in touch with my mother's doctors. We need an ambulance and maybe a hospital. Tell them what happened and what's going on here. They'll know what to do."

"You really think an ambulance is the way to go?" Gregor asked. "That's likely to increase the fuss rather than calm it—"

"An ambulance can be backed up almost to the door," Jimmy Card said. "It's the only way we're going to get Liz's mother or the nurse out of here without getting them mauled. If we can get the ambulance and my driver here at the same time, we might be able to create a diversion that will allow us to leave without—"

"I don't think so," Liz Toliver said. "Neither do you, really. We've got dark glasses. If we can get your driver here and a few police officers—did I tell you you should call the police, Mr. Demarkian?"

"I was intending to call the police," Gregor said.

"Yes, of course you were, good," Liz Toliver said. "I'm sorry. I don't handle this kind of thing well yet. I'm not this kind of famous. Here, take my keys. You can take the Mercedes—"

"Do you really think it makes sense to trust me with a hundred-fifty-thousand-dollar car?" Gregor asked gently. "I'm sure I can make it far enough up the road to get to a pay phone, but I haven't been behind a wheel in eight years."

"The Mercedes is in the driveway, parked facing out to the street," Jimmy Card said. "And it's automatic transmission. You don't have to do anything but turn on the engine, step on the gas, and go forward until you hit the road. Then you turn right and go forward until you find the whatever it is—"

"Andy's Body Shop and Garage," Mark said, sounding thoroughly exasperated.

"The thing is," Jimmy said, "we're trying to make it easy for you. If you bang up the car a little, it can be fixed. But at least you'll get where you're going."

"Right," Gregor said. He took the keys Liz Toliver held out to him. Then he went out of the living room, into the kitchen. "Why don't you all go back to the living room," he said when he realized that the rest of them had followed him, even Geoff, who had that bright, bright look on his face that children get when the grown-ups are doing something very, very fascinating. "There's no point in letting them catch you at the door."

"Somebody has to lock up after you," Mark said.

"I'll do it," Jimmy said.

"Stuff it," Mark said. "You're the prize turkey in this turkey shoot. Mr. Demarkian?"

"Ready," Gregor said.

Mark DeAvecca undid the bolts and locks on the kitchen door and pulled it out so that Gregor could pass.

As soon as he did, there seemed to be a thousand people rushing the building at once.

2

It was both worse and better than he had expected it to be. It was worse, because the crowd was far more aggressive than he had counted on. He *had* seen crowds like this before. He'd been in the entourage of presidents—in an official capacity—and he'd had a number of clients with "high name recognition." He'd never been near anything this wild. What he couldn't put out of his mind was the one time he had allowed Bennis to take him to a rock and roll concert, to see the Red Hot Chili Peppers perform in Philadelphia. It had been an eerie evening, full of an energy and anger he had never been able to trust. This was like that, except that there was no overlay of good feeling and anticipation. People were just revved up and angry as hell, and as he made his way to the car they pushed against him and pulled at his clothes. It was like swimming in mayonnaise. Gregor found himself forgetting what it was he was supposed to be trying to do and just plowing along.

Gregor had just started in on the kind of mental nattering that drove Bennis crazy—what did it mean, for instance, that a former rock and roll star got more press and more exposure than any public policy initiative floated by the United States Congress?—when he reached the door of the car. The day was overcast and just a little chilly. The clouds overhead were black and heavy. Now a wind kicked up and it began to rain, softly but steadily, in large scattered droplets. Gregor made his way around the car by holding on to metal all the way, so that when photographers pushed cameras into his face and set off their flashes, it didn't matter if he was blinded. He got to the driver's side door and took out his keys. For the last five years, he'd been nagging Bennis and everybody else on Cavanaugh Street to lock their cars and lock their doors. Now he wished Liz Toliver hadn't been so conscientious. There was more than one key on the ring she had given him. There were dozens. He was scared to death he was going to drop the ring on the ground and spend the next half hour trying to figure out which key went into the car door lock.

He got the car open. He got behind the wheel. He got the door closed after him. There was a photographer lying across the hood in front of him, pointing a camera at him through the windshield. The photographers seemed to be taking pictures of anybody and anything. Gregor got the key in the ignition and let the motor roar. He looked down at the instruments and saw, with some relief, that they weren't too confusing. "D" would be "drive," and "P" would be "park," which is what the indicator pointed to now. He stepped hard on the brake and got the automatic gear thing shifted to "D." He lifted his foot a little and the car began to roll. The photographer hopped off the hood. Half a dozen people scattered away from his front end. He was afraid to step on the gas. He might roll over one of the reporters. It was a relief to see that they pulled away from him as he came along the drive.

The good news was that it was much easier to handle the car than he had expected it to be. Getting out of the driveway was no problem. Except for one small correction with the steering wheel, all he had to do was roll forward. He got to the road and put on the brakes again. He turned the steering wheel before he started to move, and then, as he did start to move, he had to let up on it a little. He knew he couldn't just bump along the road at a roll, the way he had along the driveway, so he put his foot on the gas a little and waited to see what would happen. He picked up speed. None of the reporters or photographers was getting into a car to follow him. He wondered why not.

The road itself was nowhere near as clogged as it looked from the house. What seemed to be a sea of cars was broken in the middle by a thin ribbon of unobstructed road. Gregor was not comfortable navigating this ribbon, because he was sure he was going to sideswipe one of the parked cars, and that would mean a moral dilemma. He couldn't very well get out and leave a note on the windshield with his name and address on it, but it wouldn't feel right to just let it go.

This must be stress, Gregor thought, and then, just like that, he was past the cars. There was nothing around him but grass and trees and the occasional driveway that went nowhere, since there were no houses in sight. He sped up and decided that that wasn't too bad. He did not feel completely out of control of the car just because he was doing thirty-five miles an hour. He kept his eyes on the right side of the road, where Andy's was supposed to be. Part of him thought that he shouldn't be able to miss it. There were so few buildings out here, Andy's would surely stand out. Part of him thought that the garage would be hidden the way the houses were. You'd only be able to find it if you knew exactly where it was and exactly what to look for in the way of a driveway into the trees.

As it turned out, Andy's was impossible to miss. It sat right on the road, in a big clearing, entirely surrounded by weather-beaten cars and trucks that looked as if they would never move again. Gregor had no idea if the vehicles were abandoned or in for repairs. He made his way carefully between them. The last thing he needed was to have escaped an accident at the house only to get into one here. There was an open space on the garage's side. There was another open space near a chain-link fence at the back, straight ahead. Gregor took that one.

He got out of the car and looked around, and the first thing he saw was Luis sitting in a plastic chair at the garage's open front door. Luis saw him a split second later, and stood up.

"Mr. Demarkian," he said in a flat Queens accent that had nothing at all Hispanic about it. "Why didn't you call me? Mr. Card said you didn't know how to drive."

In other circumstances, Gregor might have spent some time wondering at the fact that, after all this time, the man was actually able to talk. Under these circumstances, he just walked over to where Luis was standing and wished he'd brought an umbrella.

"I can't," he said. "At least, I haven't driven in years. I didn't kill anybody. There's a little problem out at the house."

He gave Luis a rundown on what was going on with Jimmy Card, Liz Toliver, and all the rest of the people in Stony Hill, and Luis nodded his way through the explanation, unfazed.

"Right," he said. "We should have expected it. You should have seen what it was like when Mr. Card got divorced from Miss Handley. You want I should go out and pick the bunch of them up?"

"I think they want Mr. Card's driver to do that," Gregor said, "and they have to wait for the ambulance anyway. Is there a phone where I could—?"

"It's a nuisance, not being able to use the cell phones."

There was a pay phone just inside the garage's office, hanging open on a wall, with not so much as a little perforated head barrier to make for privacy. Gregor got out the little card Liz Toliver had given him and all the change he could find and started dialing numbers. He dialed the doctor's offices first, and was relieved to find that there was somebody actually on hand. He had no idea what he would have done if he'd gotten the answering service. He explained who he was and what the problem was and got a promise of an ambulance, as soon as possible, at the Toliver house.

"At least in this case, we don't have to worry about the insurance," the young woman on the other end of the line said, and then hung up, apparently not at all curious about reporters, cut phone lines, or rock and roll stars.

Gregor dialed the number of the hotel where Jimmy Card's driver was staying. The phone in the room rang and rang without being picked up. He hung up himself, called the hotel back, and made a point of the fact that this was an emergency. If they didn't believe it, they could turn on any television station. He had no idea if that were true, but he thought—given the insanity at the house—that there was a good chance it would be. In the end, he got Jimmy's driver, fresh out of the shower, and told him what was going on.

"Right," the man said. "Here we go again. Let me tell you, Mr. Demarkian, I've seen enough of it. I never want to be famous."

Gregor declined to talk to him about it—although it would be an interesting speculation, whether the things you got from fame like this were worth what else you got with it—and hung up. Outside the garage's big plate-glass front window, the rain was coming down hard. The sky was full of thunder and lightning. Luis had come inside, as had the three men who had been sitting in plastic chairs near Luis when Gregor first showed up. It was raining the way it did in hurricanes and floods.

"Maybe this will thin out the crowd in front of the house," Gregor said, to Luis as much as to anybody.

"Nah," Luis said. "They put up with anything. Fire. Rain. Flood. Tornadoes. This is what they do. This is what they're famous for. They always get the story."

"Right," Gregor said. He went back to the phone and searched through his change for another couple of quarters. He dialed the police department and waited. A woman's voice answered and didn't sound happy about it.

"This is the police department," she said. "If you're a reporter you can just hang up and talk to yourself, because I'm not going to talk to you."

Gregor explained who he was. He knew that voice. It belonged to the woman he had met in the department the first time he'd met Kyle Borden.

"Oh," she said. "All right. What do you want?"

"Kyle Borden," Gregor said.

"He isn't in yet. I did call him. And I called Ben Shedman, too, he should be here. Nobody's here except me."

"Is Kyle Borden coming in?" Gregor asked.

"As soon as he can get here," Sharon Morobito said.

The rain outside was coming down in sheets. The thunder sounded like mortar fire. The lightning streaked and rattled, lighting up the sky more often than leaving it dark. If those reporters didn't get off the Toliver lawn, one of them was going to get electrocuted.

"When Kyle comes in, tell him I'll be there as soon as I can," Gregor said. "If I were you, I wouldn't let any of them into the station house if you can help it."

"Well, I can't help it, can I? It's a public building. The doors opened to the public half an hour ago."

"I'll be in as soon as I can," Gregor said. Then he hung up. Now *there* was a thought: dozens of reporters from every single one of the national magazines and important newspapers, crowding the waiting area at the Hollman Police Department.

Gregor got out his phone card and called Cavanaugh Street. He tried his own number, and then Bennis's, and then Tibor's. Nobody was home. He wanted to scream.

Instead, he swept the rest of his change into the palm of his hand, put it back in his pocket, and went over to where Luis was once again sitting in a plastic chair, only inside this time instead of out.

"I guess we'd better go out to the house and make sure they all get away the way they're supposed to," he said. "Then I'd appreciate it if you'd drive me into the police department. They're having a little disturbance over there this morning, too."

"Foreigners," one of the other men in the plastic chairs said solemnly.

Luis got up. Out in the wind and the rain, a siren sounded. A moment later, an ambulance went hurtling by with its lights all flashing and its noise cranked up as far as it would go.

Gregor was relieved. No matter what else did or didn't manage to get done, there would at least be this—unless, of course, the ambulance managed to crash before it got to the house.

3

At first, Gregor thought he would have to go all the way back to the Toliver house to make sure Jimmy and Liz and the boys got away as they needed to, and that the ambulance for Liz's mother actually got hold of Liz's mother.

In the end, he hadn't had to go to that kind of trouble. It was a good thing, because he was as tense as he could ever remember being. It was the lack of logic and of linear thought that got to him. He hated states of unalloyed chaos, where decisions seemed to be made on the basis of hysteria or on no basis at all. He couldn't believe that any of the photographers trying to storm the Toliver home were thinking, logically or otherwise. At least some of them had to realize they were a disaster waiting to happen. He hated sitting in the gas station, listening to the men on the plastic chairs talk about local sports and national politics. He hated the rain, which was not letting up. At half past nine, when Jimmy Card's driver pulled in to the garage's parking lot to tell Gregor he was headed out to the house, the rain was coming down just as hard as it had been when Gregor had first called the police department. It was hard not to think about Noah and the forty days and forty nights. It was hard not to think about floods.

At quarter to ten, Jimmy Card's driver came back by the gas station, blowing his horn in three hard, sharp bursts, to let Gregor know that everything had gone well at the house and there was no need for him to return there to check on the inhabitants. Gregor watched as a dozen cars crowded up so close to the limousine's rear that there would have been a multicar pileup if Jimmy's driver had done as much as stop short at a traffic light. Then he went back to Luis and asked to be taken into town to the police station.

Luis had gone back to being uncommunicative. The town, once they got to it, looked like it had always looked. There were no signs of invasion by hordes of salivating celebrity journalists. Grandview Avenue was empty of people and nearly empty of cars. The one or two parked along the curbs were so wet they reminded Gregor of what it felt like going through a car wash.

The police station, when they got there, did not look inundated with reporters. Luis turned off onto Grand Street and pulled into the driveway and back into the parking lot.

Gregor got out of the car and pulled his suit jacket up over his head. He hunched his shoulders and made a run for the front of the building. The asphalt on the driveway was slick, and the pavement that led around to the front was even slicker. He pounded up the steps and hurtled himself in through the front doors.

The vestibule just inside the doors was empty. It was only when Gregor went through the next set of doors—plate glass; even if it was bulletproof glass, it wouldn't help, because bulletproof glass wasn't really bulletproof—that he saw that Sharon had had some reason for being worked up. The big reception room was full of people, all on the right side of the counter for the moment, but all restless. Some of them were taking up the long waiting benches that lined the wall. The rest of them were pacing around, not doing much of anything.

When Gregor walked in, one or two of them perked up.

"Mr. Demarkian!" the youngest of them called out. "Have you been called in to consult on the Toliver murder case?"

"No," Gregor said, quite truthfully. He hit the bell on the counter.

The men on the benches were restless. Gregor wondered why there were so few women. He rang the bell again and held his breath. Finally, Kyle Borden stuck his head out of one of the rooms at the back and looked relieved.

"It's you," he said, rushing up to the counter to let Gregor through. "I thought you'd never get here."

"Then you *have* been called in to consult on the Toliver case," the young man said, jumping up to follow Gregor through the opening Kyle Borden had made in the counter, and being pushed back just in time.

"No," Gregor said again.

Kyle grabbed him by the arm and dragged him along. "This is insane," he said in a voice so low even Gregor had trouble hearing it. "I've never seen anything like it. Sharon is hiding in the bathroom. That's because I yelled at her."

They were at Kyle's office door. He pushed Gregor through it, came through himself, and shut the door behind them. Gregor immediately began to feel claustrophobic.

"What happened to your man out at the Toliver house?" Gregor asked. "I just came from there, and I didn't see a policeman anywhere."

"There wasn't one," Kyle said. "We don't have a whole department. That was a part-time deputy I left there yesterday evening and he had to go home at midnight. I didn't have anybody to assign until this morning, and it isn't usually a problem, and oh, for Christ's sake, this is such a mess."

"I think you can safely assume that your crime scene is now thoroughly contaminated," Gregor said. "I'd say it was now thoroughly destroyed. With any luck, you got everything you needed last night. When do you get an autopsy report?"

"They're promising us preliminary findings at noon."

"All right. There isn't going to be a whole lot you can do until then, except maybe trace this woman's movements during the day. And keep your mouth shut. I wonder if any of them will figure it out."

"Figure what out?"

"I may be wrong," Gregor said, "but from what I remember of our discussions yesterday, the woman who died is the same woman who gave Michael Houseman his ride to work on the last day of his life, and would have given him a ride home that same day if he'd been in any shape to come home."

Kyle Borden had been pacing around the office. Now he stopped still. "I hadn't thought of that."

"It was the first thing I thought of. The question is, will *they* think of it?"

"How could they?"

Gregor shrugged. "I've got to assume that at least some of them have been through whatever newspaper archives exist on the Houseman murder. Granted, those will almost assuredly be the men from the supermarket tabloids, but once the information is out and confirmed, they'll all use it. Of course, it's a small detail, or it would have been, in that case. It only becomes important now because Miss Inglerod—Mrs. Barr—is dead. But trust me, in the next day or so, they're going to go back to those archives and go over them half a dozen times, and eventually they *will* pick up on it. Even if that particular detail isn't in any of the newspaper reports, the fact that Miss Inglerod was in that park that night almost certainly will be."

"Crap," Kyle said. "Yeah, that'll be there, I remember it. It went around town for weeks, who had been out at the park that night and who hadn't. And who, you know, was involved in nailing Betsy into the damned outhouse."

Gregor pulled out a chair and sat down. "So," he said. "Do you think it's connected? The murder of Michael Houseman and the murder of Chris Inglerod?"

"How the hell do I know? It doesn't make too much sense, does it?" Kyle said. "Why would anybody bother to kill Chris over something that happened over thirty years ago?"

"There's no statute of limitations on murder," Gregor said. "Somebody may still have good reason to fear being caught."

Kyle Borden snorted. "Crap on that," he said. "How'd we ever convict him? Thirty years will wipe out reasonable doubt faster than Windex will wipe out water spots."

"Not necessarily," Gregor said. "I've seen old cases end in convictions more than once. If you don't think the murders are connected, you're stuck with figuring out why Chris Inglerod was killed now, in that place, and in that way. Do you know of a reason why somebody would murder Chris Inglerod now?"

"She was an insufferable snot," Kyle said. "But a lot of people are that, and we don't off them. Maybe we should."

"Can you think of a reason why Liz Toliver would murder Chris Inglerod now?"

"Betsy Toliver?"

Gregor sighed. "There's a certain amount of logic to the idea Maris Coleman was putting forward yesterday. Michael Houseman was murdered when Liz was living here, and nobody else was murdered until Liz came back. Now that she is back, somebody is dead, and dead on her own mother's lawn. The only problem is, there doesn't seem to be any reason for it, unless you're going to assume that Liz Toliver is secretly a sociopath carrying out some kind of vendetta against all the girls who hated her in high school."

"There's also the fact that Betsy Toliver is the one person in this town who couldn't have murdered Michael Houseman," Kyle said. "This is not a murder mystery. The outhouse isn't going to turn out to have had a back door or a crawl space she could have gone in and out of. She was nailed into that thing and by the time she was found, she'd lost so much blood, she had to be taken to the hospital for a transfusion. She spent the whole rest of that summer bandaged up like a mummy. It's a good thing Vassar didn't start classes until after Labor Day. She'd have missed the first week of school."

"I know," Gregor said.

"So what is it you're getting at?" Kyle said.

Outside, somewhere beyond the door, there was a sudden burst of loud, frantic activity. The bell on the counter rang out sharply. A hundred people seemed to be talking at once.

"Damn," Kyle said.

Gregor moved out of the way. "You've still got a town here. Maybe there's some business today that doesn't have to do with Elizabeth Toliver."

Kyle threw back the door and walked out, just as a woman wrapped in layer after layer of rubber poncho flipped back the counter's hinged opening and stepped through.

"You can't just walk in here," Kyle shouted at her. "Visitors have to stay on the public's side of the counter."

"Jesus," Gregor said as the woman began to flip layers of rubber off her head and shoulders.

"Jesus yourself," Bennis Hannaford said. "I've been driving all night. I got lost on the Pennsylvania Turnpike, my cell phone won't work, and I'm wet. The last thing I need is a lecture on how I goddamned have to stay on the goddamned public's side of the goddamned idiot counter. If somebody doesn't give me a cup of coffee now, I'm going back to smoking cigarettes."

FOUR

1

Maris Coleman knew, in that deep-gut visceral way that was the only way she ever really knew anything, that the way she was behaving now could—possibly—be considered out of control. She left the qualifier there because she wasn't sure if she meant it. Sometimes, like at the Sycamore at lunch with Betsy, or out there on the lawn after Chris's body had been found, she heard her voice spiking up into the stratosphere. Sometimes it seemed to her that she had been going at this for years, for decades, ever since she had first seen Betsy Toliver in the kindergarten classroom at Center School. That left out a lot of her life, including the seven years from the time she had finished college and run into Betsy again in New York, and the seven years after that when they had been in the same city, on and off, but never seen anything of each other. There really had been a time when she had not been obsessed either with Betsy or with Hollman. Or she thought there had. When she tried to think of the way she had been then, her mind went blank. The only image she saw was one of herself in Bloomingdale's, carrying bags and wearing espadrilles. She had no idea why, when she imagined herself, she always saw herself wearing espadrilles.

Now she lay very still, listening, and decided that they had finally gone—Betsy and Jimmy Card and the two boys and the mother and the nurse. She had been lying very still for the better part of three hours, refusing to allow herself so much as a swig out of her Chanel bottle. She was most afraid of having to get up to go to the bathroom. The nearest one was half a level up and there were often people in it.

She'd still been drunk as hell when she'd made the phone calls the night before, and all she'd been able to think of was that if there was enough fuss and she stayed out of sight, nobody would remember she was in the house. Then she'd had to wait until Geoff was asleep and Mark had come upstairs to get something from the refrigerator, so that she could go downstairs, unseen, and set herself up in the little basement room. Then she had remembered that she'd forgotten about the phones, and had to do it all over again. She waited until Mark went to the bathroom, that time, and went out the sliding-glass doors to the patio and up against the side of the house to where the single phone line snaked in from the poles that lined the road the way they had in that Alfred Hitchcock movie about the birds. After all, they couldn't be trapped if they could call out. It had been late, and dark, and she had been frightened the whole time that one of them would come into the pantry and see her at the side of the house. The little window in the pantry looked right out on where she was. There was no sign of the cop who had been left to guard the crime scene. Maris suspected that he had gone home to bed. Leave it to Kyle Borden to do his job in a thoroughly half-assed way.

Right now, the house was not just quiet, but dead silent. She tried to see the time on her watch, but it was too dark. There were no windows here at all. She sat up and swung her legs off the couch she had been sleeping on. It was something worse than lumpy.

If there was a cop upstairs, or anybody else, she could say that she'd fallen asleep down there, and just woken up, and didn't know what was going on. It came in handy when people thought (falsely) that you were an alcoholic. She went up the half flight of steps to the family room. The sofa beds were still pulled out and their sheets and blankets rumpled.

Maris stopped in at the bathroom and washed her face and hands. She felt positively foul, but there was nothing she was going to be able to do about it until she got back to Belinda's. She went up the steep flight of stairs to the main floor and came out near the kitchen. There were kitchen things left on the table in the breakfast nook, cups half full of coffee and curdling milk, a half-eaten piece of toast with margarine on it. Betsy always had margarine, never butter, the way she always had store-brand canned goods instead of the brand-name kind. It made Maris insane. She went through into the living room and then down the little hall to the bedrooms. Nobody was anywhere. Betsy's mother's room was so empty, it could have been a guest room nobody ever slept in. Maris went back into the kitchen and looked out the window at the backyard, but there was still no policeman where the crime-scene barriers had been put up. It was raining the way it did during hurricanes.

Maris went into the living room and opened the front door. Rain spattered on her shoes and face. The one car still parked at the edge of the road was not one she recognized, but she hadn't expected to. All the other times she had met with Eddie Cassiter, it had been in New York, and he hadn't been driving any car at all. Now she stood very still with the door open and waited. The blue Ford Taurus sedan waited, too. Maris counted to fifteen. Eddie Cassiter got out of the car when she reached twelve.

"It's late," he said, coming toward her at a run, his head and jacket drenched black. "For a while there, I thought you'd taken off with the rest of them."

"Did you see me taking off with the rest of them?"

"Honey, I didn't see anything. The drivers pulled those cars right up to the doors, and the ambulance got even closer. What is it with the ambulance thing, by the way? The old lady have a heart attack?"

"I don't know. I've been busy staying out of sight. If I hadn't stayed out of sight, you wouldn't be getting in here."

"God, this is a dump, isn't it?" Eddie Cassiter said, stepping through the front doors. "It was probably hot stuff back in 1965, though. I can see that. What about you? Doesn't this place make you nuts?"

"I never think about it."

"Show me where they slept. Liz Toliver and Jimmy Card. If the bed's still a mess, I can get a photograph."

Maris considered telling Eddie what she had already told him half a dozen times before. Liz and Jimmy did not sleep together when the boys were in the same house. Liz thought it was tacky, since they weren't married. She showed him down the hall to the bedrooms instead, and was glad that Liz was using the master with the big double bed and not one of the side bedrooms, which just had twins. Then she left Eddie there to root around in the mess of makeup and costume jewelry still spread across the top of the vanity table. If she hadn't cut the phone line, she could have called Belinda. If she wasn't so worried that they'd get caught, she could relax.

She set herself up at the kitchen table with a large glass of orange juice and a cup to put coffee in, and spiked the juice from her Chanel bottle. She really did have to get back to Belinda's. She was getting low, and her reinforcements were packed away in her big traveling case. She put the kettle on to boil. There was percolator coffee and a percolator, but it hadn't been used this morning. She sat down and took a big long drink of orange juice. She put her head in her hands and willed it to stop throbbing.

Eddie came back from the bedrooms, looking happy. "That was great," he said. "She uses cheap makeup, did you know that? Max Factor. Revlon. The stuff you buy in drugstores. None of that designer salon stuff at all. Maybe that's what our angle should be. Liz Toliver, El Cheapo Supremo. Too cheap to get a professional out here to help with her mother. And now, what, her mother's had a heart attack because of all the commotion and somebody is dead and she's probably got something to do with it—"

"You don't know that her mother's had a heart attack," Maris said.

"No, I don't, and I won't write anything until I do know, but it's fun to speculate. Christ, I hate women like that. They think they're so damned superior."

The kettle went off. Maris got up and poured water over her coffee bag, but only halfway up the cup. The Gordon's was clearing her head a little, and it had occurred to her that they ought to be in something of a hurry.

She wished Jimmy Card would go back to New York. Betsy was a lot easier to handle when Jimmy wasn't around.

Maris sat down in front of her coffee and said, "I'm going to chug this down, and then we ought to get out of here. There's supposed to be a cop guarding the crime scene out back. There probably will be one any minute now."

"It's not much of a crime scene," Eddie said. "I've looked at it. It's just a lot of flattened grass. It would have been better if there'd been a concrete walkway or something like that. Concrete soaks up mud."

"Right," Maris said.

"There wasn't any dirty underwear, either," Eddie said. "I checked the hampers. We can always use dirty underwear. We got a shot of Nicole Kidman's that we ran when we broke the story about the miscarriage. Liz Toliver must change hers three or four times a day. The stuff that's there looks like it's there by mistake. Clean as a whistle. Not a single stain."

"Right," Maris said again. She drained the coffee. She drained the orange juice. She was beginning to feel awake again. The rain was still coming down outside. She could remember a flood here once, although floods were rare in the mountains. She'd been four or five years old at the time, and the waters had washed out all the bridges between Hollman and the main roads.

"You want to get paid?" Eddie Cassiter said. "I brought it with me."

"I want to get paid," Maris said. "But I also want a ride back into town. I need to get a shower and some clean clothes. Let's get out of here."

Eddie reached into his back pocket and brought out his wallet. He took out twelve one-hundred-dollar bills and left them faceup on the table. "There you go. Not bad for one phone call and twenty minutes' worth of work."

Maris picked the money up and put it in her purse. "Why do you always have so much cash?" she asked him. "Do you guys keep it in a safe in the office so you can hand it out when it's needed?"

"Maybe we get it out of the side of the bank," Eddie said.

Outside, thunder rolled across the sky that sounded like bombing. It came close enough so that the house began to shake.

2

If Belinda had had to go into work today, she would have called in sick. She had a hard time putting up with the library on the best of days. The smell of books made her feel as if she were strangling. The loud-voiced older men who spent the day in the reading room made her lose her patience. The unattractive teenagers who came in after school made her positively crazy, as if teenagers didn't have better things to do with their time than read. At least, *she'd* had better things to do with her time when *she* was a teenager. Sometimes she suspected that the teenagers who came to the library were all potential school shooters. Their minds were so addled with books and their souls were so starved for fun and light and air that one day they would just snap. She knew there were people who said they liked books, but she did not believe it. She thought they were putting on airs, the way people put on airs about liking the opera or watching only art shows on PBS instead of real television. Whatever it was, it was not something she liked to be involved in, and she would forever resent the fact that no other place had offered to give her a job, not even as a waitress. She could do what receptionists did. She could do what customer service representatives did, too. She would have preferred to have been in a place where people could talk out loud and laugh and have fun, and where nobody at all wanted to know if she'd read some book or the other that had come out only last week.

This morning, she would have preferred to be anywhere but in her apartment. She had spent most of the last hour going over her options. She could go down to JayMar's. She could go over to Mullaney's. She could get into the car and drive out to the Mountain View Shopping Center. She could drive a really long way and go to the mall. It made Belinda queasy in the pit of her stomach to think that she would never see Chris in the mall again. It made her even queasier to think of Chris with her insides spread out across Betsy Toliver's lawn, white and oozing, tangled in the grass. This was another reason why Belinda didn't like to read and didn't like to listen to the news, either. It made images in your brain, and no matter how hard you tried to get rid of them, you couldn't get them out.

The apartment was too quiet. The radio was on, which usually helped, but this morning the oldies station was not playing its regular round of songs that she recognized and could sing along to. There were only songs from the sixties, Bob Dylan and Janis Ian and folk music, which Belinda had always thought of as grungy.

If she didn't go down to the mall and didn't want to go to the shopping center—it bothered her to shop when she knew she couldn't buy anything—she could go to Hollman Pizza and have lunch there. She thought about turning on the television and rejected the idea. Television shows at this time of day were all talky-talky and full of people with problems. The local stations had bulletins and news updates all through the day. The last thing she needed was some announcer coming on to tell her that Chris had been secretly pregnant or that her intestines had been carried off in the night by dogs.

She looked at the clock on the kitchen wall. It was almost eleven.

"It isn't fair," she said, out loud, to the air, and then she clamped her mouth shut. Surely it was a sign of mental illness to be talking to yourself in an empty apartment.

The radio was playing a song by somebody named Dave van Ronk. Belinda had never heard of him, and he had a terrible gravelly voice that sounded like it belonged to a bummy old drunk. She thought of Emma and herself—sitting in the car in front of the walk that led to Betsy's front door and talking to Betsy's tall teenaged son about what he liked to do in his spare time. *That* had been an event she wouldn't want to repeat. It was like talking to an alien from a science fiction movie. How could anybody that *cute* want to spend his time going to art exhibits about Abstract Expressionism?

She heard the sound of footsteps. That had to be Maris coming home. She sat down at the table and began to play with the flowers, although there was nothing that needed to be done to them. It wasn't as if they needed to be watered, or there were so many of them that they could be infinitely rearranged.

There was a fumbling at the apartment's door. Belinda had given Maris a key. The key turned in the lock. The front door swung open. Belinda turned around on her chair and smiled.

"Where were you all last night?" she asked brightly. "I thought you'd been mugged and murdered and left on Betsy Wetsy's doorstep with everybody else we know."

Maris threw her own large shoulder bag down on the table and pulled out a chair. "This is the biggest frigging mess we've ever been in," she said. "Don't make jokes."

3

The trouble, Nancy thought, was that this was such a small town. In even a medium-sized town, there would have been a good chance that most of her students would never even have heard of Chris Inglerod Barr. Now, of course, she had dozens of girls who had worked with Chris at the food bank as part of the country club's "Good Samaritan Christmas Project," or who'd been to her house with their parents for a holiday party, or who had waited on her in Elsa-Edna's or Mullaney's. It didn't help that the gory details had been all over town in a split second, either. Just walking through the halls after third period, Nancy had heard at least six different versions of the murder scene, each more outrageous than the last. At first, Chris had just been stabbed, albeit eighty-five times. At last, Chris had been cut up into chunks and placed in a pile at Betsy Toliver's back door—except they didn't call her "Betsy," they called her "Elizabeth," and they seemed to assume that she was being persecuted. It was a privilege of celebrity. Nobody wanted to believe you'd really done anything wrong. If it appeared you had, they made excuses for you. That was how Nancy explained O. J.

It was now quarter after eleven, and Nancy needed at least two ibuprofen, which she wasn't eligible to get for another half hour. She had found a substitute to take Peggy's classes, but she'd had to teach the first one herself. There just hadn't been time to jury-rig anything else. Nancy truly hated teaching. She had hated it from the first, and the five long years between the time she got her master's degree and the time she had been able to find a job in administration had been the longest of her life. She would rather have gone back to that summer after her senior year in high school than do those five years over again.

What she really needed to do, she thought, was to take half an hour and drive out into the country with the radio off. If she could just spend a little time without having to see or talk to people, she knew she would be able to calm down. She was not, really, upset about Chris. She was only upset about the things that were going on around Chris, about the stories, about the hysteria of people like Emma. She had half expected to have a call from the superintendent this morning, suggesting they bring in "grief counselors" for the students who "might need them," but no call had come from that source, even to offer condolences. She had been reduced to pacing up and down the halls, from one floor to another, from one wing to another, looking into classrooms, listening to the talk in the halls when the bell rang and classes changed.

Nancy looked around the foyer and made a note to herself to get the clubs to change the display cases. She was tired of everything she saw. She went into her office and nodded to Lisa as she passed through the outer room. She passed into her own office and went to the window at the back. The view wasn't good at the best of times, and today the rain was so hard and the sky was so black that there wasn't anything to see but water, coming down. She pulled out the chair behind her desk and sat down. There was work she had to do. She ought to do it. She didn't want to. Lisa Bentkoop came in, and Nancy looked up, relieved.

"I'm having the worst day today," she said. "It's not that anything in particular is going wrong, it's just—" Nancy fluttered her hands in the air.

"I think that's understandable," Lisa said. "You're probably more upset than you realize. She was a friend of yours forever."

"Well, yes," Nancy said. "That's true, I guess, but since we became adults we haven't been particularly close. Oh, we saw each other. It's hard not to go on seeing the people you grew up with in a town like this. But there was a divergence, if you know what I mean. Chris was so involved with being a wife, and a wife is the last thing I ever wanted to be."

"I know what you mean. And I hate to make your day any worse than it already is, but there are a couple of things."

"Like what?"

"Well." Lisa took a deep breath. "We got a heads-up from Kyle at the police station, for starters. Apparently, Hollman has been invaded. There were so many reporters out at the Toliver place this morning, the inhabitants had to flee. Those aren't my words, they're Kyle's. 'The inhabitants had to flee.' Hundreds of them, from his description—"

"He went out there?"

"No," Lisa said. "That detective person was out there. Gregor Demarkian."

"I can't believe there was that much fuss over Betsy Toliver," Nancy said. "Yes, she's sort of famous, but it's only sort of. Most people don't even watch those talking heads shows."

"I don't think it was about Elizabeth Toliver. Kyle said Jimmy Card was here, he was here last night when they found the body. So I think it's him they're after."

"Yes," Nancy said.

"And Kyle said they got inundated awhile at the police station, too, with the reporters crowding into the vestibule and the waiting room, but they got that under control. He wanted us to be ready, though, because he thinks—or maybe it's Mr. Demarkian who thinks—anyway, he thinks that they might come here."

"Who? Kyle and Mr. Demarkian?"

"No," Lisa said. "The reporters. Or some of them, at any rate. Remember how that one came down here a couple of months ago, from the *Enquirer*? Except he didn't tell us he was from the *Enquirer*. He wanted to photograph the school."

Nancy did remember. That was when the stories had first started appearing in the tabloids about the night Michael Houseman was murdered. She drummed her fingers on her desk. "Has anybody actually been here today?"

"If you mean reporters, not that I know about. But you know what they are. They could be waiting in the parking lot for the students to come out. They could just waltz through one of the doors. We talk about making this school secure, but we never do anything about it. And we can't lock too many doors. The fire regulations—"

"No," Nancy said. "No, that's all right. I don't see that they'd have much to get if they did come here. I can't see that it would hurt the school anyway. It isn't even the right building. This wasn't where we all were when all that stuff happened with Betsy."

"Yes," Lisa said. "Well, the thing is, there may be another complication."

"What complication?"

"David Asch is here to see you."

"Who's David Asch?"

"Diane Asch's father."

Nancy's head snapped up. "He's here? Waiting outside someplace? He didn't call for an appointment?"

"No, he didn't call for an appointment, and I don't think that's a good sign. He looks like the kind of man who does call for appointments. He's—well, you'd have to see him."

"I don't intend to see him. Go right back out there and tell him I don't have any time today. Make him make an appointment."

Lisa hesitated. "I've tried that," she said. "I tried it several different ways. He said he'd wait. 'Nobody schedules every breathing minute of the day,' is what he said."

"Was he belligerent?"

"Oh, no. He was quite pleasant."

Nancy drummed her fingers on the desk again. "What about Diane? Is she in school today?"

"Same as always. I saw her on her way to biology."

"Has there been any trouble?"

"Nothing unusual." Lisa shrugged. "I mean, I heard a couple of people call her 'fart face' in the hall, but that's—"

"Par for the course," Nancy finished. She stood up. If she had been one of the students this year, she would have called Diane Asch "fart face," too. She wondered what Mr. Asch was like. Maybe he was Rick Moranis. "Send him in," she said. "Tell him I've got exactly five minutes. It's a busy day. When I buzz, I want you back in here faster than you can think about it. And I'm going to want him out."

"Right," Lisa said.

She hurried out of the room, and Nancy remained standing. A moment later, Lisa returned ahead of a tall, elegant-looking man in a good tan suit. He was far too elegant, and the suit was far too good, for Hollman. Nancy held out her hand.

"Mr. Asch," she said.

"Ms. Quayde."

Lisa retreated out the door and closed it behind her. When she was gone, it seemed too silent. The rain outside was too loud. David Asch had an attaché case. He was smiling.

"Well," Nancy said. "I suppose you're here to talk about the trouble Diane has been having, getting along with her classmates."

"No," David Asch said. "I'm not."

"You're not?"

"There wouldn't be any point, would there? I've heard enough conversations of that kind—not about Diane, mind you, but about me—to know how they go. I complain. You tell me it's really mostly Diane's fault, we need to get her a therapist, she has a problem, and besides, there's nothing you can do to *make* people like her. That *is* the way the conversation would go, isn't it?"

Lisa was right, Nancy thought. This man was pleasant, but it was not a nice pleasantness. "If you don't want to talk about Diane," she said, "what do you want to talk about?"

"You."

"Excuse me?"

David Asch's smile became wider. He sat down himself, in the visitor's chair, and put his attaché case on the desk. "You," he repeated. "Because there are things you can do about the situation with Diane, although you won't do any of them. It's true you can't make people like her, but you can stop collaborating in their bullying. Because we both know, don't we, that this kind of ostracizing behavior does not occur in isolation. It does not occur where there is not adult support."

"I don't know what you're talking about."

"I think you do."

Nancy watched in fascination as David Asch snapped open the brass fixtures on the attaché case. "You're not from around here, are you?" she said. "If you were, I'd know you. You look like you come from someplace far more cosmopolitan and—"

"I come from Armonk, New York."

"Well," Nancy said.

"Armonk is not what I'd call cosmopolitan," David Asch said. "Although it certainly is a good deal more sophisticated than this area around here. We moved here so that I could teach at UP-Johnstown. I have another year to go on my contract and then I'll be gone. That will be Diane's senior year."

"What do you teach?"

"Psychology," David Asch said. "But I'm not a clinical psychologist. I'm a behavioral one. I deal in statistics and probabilities. I don't have much use for touchy-feely. Do you know what this is?" He took a thick wad of paper out of the attaché case and dropped it down on the middle of her desk.

"No," Nancy said.

"It's a copy of the summary of the police report on the murder of one Michael Houseman, until last night the most famous crime to have been committed in this town. It's not hard to get hold of, by the way. It's a public record. I actually obtained it nearly six months ago, after that incident when two girls pushed Diane into the trash Dumpster out by the athletic field and then piled the door of it with heavy objects so that she couldn't get out. Do you remember that incident?"

"Yes," Nancy said. "We did—"

"You did nothing," David Asch said. "My wife came in to see you at the time. You gave her a lecture on how we should send Diane to therapy to 'help her with her problem.' "

"She does have a problem," Nancy said. "She has several of them. And we did try to do something about the incident with the Dumpster, we just couldn't—"

"Prove who had done it? Yes, of course. Except that Diane told you who had done it."

"We can't initiate disciplinary proceedings that might end in expulsion on one student's say-so," Nancy said. "And that's especially so in this case, because Diane has an almost paranoid obsession with the girls she accused—"

"*Diane* has an obsession?"

"Yes, she does. She—"

"They follow her around while she tries to avoid them. That doesn't sound to me like she has an obsession. It sounds to me like they have an obsession. Just as it sounds to me like they have a problem. Not Diane."

"I realize that as her father—"

David Asch leaned forward and flipped open the report. "I bookmarked the page for you," he said. "And I highlighted the relevant passages. Don't worry about making a mess of it. I made copies. One to leave with you. One to keep for myself. One to give to other people."

"What other people?"

"This morning, I gave it to a reporter for the *National Enquirer* that I met in JayMar's. He wasn't keeping it to himself. We had a very nice talk, he and I. About you. And Elizabeth Toliver. And Diane. Do you know what a parallel case is?"

"Nobody listens to the supermarket tabloids," Nancy said stiffly.

"Oh, everybody listens to them," David Asch said. "But I'm not leaving it at that. My old college roommate now works on the national desk of the *New York Times*. I've talked to him, too. I talked to him a good long time ago, if you want to know the truth, but now the—problem—with Diane is newsworthy. You're newsworthy. And that makes all the difference."

"I don't see what you think you're going to accomplish," Nancy said, and now she was not just stiff. She was frantic. "I really can't make the other girls like her. I can't do anything. What do you think it's going to get you to blackmail me?"

"I'm not blackmailing you," David Asch said. Then he laughed. That wasn't very nice, either. "I wouldn't bother to blackmail you. There's no point. I'm not telling you what I'll do if you don't help Diane. I'm telling you what I've already done. Oh, I'll do a little more of it. There's no reason not to. But by and large, it's already done."

"I don't get it," Nancy said. "I really don't understand what you want. What's the point here? What are you trying to accomplish?"

"Let's just say payback's a bitch," David Asch said. He was still smiling when he stood up. "The year after next, we'll be gone, Diane will be at a good college and I'll never have to speak to you again. But it would be interesting to see if I can get you fired long before that. Don't you think?"

He closed the attaché case and picked it up. The report was still lying in the middle of Nancy's desk. He made no move to take it. Nancy thought the air was waving, but she couldn't be sure. It was hard to tell what was going on in the real world, and what was just her mind, reeling. She'd heard about minds reeling, but she'd never believed they actually did, until now.

A second later she looked up and was surprised to see that she was alone. David Asch had left without saying good-bye, or taking her hand, or doing any of those other things that are required by politeness. The rain outside was coming down harder than ever, and the thunder was harsh and close. The only light in the world came from the lightning that broke out in sheets to backlight the sky. *This cannot be happening to me*, she thought.

Then she put her head down on her desk and closed her eyes.

FIVE

1

The rain got worse. Gregor had never seen so much rain. He kept worrying about floods, but nobody else seemed to. Even Bennis ignored the weather, except to say once or twice how awful it had been to drive in it. Kyle Borden ran in and out of the station house as if nothing were going on. When the thunder got bad enough to rattle windows, Sharon Morobito complained that the storm might take out the power.

Bennis got on the phone and found them a hotel room. "I knew you wouldn't think of it," she said, heading off to a spare desk in the big outside room with a list of hotels made out by Kyle Borden. He'd put little stars next to the ones he thought were "expensive," which included the Ramada Inn. "You'd have gotten to tonight and then realized you didn't have anyplace to stay, and by the time you went looking everything would be booked up, and then you'd be stuck in some fleabag on a back road somewhere, wondering why you couldn't sleep."

"We could just go back to the Toliver house," Gregor said. "Somebody ought to. If they leave that place empty overnight, somebody is going to break into it."

"Somebody probably already has," Bennis said. "And I don't want to go back to the Toliver house. I've never been there in the first place. I've never met the woman. And what would I say? Hello, Ms. Toliver, I'm Bennis Hannaford. I used to be your lover's lover."

"She isn't worried about you," Gregor said calmly. "She's worried about somebody named Julie."

"Julie Handley, yes. She's a supermodel. I'd worry about her, too. Jimmy was married to her. She was in *Sports Illustrated.*"

"Why was a supermodel in *Sports Illustrated?* Was she in the Olympics before she started modeling?"

Bennis and Kyle Borden both gave him very odd looks, and then Bennis disappeared, mumbling to herself as she went. Kyle pulled out a piece of paper and started to make a list.

"The real problem is not knowing where Betsy Toliver went," he said. "There are things here from last night that I'd like to nail down. Are they going to skip town, do you think?"

"They weren't meaning to," Gregor told him. "At the house this morning, they were talking about finding a hotel in the vicinity so that they'd be available for the investigation. From what I've seen of Elizabeth Toliver, she probably meant it. I've never seen enough of Jimmy Card to even guess what he'd do."

"There aren't a lot of places in the vicinity," Kyle Borden said. "Especially not ones that a big pop star would want to go to. We could call around."

"They'd be crazy not to use an assumed name," Gregor said.

"Right," Kyle Borden said. He looked down at the piece of paper he had placed on his desk. "Okay, first person I want to talk to is Mark DeAvecca, and I can't. Next people I want to talk to are Emma Kenyon and Belinda Hart. That's right, isn't it? That's who he said gave him a ride home from the library?"

"That's what he said. And they were stupid."

"At his age, all adults are stupid," Kyle said. "Except Belinda really *is* stupid. I don't mean mentally retarded or like that. She's just stupid. It's incredible to try to talk to her."

"She can't be too stupid, can she? She was one of the girls that night in the park?"

"You think she couldn't be stupid and be one of the girls that night in the park?"

"No, I mean they'd all graduated from high school, from what I remember," Gregor said. "So she couldn't be too stupid. She graduated from high school."

Kyle Borden snorted. "Listen," he said, "it isn't the Main Line out here. You could graduate high school with a brick for a brain if you were just willing to slog it out. And she did slog it out. I think she did a couple of years at a community college or a secretarial school or something afterward, too. Not that it mattered. She got married as soon as she could. He divorced her as soon as she got a little saggy and he got a little itchy turning forty. When you marry a woman because she's got perfect skin, the relationship has a short trajectory."

"She had perfect skin, I take it," Gregor said.

"She had perfect everything. You should have seen her. I can still remember the first time I saw her. Perfect skin. Big china-blue eyes. These days, she'd probably go off to New York to see if she could be a model, except maybe she's not tall enough. But there wasn't anything else there. None of them are too bright, except for Maris, but Belinda is—whatever."

Gregor looked down at Kyle's piece of paper. He'd written the three names in a line: *Mark DeAvecca, Belinda Hart, Emma Kenyon.* He knew that Emma

Kenyon's married name was Bligh. He wondered if Belinda Hart used her married name, too.

"So," he said. "This Emma Kenyon we're talking to. That's the one at the Country Crafts store I went into in town?"

"That's the one. She's easy to find. The store used to be their house—the Kenyons' house, I mean. Emma grew up there. When she got older and her father died, her mother turned it into that little store, and then when her mother wanted to retire Emma and George took over the store and moved into the rooms above it. George works a little real estate at an agency on Grandview. We can go right over."

"What about Belinda Hart?"

"She lives in an apartment in a building near English Drugs," Kyle said.

"Does she work?"

"At the library. I don't know if today is one of her days. The thing is, though, Maris Coleman is staying with her. It's kind of weird, really. Maris doesn't usually stay there because, you know, it's hard to stay there and not go nuts."

"So why is she staying there?"

Kyle shrugged. "I don't know. Maybe because Nancy Quayde bought a house out in Stony Hill last year. Nancy used to live in town, you know, so Maris could walk—"

"She doesn't drive?"

"Well," Kyle said cautiously, "she used to. And she does have a car, nice rental Volkswagen, one of those new bugs. She's got it parked back of English Drugs. So I suppose she's still got a driver's license. All you have to do to keep that up is show up to have your picture taken once a year. But she doesn't drive when she comes here."

"Why not?"

"You ever seen her one hundred percent sober?"

"Ah," Gregor said.

"Like I said, Maris isn't stupid. A bitch of legendary proportions, maybe, but not stupid."

"Well, at least they're together in one place," Gregor said. "Maybe we can get to both of them at once."

"We ought to talk to Nancy Quayde, too," Kyle said. "She was Chris's best friend, all the way back to when we were all in kindergarten. Dan will be back from Hawaii today. We can talk to him. Then I guess we should think about talking to Peggy Smith. Do you really think this is going to turn out to be about what happened back in 1969?"

"I don't know."

"I don't either. Peggy was there. Peggy was a part of that popular crowd, but she's sort of out of it these days."

"Why?"

"Married a guy from our class. He drinks himself blind, stokes himself up on cocaine, and beats the crap out of her. If we could ever catch him with dope on him, we'd send him away, and maybe she could get free. But don't count on it. I've been out there myself half a dozen times when she's had to go to the emergency room and she will not rat on him. Will not."

"That's a syndrome, you know," Gregor said. "There are therapists—"

"Yeah, well," Kyle said, "that's all well and good, but when you're standing in the emergency room at three o'clock in the morning it doesn't help you much. He blames her for us coming out to begin with, even though she never calls. The neighbors hear it and they call, but Stu won't listen. If we arrest him, he'll blame her for that, too, and if we can't get him successfully prosecuted or she insists on taking him back home he's only going to beat her up worse because of it. *You* tell me how to handle that, Mr. Demarkian, I'd love to know."

"Gregor," Gregor said.

"Here's the thing," Kyle said. "Peggy Smith doesn't have a car. Stu won't let her have one. I think he thinks that if she did have one she'd get in it one day and take off, and he can't have that. She supports him."

"Does he have one?"

"Yeah," Kyle said, "but don't go jumping to conclusions. He keeps the keys on a chain around his neck. I suppose she could get hold of them if he passed out cold, but you'd be amazed with these guys. They don't pass out cold all that often. You'd think they'd spend their whole lives passed out cold."

"They learn to accommodate the alcohol," Gregor said.

"Nancy Quayde picks her up every morning and takes her to school, because now that the school is out in Plumtrees, she can't just walk there."

"What about, who is this, Belinda Hart? Does she have a car?"

"Little Escort, bright blue. Keeps it parked behind English Drugs, and they let her. Because they've known her forever. They knew her parents."

"So," Gregor said, pulling a chair out of the corner of the room and sitting down himself. "Let's see what we've got. Belinda Hart, Emma Kenyon, Nancy Quayde, Elizabeth Toliver, all have cars and can drive them. Peggy Smith and Maris Coleman can drive, but Peggy Smith doesn't have access to a car, and Maris Coleman tries never to drive hers."

"What are you getting at?"

"Well," Gregor said, "Elizabeth Toliver's mother's house isn't within walking distance of town. It isn't within walking distance of anything. That means that to get there, to kill the dog, to kill Chris Inglerod Barr, somebody had to drive. And we know already that some of them did drive. Emma Kenyon and Belinda Hart gave Mark DeAvecca a ride back out there from the library. They went out of their way to do it, because they both live in town. They could just have been being helpful, or they could have been driving out to Stony Hill to see somebody else, or they could just have been curious about what Mark was like. Maybe they were even hoping to see his mother."

"You'd think they'd want to stay the hell away from her," Kyle said, "but I know what you mean."

"It's too bad about the way the dog was found. Anyone could have put it there at any time. It's all well and good to say that the dog was still alive when it was found, but we've got no way of proving that. I wonder if there's some kind of significance about late afternoons."

"It's a time when most people are able to take off work if they really want to?" Kyle suggested.

Bennis came in from the other room. "There's a Radisson," she said. "I got us a suite. If Elizabeth Toliver and Jimmy have any sense, they'll be there, too. I couldn't find another place within a hundred miles that had suites at all. Mostly, what you've got here is Holiday Inn."

"I like Holiday Inn," Gregor said.

"I know you do. I like suites. I'm going to drive out there and register. We'll be under the name Mr. and Mrs. Tibor Kasparian."

"Oh, Jesus," Gregor said.

"I was just picking something everybody could remember. It would be nice if you could come on out for dinner and like that this evening, just so I could see you. It was your idea to have me come out there. It was nice to meet you, Mr. Borden."

"It was nice to meet you, too," Kyle Borden said.

Bennis gave Gregor a peck on the cheek. "Talk to you later," she said. She turned around and went quickly out of the door. The reporters were gone.

Gregor sat back and wished that he'd remembered to grab his raincoat before bolting out of Elizabeth Toliver's house.

2

They went to Emma Kenyon Bligh's place first, because it was one of the closest, and because she was the most likely to be where she was supposed to be.

"We could try Belinda," Kyle said as he eased one of Hollman's two police cars out onto Grandview Avenue. "She's just up the block. Thing is, though, she might be at work, or out at the mall, or anyplace. I think she'd live at the mall if she could afford it. And Peggy'll be teaching until three."

Gregor thought that Grandview Avenue in the rain was much like Grandview Avenue in the sunlight, except that it had a faintly biblical air about it. *God was mightily displeased*, Gregor thought, and then got an image of Hollman in a deluge, rowboats drifting through the water between the tops of nineteenth-century false-front commercial buildings.

Kyle found a parking space as close to Country Crafts as he could. "It's a good thing for the rain," he said. "Grandview is usually parked solid this time of day. I hate parking in the lot at English Drugs."

Gregor gave one more thought to his trenchcoat, still hanging in the closet in the little guest room out at the Toliver House. He stepped out into the wet, and slammed the door behind himself. Then he turned and made a run for the Country Crafts porch. When he got up onto the porch itself, Kyle was waiting for him.

"I hate this weather," Kyle said.

Gregor thought, not for the first time, that it was a good thing the store had an OPEN sign to hang in the window, because there would be no way otherwise to tell if the store was open or shut. He wondered why the Blighs hadn't retrofitted the house with real display windows and a glass front door. Kyle held the front door open and let him through. Gregor went in and was caught, yet again, by the amount of froufrou and knickknacks and sheer clutter everywhere.

Emma Kenyon Bligh was at the back of the store, polishing shelves. She looked up when they came in, then turned away quickly. Kyle and Gregor walked to the back to where she was.

"Don't bother," she said when they came close. "I talked it over with George last night. I don't have to talk to you if I don't want to. I can have the lawyer here to listen in to anything I have to say."

"Jesus Christ," Kyle said. "I'm not asking you for a statement, Emma. I'm just trying to nail down a couple of times for yesterday afternoon. This is Gregor Demarkian."

"We've met," Emma said. "Well, I mean, we haven't been formally introduced. He was in here a couple of days ago. How do you do."

She held out her hand. Gregor took it and kept his mouth shut.

"Mark DeAvecca said that you and Belinda gave him a ride yesterday," Kyle said. "You and Belinda did give him a ride, right? From the library?"

"Oh, yes," Emma said. "We did that. And we didn't even get out of the car, so you don't need to start thinking I killed Chris while we were at it. Belinda will back me up. We never got out of the car."

Kyle sighed. "If I were you, I wouldn't use Belinda frigging Hart as an alibi. She'll forget what day of the week it was. What time was this, anyway?"

"Three o'clock, maybe quarter after. I don't know. I wasn't paying attention."

"Was the store closed?" Gregor put in.

Emma looked up from the pile of porcelain display plates she was wiping off and said, "My husband was minding the store. Usually he does real estate, but he didn't have any appointments yesterday afternoon. Why do you let him ask questions? Aren't you royally upset that some hotshot from Philadelphia is coming down here and telling you how to run your police department?"

"I could use a few more. Mr. Demarkian is usually very expensive, and this time he's agreed to work cheap. Why'd you have Belinda with you? She has her own car."

"We weren't in the car," Emma said patiently. "At least not originally.

George came and took over the store to give me a break, and I ran across the street to see if Belinda had a minute to talk."

"And?" Kyle said.

Emma got the last of the plates wiped off and put back on the shelf. She leaned forward and put her palms down flat on the floor. Then she put her weight on her hands and slowly began to twist her body until her knees were on the carpet. This, Gregor realized, was what she needed to do to get up.

Emma shrugged. "And nothing. He was there, Mark what's-his-name. Sitting at one of the big round tables in the front room reading something really weird. And Belinda said he was Betsy's son."

"And?"

"You can't just go on saying 'and' all the time, Kyle," Emma said. "It sounds stupid. And nothing, I suppose. We were curious. Belinda and me both. About what he was like. He looked—expensive, if you know what I mean. I mean, he wasn't wearing anything in particular, just jeans and one of those, what do you call them, polo shirts. But you could tell he came from money. He had that kind of aura."

Emma started moving toward the front of the store, and they moved with her. She went behind the counter and arranged a few things there, needlessly. Kyle came up and pushed a box of pipe cleaners out of the way so that he could lean on his elbow.

"So then what?" he said. "Did you just go up to Mark and haul him off to your car? How did you end up driving him home?"

"It was just one of those things," Emma said. "Belinda really wanted to talk to him, but you know what she's like. And he kept looking up at the clock. So I sort of drifted over to him and the next time he looked I asked him if there was anything wrong. And we got to talking. And that's how we ended up offering him a ride out to Betsy's house. Her mother's house. You know what I mean."

"I'm surprised he let you take him," Gregor said.

"Well, Betsy was late," Emma said. "She'd forgotten all about him. Which is typical, if you want to know what I think. And anyway, he seemed to have heard all about us."

"Did he really?" Gregor asked.

"Well, he knew I'd been captain of the varsity cheerleading squad in high school, and he knew Belinda had been homecoming queen our senior year. Belinda and I thought Betsy must have been talking to him. It seemed odd at first, you know, because if I'd been like Betsy was in high school, I'd never have mentioned it to anybody for the rest of my life. But I think he must have seen her old yearbooks, or something, because he knew an awful lot."

"He's a bright kid," Gregor said.

Emma shrugged. "He's weird, really. Just like she was, except that he's less, I don't know, less prickly. More sure of himself. She was always cringing around, acting like a big crybaby. He's almost—if it wasn't for the books and that stuff I'd have thought he was popular, you know, wherever he went to school."

"So," Kyle said. "You got to talking to him, and Belinda got to talking to him, and you offered him a ride home. And he accepted."

"Yes. Well, you know, Laurel, the librarian. She promised to tell his mother where he'd gone if Betsy came in looking for him, and she told him she knew who we were, and that kind of thing. And then he accepted."

"Good," Kyle said. "So, you all went around where, to the back of Country Crafts, to get your car?"

"Right."

"And Belinda just came along for the ride because she was curious?" Kyle said.

"We were both still pretty curious. We thought maybe Betsy had gone home and gotten tied up and not gotten to the library in time, and we would get there and she would be in the house and we would see her. I'd give a lot to actually be able to see her. In the flesh, if you know what I'm saying."

"But she wasn't home," Kyle said.

Emma shook her head. "Nobody was home. It was disappointing. There we were, out in the middle of nowhere."

"Mark didn't invite you inside?" Gregor asked.

"Oh, he invited us," Emma said. "He even offered to make us coffee, although I don't know how a man is going to make coffee. You see all these chefs in famous restaurants who are men, but they're all gay, and I could tell right off Mark wasn't gay. And there didn't seem to be any point. If Betsy had come home and found us sitting at her kitchen table, she'd have thought we were lying in wait for her."

"Right," Kyle said. "Did you pull into the driveway, or did you park out on the street?"

"We parked out in front. I hate that driveway. It's too long."

"Could you see down the driveway?" Gregor asked.

Emma shook her head. "If you mean, did we see Chris's car, the answer is no. But why would it be out there, anyway? Nobody was home."

"Chris could have just arrived and not realized nobody was home," Kyle said. "She could have been parked out there meaning to knock on the kitchen door, and when she did nobody would have been there. So—"

"Don't be ridiculous," Emma said. "If she'd been there and been just getting out of her car, she'd have heard us. Mark stayed on the walk for a good minute talking to us before he went inside, and we sat watching him until he was safely in the house, too. You know how you do that. But he's got a really loud voice, and there isn't anything else around there. She'd have heard. She'd have come around to see."

"Maybe she was already back in her car and on the way out," Gregor suggested.

"Then we'd have seen her come out," Emma said. "I told you. We sat there waiting until we were sure he was back in the house. It's a long drive, but it's not Manderley, for God's sake."

"Right," Kyle said.

"Face it," Emma said. "Chris wasn't there when we were. Why don't you ask Dan what he was doing that afternoon? Isn't that the way it's supposed to be? The husband is the one who's always responsible."

"He was in Hawaii," Kyle said. "At some kind of medical convention."

"Maybe he hired a hit man," Emma said. "I wouldn't put it past him. He's cold as anything. She wasn't there when we were there. If she was, we would have seen her, one way or the other."

Of course, Gregor thought, there was always the possibility that Chris Inglerod *had* been there when they were there, but hadn't been alive—or alive enough to let them know where she was. It was always so hard, in real life, to establish where anybody was, and when. It was only in murder mysteries that the detective could construct a timetable, and all the times on it would come out right.

3

Belinda Hart Grantling's apartment turned out to be barely half a block up Grandview Avenue, in one of those brick storefront buildings whose false fronts made it difficult to know just how many stories they really were. In this case, Gregor found, there were two, the one that held the store on the ground floor, and the one reached by a single, narrow staircase to the left of the store's front door. It was the kind of climb that needed a landing. The ground-floor story must have had fairly high ceilings, because the railing was needed as much to help the ascender pull himself up as to steady him on the way down. It was also absolutely dark. There was a single bare lightbulb in the ceiling of the floor above, but it was inadequate for anything but a horror movie special effect. Gregor was winded before he'd gotten a third of the way to the top.

Gregor thought he might do nothing more than see spots, but they were at the top of the stairs, finally, and he had a chance to stand still and breathe in. When Bennis was first quitting smoking, she used to say that there were times when she thought she would never be able to get enough air. He thought he now knew what she meant.

Kyle Borden knocked hard on the single door on the floor. Gregor heard a bustling and a coughing on the other side of the door.

"If you've lost your keys again, I'm going to scream," a woman said, and then the door swung back, and Gregor was faced with one of the oddest-looking people he had ever seen. In some ways, she was still a child. Her dress was frilly and pastel. Her hair was dyed blond and curled up and back in a way that was thirty years out-of-date, and even when it had been in style it had been a style for a teenager. In other ways, she was peculiarly ancient. Her skin was a mass of wrinkling and deep trenches. Her hair was far too thin on her scalp. Her eyes drooped. She looked them up and down and said, "Kyle, for God's sake. I thought you were Maris. Come on in. Who's your friend?"

"Gregor Demarkian," Gregor said.

"He's a consultant," Kyle said, coming in and signaling Gregor to come after him. "He's a consultant to the police department. We thought you might be at work."

"I'm only at work *sometimes*," Belinda said. "Honestly. It's only fifty dollars a week, and no matter how I try, I can't get anything else. How I'm supposed to live on fifty dollars a week, I don't know."

"Did you say that Ms. Coleman lost her keys?" Gregor asked.

Belinda blinked. "Oh. Well, I don't know. I mean, she did, about a week ago, when she first came. Lost them in the Sycamore one night when we were all there to catch up, you know. Before Betsy Wetsy came back to town. We all went one afternoon right about five, and of course I drove her, because Maris won't drive, even though the car she's got is better than mine, it's new and mine has a hundred thousand miles on it. She didn't even realize she'd lost them for two days, and then she had to go back over everything and trace her steps and like that, and I had to drive her out to the Sycamore, and there they were. It's just selfishness, if you ask me. She just likes riding around like she's got a chauffeur. It drives me crazy."

By now, Gregor and Kyle were fully into the apartment.

"Listen," Kyle said. "Maris had her keys last night, didn't she?"

Belinda blinked again. "I suppose so. I don't know. I didn't see her. She went out to Betsy Wetsy's around five o'clock or so and she didn't come back. She probably spent the night over there. She's got to suck up to Betsy because Betsy has money now. It really isn't fair."

"Right," Kyle said.

Belinda sat down in a big overstuffed armchair upholstered in white violets and cherries on twigs and gestured for the two of them to sit down, too. "This is all my own furniture," she said. "I brought it from the house. It was all I could hold on to. It was terrible the way that worked out. He should have been arrested."

"What did he do?" Gregor asked, curious.

"He refused to go on paying the mortgage," Belinda said. "He just stopped paying it, as soon as he moved out. The bank came and padlocked the house. It was humiliating. The only good thing was that Hayley was grown and out on her own, because if she'd still been a child I think I would have killed him. And then the lawyer said there was nothing I could do about it. It was only his name on the deed and only his name on the mortgage. Imagine that. I mean, of course I didn't work when Hayley was small. I'm not one of those lesbian feminists like Betsy Wetsy. But everybody knows that a husband and a wife own everything together. That's what marriage is all about."

Kyle cleared his throat. Gregor sat down on the edge of the couch, which was some kind of pink.

"So," Kyle said. "We were just over talking to Emma. About how you and she took Mark DeAvecca home from the library yesterday."

"DeAvecca? Is that his name? I thought his name was Toliver. Betsy Wetsy kept her name after she got married. I read it in the newspapers."

"Just because she kept her own name doesn't mean her children wouldn't have her husband's name," Kyle said patiently. "Now, the thing is—"

"I think it's really terrible, the way she behaves," Belinda said. "I mean, who is she, anyway? She's nobody at all. Nobody even said hello to her in high school except to tell her what a jerk she was being. It's Maris who should be the famous one."

"Right," Kyle said.

"And I do know Maris drinks," Belinda said. "I'm not that stupid. But I know why she drinks, Kyle Borden, and so do you. She drinks because she can't stand seeing what Betsy Wetsy's done, that's why. It isn't fair."

Kyle cleared his throat again. Gregor bit his lip.

"Belinda," Kyle said. "About yesterday afternoon. You and Emma took Mark back to the Toliver house, from the library."

"Right," Belinda said. "I was getting off work. We wanted to know what Mark was like. He was terrible. I really hated him. He was such a snot. I told him all about Hayley and you could see he was impressed, but he wouldn't say so. He just went on about the library and how he couldn't find this book."

"What book?" Gregor asked.

"I don't know," Belinda said. "I never spend much time with books except, you know, at work, and then I don't read them. They give me a headache. It was a book about carpentry, I think."

"Carpentry?" Gregor asked.

"It had carpenter in the title," Belinda said. "He couldn't find it. He went looking for it, and he got Laurel to help him, but she had to tell him we didn't have it. We used to have it, and it was in the card catalogue, but it disappeared and we never got it back, because nobody used to take it out anyway. Honestly, you'd think, with a book on carpentry, at least some people would want to take it out. At least it was about something useful. It wasn't like Betsy Wetsy's books. They're just a lot of bull about what everybody thinks and why they think it and how we're all too stupid for liking to wear makeup and going on diets."

"You've read one of Betsy's books?" Kyle said.

Belinda shrugged. "Parts of one. It wasn't a whole book straight through. It had chapters in it that were separate, you know, and not all about the same thing."

"Essays," Gregor suggested.

Belinda shrugged again. "Something. It was stupid. The first chapter was all about high school, and how we all have this sound track to our lives like our lives were a movie, and so instead of really living we have other people's words and emotions and, I don't remember. It was really, really stupid. It was like she was saying we shouldn't ever listen to music except maybe classical music. Or like that."

"Right," Kyle said.

"It was stupid," Belinda repeated.

"Look," Kyle said. "About driving Mark DeAvecca out to the Toliver house. We're trying to get a few things straightened out. Emma says it was around three. Is that right?"

"It was a little before," Belinda said. "Betsy Wetsy had gone and abandoned him, so Emma and I decided to take him home."

"Okay," Kyle said. "Now. You take him out to the Toliver house, and then what?"

"He asked us in for some coffee, but Emma wouldn't go," Belinda said. "I thought she was being stupid, myself. I would have loved to go in. Betsy Wetsy could have come home anytime and then we'd be able to see for ourselves."

"But she didn't come home," Gregor said.

"No, she didn't, and we didn't even get out of the car." Belinda pouted. "We just stayed parked there at the curb while Emma talked to Mark, which was awful, because he's just like Betsy Wetsy was. Stuck-up. Snotty. You wouldn't believe the books he had. I don't think anybody ever really reads books like that. They just pretend to."

"Now, pay attention," Kyle said. "Did you see Chris when you were out there?"

"Of course we didn't."

"Could she have been parked in the driveway behind the house?"

"No," Belinda said positively. "If her car was parked in that driveway, I'd have seen it."

"Are you sure?" Kyle asked. "Because I asked Emma, and she said she couldn't see anything."

"That's because Emma was driving," Belinda said. "She was on the other side of the car. She wasn't right up next to the curb. I was right up next to the curb, and I was practically in front of the driveway entrance, and I could see right down it. The only car there was that Ford Taurus the nurse drives Betsy Wetsy's mother around in."

"Could there have been cars in the garage?" Gregor asked.

"Oh," Belinda said. Then she put on a show of thinking really hard. "I suppose there could have been. I don't remember the garage doors being open, but I don't remember them being closed either. Was Chris's car in Betsy Wetsy's garage?"

"No," Kyle said.

Gregor got up. He was finding it almost impossible to sit still in this room.

"You've got a good view here," he said. "And that's where you work? Right across there?"

"It means I don't have to drive when the weather gets bad," Belinda said. "But it's not like it was when I was growing up. My parents had a really nice house in those days, and we had big trees. Even when I was married, I had a better house. It's a good thing Hayley was grown when her father decided he wanted a divorce. She'd have been ashamed to bring her friends here."

Gregor wished he could open a window. The room was virtually airless. Unfortunately, although the window had screens, they wouldn't keep out the rain, and the rain was still coming down in sheets.

"It's so weird," Belinda said pleasantly. "Do you know what I was thinking? It was raining just like this, the night Betsy Wetsy got stuck in the outhouse. Not in the beginning, you know, but at the end, when we were all at the river and then—then—" She looked from one to the other of them and blushed.

"And then Michael died," Kyle Borden said. "What is it with you people that you can never say that right out loud?"

Belinda got out of her chair and bustled off in the direction of the kitchen. She was one of the few people, Gregor thought, who could actually be said to bustle.

"I don't know why everybody makes such a big deal about it," she said. "It's as if it were some kind of catastrophe or something. *Chris* is the catastrophe. She was somebody who really mattered."

SIX

1

The really odd thing, Liz Toliver thought, was that, when it was happening, she'd behaved as if she'd been through it all a dozen times in the last six weeks. The reporters were storming the house. The phone lines were cut. Her own picture was on the news segment of the *Today* show, as if she were O. J. Simpson—in fact, exactly as if—and yet through it all she had been perfectly calm, and perfectly clearheaded, and perfectly focused.

Now she turned over on her side and looked out the window. They had commandeered an entire floor of the Radisson, almost as much space as they had on the first floor of the house in Connecticut, and maybe more. She was lying on this bed because it had been handy when she wandered out of the shower, and she had taken a shower because she'd needed something to do that wouldn't require her to talk to anybody for a while. There was so much thunder and lightning it amazed her that they still had power.

She got up and went to the door of the room and looked down the hall. Several of the other doors were standing wide open. Through one of them, she could hear the sounds of Mark and Geoff playing a video game. She went back into the room she'd come from and got the robe she'd left lying across the little desk near the window. She got the robe wrapped around her and went out into the hall again. She bypassed the room where the boys were playing—if Jimmy had been in there playing with them, which he sometimes did, she would have been able to hear him cursing at the joystick—and went down to the other end of the hall where she could see a door standing wide open and hear the sounds of classical music spilling out. The music was Paganini, whom Jimmy claimed was his favorite composer after Paul McCartney.

When she came to the door, he was still on the phone. When she knocked, he was just hanging up. He looked at her and smiled. "Hey," he said. "I wish I'd known it was you. I was talking to Debra."

"My Debra?"

"Your Debra, yeah. I thought I'd check in and see how things were going. There's been a certain amount of fuss over there this morning. You might want to call her back when you get the chance. She was a little frantic."

"My Debra? Frantic? The world must be coming to an end."

Jimmy picked up a cup of coffee from a large round table beside the bed, and Liz realized he'd ordered room service while she'd been showering. She went over to the table and found enough hot water and Constant Comment tea bags to last the afternoon.

"So," she said. "I've been thinking."

"I've been thinking, too," Jimmy said. "Debra said you were supposed to fire Maris when you were up here. Have you?"

"I was only going to stop her from going back to the office," Liz said. "Debra's right about that. She's a distraction. I was going to keep her on as a research assistant, or something like that. Keep Maris on, I mean."

"I know who you mean," Jimmy said. "Why?"

"Because she probably couldn't get another job. Because I don't really want to see somebody I've known since kindergarten sleeping in the street. Why do we have to go through this again?"

"Because," Jimmy said, "I'm the most loyal person on the planet, and you know that, but even I wouldn't go on taking care of somebody who spent all her time trying to screw me up. Is that why you won't marry me? Because you're afraid I'll make you fire Maris?"

"Be sensible," Liz said. She got a cup of tea rigged up—why was it that places always gave you little tiny cups to drink tea in, as if they thought that only coffee drinkers were in it for the caffeine?—and took a seat on the edge of the bed. "Think about Maris for a minute," she said.

"Where is she?"

"How should I know where she is?" Jimmy said. "Not here. That's enough for me."

"Why isn't she here?"

"Is this a trick question? Maybe if we, you know, did a little rock and roll, it would clear my head and I could answer better."

"Behave yourself," Liz said. "Think about this for a minute. Last night, when Chris's body was found, Maris was at my mother's house. Right?"

"Right."

"And then she fell asleep on the couch," Liz said. "Passed out, really. You remember that? You went off to take a shower, and Mr. Demarkian came in to talk, and then Mr. Demarkian left and I went to bed and Maris was still asleep on the couch. I think I mentioned something to you about it at the time."

"I think I said something about Maris going down one more step of the alcoholism ladder. I still don't see what you're getting at."

"Well," Liz said, "if she was asleep on the couch when we all went to bed, where was she when we all woke up?"

Jimmy shrugged. "Maybe she woke up in the middle of the night and went home. Or to wherever she's staying."

"At Belinda Hart's place. How?"

"How what?"

"How did she get home?" Liz insisted.

Jimmy looked thoroughly confused. "She got home the same way she got to the house in the first place," he said. "She must have driven out, right? So she got back in the car and went home, and it's probably a miracle she didn't kill herself or somebody else."

Liz shook her head. "She didn't drive out. Or at least, she didn't drive herself out. She's got a car she rented, yes, but it's a bright yellow Volkswagen, one of those new bugs. She told me. There was no bright yellow Volkswagen in the driveway at my mother's house when Chris's body was found, and there wasn't one in the garage, either, because my mother's car is in there. Maris hates to drive. She even walked all the way back from the Sycamore yesterday after we had lunch."

"Maris is scared shitless that she'll kill somebody," Jimmy said. "It's one of the few signs of common human decency I've ever been able to attribute to her."

"The thing is," Liz said, "if she didn't have a car, then where did she go? Where was she this morning? And what bothers me, what I keep thinking about, is maybe that nothing happened to her this morning. Maybe she's still out there. Back at the house."

"Doing what?"

"Waking up to find the house deserted," Liz said. "Waking up to find the phone lines cut. Or, if you really want to write a worst-case scenario, waking up maybe an hour and a half ago and finding some reporters still outside the house and nobody in it and needing a ride into town and having only one place to get it from. If you see what I mean."

"Shit," Jimmy said.

"Exactly," Liz said. "She could have been half a dozen places in that house and we'd never have seen her if we weren't looking for her. All she had to do was get up in the middle of the night, still mostly drunk, and go wandering around looking for a bathroom in the dark. Is there a way we could send somebody out there to check?"

"There's supposed to be a policeman posted," Jimmy said. "Maybe he can check. Maybe he can find another cop to get her a ride back into town. Assuming she's still there. Shit, shit, shit. I forgot all about her."

"I forgot all about her, too," Liz said. "Oh, damn. This is going to be messy, too. Maris, stranded while we flee, giving no thought to her comfort or well-being. Or however the papers will put it. And *People*. I'm beginning to be very glad that *George* folded when it did."

"You wouldn't have to worry if she didn't spend half her time talking to the papers."

"Do you ever wonder what you'd be like if you hadn't ended up being a famous person named Jimmy Card?" Liz asked him. "Do you ever wonder what kind of jerk you would be if you'd tried all the things you tried but they hadn't worked out and you were still playing bars in Long Island City? You don't give any consideration to context."

"I give my consideration to you," Jimmy said.

He stretched out his hand and ran the tips of his fingers across her cheek, very slowly, the way he sometimes did when they first met at the apartment for an afternoon of making love. Liz knew that nothing like that was going to happen right here, right now. Her rule about sex in any place the boys were was absolutely unbreakable. It was just that she wished they really were married, as married as she had once been to Jay, so that she could stretch out on the bed with Jimmy beside her and not have to care at all what Mark thought might be going on on the other side of the door. It wasn't that she was horny, as Mark liked to put it. It wasn't as if she wanted sex the way she sometimes did when she was working in the city and knew she would be meeting Jimmy later, for lunch, or at the end of the day. She was not craving orgasm, but the comfort of a catharsis, something to prove that she was not Chris, she was not dead in somebody else's backyard, she was not dead at all, and she was not likely to be indicted for a murder she didn't commit. She wanted to twist around and wrestle Jimmy down to the bed and go at him the way she'd never dared to do when she *had* wanted sex.

"Are you all right?" Jimmy asked her.

"I'm fine," she said, but she wanted to say something else, and it scared her. So she got up and went to the room-service table and made herself another cup of tea.

2

Emma was working on the checkbook when Peggy Smith came in, and for a moment she was even more disoriented than she had been. Was it after three o'clock already, that Peggy should be here? Had it really been raining all day? Peggy was as wet as Emma had ever seen anybody. Droplets as thick as the ones on chandeliers were falling from her hair.

Peggy seemed a little dazed. There was a slight swelling in her left eye socket that was going to turn into a shiner. At the moment, it only looked raw and painful. Peggy did not seem to notice it. Emma moved the checkbook around on the counter and bit the end of her pen. She didn't like having Peggy in the store at the best of times—there was always the danger that Stu might show up—and she really hated it when Peggy was banged up.

Peggy stopped at the counter and put her handbag down. Her handbag was as wet as the rest of her.

"I didn't realize it was raining so hard," she said. "If I'd realized, I'd have worn my raincoat. Or brought my umbrella."

"Right," Emma said. She shut the checkbook, which was one of those big folderlike things for business checks. She had a regular-sized checkbook for her and George's personal account upstairs in the apartment. "So," she said, "it's later than I realized. You're already out of school."

"What? Oh, I didn't go in to school today. I wasn't feeling well. But then, I thought, you know, staying cooped up in the house. It didn't make me feel any better. So I thought I'd go for a walk."

"In the rain?"

"It's like I said. I didn't realize it was raining so hard. I don't think it was, when I first started out. At least it wasn't enough so that I noticed it."

Emma did not say that it had been raining in sheets since early this morning. She took a clean rag from the shelf under the counter and began to polish fitfully. "So," she said. "How's Stu this morning? I haven't seen him around."

Peggy gave her a sharp look. "Stu's fine. He was sleeping when I left the house. I didn't see any reason to wake him up."

"Did you call in to the school to tell them you'd be absent?"

"Early this morning. God, Emma, what do you take me for?"

"You look sick," Emma defended herself. "You look absentminded. People get that way when they're sick."

"I even turned the ringer off on the phone before I left," Peggy said. "I'm really not a complete fool, Emma. I know Stu gets upset when his routine is interrupted. Did you and Belinda really go out to Betsy Toliver's house yesterday afternoon?"

Stu got upset as a matter of principle, Emma thought. That was why you couldn't trust him. She put the clean rag back on the shelf. The counter did not need to be polished. "We drove her son back there from the library," she said carefully. "Where did you hear about that?"

"I heard about it from Laurel. I was in the library for a while. It was quiet there, you know, but after a while I began to think that there might be other people. Somebody from the board of education. You know how it is in a town this size. Have you ever been sorry you didn't get out and go do something? Like Betsy?"

"No," Emma said.

Peggy looked around the shop. "I was looking through our yearbook the night before last. Do you ever do that? It was surprising me how many people we know are already dead. And that was before Chris was killed. People who died in Vietnam. People who died in car accidents. Nobody turned out the way you would expect them to, except maybe Chris. Nancy Quayde didn't even manage to get married."

"Is there some point to this conversation?" Emma asked. "Did you just drop in to muse? Because if you did, I've got a lot of work to do."

Peggy smiled slightly. "You and I," she said. "We didn't turn out the way we were supposed to, either. We just sort of—approximated it. You've got a happy marriage, but you're still living over the store. And I've got a house, but—" She shrugged.

"Don't tell me you're finally going to admit that your marriage isn't happy," Emma said. "I'll sing glory hallelujah, I promise. Nancy will find you a good attorney. We'll all go to court and testify against him, and maybe he'll rot in jail for forty years."

"You don't understand him," Peggy said.

Emma wanted to say that she understood Stu perfectly, and so did everybody else, but Peggy was getting that look on her face that she always did when she talked about Stu, the one Emma associated with religious fanatics. It was not true that Peggy hadn't ended up where everybody had expected her to. She had ended up exactly where everybody had expected her to. She had ended up married to Stu.

"Well," Emma said.

"Did you go out to Betsy's yesterday afternoon? When Chris was killed?"

"We weren't there when Chris was killed," Emma said. "We just drove Mark out there from the library and sat parked at the curb for a minute or two. We didn't see Chris. We didn't see anything."

"You didn't see Betsy?"

"She wasn't home." Emma shook her head. "You're reminding me of Belinda. She wanted to see Betsy, too. I don't know why. If you really want to see her, she's on Grandview Avenue enough these last few days. She's been in Mullaney's. She's been in English Drugs. I've seen her half a dozen times, getting in and out of that Mercedes."

"Haven't you wanted to talk to her?"

"What for?"

"I don't know. To see what she's like. She used to hate Stu when we were all in high school, did you know that? She told Maris about it when they were in college. Maris says it was really just a cover story about her coming back here to take care of her mother. Jimmy Card was going to send people down here to do that for her. Maris says what she's really here for is to write an article about us for one of those magazines. You know, the ones nobody reads."

"Where did you see Maris?"

"She was in the library." Peggy looked around, vague and vaguely startled at once, as if she had had no idea, until now, just where she was. "We've made it a kind of meeting place, Maris and I. She's the only one of you I can talk to anymore. She's the only one of you who doesn't treat me like some kind of leper. Or mental defective. God knows I can't talk to Nancy."

"People are just worried about you," Emma said stiffly.

Peggy smiled stiffly and drifted off between the shelves, picking things up and putting them down again. Emma had the almost desperate need to run down to where she was and grab her, as if Peggy's touching the things in the shop would taint them somehow. She wished she wasn't sweating so heavily that the sides of her dress had begun to feel damp.

"Look," she said. Her voice sounded shrill even in her own ears.

Peggy looked up from a shelf full of hand-painted porcelain teacups and said, "I was just wondering if you knew anything about it. If you'd talked to her and what she'd said. That she was going to write an article about us. Maris said it was supposed to be some kind of true crime about Michael Houseman and her being stuck in the outhouse and all that. Because of the stories in the tabloids. To clear her name."

"I don't know, Peggy," Emma said. "How would I know?"

"I went to the library," Peggy said. "I went a couple of times. And I read some of her articles and her books, and it isn't the sort of thing she writes about. But maybe I was looking at the wrong things. I don't really understand how those things work. So I figured, if you'd talked to her—"

"I haven't."

"We'd all look awful, if she wrote an article about us. We'd all look like Nazis. I don't know what the board of education would think."

"The board of education is made up of people who've known us since we were all in diapers, mostly because they were in diapers, too. This is a silly line of thought, Peggy. It doesn't matter what Betsy Wetsy does. After yesterday, she won't ever show her face in town again. Leave it alone."

"Why after yesterday? Do you think she murdered Chris?"

"I don't know if she murdered Chris," Emma said, "but there've been reporters in town all day, and I heard from Mrs. Cadwallader who lives out in Stony Hill that there were hundreds of them out in front of Betsy's house this morning. They practically stormed the front door. Betsy and Jimmy Card and the boys have all disappeared somewhere. I don't even know if they're in town anymore. And Betsy's mother is in the hospital. It doesn't matter what she was intending to do. This changes everything."

Peggy put down whatever it was she'd been holding. Emma couldn't tell what it had been.

"Well," Emma said.

"Is it still raining?" Peggy said. "I ought to go back to the library. I ought to go up and see Maris and Belinda, if they're home. I so rarely get a day free to myself."

"I know what you mean."

"It's too bad you didn't see Betsy in person," Peggy said. "It's too bad she's hiding out now or whatever she's doing. I would have liked to talk to her."

"Call her office in New York and make an appointment."

"You don't take it seriously. You never take anything seriously. But she could make us sound like Nazis, if she wanted to."

Emma couldn't get past the feeling that there was no reason why Betsy Toliver should want to, but on this matter she knew she was in the minority.

Peggy came up from the shelves to the counter and picked up her pocketbook. She'd left it there when she first came into the store. "Well," she said, "I'll be going."

"If you're trying to fool Stu that you've been at work, you'd better be careful."

"I can't fool Stu about anything," Peggy said. "You don't understand. None of you do. Stu is a genius."

Stu is a jerk, Emma thought, but that was something there was no point in saying, and she just clamped her mouth shut and watched Peggy go back on out the door. When the door opened the sound of the rain was deep and thunderous. When the door closed, the cowbell tinkled faintly in the wind the door created. Peggy went down the front steps. She did not hold her pocketbook over her head to stave off the rain. She did not hunch her head. She walked as if not a drop of water was landing on her.

Maybe, Emma thought, Peggy had always been schizophrenic, or whatever it was, and they had never noticed.

SEVEN

1

Gregor Demarkian had no idea how difficult it would be getting anything done in this kind of downpour. More than once over the course of the morning, he wondered desperately if Kyle Borden wasn't engaging in some kind of criminal stupidity. For all Gregor knew, the National Weather Service might already have declared an emergency. The whole area might already be under orders to evacuate to higher ground—although it would be difficult to get much higher than they were now without climbing into the trees and brush that carpeted the mountains above them. It was eerie. Nobody they saw on the street seemed to be panicking, either. The stores were all open. The lights were all on. The people drinking coffee in JayMar's were reading newspapers. The reporters were easily recognizable as people trying to use cell phones that didn't work.

Now Kyle pulled into the parking lot behind the police station and shut off the engine. "That wasn't very helpful, was it?" he said. "You got anything in those notes you took?"

Gregor flipped the pages of the notebook back and forth. "I was thinking about something. What about the others?"

"What others?"

"The other girls who were part of the group that night in 1969. So far, everybody we need to investigate seems to be part of that group. The victim was part of that group. Mrs. Grantling and Mrs. Bligh were part of that group. What about the others?"

"Well," Kyle said, "Maris Coleman was part of that group. She's on our list for investigation, too."

"That makes four. There were six," Gregor said.

"Peggy Smith and Nancy Quayde," Kyle said. "They don't have anything to do with this, do they?"

"I don't know. Had they remained friendly with Chris Inglerod? We can't just assume that the solution here will be restricted to the people we already know were at Elizabeth Toliver's house. What about these two? Do we know where they were? Are we going to talk to them?"

"Oh," Kyle said. The rain was drumming on the roof. He rubbed his hand against the side of his face and shook his head. "We could talk to them if you want. But it wouldn't be a very convenient time, right now."

"Why not?"

"They work at the high school. Peggy teaches something, I don't remember what. Nancy is the principal. She'll be superintendent a couple of years from now if she has her way."

"All right," Gregor said. "So, what, school's in session until three o'clock? We can see them after that. But you still haven't answered my question. Were they still friendly with Chris Inglerod?"

"Nancy was," Kyle said. "Peggy—" He shrugged his shoulders. "Peggy married Stu Kennedy. I told you what that was like. He doesn't like her to leave the house."

"But she must leave it, for work if nothing else."

"Oh, he doesn't mind work," Kyle said. He popped his door open and got out into the rain. Gregor got out, too. "He does mind socializing. Funny how things work out, don't you think? She chased his ass for years, all through kindergarten, all through grade school. She chased and he ran. When they finally started going out, we were all betting it would last a week and Stu would be off looking for his freedom. And now he won't let her out of his sight."

"It's the way men like that work," Gregor said. "It's an issue of control."

"I know what it's an issue of," Kyle said sourly.

They headed to the back door of the police station. They were both so wet, there didn't seem to be any need to run. They got into the back corridor and Gregor took his jacket off to hang on a peg. Sharon stuck her head in from the main room and said, "That *Miss* Hannaford called for Mr. Demarkian. She left a number where she could be reached. She said it wasn't urgent."

"Ah," Gregor said. He and Kyle came out of the corridor into the main room. There was now only a single reporter waiting on the bench in the reception area, and he seemed to be paying more attention to what was on his laptop than to what was going on with them. Kyle led the way into his own office. Gregor looked around. "Could I make a phone call somewhere? Privately?"

"Want to call Ms. Hannaford, do you?"

"No," Gregor said. "I want to call long distance back to Philadelphia. Don't worry about it. I'll use my phone card."

"Use the phone, for all I care," Kyle said. "You close yourself in here. I'll go see if I can get somebody to go get coffee at Dunkin' Donuts."

Gregor wondered where the Dunkin' Donuts was—he could use some Dunkin' Donuts—and then, when Kyle was gone, picked up the phone. He did use his phone card. He didn't want to get into the habit of making personal calls on police telephones. He heard the phone ring on the other end and almost held his breath. You could never tell when anybody on Cavanaugh Street would actually be in and available to answer his phone, unless you called dead in the middle of the night, and even that might not be good enough for Tibor.

The phone rang. Once. Twice. Three times. Six times. Eight. Gregor checked his watch. It was after Tibor's usual lunch time. *When it's rung twenty-two times, I'll hang up*, he promised himself. Then the phone was lifted on the other end, and he heard a rough gravelly voice say, "*Hehn*."

"Tibor?"

"Oh, Krekor, excuse me. I forget my manners. In American, you don't answer the phone by saying '*hehn*.' Of course, to say 'hehn' is to be more polite than the Greeks are. They answer the phone by screaming and they scream '*embross!*' It means '*talk!*' It's very intimidating."

Gregor assumed that Tibor was talking about the modern Greeks, not the ancient ones, a good bet since the ancient Greeks hadn't had phones. He had been talking to Tibor for less than thirty seconds, and already he was off track.

"Listen," he said. "Bennis is here. Did you know that?"

"I knew she was going up to you, yes, Krekor, she told us all about it. At length. Also, Donna helped her to pack something, I don't know what, Lida and Hannah put it together. They say there is never any decent food in these small towns."

"I wouldn't know," Gregor said. "I've barely had time to eat."

"If they'd heard that, they would have packed twice as much," Tibor said. "So, you are all right? Bennis is all right? We listened last night to the story about the murder. It was on the eleven o'clock news."

"As far as I can tell, it was on the eleven o'clock news in Timbuktu," Gregor said. "Okay, can you do me a favor? I need to get in touch with Russ Donahue. I would have called Donna, but she's got class this time of day, hasn't she?"

"She has class, yes, until four-thirty. Why didn't you call Russ at his office?"

"I didn't have the number. You can give him my number, if you want, except that I'm not entirely sure where I'm going to be. I need to get hold of something, called a Regional Crime Report. I'm not sure if they had them for the year I'm looking for."

"What year is that?"

"1969. In 1969, I was with the Bureau. I wasn't even in the Commonwealth of Pennsylvania. But if there isn't actually a Regional Crime Report, there might be something similar, some reporting mechanism that came before it, I don't know. Russ would know, though, or if he didn't he'd know how to find out. What I need to do is to get in touch with him and tell him exactly what I'm looking for. Except that I can't get in touch with anybody, because cell phones don't work up here. So."

"So," Tibor said. "I will get in touch with Russ, and tell him what you want. A Regional Crime Report."

"For this county, wherever I am," Gregor said. "Hollman, Pennsylvania. He'll have to look it up. I'm sorry. I didn't think to get the information."

"It's not to worry about. We'll think of something."

"Now, write this down." Gregor did not doubt that Tibor would write it down, but he did doubt that Tibor would ever again be able to find the piece of paper he'd written it down on. "I need a complete crime survey report for the months of June, July, August, and September 1969. Wait. Make it May and October, too. If Russ asks what I'm looking for, tell him you don't know, because I don't know."

"You don't know what you're looking for?"

"Not specifically, no," Gregor said. "I just—it's a matter of proportion, that's all. There has to be something else. Something else then and something else now."

"Krekor? What are you talking about?"

"Never mind. It might make you feel better to know that I know who killed Michael Houseman."

"This is the person who died yesterday at Elizabeth Toliver's house?" Tibor said.

"No, this is the person who died in a park up here in 1969."

"But, that is good, isn't it? Isn't it usually that if you find the person who has committed the one murder you find the person who has committed them all? You told me yourself—"

"Yes," Gregor said. "I know. And you're right. I just can't make some things fit together, and the times are all off, and the opportunities are all skewed, and there are five million reporters up here gumming up the works and they give me a headache. And Bennis is here, and you know what that means."

"Well, yes, Krekor, I do know, but most often I am discreet enough not to mention it."

Gregor laughed. "Listen, get Russ, tell him what I need, ask him if he'd mind being sure to be in his house and at his phone at, say, around ten tonight. That way I can call him directly and we can talk. How is everything on Cavanaugh Street? How is the woman with the harpsichord?"

"Grace. She is very nice, Krekor, what would you expect? She has played the harpsichord for me and for old George Tekemanian yesterday evening. It is a very beautiful instrument."

"Good. If she plays it too loudly, I can always go and sleep on Bennis's couch."

"It's been a very long time since you slept on Bennis's couch, Krekor. What do you take us for? Lida has been saying—"

"Never mind what Lida has been saying," Gregor said. "I'll talk to her when I get back. I'll talk to you later. Remember. Ask Russ to be at his phone at ten. By then, I should know where I'm spending the next few nights. Did I tell you we'd all been driven out of the Toliver house by reporters?"

"It was on the noon news, Krekor."

"Right."

Gregor put down the phone and stood up. Kyle Borden was sitting next to the counter, talking on the phone there. When Gregor came in, he looked up and waved.

"That's Nancy Quayde over at the high school," he said, pointing to the receiver. "She sounds really upset. She says we can come right out and talk to her if we want to."

"Good," Gregor said, coming over. "What about the other one? Peggy Smith?"

"Peggy Kennedy these days. No such luck. She's not at work today." Kyle covered the receiver. "From what I'm gathering here, Nancy thinks Peggy got beat up last night. Peggy called in sick."

"Does that mean she'll be home?"

"Well, yeah," Kyle said. "But I told you. I don't like the idea of going over there when Stu is home and he's always home, because he—"

"We'll talk about it later," Gregor said.

Kyle went back to the phone. "It's okay," he said. "We'll be right over. You sound like hell . . . yeah, yeah . . . I know . . . I know . . . I've told him. We'll be over right away. Hold on tight." He put the receiver back in the cradle.

"So," Kyle said, "you ready to go?"

2

The Hollman public schools—or a lot of them—were on the top of a hill in the Plumtrees section of town, cordoned off from the rest of the world by a low brick wall and a fancy stone gate with the words "Hollman Educational Park" embedded in one side of it. Above him, in the rain, the "educational park" rose up in a scattershot pattern of low brick buildings. The buildings all had metal letters on them that looked like brass, like the gate. The first one they came to said "Frank A. Berry Elementary School." Hollman High School was three buildings up.

"What do you think?" Kyle asked.

"I think it looks like a women's prison," Gregor said.

Kyle laughed. "They built it our senior year. We didn't actually get to go here. The town was really excited about this. Our leap into the twentieth century."

"This is the twenty-first."

"That was back in 1969. We don't get around to things real fast up here. We'll probably hit the twenty-first century in about 2088." He pulled the car up to the curb in front of the largest building in the "park."

"You want to make a run for the door?" Kyle said.

Gregor did want to make a run for the door. It was quite close—Kyle had parked right outside, in the fire lane. Gregor stepped out into the wet and bolted for the enormous plate-glass front of the lobby. Kyle was right behind him.

"You wonder what they're thinking when they build places like this," Kyle said. "It's like living in a fishbowl. Literally. All glass." He grabbed the possibly brass metal handle of the glass door and pulled it open for Gregor to go through. "Principal's office to your right. There's a sign."

There was a sign. Gregor headed through it and found himself in a room very much like the room at the police station, a big space with a counter running across the end of it nearest the door, leaving a small area for people to wait until they could be spoken to. Unlike the area at the police station, though, this one contained more than a single receptionist. There had to be half a dozen secretaries, all working away at computers. Kyle came in and said, "Yo, Lisa. Where is she?"

A dark young woman rose from a desk at the back and came up to the counter. "Hello, Kyle. You must be Mr. Demarkian. She's in her office. You don't want to know."

"We have an appointment," Kyle said.

"I know you do. She told me. But it's like I said, you don't want to know. She's been absolutely nuts all day, and I don't mean her usual nuts. She's been berserk. I've never seen anything like it."

"Perhaps she's upset about the death of, ah . . ." Gregor drew a blank. He kept thinking of the dead woman as "Chris." He always seemed to think of all the women in Hollman by their first names, even if he hadn't met them.

"She isn't upset," Lisa said as she opened the counter to let them through. "She's furious. She's having one of those full-scale attack things where she thinks she can storm the walls of Troy and bring it down single-handedly. Just a second and let me knock."

Lisa knocked on a door at the very back of the big room. There was a sound from inside, and she opened the door and stuck her head in. "Kyle is here. With Mr. Demarkian." There was another sound from inside the inner office, and Lisa stepped back to let them in. "I'll get coffee," she said, disappearing behind them.

Gregor let himself get ushered into an office that was small by federal standards, but probably huge by the standards of a small-town school system.

The woman behind the desk rose to greet them. She was a thin, driven-looking woman with hair much too black for her face, or for nature, but other than that she looked like hundreds of "professional" women in small towns across the country: a tailored blazer and equally tailored blouse topped a wide, floral-print skirt that fell low on her leg. She could have been on the cover of the latest Talbot's catalogue.

"Well," she said as they came in. "Kyle. Introduce me."

"Right," Kyle said. "Nancy Quayde, this is Gregor Demarkian. Gregor Demarkian, this is Nancy Quayde."

"Dr. Quayde," Nancy said.

"Dr. Quayde," Gregor repeated politely.

"I just don't see what the point is of going through all the trouble to get yourself a Ph.D. if you're going to be ashamed of it," she said. "Oh, never mind. Sit down. I'm not having a good day. Do you know there isn't any way to sue somebody for telling lies about you to the newspapers? I've been on the phone to my attorneys for half the day."

"Who's telling lies about you to the newspapers?" Kyle asked.

"Never you mind. The parent of a student. God, I hate parents. I really do. They are *such* self-righteous sons of bitches. And don't look at me like that. I don't talk that way in front of the students. Although I should. God only knows *they* talk that way, and to my face, too. They don't give a damn. And then there's Peggy. Whatever the hell am I supposed to do about Peggy?"

"I heard she was out sick," Kyle said mildly.

"Out *sick*?" Nancy Quayde nearly exploded. "You know as well as I do what she's out for, Kyle. Stu bashed her face in again last night and now she's got a shiner the size of a dinner plate and she's afraid to be seen with it. That's the third time this term. If she didn't have tenure, she'd be out on her ass. If he ever shows up here looking for her, she *will* be out on her ass. God, that whole situation drives me insane. Why doesn't she leave him? Why doesn't she turn him the hell in? Christ, given the amount of cocaine that man snorts, she ought to be able to put him away for thirty years. If she'd turned him in thirty years ago, she'd be much better off."

"Thirty years ago?" Gregor asked.

"Thirty years ago," Nancy said. Then she laughed. "God, don't you know? Stu sold marijuana to the entire senior class. Well, not all of it, just the 'cool' people and the hoods. Peggy thought he was going through a phase. But you could see it even then. You could tell he was going to end up an addict. It was written all over him."

"Well, not so I could read it," Kyle said. "Maybe we ought to go a little easy on just who Stu was selling marijuana to senior year."

"You mean because it included you?" Nancy said. "Never mind. It included me, too. It was a novelty, at the time. Now we practically execute people for smoking a couple of joints. We're all so afraid they'll end up like Stu. Christ. So what do you want to know? I was here yesterday. I didn't have anything to do with what happened to Chris."

"Right," Kyle said. "Mostly, I think what we want to know is what has been going on with Chris for the past few days. We could ask Dan, but he's been in Hawaii, and besides—"

"Besides, he probably wouldn't know," Nancy said. "That was a marriage of convenience. Or mutual assistance. I don't know. Anyway, what's been going on with Chris is what's been going on with the rest of us. Betsy Wetsy triumphantly returns. Chris was organizing a cocktail party for her."

"Are you serious?" Kyle said. "That's crazy. Whatever made Chris think she'd come?"

"Well, that's the point, isn't it?" Nancy said. "That's why Chris went out there yesterday, to try to talk to Betsy face-to-face. She was the best one to send, really. I don't have the patience, and the rest of them—" Nancy shrugged.

"When you say she was the best one to send," Gregor said, "do you mean this was something you all cooked up together? It was a group project?"

"Well, sort of," Nancy said. "It was—well, she was going to be here. And she's famous. And a lot of people, the superintendent of schools, the head librarian, thought it would be a good thing to have her speak, you know, to classes and to the Friends of the Library and like that. And we thought—Chris and I thought—that we ought to do something to calm everything down."

"Calm what down?" Kyle said. "It's been over thirty years."

"It may have been over thirty years," Nancy said, "but it's not like she disappeared and was never heard from in all that time. She's been in our faces now for a decade at least. And it . . . rankles . . . some people."

"Some people such as whom?" Gregor said.

"Mostly," Nancy said, "there's Belinda, who's just livid. I think Belinda's entire worldview came apart at the seams when Betsy got famous. And there's Maris Coleman, of course, but she doesn't really live here anymore. I don't know if she counts."

"So," Kyle said. "What was it exactly that you and Chris thought you were going to do?"

"Chris was going to throw her a party," Nancy said, "and I was going to take her out to dinner—not by herself but with all of us, or nearly all of us. Stu being what he is, Peggy can't usually make it. Anyway, all of us except Peggy and Belinda were going to do something and see if we couldn't sort of just bury the hatchet, so to speak. So Chris drove out there to talk to her. She was trying to make an effort."

"How did she know Betsy would be home?" Kyle asked. "Did she call ahead?"

"She tried to call ahead," Nancy said sourly, "but you just couldn't get through on that phone. It was hooked up to an answering machine. Chris left a few messages, but she could never get Betsy to call her back."

"I'll bet," Kyle said.

"You don't need to be such a snot about it, Kyle. You're the one who said it had been over thirty years. It *had* been over thirty years. You'd think some people would grow up. Especially famous people. Somebody as successful as Betsy Wetsy shouldn't still be obsessing about high school."

"Right," Kyle said.

"You said she drove over there on her own," Gregor said. "Do you know what time that was? Did you go with her?"

"I didn't go with her, no," Nancy said. "I'm almost never out of here before five, even though the school day ends at quarter to three. She intended to go out there at around three-thirty or four, but I don't know if she went then or earlier or later, at least not for sure. I do know she was intending to go alone."

"This Miss Smith," Gregor said.

"Mrs. Kennedy," Nancy corrected.

"Was she out sick that day, too?" Gregor asked.

Nancy shook her head. "She was right here, all day. Trust me, if she ever pulls one of these two days in a row, Hollman will hear about it. No, Peggy was in as usual, yesterday. I picked her up and drove her in. But I forgot to pick her up this morning."

"How could you forget?" Kyle asked.

"I met Emma in JayMar's and she made me furious," Nancy said. "So I came in early to do some work. If Peggy had called to say she was stranded, I would have gone back out to get her."

"Back to Chris," Kyle said. "She was supposed to go out to Betsy's house between three-thirty and four. As far as you know, she did it."

"As far as I know, yes."

"You were here. Peggy was here—"

"Well, not at three-thirty, she wasn't. Shelley Brancowski gave her a ride home at three. Shelley does that when I have to work late. Peggy only stays late when she's got French Club, and they only meet twice a week."

"Right," Kyle said again.

"Christ," Nancy said again. "Do you really think any of us would kill Chris off? Whatever for? I mean, I know she was a pain and a snot and all the rest of it, but there's just no reason for any of us to have done it. And you can't really think Betsy did it, no matter what Belinda says. Why would she kill Chris? If she was going to kill any of us, it would be Belinda. And I say if she hasn't killed Maris yet, she's not capable of killing anybody."

The door opened and the young woman named Lisa poked her head in. "I'm sorry to bother you," she said, "but somebody from the police department is on the phone for Kyle."

PART THREE

"Babylon"

—DAVID GRAY

"Don't Think Twice, It's All Right"

—BOB DYLAN

"My Life"

—BILLY JOEL

ONE

1

Not all small towns are alike. Some are small because they are kept that way, deliberately, by residents whose lives are really in a city not too far away, by people who know very well that a modern and efficient police force is indispensable, even if it seems not to be on a day-to-day basis. Other small towns are really small towns. They exist naturally. The people in them live in a bubble that allows them to think that they are immune from the disease of violence that infects every other place, and that has infected even small towns from the beginning of time. Gregor often thought that if you wanted to do something effective to teach people about crime—and to convince them to protect themselves from it—you would run a sixty-second commercial that did nothing but spell out the mayhem that had occurred in small towns in the last two years, any two years, pick them. Serial killers in Richmond, Nebraska. Domestic violence deaths in Mortimer, South Dakota. Drug gang wars in Leeland, Oklahoma. Envy, jealousy, and spite—everywhere, Gregor thought, because those things were part of being human. He had no idea where so many people had gotten the idea that crime was an aberration. To him, it seemed that crime was a constant. Anthropologists found evidence of murder in fossil remains.

In Hollman, they found it on Grandview Avenue, and they found it in full view of at least a hundred people. Kyle Borden hit the brake as soon as he saw them, crowding out over the sidewalks and into the street, heedless of the rain. Gregor leaned forward in his seat and tried to make some sense of what he was looking at.

"What is that?" he said.

"That's why we called the state police," Kyle said. "That's just about everybody in town who could walk up here. Plus some people I don't recognize. They must be the reporters."

Gregor was sure there would be reporters. He knew about reporters. He also knew about rubberneckers. This looked as if the whole town had come out in a body to stand on the porch of Country Crafts, and the ones who hadn't were in the street, waiting, pushing forward every once in a while to see if people would move.

"To hell with this," Kyle said. He jerked his steering wheel to the right and bumped up onto the sidewalk on the other side of the street, then up onto the lawn of the Hollman Public Library. Gregor felt the wheels of the police car sink a little in mud. "If they don't like it, they can sue me. Let's go."

Gregor snapped off his seat belt and climbed out. His shoes sank into the ground just as the wheels of the police car had. He moved as quickly as he could without falling, off the grass and onto the sidewalk. Kyle came up beside him and cupped his hands. How could people stand in the rain like that? Gregor wondered. Some of them had umbrellas, and some of them had bags or newspapers they were holding up for protection, and some of them had hats, but most of them were bareheaded. Gregor ran a hand through his own hair and water flew out of it as if he had splashed against the surface of a pond.

"This is the Hollman Town Police," Kyle shouted. "Please move out of the way. Please move out of the way."

Some people on the edge of the crowd closest to them heard, and turned, and moved away, and that was enough to get them started. They waded in, with Kyle shouting through his hands at intervals and sometimes tapping somebody he knew on the shoulder. It was hard to hear above the rain and even harder to hear above the low hum of people talking. Gregor kept his hands close to his sides and himself as close to Kyle as he could, nodding at people when they stared at him. He had no idea if he was being recognized or not. Nobody talked to him. Nobody he heard said his name.

"This is the Hollman Town Police," Kyle said, over and over again, as they inched forward. "Please get out of the way."

They reached the porch before Gregor was expecting to. At the steps, Kyle Borden had to shove a few people away. They wouldn't move just because he told them to. Gregor would have thought that these people were the reporters, except that some of them so obviously weren't. One was the middle-aged woman who had waited on him the day before in Mullaney's, when he had run in for a newspaper. Another was the woman he recognized as the waitress from Hollman Pizza. Kyle pushed at these people without ceremony and reached the door. He turned the knob and found it locked.

"Open up," he said, pounding on the glass front. Far away, Gregor could hear the cowbell tinkle.

The face of a man appeared in the glass on the other side of the door. It seemed to stare at Kyle for a moment, and then nod. There was a rattling and then the door swung open on blank space.

"Hurry," Kyle said, grabbing Gregor by the sleeve and pulling him inside.

Several people tried to follow. Kyle whipped around and shut the door in their faces. Then he looked up at the man who had opened up for them. "George. What's going on? What is this?"

"I knew they'd come," George said. His face was as white as good quality typing paper. "I knew they'd all be here as soon as they heard, and they'd hear. They always hear. Why is that? Why do people behave that way?"

"I don't know," Kyle said. "I've called the state police. They should be here any moment. They'll clear the crowd out. Try to tell us what happened here."

"I don't know what happened here," George said. "I just—came home, that's all. I was showing a house out in Stony Hill and then I, I don't know, I just thought I'd come home and talk to Emma for a while and sit in the store if she wanted to go out, you know, down to JayMar's or something and when I came in—" He looked quickly to the back of the shop. "They're still there, I think. Both of them."

"Both of them?" Kyle was startled. "There are two bod—people hurt?"

"I called the ambulance, but I know it isn't any good," George said. "You can see she's dead. There are, I don't know, parts of her—pieces of her—"

"Where?" Kyle asked.

George looked astonished. "Back there. In the storeroom. Behind the curtains. I called out and she didn't answer me so I went back there first thing because that's where she usually is. I should have known something was wrong. She always comes out when the bell rings. And I went back there and there they were, the both of them—"

There were sirens outside, very close. "That's the ambulance," Kyle said. "George, listen to me. I'm going to go back to look. When the ambulance men get to the door, let them in. Okay? Do it fast. Just in case. Come on, Mr. Demarkian."

Gregor came. They walked to the back of the store, through another small room filled with even more shelves. These shelves were full of materials—pipe cleaners, cloth, construction paper, glue, glitter, beads. At the back of this small room was a curtain. Kyle hurried toward it, pulled it aside, and sucked in his breath.

"Jesus Christ," he said.

Gregor came up beside him. Behind the curtain there was another small room. Unlike the two in the front, this one had not been decorated, and it had no shelves. Instead, there were boxes everywhere, most of them open and half-empty. On the floor among them was the bulky body of the woman Gregor had come to know as Emma Kenyon Bligh. The front of her dress was ripped, slit partly open—but George Bligh was wrong. There were no "pieces" of Emma anywhere. There was a lot of blood, but only pieces of her dress. It looked as if somebody had tried to carve her up from the front. Gregor's head swiveled around, looking for the other one—and found her, sitting up and entirely conscious. She was not someone he recognized, but she was just as bloody as Emma Bligh, and maybe more, and she had a long razor-edged linoleum cutter in her lap.

Gregor ignored her and dropped down by Emma Bligh. He put his head on her chest and listened to the heartbeat. It was a little rapid, but it was not faint. "Are those ambulance men through the door yet?" he asked. "Tell them to hurry. This one's alive."

"What?"

Gregor stood up. "She's alive. I doubt if she's unconscious from anything but the pain. The artery isn't cut. If it was, there'd be a lot more blood."

"How much blood do you want there to be?" Kyle asked.

"Trust me. This is not enough. Tell her husband to thank God that his wife got fat. It saved her life. Who's the other one?"

The ambulance men were at the curtain. They took one look at Emma Bligh's body on the floor and went to it. Seconds later, one of them looked up and said, "She's alive. Holy shit."

Kyle went over to the woman sitting on the box. "Peggy?" he said. "Peggy, what happened here?"

This must be Peggy Smith Kennedy, Gregor realized. He looked her up and down, but it wasn't a good time to check her out. She was dazed. She was covered with sticky blood.

"Peggy," Kyle said.

Peggy looked up. "It was sticking out of her," she said. "I looked down and it was sticking out of her and then I just grabbed it and pulled and I fell, and when I was trying to pick myself up George came, I heard him come in the door. And then I don't know what happened. Is she dead?"

"No," Gregor Demarkian said. "And if we get lucky, she won't be."

"She isn't dead?" Peggy looked confused.

One of the ambulance men must have been a paramedic. He had done something to stanch the flow of blood, and now two other ambulance men were lifting Emma Bligh carefully onto a stretcher. Peggy looked at them in astonishment.

"How could she be alive after all that blood? How is it possible?"

"Mr. Demarkian here says she had armor made of fat," Kyle said. "Listen, Peggy, I think you should go to the hospital, too. You're in shock. You need to be taken care of."

"I don't want to go to the hospital."

"I don't care if you want to go," Kyle said. "You should go. You need to be looked at. You need to find out if—"

"If Stu finds out I was here, he'll kill me," Peggy said. "He really will. I stayed home from school today because I was feeling, well, you know, not well, and he hates that. He really hates that. He has to stay out sick so much himself. He's always sick. He goes crazy when he thinks I am. He thinks I'm at school. He thinks—"

"Shh," Kyle said.

"It isn't just blood from Emma Bligh," Gregor said. He got a handkerchief out of his pocket, reached forward, and took the linoleum cutter out of Peggy Smith Kennedy's hands. The parts of the blade that were not streaked with blood gleamed. "She's got a black eye. She's got bruises on her arm. I think her left pinkie finger is broken."

"Jesus," Kyle said.

Peggy Smith Kennedy stared at the linoleum cutter. "That was inside her. It was sticking out of her. And I thought, you can't leave it like that. You can't leave Emma on the floor with a thing like that in her. So I took it out, and then there was blood everywhere. There was blood all over me. I'm never going to get it out of this dress."

The ambulance men took the stretcher with Emma Bligh on it out of the room. A few moments later, George Bligh stuck his head through the curtains.

"Is it true? Is she really still alive?"

"She was when I listened to her heartbeat," Gregor told him. "In spite of how awful it looks, my guess is that the wound isn't anywhere near as serious as it would have to be to kill her. She—"

"I'm going to follow the ambulance to the hospital," George said. "If you want to arrest me, you can do it later. I'm going to the hospital now."

He ducked back out of the curtains, and Kyle shook his head. "It's not like he's going anyplace we can't find him. Jesus, Jesus, Jesus."

"There was blood everywhere even before I took it out of her," Peggy Smith Kennedy said. "I stepped in it."

All of a sudden, there were sirens, lots of sirens. Some of them would be the ambulance taking Emma Kenyon Bligh to the hospital. Some of them turned out to be the state police. Gregor heard them as they came up the porch steps, barking orders. Gregor went out into the little room and then beyond it into the bigger one. He watched as one of the state police officers tried to push people back onto the porch. The other officer came up to him.

"Mr. Demarkian," he said.

"How do you do." If he'd met the officer by name, Gregor didn't remember him. "You'd better go on back, through the next room and then through a curtain. There's another one."

"Another body?"

"Another woman. The woman the ambulance just took is alive. That's why she's gone. Go on back. There's something I've got to do. I'll be with you in a moment."

"Is the other woman dead?" the officer asked.

She might as well be, Gregor thought, but he didn't say it. He watched the officer at the door finally get all the unauthorized people out onto the porch and then lock the door behind him. Then he sat down behind Emma Bligh's counter and picked up the phone.

2

Bennis Hannaford was not only in but showered and dressed, and just two floors down from Jimmy Card and Elizabeth Toliver.

"Nobody knows we're here yet, if that's what you're worried about," she said, when she'd heard Gregor out. "Although I don't expect that's going to last long. If I recognized the car, somebody else will. I mean Jimmy Card's car. Didn't you say you had Elizabeth Toliver's car? Where is it?"

"At Andy's garage," Gregor said. "Do you think you could go up there and ask them if they've seen anything at all of Maris Coleman?"

"Who's Maris Coleman?"

"Somebody who works for Ms. Toliver. It's a long story. Do you think you could—"

"What, Gregor? Just march upstairs, muscle my way onto their floor and walk up to Elizabeth Toliver and say 'Hello, Ms. Toliver. It's nice to meet you. I've always enjoyed your work. Where is Maris Coleman?' "

"Bennis, for God's sake. I don't have the phone number. I wasn't even sure where they were until you told me. I was just calling you up to see if you could find out. Since you're there, go ask them if they've seen Maris Coleman at any time this morning. All right? There's a woman half dead out here and—"

"Another one? Where? At Elizabeth Toliver's house?"

"No. Nowhere near there. In town. It's a long story. Now will you please—"

"It'll take forever. Five minutes. Ten."

"I'll wait."

"But—"

"I'll *wait*," Gregor said. "I've got to know if they've seen anything of Maris Coleman this morning, all right? Go. It's only going to take longer if you stand there arguing."

"Hell," Bennis said.

Gregor heard a clunk that he supposed must be the phone receiver hitting some kind of surface—the night table, the floor—and sat back to watch the state police help Peggy Smith Kennedy out of the back room and through the front rooms toward the door. There were still dozens of people on the porch outside, but there was also a state police officer.

Peggy Smith Kennedy was hobbling when she walked. The chalk whiteness of her face made the growing bruises around her eyes all the more noticeable. If she'd been trying to hide what was going on in her marriage, she was about to lose the fight—but Gregor knew she'd already lost it. She went out onto the porch holding on to a state police officer the way swooning maidens held on to rescuing lovers in bad nineteenth-century novels.

Kyle Borden came up and said, "Who're you calling? We've got to get back to the station."

"Give me a minute," Gregor told him. There were suddenly voices on the other end of the phone, and Gregor distinctly heard Bennis say "halvah." He shook his head. "Bennis?" he said into the phone.

"Mr. Demarkian?" It was not Bennis's voice. "This is Liz Toliver. I'm sorry. From what Bennis said, it seemed to make more sense if I talked to you directly, but—oh, thank you, this is wonderful—but we didn't know where you were to call you back from upstairs. Bennis says someone was attacked but not killed. Was that Maris? Is Maris hurt?"

"What's she feeding you?" Gregor asked.

"What? Oh, halvah, you know, the stuff that's like a brick with a tahine base. You can get it in New York in some places. This is better. Is Maris hurt?"

"I have no idea," Gregor said. "I don't know where she is. I was hoping you did."

"Oh, no. I don't. We haven't seen her all morning. We were worried about it earlier. We thought she might still be back at the house."

"Still? You mean, she was there this morning?"

"We don't know," Liz Toliver said. "I remember last night. She passed out on the couch. And that was the last time I saw her. But she didn't have her car, so if she was passed out on the couch last night she should still be in the house, because she wouldn't have any way to get home. Back to Belinda's, I mean."

"I didn't see her," Gregor said. "Not at the house this morning."

"She isn't usually at the house in the morning," Liz said, "so you don't expect to see her. But we're very worried that she wandered off and fell asleep somewhere and didn't hear all the commotion this morning and got left behind, and maybe she's still out there. She couldn't call anybody. Not with the phone lines cut. She could be stranded."

Gregor almost said that if Maris Coleman were stranded in that house, it was because she had stranded herself there. There was no way that anybody who wasn't in a coma could have slept through that hysteria this morning.

"We'll go out there and check," he said, waving away Kyle's protest. "What I wanted to know was if you'd seen her, and now I know. I take it you've been with Jimmy and the boys ever since you left your house this morning?"

"Well, I took a shower by myself, but it was only for about twenty minutes."

"That's fine," Gregor told her. "That's much too short a time to have done what you'd needed to do. What about in the last hour? Have you been mostly visible?"

"Oh, yes. Jimmy and I have been—discussing things."

Gregor heard Bennis whoop with laughter in the background. He ignored her. "Good," he said. "That puts you out of it, at least for this attack. That's helpful."

"Who was it? Who got attacked? You said she isn't dead?"

"Not dead, no, but badly hurt," Gregor said. "It's a woman named Emma Kenyon Bligh."

There was a silence on the other end of the phone. "Emma Kenyon. My God."

"I'm not a doctor, but I've seen enough people who'd been attacked to say with some certainty that she's likely to be all right in the long run. I don't know how long a run."

"Maris said she'd gained a lot of weight," Liz Toliver said.

"I'd estimate that she weighs close to four hundred and fifty pounds," Gregor said. "She's very large. It probably saved her life."

"Well," Liz Toliver said.

"Would you mind if I talked to Bennis again?" Gregor said.

There was more talking in the background, and more passing around of food. Bennis was promising to pack up a box of pastries for the boys, and Liz Toliver was insisting that she come upstairs and have coffee with Jimmy and the rest of them. So much for Bennis's worries about how Liz would take to being around one of Jimmy's former lovers. Gregor thought it was interesting that Bennis never seemed to have worried for a moment about how *he* would feel about being around one of *her* former lovers. She picked up the phone.

"Gregor? Are you coming on out? Because if you are, I'm going upstairs for some coffee and you might as well meet me up there."

"I probably won't be home for hours," Gregor said. "Have you called Russ for me?"

"Yes. Already did it. You asked Tibor to check, too. Russ said to tell you that he'll check, but he isn't very hopeful. He said it would be easier for him if you knew exactly what you were looking for. Do you?"

"Yes. But if I tell him, he'll go looking for that in particular, and I might miss something I'm not expecting. There's always a chance that there's something I'm not expecting. Although I don't believe there will be, in this case. Go up and have coffee with Liz Toliver. Say hello to Mark for me."

"All right. Where are you? How do we get in touch with you?"

"I'm at a store on Grandview Avenue called Country Crafts, but I won't be here for long. Your best bet is to call the police department, but I'd feel much better if you don't have to. There's more going on here than I can tell you about yet. Take care of yourself."

"You take care of yourself. You sound funny."

"I feel fine. I'll talk to you later, Bennis."

Gregor put the phone down in the cradle and looked up to see that Kyle Borden was hovering over him, glowering.

"We can't go back out to the Toliver house now," he said. "We've got to go back to the station. We've got reports to file. We've got the Staties to worry about. We've—"

"I'll go back by myself if you want me to. Maris Coleman seems to be missing."

"Missing from where?"

Gregor gave Kyle a rundown of the events of the night before and this morning, and Kyle kicked the side of the counter.

"Shit damn," he said. "She must still be out there, right? She's probably wandering around in that house drinking coffee spiked with whatever she spikes it with and pretending nobody ever notices. Shit damn. We'll have to go get her. Or send somebody else to."

"Oh, I don't think she's still out there. There were a hundred people who could have given her a ride, if she was willing to pay for it by talking a blue streak, and I think she'd have been willing to do that. Don't you?"

"She'd have paid them to let her. If we're not rescuing Maris, what are we doing? Why are we going out there?"

"I want to make sure something isn't there."

"What?"

"Just something," Gregor said. "Listen, what about here? What's left to do? Did the state police bring in some decent forensics this time? What about the linoleum cutter?"

"One of the Staties picked it up with a handkerchief and put it in a plastic bag. It's probably got my fingerprints on it. I took it away from Peggy and it didn't occur to me to use a handkerchief. It's been coming home to me, lately, just how well I was trained for this job. Meaning not at all. You have no idea how much I feel like a jerk."

"It's a waste of time," Gregor told him. "Right now, the real issue is that that linoleum cutter is almost certainly going to turn out to be the murder weapon in the death of Chris Inglerod Barr. It would be a good thing if we didn't lose it. Go back and tell the state policemen that. Whatever. Then let's pack up and go on out to Liz Toliver's house. With any luck, there won't be much of anybody left there to bother us."

"Right," Kyle said. He gave Gregor a long, puzzled, and faintly resentful look and then went on back to the curtained space, where more state police officers were crowded than it seemed that the building could hold.

Gregor sat down in the heavy chair Emma Bligh kept behind the counter and took his notepad out of his inside jacket pocket. He flipped to the front and found the list that Jimmy Card had given him when he first agreed to look into the death of Michael Houseman. The list was not complete. Jimmy had been working off the things Liz Toliver had told him, not as part of a coherent story but as pieces in an ongoing conversation. The list did not include Stuart Kennedy's name, or Kyle Borden's. Gregor checked off the names of Chris Inglerod and Emma Kenyon, and then wrote Stuart Kennedy's and Kyle Borden's at the bottom of the list.

Kyle came up from the back of the store. "That's done," he said. "They think it's going to turn out to be the murder weapon, too. Where would you get something like that?"

"In a hardware store," Gregor said. "At Home Depot. A lot of people who do odd jobs around the house have them."

"I think I'd cut half my hand off just trying to pick one up."

Gregor stood up and shook the wrinkles out of his jacket. "Let's go," he said. "Let's go see what's still out at the house and then let's try to do something sensible with what we find."

3

It was odd, Gregor thought, that Elizabeth Toliver's house should look so much like he had seen it for the first time, and not at all as he had been seeing it since—experiencing it since, Bennis would say, to indicate that he was really talking about a kind of emotional atmosphere. This afternoon, there was no atmosphere around the place at all. There was only rain, which was now slightly, but only *slightly*, less furious than it had been an hour or two before. Gregor looked up and down the road as they drove into the Toliver driveway, but it was as completely deserted as anything he had ever seen, which was a relief.

Kyle pulled the car into the driveway halfway to the garage and cut the engine. "Here we are," he said. "What exactly is it that you want to do?"

"I want to look for something," Gregor said. "Let's start with the garage first. And let me ask you something. Does Elizabeth Toliver make you angry?"

"Betsy? No, of course she doesn't make me angry. Why should she?"

Gregor got out of the car and headed for the garage. Kyle was behind him in a moment. "She makes a lot of people angry," Gregor said, pulling up the first garage door he came to, "have you noticed that? I don't mean just envious or jealous or even resentful, but really down dirty furious. Belinda Hart could barely say Liz's name without spitting it. And then there's Maris Coleman. You haven't been watching Ms. Coleman's behavior from up close these last few days. I have. 'Angry' is almost too mild a word for it. The emotion runs so deep, I don't think Maris Coleman even wishes Liz Toliver dead. I think death would be too quick. The pain would be over. Maris Coleman wishes Liz Toliver a long life lived in unending pain and humiliation."

"Don't you think that's a little strong?" Kyle said.

"No." Gregor looked around the garage. It was dark at the best of times. Now, with so little light coming from outside, it was virtually pitch. "Are there any lights in this place?" he asked.

"Right here." Kyle fumbled around for a moment, and then three weak bulbs, screwed into ceiling fixtures without benefit of shades, glowed on.

Kyle blinked. "I guess I can't imagine Maris Coleman working up all that much energy about anything," he said.

"But you've noticed the anger with Belinda Hart Grantling."

"Oh, yeah," Kyle said. "And it isn't only her. It's Emma Kenyon Bligh, too, if you want to know the truth, and Chris and Nancy weren't too calm about the whole thing, either. I don't know about Peggy. I've never heard her talk about it."

"What about everybody else in town?" Gregor asked. He had begun to move slowly along the garage's perimeter, studying the walls. "Are they angry at Elizabeth Toliver, too?"

Kyle cleared his throat. "Well," he said, "a lot of them, it's sort of the 'who do you think you are?' thing. They all knew her when she was growing up. They didn't think she was anything special. And now she's—We don't feel very comfortable with people who are different. People who go away and become famous are different."

Gregor finished with the first wall and began on the second, moving carefully, running his eyes up and down as well as back and forth. "But that's not the way all small towns behave about all people who go away to become famous," he said. "There's that country singer, what's her name, Shania Twain. Her hometown held a big celebration for her when she returned. And that movie star. Meg Ryan. Her hometown—"

"But that's different," Kyle protested. "They were big deals even before they left. Meg Ryan was a prom princess. So, you see—"

"Yes," Gregor said. He finished with the third wall. The fourth wall was garage doors. He looked around one more time, to make sure. "Where else would somebody keep tools?"

"Tools?" Kyle looked blank. "You can't be looking for tools here. Mrs. Toliver has Alzheimer's disease. Even if the Tolivers ever had any tools, they wouldn't have them around now. She could get hold of them and be dangerous."

"Did they have any tools?" Gregor asked.

"Not a chance. Mr. Toliver was a hotshot lawyer. He never touched a tool in his life."

"Elizabeth Toliver has a brother, doesn't she? Did he have tools?"

"He kept them at Andy's Garage," Kyle said. "And it's been years since he's been back here, too. He moved out to California about two decades ago. What is it you're getting at?"

"We ought to go check the basement, just in case," Gregor said.

"I can't do that without a search warrant," Kyle said. "You don't want to get me into a position where—"

"Don't worry about it. I won't get you into any kind of position. There will be no searching the house in the ordinary sense. We will not be conducting a criminal investigation. I've got the key. I'm going in to get some of my things, which I'm going to need. You coming with me?"

"Shit," Kyle said.

"Turn off the lights," Gregor told him.

Gregor waited until the lights were out and then went out into the driveway again through the bay. He waited until Kyle got out and then pulled the garage door down. The rain really had let up by now. It was still coming down, but it was of only ordinary force, and there was no thunder in the distance. Gregor led the way across the backyard toward the kitchen lawn.

"For a long time," he said as he and Kyle let themselves into the mudroom, "I was very confused. I didn't go to what you'd call a normal high school. I grew up in central Philadelphia, in what was at the time I suppose a slum. I went to high school with a lot of other people just like me. We had parents who'd come from Armenia. English was not our first language. We didn't have proms and prom princesses and cheerleaders and any of that sort of thing—well, the school did, to an extent, but that had nothing to do with us. Our parents wouldn't have let us near things like that. If we wanted to meet members of the opposite sex, we went to dances at the neighborhood church. So you see, it didn't make any sense to me. The 'popularity' thing. Have you noticed how odd that is? The 'popular' people are 'popular' by virtue of being envied and hated by ninety-nine percent of the people they go to school with. Does anybody but me think that's very strange?"

"No," Kyle said. "It had occurred to me on occasion, too."

"Here"—Gregor held open a door on the other side of the mudroom—"there's a basement down here. 'Finished.' That way's the main house. Down here there's a recreation room and some kind of workroom."

"I'll bet there aren't any tools in it," Kyle said.

Gregor led the way down the stairs. "I got very tangled up in it at first," he went on. "The emotions were so strong, it seemed to me that they could lead to the murder of just about anyone. But the longer I thought of it, the more I realized that if somebody was going to get killed over this kind of thing, it would be Liz Toliver herself who ended up dead. Because the key here is the disjunction. What people really hate is that things haven't turned out the way they expected them to."

They were at the bottom of the basement stairs. Gregor knew where the light switch was. He flipped the flat of his hand against it and turned on half a dozen lights at once. "It would be different if Liz Toliver was still what she had been. That's how you get school shooters. You think that kind of anger and hurt would dissipate in time, but I don't think it does. I remember a woman who wrote to the Philadelphia *Inquirer* after the Columbine incident who said that whenever she heard about a school shooting, she cheered, because it was a triumph for the losers. She was forty-three. I thought she was psychotic when I read the letter. Now I'm not so sure. If she's psychotic, practically everybody else in the country must be, too."

"Is this going anyplace?" Kyle asked.

Gregor led the way through the recreation room—which was large, and carpeted, and contained a television set the size of Oklahoma. He tried the first door he came to on the back wall of the room. It opened onto a closet. He tried the next one and met blackness. He snaked his hand inside against the wall and found the light switch. The lights went on, big fluorescents behind patterned plastic panels. There was a table in the center of the room. There was a sewing machine. There were a lot of things in boxes.

"Here we are," Gregor said.

"You do spend a lot of time talking about nothing," Kyle said. "And then you don't finish your thought."

"My thought? Well, my thought is that reality is not very much like the movies. You know those movies, where the small-town loser goes off to the big wide world and comes back a success and everybody finally loves him?"

"It's the American dream."

"Exactly. And it's full of it. When the small-town loser comes back a success, everybody hates him, or is indifferent. But mostly there's the hate. And if you're not prepared for that, you're likely to get thrown very badly. I don't think Liz Toliver was prepared for that. I don't think she was expecting a hero's welcome, mind you. She's not that naive. But I don't think she was expecting the animus."

"Why not?" Kyle said. "It's the way they always did treat her, before. The woman is completely phobic about snakes, and they knew that. And they nailed her up in that damned outhouse with nearly two dozen of them. I'd say that's enough animus for anybody to notice."

"True. I just don't think she was expecting it to have lasted. To tell you the truth, if I'd been in her position, I wouldn't have expected it either. It's not really very sane, is it?"

"Do you have what you came for?" Kyle asked. "It gives me the creeps, being in here like this. We could get nailed."

"We could not get nailed. I have a key. I have the right of access. And, yes, I have what I came for. No tools. Not only that, no sign that there ever were tools. No drills. No saws. No linoleum cutters. No pegs in the wall. No toolboxes."

"I told you so."

"I know. I had to see for myself." Gregor looked around. "It looks like it was used as a sewing room once. Now it's a storeroom. That's sensible enough. Here's another question. Is there some reason why the fever about Liz Toliver is so much higher in Maris Coleman and Belinda Hart Grantling than in the rest of them I've met so far?"

"Well," Kyle said, "they were the ones who pulled the most crap on Betsy in high school. And before high school. Betsy's problems didn't start in high school."

"Yes," Gregor said, "I know. It's odd the way people are, don't you think? There's so much emotion expended over things that don't matter. Most people who are murdered are murdered over trivialities. Over emotions. Over slights and disrespect and arguments and dozens of other things that make no sense. Harris and Klebold murdered fifteen people over things that shouldn't matter to anybody, except that we make them matter. You'd think we'd learn."

"You're not making sense again," Kyle said.

Gregor sighed. He supposed he wasn't making sense, although he was making perfect sense to himself. He headed for the door again. "We'd better get out of here," he said. "I'd better pick up some clothes upstairs. I should go out to the Radisson to see Bennis. Do you think you could call me there and let me know about Emma Kenyon Bligh's medical condition? Or I could call you."

Kyle said something about how Gregor should call him, and they both went far too quickly up the stairs. The house felt deserted, even though they were in it.

TWO

1

There came a point when Liz Toliver couldn't sit still any longer. She had never been very good at sitting still—that, and not talent or drive or an unhappy childhood, was what she thought really explained her success—and she found sitting still under pressure virtually impossible. She had been pacing up and down the long corridor of the hotel floor they had rented all morning. She'd put down a half-dozen half-empty cups of tea and forgotten where they'd gone. She was scared to death that she was about to commit one of the great sins in her ethical lexicon and leave a mess for the maids. It didn't matter. The world felt like a claustrophobic place, all the more because she now knew that events were going on without her. She kept getting an image of Emma Kenyon with a knife stuck out of her belly, a knife that didn't go all the way through because, in Liz's fantasy, Emma was as enormous as a circus freak. She turned on a television in one of the rooms and sat down to watch CNN. There was nothing on it of any interest. She surfed through the channels until she found some local news, and there was nothing on that, either. She had forgotten what it was like to live in a place where people did not expect fresh, up-to-the-minute, breaking news about their area twenty-four seven. Her muscles ached. She wished she were herself only five years ago, when nobody would have cared if she walked stark naked down Fifth Avenue at high noon. Most of all, she wished she understood herself. She ought to feel vindicated. She ought to feel that she'd scored some big triumph. That was how Maris expected her to feel. Instead, whenever she could get her mind off herself, the whole thing made her tired. How could anyone—*anyone*—spend their entire lives in a town like Hollman?

She went to the end of the corridor and looked out. Her car was at Andy's Garage. Jimmy's car was in the parking lot, and his driver was in one of the rooms on this very floor, but that wouldn't work. Everybody in creation knew what Jimmy's car was like. There was Mr. Demarkian's car, but Mr. Demarkian had it. There was Maris's unused little rental, but Maris had that, or it was parked behind English Drugs, which came to the same thing. Liz could remember one day when she was fourteen years old, walking alone down Grandview Avenue, on her way up the hill to go to the Booklet. Belinda and Maris and Emma had been coming at her from the other direction, and when they got less than a foot and a half away, they burst into giggles and jaywalked at a run to the other side of the street. 1965, she thought. That had been in *1965*.

She went back down the corridor to the room where Jimmy had set up shop and stood in the empty doorway. He had his back to her, talking on the phone, the good black light summer wool of his city jacket making him seem just a little taller and a little thinner than he was.

Jimmy was pacing around, just as she had been. In the middle of one tour of the room, he saw her standing in the doorway and stopped.

"Just a minute," he said into the phone. He put the receiver against his chest. "Are you okay? Do you need me?"

"I always need you. It's not important. I'm feeling a little crazy."

"Just a minute," he said again, but this time to her. He put the receiver back up to his ear. "Listen, I'll call you back in an hour, how's that? I know. I know. Something's come up. It can wait, Creighton. It can certainly wait an hour. Yes. Yes. I'll talk to you later."

Creighton Allmark was Jimmy's agent. Liz waited while Jimmy hung up the phone and came across the room to her.

"You look awful," he said. "You really look awful. Is there something I can do?"

Liz shrugged. "The problem is, there isn't anything I can do. I've had a shower. I've played backgammon with Mark. I've played Go Fish with Geoff. I've drunk enough tea that my kidneys are floating. I've eaten half a pound of that pastry thing Ms. Hannaford brought up for me. I've talked to you. I've talked to the doctors. I've talked to the hospital. I've even talked to Mr. Demarkian. I'm going insane."

"States of siege are sort of like that."

"But we aren't in a state of siege, are we?" Liz asked. "There isn't anybody outside. Nobody knows we're here."

"They will."

"I know they will. And then we will be in a state of siege. I want to get out of here before that happens."

"Get out how?" Jimmy looked alarmed. "You mean get out of Hollman? Mr. Demarkian explained how that wouldn't be the best idea, and—"

"No," Liz said. "I want to get out of the hotel. I want to take a drive. I want to do something, even if it's nothing in particular."

"Somebody will see you. And recognize you."

"Maybe."

"They'll follow the car when you try to come back here," Jimmy said.

"Maybe," Liz said again.

"Besides"—Jimmy took a deep breath—"what would you take a drive in? Your car isn't here. Mine is too recognizable. Taking that would really be psychotic. And you couldn't rent one, not from here, not now. If you tried it, we'd be inundated in no time flat."

"She's got a car," Liz said.

"Who's she?"

"Bennis Hannaford. She's got a tangerine-orange Mercedes two-seater. Parked in this parking lot. I know. We talked about it."

"Well," Jimmy said. "That's not exactly being inconspicuous either, is it?"

"Maybe not. But it would at least get me out of here. And I do have to get out of here. I know what you're saying. I've seen it happen to other people, the Clintons during the impeachment, Caroline Kennedy Schlossberg right after John Kennedy disappeared in his plane. I know what you're trying to say. But even Caroline Kennedy went out for a bike ride. She didn't stay indoors for the whole week until the reporters went away."

"When she did go out for a bike ride, she was followed by camera crews in vans," Jimmy said. "I know you're feeling shut in. I'm just trying to counsel something like prudence. You said yourself that Demarkian was asking you about where you were when this latest murder happened—"

"It wasn't a murder. It was an attack. She's still alive."

"Attack, whatever. You said yourself he was asking about where you were. And you know you were here, in full view of everybody, for the whole time. And you know that means that you're going to be off the hook, probably sooner rather than later. So if you'll just—"

"If they don't arrest somebody for this crime," Liz said carefully, "the tabloids will pin it on me, forever, and it won't matter at all that I couldn't have committed the attack on Emma Kenyon. The legitimate press will pin it on me, too, they'll just be more polite about it. You know all that as well as I do."

"The police usually do catch murderers," Jimmy said.

"I know. On the other hand, I also know that the police in this town consist of exactly two men, one of whom I have known since birth. And he was nobody's Einstein even then."

"They have the state police in on this as well. And Demarkian."

"I know. I know." Liz walked over to Jimmy's window and looked out. There was more parking lot on this side of the building. The hotel seemed to have been set down in a vast sea of parking lots. "Take me seriously, for a moment. I have to get out of here for a little while. I'm really beginning to lose control. And that won't be any good for any of us."

"You won't lose control, Liz. You never do."

"You know," Liz said, "that's not true. I did when Jay died. I didn't lie down on the floor and roll around and kick and scream. I looked all right.

But I didn't work at all for nearly two years, and that in spite of the fact that my financial world was collapsing and we lost the house and had to live in that god-awful cabin and one Christmas there wasn't a Christmas. And none of that picked me up and got me moving again."

"Something did."

"Yes. Something did. But it was mostly time. I do lose control of myself. I do. And I do make an idiot of myself. I do handle things badly. I do. I just want to get out and ride around in the air for a little while. Is that really too much to ask?"

"I don't know," Jimmy said. "Ask the guys who are trailing you. What is it exactly that you want to do?"

"I thought I'd run downstairs and see if Bennis Hannaford would give me a ride into town. Either that, or let me borrow her car, but I wouldn't let anybody borrow a car like that from me. Tangerine-orange. She must have had it custom-painted."

"I think it's really odd that you and Bennis Hannaford get along so well."

"Why? You fell in love with both of us."

"I fell in love with Julie and you can't be in the same room with her without spitting nails. You going to tell the boys you're going?"

"No. You tell them. I don't want them asking to come with me. They're probably as stir-crazy as I am. And relax. She may turn me down."

"Lately, I don't have that kind of luck."

He came over to her and kissed her, seriously, the way he did when he couldn't wait for them to get into bed. Then he leaned back and smiled at her, as if it had been a joke.

"No harm in trying," he suggested.

She pecked him on the cheek and went out of the room. She saw Mark and Geoff sitting on the floor of one of the rooms in front of a television set, blasting away on another video game. She went to the end of the corridor and out onto the landing and down the stairs.

As soon as she was moving in the stairwell, she knew she had made the right decision. She already felt a million times less tense than she had. Her muscles were already beginning to unkink. She went through the fire doors at the second floor and out onto Bennis's corridor.

She watched the door numbers pass by and stopped at 223. She knocked on the door and waited, patiently, while somebody came up close and probably looked through the spy hole. Then the door locks turned over and the door opened on Bennis Hannaford, looking disheveled and just out of the shower in a clean green robe.

"You want to borrow the car," she said, holding up a set of keys on a plastic key ring. It was one of those fish with feet with the word "evolve" printed inside it.

"Do you always give the keys to your car to strangers?" Liz said. "And how did you know I wanted to borrow the car?"

"I knew because you asked me thirty questions about it when you were down here before. Besides, I've been claustrophobic in my life. I know the signs. And no. I don't loan the car to strangers. I don't loan it to anybody. I figure, at the moment, that I'm loaning it to Jimmy, and I owe him a little."

"Well, I'd like to hear about *that*."

"Maybe we'll skip it. Do you want these?" Bennis jangled the keys in the air.

Liz took them, and looked at them, and then looked up. "Listen," she said, "come with me. I mean it. I don't want to talk to Jimmy, and I don't want to talk to the boys, and God only knows I don't want to talk to the police or the reporters or even to Mr. Demarkian. But I could use someone to talk to."

"Someone you don't know?"

"Maybe. But not any somebody."

"Are you all right?" Bennis said.

"*No*," Liz said furiously. "No, I'm not. Deep down, in the pit of my stomach, I have this awful sick feeling that I've been a complete idiot nearly all my life. I've based everything I've done, everything I've felt—I've based it all on a delusion and it's all my fault. It's been my delusion. Nobody lied to me. Nobody tried to confuse me. The truth was right there in front of my face all along and I just chose not to see it. Oh, Christ. Am I making *any* sense at all?"

"No," Bennis said, "but you've convinced me. I'll drive. Why don't you come in and sit down for a minute while I put something on. Do you know where it is you want to go?"

"Sort of."

Bennis made a little grunting noise and disappeared into the room's bathroom. Liz came in and shut the door behind her and went over to the window. There was more parking lot out this side, too. At least, with Bennis Hannaford, she wouldn't have to listen to a lecture about how she shouldn't be spending her time—right this minute, under the circumstances—looking for Maris Coleman.

2

It had seemed to Maris Coleman that the best possible course of action would be silence, and that the best possible way to maintain silence would be to disappear for a few hours. When she'd gotten back to town from the Toliver house, she'd gone up to Belinda's apartment dreading the kind of conversation she was going to have to have to keep Belinda happy, but she'd only been happy herself for a moment or two. After that, she'd started flipping back and forth through the channels on Belinda's cable system, getting nowhere. It was like that old joke: *fifty-two channels and nothing on*. There *was* something on CNN and the twenty-four-hour news shows, but not nearly as much as Maris would have liked. For the moment, the legitimate press were being very careful about what they said about Betsy Wetsy's involvement in Chris Inglerod's murder, and what coverage there was of the case seemed to focus on the return of Chris's husband Dan from his convention in Hawaii. What was really disturbing was the fact that CNBC seemed to be treating Chris's death as if it were an attempted attack on Betsy, gone wrong, making Betsy look like a martyr or a victim, not like somebody who could have been responsible for a woman being eviscerated on her lawn. Local news was nonexistent. It wasn't the hour for it. They were showing syndicated episodes of Maury Povitch and Sally Jesse Raphael and Ricki Lake. The Cartoon Channel had cartoons. Comedy Central had reruns of *Saturday Night Live* shows. Court TV was broadcasting a drunk driving trial in North Carolina. Maris paused a little on that one to listen, but she couldn't understand much of what was going on.

When the commotion started up Grandview Avenue, she went out and tried to blend into the crowd around the door to Country Crafts. It took her a while to figure out what was going on inside, and to hear the story of Peggy Smith Kennedy and her "near *coma*" as one woman put it, while another corrected that to "near *catatonia*, poor dear, it must have been such an awful thing to find." The crowd was full of reporters, some of whom knew her, and that was the last thing she wanted at the moment. She wasn't ready to talk to the *Enquirer*, or the *Star*, and she had a feeling that they would not be ready to talk to her. The big prize now would be Emma, who had survived being cut in the belly with something that sounded like a Saracen's sword. She wanted to make sure she hadn't made some kind of terrible mistake. That was why she hung around in the rain only long enough to find out what had happened, but not so long that the crowd started to thin out and leave her stranded.

She went back to Belinda's apartment and locked herself in. She threw all three of the bolts—whatever did anyone want bolts for in a place like Hollman? Maris didn't have bolts on her apartment door in New York—and went into the bathroom. As soon as she saw the sampler on the wall next to the medicine cabinet, she felt her stomach start to heave. She arched up over the toilet bowl and let it out, all at once, a thick hot stream of it that came from so deep inside her she thought she was pulling up her own organs. She had no idea what it was. She hadn't eaten anything in hours. She hadn't even had much in the way of dinner the night before, just a half a tuna-fish sandwich that Mark DeAvecca had made her. She seemed to be finished heaving. It was gone as capriciously as it had started. She stood back, flushed the toilet—she'd clean up later, when she had a chance to relax for a while—and washed her face.

Out in Belinda's kitchen, Maris suddenly realized that she really only had one option. She couldn't just sit in Belinda's apartment for another two weeks. She couldn't just act as if nothing had happened, and she had some repair work to do. She got a thick white coffee mug out of the cabinet and put a spoonful of Taster's Choice coffee in it. She put the little kettle on to boil and waited until it began to whistle through its spout. She filled the mug half full of water.

Then she got the Chanel No. 5 bottle out of her bag and filled the mug half full of gin. She stirred the whole thing with a spoon and took a long drink off the top of it. Her throat felt scalded. Her nerves felt calmed. She took the mug into the living room and sat down next to the phone.

Belinda was always talking about how expensive the phone calls were, but this was an emergency. Maris had to make a long-distance call, and she didn't have a calling card anymore since AT&T had taken hers away. They'd taken her Universal Card away, too, in one of those periods when Maris was having a hard time remembering anything, and didn't remember to pay her bills. Right now, though, she did remember the number of the office and, more importantly, the number for Debra's private line. She didn't want to be stuck on the phone waiting while the others put her on hold and discussed whether Debra was willing to talk to her at all. Without Betsy in the office to rein them in, they were as likely to hang up on her as to help her out—and Betsy had not been as enthusiastic about disciplining them lately as she had been in the past. Still, Maris thought, they had to talk to her. Until Betsy told them not to, they had to.

The phone was picked up on the other end and Debra's voice said, "Elizabeth Toliver's office."

"It's Maris," Maris said. "And don't you dare try to lecture me. I'm a wreck. We're all a wreck. I need to know where she is."

"You need to know where who is?" Debra said.

"Oh, cut the crap. I need to know where Betsy is, and you know it. She left me stranded out at her mother's house this morning, without a phone, without any means of transport, surrounded by hostile press—"

"Liz Toliver never left anybody stranded in her life," Debra said. "Not deliberately. And especially not you. And you know it."

Maris took a long drink of coffee. "I take it you talked to her. She knows she left me stranded. They all took off out of there and just left me asleep in the basement. Doesn't she want to know where I am?"

The pause on Debra's end was even longer than the one Maris had taken to fortify herself with gin. "She did mention that she didn't know where you were. And that she was worried about you. I don't know why. God takes care of drunks and little children."

"I need to know where she is and I need a number where I can reach her," Maris said. "You probably don't realize it, but there's been another one. Right down the street from where I am. I want to get out of here."

"Another what?"

"Another murder."

"Well, she couldn't have committed that one, can she?" Debra said. "No matter what you try to make it look like. She's been in full view of half a dozen people all day."

"How the hell am I supposed to know who committed it?" Maris said. "I just don't want to be in the middle of it, which is what I am right now, because it happened just half a block up the street from me. I want to know where she is and I want a number where I can get in touch with her."

Debra paused again. "No," she said finally.

"What?"

"No," Debra said again. "There's no use screaming at me. I'm not authorized to give out that information. What I can do is to call her and tell her where you are and to give her the number you're calling from so that she can call you back. Then she can decide what to do about you herself. But the information you want is privileged. I'm not going to give it out unless she's given me direct instructions to give it out."

It was obvious that Debra expected her to argue, but Maris was better than that. She knew that Debra was telling the complete truth—it was Debra's job, as Betsy's personal assistant, to guard information, even from close friends and relatives.

"All right," Maris said. "Tell her I'm at Belinda's. That's 555–2627. She ought to know that number by now, but she probably doesn't."

"I'll call her right away."

"You do that."

"I *will* call her right away, Maris. It isn't everybody who thinks her responsibilities are a joke. Sit tight where you are for a few minutes."

Debra hung up in her ear. Maris put the phone back in its cradle and finished off her coffee. Then she got up and made herself another cup. The rain had now eased to nothing but gray and drizzle. The gin had begun to taste bitter. She went back to the couch and put her hand on the phone.

It took much longer than she had expected it to, and the longer it took the more uneasy she got. She was sure, really, that Betsy would call her back. It spite of the craziness of the last few days, Betsy was nowhere near ready to cut her off just yet. Maris was fairly sure Betsy would *never* be able to cut her off. Even with Debra, even with Jimmy Card, even with Mark all hating the sight of her, Maris could always count on Betsy being Betsy, the same girl who had walked all the way out to the White Horse and back again, the same girl who had come when she was called to the outhouse.

Still, it was hard to wait, and she had to wait a long time. The minute hand on Belinda's clock moved five minutes, then ten, then fifteen. Maris began to be afraid that Belinda would come back before Betsy rang. The last thing she wanted was to have to have this conversation with Belinda listening in. She finished her cup of coffee. She got up and made another one. She sat down next to the phone again. She thought if this went on much longer, she would be sick again.

When the phone rang, it startled her, and she jumped. Liquid jumped out of her mug and splashed against the front of her dress. She put the mug down next to the phone and picked up the receiver with that hand. She brushed at the wet spot on her breast with the other.

"Hello," she said.

"It's Jimmy," Jimmy Card said. "Liz isn't here."

"What do you mean, she's not there? She has to be there. Where else could she be?"

"I have no idea. You can ask her when she gets back. I'll give her the number. Just stay where you are."

"Why don't you give me her number, instead, and tell me where she's at so that I can get there. It was bad enough that you left me stranded at the house when you took off this morning—"

"We didn't do anything of the kind. You were nowhere in sight. We thought you'd gone home while the rest of us were sleeping."

"I'll bet you didn't think anything at all. If you had, you'd have remembered I didn't have a car with me out there yesterday. Or Betsy would have remembered it. Right now, there's been another murder—"

"There hasn't been any murder, Maris. We already talked to the police. Mrs. Bligh is very much alive. She was attacked, but she wasn't murdered."

"Wonderful. She'll be able to tell the police who attacked her. In the meantime, this town is full of reporters with appetites like vampires and I'm right in the middle of them. And you're telling me that Betsy isn't even where she's supposed to be, for all you know she could have been right here in the middle of town cutting up the front of Emma's disgustingly obese stomach—"

"Don't," Jimmy Card said.

"Don't what? Do you think I'm doing anything different from what those reporters are going to do when they get hold of this?"

"Don't," Jimmy Card said again. "I'm not Liz, Maris. I'm not even Mark. If you try to pull this kind of crap on me, I'll take you apart at the joints."

"Who the *hell* do you think you are?"

"I'm the man who knows how to put a stop to you. In the meantime, I'll tell Liz you called. She can call you back if she feels like it."

He hung up. Maris sat listening to the receiver buzz a dial tone in her ear. She put the receiver back in its cradle and picked up her mug of coffee again. Coffee and gin. It was a mug of coffee and gin. Her head was starting to hurt the way it did when she was having a particularly bad hangover. Big drops of rain were dropping down from the roof gutters outside the living-room window. The apartment was absolutely silent.

Maris Coleman thought that everything would be all right if only she was able to think.

3

It was not that Belinda Hart Grantling did not know what happened to Emma Kenyon Bligh. She not only knew, she had known for minutes before anybody else, because she had been in the store minutes before anybody else, before even George. She told herself, a little self-righteously, that she would have called the police if it had been necessary, but it hadn't been necessary. Almost as soon as she had darted out of the building and down the sidewalk, George had pulled into the best parking space out front and gone bounding up the porch steps to the front door. It made more sense to let George do what needed to be done than to get involved herself. The truth was, she had panicked. She had been really shocked at how much blood there had been, blood everywhere, blood spurting out of Emma's middle as if Emma were that fountain people jumped into in front of the Plaza Hotel in New York.

It was at that point that Belinda had run, really fast, out the door and across the porch and down Greenview Avenue in the rain—and it had still been raining then, hard, so that she was sure that if anybody had seen her running, they would only have thought it natural in the weather. She had started walking more slowly when she got to JayMar's, which was about the time she had seen George pull in. Then she had gone down the block a little more to find her car. She didn't really want to drive anymore today. She had been driving since early this morning. She had driven all the way out to Betsy's house, only to find not much of anybody home and the whole front lawn a mess. She had driven all the way out to the hospital to see if she could catch Betsy there, but when she'd arrived at the hospital, there had been no sign of Betsy anywhere, and when she'd asked the receptionist, the receptionist had clammed right up. In the end, she had been about ready to scream. Then she had driven all the way back to town and parked on Grandview and gone walking up the street to Country Crafts, and all she had really wanted to do was—

All she had really wanted to do was to talk to Emma, Belinda thought now. She was sitting in a little turnoff on Jefferson Road in Grassy Plains, right above the Sycamore. That was where she had gone when she had run out after seeing Emma bleed, although she couldn't remember why she'd come there in particular, instead of just driving all the way out onto the highway and going to the mall. She put her head on the wheel and closed her eyes. Her hands were jerking around against the steering wheel. Her body was twitching almost uncontrollably. She hurt.

Belinda took a deep breath. It was too bad she didn't have a full-time job. A full-time job would at least give her someplace to be. She got the car started and backed out onto Jefferson Road again. She headed down the hill. She went slowly, because she was still trembling, and because she didn't know what she wanted to do or where she wanted to go. Then, when she got to the very bottom of the hill, she did. She pulled into the parking lot of the Sycamore and cut the engine.

If she'd been thinking straight, she would have noticed that the parking lot was chock-full, which it never was in the middle of the afternoon, even when it was raining. Instead, she didn't realize how packed the place would be until she got inside and saw that all the booths and all but two of the stools around the counter had been taken. She hesitated for a moment, wondering if she ought to leave—she'd never seen most of these people, and she knew everybody in town—and then Bonnie Cantor had waved to her from behind the counter and she began to relax a little.

"What's going on around here?" she asked, sitting down on one of the two empty stools. "Who are all these people?"

"Reporters," Bonnie said solemnly.

"What are they reporting?" Belinda asked.

Bonnie started setting her up for a Diet Coke. "They came in because of Chris, being dead, and it being Betsy Toliver's house where the body was found, because Betsy Toliver is famous. Or they say she is. Did you know Betsy Toliver was famous?"

"I wouldn't call it famous," Belinda said stiffly. "She's on like CNN and like that."

"Oh. Well. No wonder I haven't seen her. So that's why they're here. Except," Bonnie lowered her voice, "something happened to Emma Kenyon. I don't know if you've heard about it—"

"It was on the radio," Belinda said, because it was true. It had come on the radio news on the oldies station while she was parked up on Grassy Plains. "She was—attacked."

"She was *stabbed*," Bonnie said, looking around quickly. "She was stabbed right in the stomach. I called Sue Cameron out at the hospital and she checked up on it for me. She's not dead yet, though. Emma, I mean. She's just unconscious. But Sue says she could be dead any minute now, and then there would be a double murder. Doesn't that just shock the socks off you? I've lived in Hollman all my life and nothing like this has ever happened here."

"Michael Houseman was murdered," Belinda said. "In 1969."

"But that was just the one, wasn't it?" Bonnie said. "And it was some old tramp who did it, if I remember. It wasn't like this. It didn't have famous people in it."

"I wouldn't call Betsy Toliver famous," Belinda said again. She looked down into the Diet Coke Bonnie had brought her. It had a lemon in it, just the way she always drank it.

"Listen," Bonnie said, leaning on the counter and putting her lips up close to Belinda's ear, so that she could whisper and maybe really not be overheard by everybody in the place. "You see the corner booth? The man in the black jacket with the red shirt under it? That guy is from the *National Enquirer*. No kidding. I read the *Enquirer* all the time and now there's somebody from there in here and I can't even wait on him because he's not at the counter. LeeAnne gets all the good jobs."

Belinda turned around to look at the corner booth. There was a man in a black sports coat with a red T-shirt under it, but he was not alone. The booth was full of men, odd-looking men. Some of them were wearing ties, and some of them were not, but all of them managed to look both expensive and seedy at the same time.

"Are they all from the *National Enquirer*?" Belinda asked.

Bonnie shrugged. "I've got no idea. They all seem to know each other, anyway. This really is the most exciting thing that's ever happened to me. It's driving me crazy."

"Bonnie," somebody on the other end of the counter called.

"I've got to go," Bonnie said. "Most days we don't even have a girl to wait tables in the afternoon. Just my luck we've got LeeAnne here today. Honestly. I never have any damn luck at all."

Bonnie went down the counter. Belinda turned around and looked at the corner booth again. Then she looked at all the other booths, and at the tables. Everybody drinking coffee had that look about them, the one that said they did not belong in small towns. Maris had that look. Belinda swiveled the stool back so that she was facing the counter and attacked her Diet Coke again. Her hands looked old to her. The veins bulged out on them. She didn't think there was anything like plastic surgery for the hands.

She was just starting to wonder what she was supposed to do now, when the man sitting next to her cleared his throat.

"Excuse me," he said. "I overheard you talking to the waitress."

"Her name is Bonnie." Belinda wasn't trying to be rude. She just didn't want to talk to one of the outside people.

"Yes," the man said. "I know. My name is Eddie Cassiter. I'm a reporter."

"I know."

Eddie Cassiter cleared his throat again. "I heard her talking to you and it sounded like you were a friend of that woman who got attacked this afternoon," he said. "That's true, isn't it?"

"Of course I was. We were friends all the way from kindergarten."

"Did you know the one who got killed, too? This Christine Barr?"

"Chris Inglerod," Belinda said. "Nobody thought of her as Barr."

"So you knew her a long time?"

"I knew her since I was six years old. Just like Emma. We all knew each other. We were all friends forever. Why is that hard to understand?"

"It's not hard to understand. I'm just trying to figure out what goes on here. I'm not from here. Were you a friend of Liz Toliver's, too?"

"*Nobody* was a friend of Betsy Toliver's. *Nobody* was. We couldn't stand her. And that's her name. Betsy. Not Liz. Betsy."

"Betsy," Eddie Cassiter said pleasantly. "Yes, I've heard that. And she had a god-awful nickname when she was growing up."

"Only because she deserved it," Belinda said righteously. "It's not true the way they put it in the papers. It's not true that we persecuted her. She's a terrible person, and she always was, and she's ugly, too. She *deserved* it."

"I understand that completely," Eddie Cassiter said. "Why don't you let me buy you another Coke?"

THREE

1

It took nearly three hours to find out just how badly hurt Emma Kenyon Bligh really was, and during those three hours Gregor felt as if he and Kyle Borden had been frozen solid in the middle of the road. Every investigation has its periods of stasis. They were warned about that at Quantico when Gregor was in training, and years later, he had given the same warning to the new agents who joined the Behavioral Sciences Unit. Sometimes nothing happens, and sometimes there is nothing you can do about it. If you try, you risk making a mess of the entire case.

Still, he also couldn't imagine sitting still for too much longer, especially with Kyle Borden lecturing him at every opportunity about how traumatic violent crime was in "small communities." He tried calling Cavanaugh Street again. He had no luck. Tibor's phone was on the answering machine, and it wasn't just to screen calls. Donna's phone was also on the answering machine. He tried calling the Radisson and Bennis, but there was no answer there, either. God only knew where *she* was. He looked around Kyle Borden's office, at the clutter on the desk, at the picture magazines in a pile in the corner (*People*, *Us*, *Celebrity*), at the photographs tacked to the walls.

Gregor got up and left the little office. The big open area outside was empty of everybody but Kyle and Sharon Morobito.

Gregor cleared his throat. "I was thinking that we ought to go out and make another call. There's somebody I'd like to talk to."

"There's a lot of people I'd like to talk to," Kyle said, "starting with Peggy. We'll get to it this afternoon. Who is it you want to talk to?"

"The husband," Gregor said. "Not Chris Inglerod's husband. Peggy's husband. What did you call him? Steve—"

"Stu Kennedy. You can't interview Stu Kennedy."

"Why not?"

"Because if you do, he'll end up beating the flaming shit out of Peggy and you'll have another murder on your hands."

"There isn't going to be any way you can prevent this man from knowing that his wife is at least peripherally involved in the attack against Emma Kenyon Bligh," Gregor said reasonably. "She's in the hospital now. She'll be released this afternoon. It's going to be on the news. It's going to be in the newspapers. People are going to talk. And even if nobody talks to Mr. Kennedy himself, we are all going to have to talk to Mrs. Kennedy. At the very least she's a material witness."

"He's too blasted to see straight most of the time," Kyle said. "He could miss the whole thing. If we don't tell him about it—"

"If he was really that blasted all the time, he'd be dead," Gregor said. "So I must assume he's like most alcoholics, even in the late stages, and has periods of lucidity. And I don't even need him to be that lucid. I just need him to confirm a few things for me. You did say he was in the park the night Michael Houseman died?"

"A lot of people were in the park the night Michael Houseman died."

"And so far, we've only talked to members of the witch's coven," Gregor said. "Except I shouldn't say that, because it's an insult to witches. Let's go see Stuart Kennedy."

2

Gregor had expected to find that the Kennedy house was much like the one belonging to Michael Houseman's mother, and in some ways it was. For one thing, it was in town and not out in one of the subdivisions in Plumtrees or Stony Hill. For another, it was definitely small, a square little old-fashioned Cape without any of the extensions or dormers Capes often accumulated over the years. The lack made it somewhat at odds with its neighbors, all of which showed signs of having been worked on at least by their owners, and in one case—the house with the addition with two-story-tall Gothic windows—by a professional construction company. What really set the Kennedy house apart from its neighbors was more subtle, though. It was in the fact that its paint was peeling just a little. You could see it most plainly on the wide front porch. Other things were wrong, too, things you wouldn't necessarily notice right away, but that stayed with you as an undertone: the mailbox nailed to the wall next to the front door was knocked off true; the rain gutters that ran along the front of the house were rusty around the edges; the railings on the porch were peeling wood along ridges that defined their decorative bevel. All in all, it was the kind of house that turns up haunted in one of the better horror movies.

Kyle Borden parked the police car right out front, at the curb, even though there was a driveway at the side of the house, leading to the back.

The driveway, like the lawn, was well cared for. Either the Kennedys cared more for their lawn than their house, or one of them had had the sense to hire a yard service. The house's front windows were washed, but blank. The house looked deserted.

"Well," Kyle said, "you really want to do this."

"I've talked to nearly everybody else who was in the park that night," Gregor said, "except for Mrs. Kennedy herself, and she's unavailable."

"Stu's probably unavailable, too," Kyle said. "I don't know how to break this to you, Mr. Demarkian, but Stu Kennedy is an alcoholic. And a drug addict. With a wife who makes very decent money, or at least what amounts to very decent money around here. He spends ninety percent of his time out of it, and the other ten percent you don't want to know him. And this will get Peggy in trouble. I can guarantee it."

"I've dealt with drunks and drug addicts before," Gregor said. "Let's go."

"Besides," Kyle said, not budging, "it's not like we're really all that concerned with Michael Houseman's death anymore. I know you are, you've got a job to do, but right here with the Hollman Police we're interested in who killed Chris Inglerod Barr and who nearly killed Emma Kenyon Bligh. So unless you can tell me that Stu is connected to one of those, I've got to say that I don't see the point—"

"Your problem is with the word 'connected,' " Gregor said. "Your thinking is too limited. Everybody who was in the park that night is connected to the death of Michael Houseman and the death of Chris Inglerod and the attack on Emma Kenyon Bligh and, of course, the death of Mrs. Toliver's dog. 'Connected' doesn't mean anything. God is 'connected' to all those things."

Kyle sat still for a long time, blinking. "To hell with it," he said. "I have no idea what you're up to, but I'm going to get the hospital to keep Peggy in a bed for at least a week."

"Her HMO probably won't have it."

Kyle got out of the car and looked around. "What *is* it about the dog?" he asked to the air. "I keep forgetting about the dog. I hate what happened to the dog."

Gregor got out, too, and they walked up the narrow concrete walk together. The walk was cracked.

Kyle rang the front bell, and waited. He rang it again. And again.

"Probably passed out cold," he told Gregor. "Or he's not and he's just not going to open up. What are you going to do about that? We don't have a search warrant."

Gregor tried the front doorknob. It was locked. "Lean on the bell some more," he said.

Kyle let out a raspberry, but he leaned on the bell. Gregor could hear the grating buzz from where he stood. Kyle let go of the button and pounded on the door once or twice. "Stu," he shouted. "Stu, for God's sake, open up. I've got to talk to you."

"Get the fuck out of here," somebody said from the other side of the door. It was an odd voice, Gregor thought, high and petulant and childish.

Kyle sighed. "Listen, Stu, open up. I mean it. I've got to talk to you."

"No fucking cop is getting into this house without a search warrant," the voice said.

"I don't need a search warrant," Kyle said. "I'm not searching for anything. I don't care if you have a goddamned mountain of cocaine sitting in the middle of your living-room floor. Snort the whole damned thing for all I care. It's not what I'm looking for. Open up or I'll find some excuse to arrest you and put you in jail. Then you'll have to listen to me."

"Who is it you've got with you?"

"Oh, that's Gregor Demarkian. He's—"

"I know who he is."

Gregor heard the bolt lock turn in the door, the same snap and slide that bolt locks made everywhere. The door swung open and he got his first look at Stu Kennedy. The first thing that struck him was how small the man was, not only thin—all coke heads are thin—but short, shorter than Kyle, almost as short as Jimmy Card. The next thing that struck him was that the man smelled. He'd been in the clothes he was wearing for days, and he hadn't been in the shower anytime lately. His hair hung in greasy clumped strands around his face. It was too long, and it looked as if it had been cut by an amateur the last few times. His face had a streak of dirt running down one jaw. His hands had dirt caked under the fingernails.

"Jesus Christ," Kyle said. "What's wrong with you?"

"Nothing the fuck's wrong with me," Stu said. "Who do you think you are, coming here in the middle of the afternoon knocking on the door and throwing bullshit at me about how you got to tell me something? You don't have to tell me anything. You're just a piece of motherfucking slime—"

"This is Mr. Demarkian," Kyle said dryly. "He's a famous detective from Philadelphia. He used to be head of some hotshot division at the FBI—"

"I know who the fuck he is. Just because you want to lick his boots don't mean I do. Christ, Kyle, you're such a wet wuss bag."

Stu Kennedy stepped back a little, and Kyle edged past him, sucking his stomach in so that he didn't have to touch Stu's clothes. Gregor slid past him, too, but with less fastidiousness. He got into the living room and looked around. The room was both clean and tidy, but everything in it was worn, and it was very dark. Part of that was due to the fact that the drapes were closed, but part of it was due to the fact that all the furniture was dark, too, black or navy-blue, just like the carpet. The walls were white, but they looked as if they hadn't been painted in a long time. Beyond the living room was a smaller room that looked to be the dining room. It was dark, too.

"See?" Stu said. "No mountain of cocaine on the living-room floor. What the fuck kind of idiot do you think I am?"

"What is it with you, anyway?" Kyle said. "You got out of school, you can't watch your language anymore? I can't believe Peggy puts up with this."

"Peggy puts the fuck up with what I tell her to put the fuck up with," Stu said. "Now will you tell me what the fuck you want and get the fuck out of my house?"

Kyle sighed. Gregor sat down on the couch. "Mr. Kennedy," Gregor said, "what we really want to do is to ask you something about the night on which a boy named Michael Houseman died. According to Mr. Borden here—"

"Who the fuck cares about Michael Houseman and how he died?" Stu said. "That was years ago. You couldn't arrest anybody for that. You couldn't prove anything about who did it. That's not the fuck what you want. You want to know if I murdered that tight-twatted cunt. Well, I didn't. I wouldn't bother. Why would I bother? You think just because—just because . . ." Stu seemed to lose his train of thought. He went over to the little fireplace and got something off the mantel. Gregor finally figured out that it was a pack of cigarettes. "I can still smoke in my own fucking house," he said. "You can't stop me. It's still legal. Fucking nanny state."

Gregor cleared his throat. "Let me assure you," he said, "you're not in any way under suspicion for the death of Chris Inglerod Barr, at least not from me. I'll stipulate, if you like, that I'm quite certain you did not commit that murder or even aid in its commission in any way."

"You talk like a fucking textbook," Stu said.

"He's an educated man, Stu," Kyle said. "That's more than I can say for you or me. He's got master's degrees. Do you *have* to sound like some backwoods yahoo on a bad day?"

"I'm no fucking backwoods yahoo," Stu said, almost pleasantly, "and as for Michael Houseman, who the fuck cares? The guy was a Boy Scout. And a snitch. Anybody breathed wrong, he went running right to the fucking faculty. Everybody hated him."

"I didn't hate him," Kyle said.

"Yeah, well, you were a Boy Scout yourself back in high school. That sure fucking changed, didn't it? You get some pussy off the girls you put in the tank for being high? If you don't, you're a fucking fool. Everybody else does. Christ, I can't believe the crap we swallowed when we were kids. Friendly Mr. Policeman. Be just like Dudley Dooright. And all the time the fucking faculty was screwing around, the fucking police were screwing around, everybody was screwing around except Michael fucking Houseman and he was trying to get himself made some kind of fucking saint."

"Yes," Demarkian said, "well. What I wanted to know was this, did you see Mr. Houseman on the night he was murdered?"

"I saw him on the day he was murdered," Stu said. "Everybody did. He was sitting in that fucking lifeguard's chair out at the lake most of the day. The great god Michael on his throne."

"Did you see him at any other time?"

"I saw him out by the outhouse, if that's what you mean." Stu's eyes had gone dead flat, but it was impossible to tell if that was emotion or the drugs.

"Even Kyle here was out by the outhouse, Betsy Wetsy screaming her head off inside. It was hysterical. Doesn't *that* motherfucking cunt think she's hot stuff these days?"

"I don't know who you think you saw," Kyle said stiffly, "but I wasn't out at the outhouse that night. I wasn't anywhere near it. I mean, for Christ's sake, if I had been, don't you think I'd have let her out?"

"Nah," Stu said. "Nobody was going to let her out until the cops got there and you know it. I mean, who the hell cared? And they were all scared to shit about the cunts," Stu said to Gregor. "You've got no idea. That bunch of bitches got together, and everybody in school shook like they were in an earthquake."

"Was Michael Houseman out near the outhouse?" Gregor asked.

"No, Michael Houseman wasn't near the outhouse," Stu said. "If he had been, *he* would have let her out. He was a fucking Boy Scout. I told you that. He was up near the river, in that clearing where everybody got laid in those days only you pretended you weren't doing it. Christ only knows what he was doing there. He didn't get laid. Maybe he was going to search through the underbrush for fucking couples and turn them in to the state police."

"In the rain?" Kyle said.

"I don't know fucking anything about the rain," Stu said.

Gregor cleared his throat and looked around again. There were no pictures in this room. He'd gotten so used to pictures in Hollman, the lack of them felt significant. Stu was leaning against the wall and flicking the ashes from his cigarette indiscriminately on the floor.

"Well," he said, "I think that's all I really need. Thank you for being so helpful."

Stu Kennedy laughed. "I haven't been helpful. I'm never helpful. I make a fucking point of it. Christ, you don't want to know about Michael. You want to know about the cunt. But she was a cunt even in high school, you know that? One of Peggy's best friends, and the whole time we were going out, she couldn't stand me. Couldn't stand Peggy going out with me. Couldn't stand to be in the same room with me. Christ, they were all cunts, though. Weren't they, Kyle? Every last one of them."

"Well," Kyle said, "they weren't very pleasant."

"Yeah, and now Betsy Wetsy is going to marry a rock star. An old, broken-down, washed-up rock star, but a fucking rock star. That must make them just want to spit."

"They're taking it better than you are," Kyle said.

"Well, if you and your Mr. Demarkian have everything you want from me, you should get the fuck out of here," Stu said. "You don't have a search warrant. You don't have any right to be here. Get up and get the fuck out of here."

"Right," Kyle said.

Gregor stood up. "Thank you again, Mr. Kennedy," he said, holding out his hand.

"Fuck," Stu Kennedy said. Then he walked over to the front door and pulled it open. "Get the fuck out," he said. "I've had enough."

3

By the time they got down the front walk to the car, it was raining again, not the lunatic pelting that had been going on for most of the morning, but a deep, steady, heavy fall that was almost silent.

Gregor got into the car. Kyle got into the car and started it up.

"What was that about?" Kyle asked. "You didn't mention Peggy. You didn't mention what happened to her."

"There was no need to."

"Well there was maybe one need to. Eventually this is all going to come out in the wash. Stu is going to know where Peggy was earlier this afternoon. Either it's going to be on the news, or the hospital is going to call, or Peggy is going to tell him. And then what? I've got my ass in a sling for withholding information on the medical condition of a—"

"There's a record of all the times he's beaten her up?"

"I don't know about all of them. There's probably a record a mile long about some of them, though. We've got them in the police department. They've probably got them in the emergency room over at Kennanburg. Why?"

"Because that's all you'll need not to get your ass in a sling. Some states have mandatory arrest laws—"

"We've got one here," Kyle said. "But they don't do any good, Mr. Demarkian. Oh, they sometimes do, when the woman really wants out and she's got no way to get out herself, but in a case like this—" Kyle shrugged.

Gregor shook his head. "We should get going."

"Get going where?"

"Out to that hospital. I'd like to talk to Mrs. Kennedy for a while."

Kyle put the car in gear and began to pull away from the curb. "Do you think she'll be in any position to talk? She looked like she was sleepwalking the last time we saw her."

"I need to know a few things from her, especially about the death of Michael Houseman. Does Mr. Kennedy always behave like that? With the language. Or did he put it on for my benefit?"

"He always behaves like that to me," Kyle said, "but he could be putting it on for *my* benefit. Why are you still so interested in the death of Michael Houseman? Did the same person who killed Michael Houseman kill Chris Inglerod Barr? And try to kill Emma?"

"Let's say that the same person who murdered Michael Houseman was responsible for the death of Chris Inglerod Barr and the attempted murder of Emma Kenyon Bligh. And for the death of the dog, of course, although that was something in the way of an accident."

"How do you eviscerate a large part-malamute, part-shepherd dog by accident?"

"You find it in the wrong place at the wrong time."

"Marvelous. Wonderful. I can see the prep sheet I'm going to make up for the town prosecutor right this minute—"

"You know," Gregor said, "you've got nothing to worry about. The fact of the matter is, this case is going to have a Gordian knot solution. Sooner or later, Emma Kenyon Bligh is going to wake up, and when she does she's going to hand you your solution on a plate, and hand you a star witness, too, in the person of herself. And that's going to be enough to go to trial on."

"That's going to be enough to go to trial on for the attack against Emma," Kyle said, "but does that mean it's going to be enough to go to trial on for the death of Chris Inglerod Barr?"

"You're going to have the linoleum cutter," Gregor said. "That will be a start. With any luck, what I'm doing now will get you the rest of what you need. It's odd to think, though, that Chris Inglerod would be alive and Emma Kenyon Bligh wouldn't be in the hospital with a slash wound in her abdomen if Elizabeth Toliver hadn't decided to take her younger son to McDonald's."

"What?"

"She wasn't home, you see," Gregor said. "She was supposed to be home. She had a nice set schedule that day. She was driving her mother to one set of doctors in the morning. Then she was leaving her mother and the nurse at the ob/gyn clinic in the early afternoon so that the doctors could run some tests. While that was going on, she was supposed to be having lunch with Maris Coleman at the Sycamore, and when that was over she was supposed to pick up her older son at the town library and her mother at the gynecologist's and go straight home. She should have been home by two o'clock. But she wasn't."

"We know she wasn't. Emma and Belinda brought Mark home from the library and they got to the Toliver house at three and there was nobody home."

"Exactly. Because Elizabeth Toliver and Maris Coleman had an argument at the Sycamore, and Liz took Geoff out to the Interstate to the McDonald's there, and she didn't get home until after four. And that's why the dog died. Because nobody was home."

"You just said Mark was home."

"I know. Essentially, nobody was home, because he went to sleep in that room in the basement. You can't hear somebody knocking on the front door from there, or on the back door, either. So, you see, she got to the house expecting to find Elizabeth Toliver, and as far as she could tell nobody was home. She probably walked around the yard a couple of times, with the linoleum cutter in her hand, and nobody to use it on—"

"Wait. Are you saying that whoever this is was intending to kill Betsy? I mean, Liz?"

"Of course. Didn't you know that? The thing is, it's very difficult to kill somebody in Liz Toliver's position with a knife or a razor. It's not impossible, but it's difficult, because those people usually have other people around them. It's much easier, if you want to murder a celebrity, to use a gun, because you don't have to worry about getting physically close. Either our murderer didn't have access to a gun or she didn't know how to use one and was afraid to try."

"Right," Kyle said. "Who the hell doesn't have access to a gun in a place like this? There are guns all the hell over the place. Half the town hunts."

"All right," Gregor said. "I'll give you three people who didn't have access to guns. One, Peggy Smith. There are no guns in that house. I'll guarantee it."

"Why? How could you know that?"

"Because you haven't said a single word about his shooting her, and if he'd had a gun he'd have shot her at least once by now. I don't care about background checks or laws that say you can't own a gun if you've ever been charged with domestic violence, people like Stu Kennedy have guns if they want them, and if they have them they use them."

"Hell," Kyle said. "He did shoot her. Or tried, anyway. He missed by a mile. About eight months ago. I went through the house and picked up a pistol and two rifles and read him the riot act."

"And he listened to you?"

"I'd like to think so," Kyle said, "but I have a feeling it was more a matter of finances. Stu spends a lot of money on chemicals. There doesn't tend to be a lot left over to buy guns and ammunition with. The guns I confiscated had all belonged to his father."

"Fine," Gregor said. "Now I'll give you another one. Belinda Hart Grantling. Or are you going to tell me that she keeps a pistol in her bedside drawer?"

"No. No, as far as I know, she's never had a gun in her life. Her family never had them either. There are families around here that hunt, and there are families around here that shoot at gun ranges, and there are families around here that are just plain whacko, but the Harts never were any of those things."

"Two down and one to go. Maris Coleman."

"Oh," Kyle said. "Funny, isn't it? I don't usually think of her as a suspect. I mean, it's not like she's here anymore. She's just sort of all over the place. Visiting. Like the tooth fairy."

"She also is extremely unlikely to have a gun," Gregor said. "I suppose it's possible, and I could always check the New York gun registry, but the fact is that I've been watching her for days. I've seen her do all kinds of things, I've seen her empty her handbag on a table, and there's been no sign of a gun, no sign of ammunition, and no talk from anybody around her—Liz Toliver, for instance—to indicate that Maris ever even had a gun in the city. Of course, if I had to pick one person who might decide to stab instead of to shoot even if she had a gun, Ms. Coleman would be that person. The one thing she's very, very good about is knowing what she's capable of when she's drunk, and she's nearly always drunk."

"I wouldn't call it drunk," Kyle said. "I'd call it not exactly sober."

"Call it what you will. That linoleum cutter was most likely the best weapon available, better than a knife, for instance, because it's sharper."

"Do you know where the linoleum cutter came from?" Kyle asked.

"I'm about ninety-nine percent sure. We'll have to check. It won't matter, though, the fingerprints will be clear enough and a good lab analysis ought to get a lot more."

"Do you intend to tell me where it came from?" Kyle asked. "Are you going to let me in on this? And if you think you know where it came from, why haven't we gone there and checked it out?"

"For the same reason you didn't search Mr. Kennedy's house back there. Because we didn't have a warrant. Eventually, you're going to have to get a number of warrants and search a number of places—if I were you, I'd search that house, too, on general principles—but at the moment it would just waste a lot of time, and there's no hurry. It doesn't matter where it came from much now that we have it. The trick is to get all our ducks in place so that nobody can claim we've got a case shot full of holes. I'm mixing metaphors. Bennis would kill me."

"Look," Kyle Borden said, "do you know who killed Chris Inglerod and attacked Emma Kenyon Bligh?"

"Yes."

"And it was the same person in both cases?"

"Oh, yes."

"And the same person killed Michael Houseman?"

"No," Gregor said, "but the same person was responsible for all three deaths. That's not quite the same thing."

"It'll be enough if I've got the person locked up for the death of Chris Inglerod. Was the death of Chris Inglerod a mistake, too? Is this woman—and I assume you're talking about a woman—"

"Right."

"Was this woman going around slashing people just because she wanted to slash Betsy and Betsy was never available? Because I'm going to have a hard time selling that to the town prosecutor, and he'd never be able to sell it to a jury."

"Don't worry about it," Gregor said. "It's nothing that odd. Just let's go see Peggy Smith Kennedy, and then let's hunt down Maris Coleman and insist she sit still for a talk for once. And when we do find her, let's make sure she can't go anywhere."

FOUR

1

In the end, it was Liz who drove Bennis Hannaford's tangerine-orange Mercedes. It was easier not to have to give directions every other minute. You could drive on automatic pilot if you knew where you were going, and Liz did know where she was going. She could have driven these streets every day for the last thirty years instead of not seeing them in all that time. She could have walked this landscape. She remembered things it made no sense to remember, like where old Mrs. Gorton lived and how to get there. Old Mrs. Gorton had been her fifth-grade teacher. Then there were other things. When they were all seven years old and in second grade, Chris Inglerod had started coming to school in black velvet hair bands. Soon they all had black velvet hair bands, even Liz herself, and some people, like Belinda, had started to claim that they wore them even to bed. When they were all eight and in third grade, the fashion was sleepover parties and Polaroid photographs. Girls who had sleepover parties took Polaroids and brought the photographs in on the Monday after the weekend for show and tell. For eight months straight, all Liz had wanted in the world was to have a single Polaroid photograph of herself at a sleepover party, any sleepover party, anywhere. When they were all ten and in Mrs. Gorton's class, Liz had gone from the first of October until the last week of school sitting by herself at lunch with nobody on either side of her and nobody to talk to, because—well—because. By then they had begun to be explicit about how much they didn't want to have her anywhere around. That year was the year that Harry Spedergelb planted the maple tree in his front yard. Driving by it now, it seemed to dwarf the small lot and the small house that was on it, and to menace the other houses on the street, one of which was Chris Inglerod's mother's house, except that Chris Inglerod's mother no longer lived there. Harry Spedergelb had died of lung cancer in 1974. Liz's mother had sent her the news while she was at graduate school. Liz never knew why. Mrs. Gorton had died of blood poisoning in 1986. She was ninety-two years old, and the picture in the Hollman *Home News* made her look even more like the Wicked Witch of the West than she did in person. Liz's mother had sent her that article, too, or rather that copy of the *Home News*, the way she'd sent a copy of the *Home News* every week for eleven years, on the assumption that Liz would eventually get homesick enough to want to come for a visit. Liz had not come to visit. For a while, everything in the *Home News* had seemed to be an obituary. Dave Grieg and Tom Bellson both dead together in a car crash. Jimmy Strand, Nelson Harvey, and Tim Stall all dead in Vietnam. Cathy Conway dead in the crash of a prop plane outside Omaha, Nebraska.

In the other front bucket seat, Bennis Hannaford seemed to be trying very hard not to panic. Liz would have put some music on if she could have, but although the tangerine Mercedes had a CD player, the CDs Bennis had were restricted to one Charles Mingus album, one copy of the Chicago Philharmonic's rendition of Beethoven's Ninth Symphony, and the Three Tenors. Liz hadn't believed anybody really listened to the Three Tenors.

"So," Bennis said finally. "Are we going anyplace in particular? And do you know how to get there?"

"Yes, and yes," Liz said. "We're going out to the park, and I could get there sleepwalking."

"Do you think this is healthy, the amount of time you spend obsessing about all this? Wouldn't it make more sense to give them all a great big raspberry and get married to Jimmy and live happily ever after?"

They were at that fork in the road at the edge of town where the right veer went Liz didn't know where and the left led out to Plumtrees. Liz took the left. "Do you know a science fiction writer named Lisa Tuttle?"

"I've met her a couple of times."

"I've never met her," Liz said, "but I read a short story of hers once in a collection. It was one of Mark's collections and we were on a plane and I was restless and it was the middle of the night. I can never sleep on planes. Can you?"

"If I'm tired enough. Did you like this short story?"

"Well, yes, I did," Liz said, "but that's not the point. The point is, the story was about this woman who had been this ugly, acne-ridden, bespectacled hick in her little town in Texas or wherever when she was growing up, and then she left for college and started writing and she wrote this one science fiction novel that was just huge. Sold tons of copies. She was living in London or somewhere and she had contacts and the acne had cleared up and she was sophisticated and all that kind of thing. The only problem was, she couldn't write. She tried and she tried, but she had something worse than writer's block. And it went on for a couple of years."

"And that was it? That was the story?"

"No, no, no," Liz said. "The story was, she got an invitation to speak at this convention near her old hometown. And she went there to show off, but then she got caught up by a couple of geeky, acne-ridden fans. And the longer she stayed with them—she had to stay with them, they wouldn't let her go—anyway, the longer she stayed with them, the more she sort of morphed back into being the geek she'd started out being. And then they started abusing her, calling her names, telling her how ugly she was. And it was true. She lost her contacts and had to put on glasses. Her skin started to break out. Her clothes started to look funny and wrong. She just got sucked right back into being the person she'd been in high school. But she could write."

Bennis cocked her head. "Is that what all this has been about? You've got writer's block and you're trying to recapture the inspiration?"

"Not exactly. I think that the point of the story is that nobody gets to be successful at anything without something driving them, and that for a lot of us it was being what I was in this place thirty years ago. There's an awful lot of people out there who are still playing In Crowd and making up for what they resent not having had by re-creating it—oh, God, you know. Private clubs with blackball votes. Co-op apartment buildings where the board gets to reject people who want to buy in. Private schools where membership in the parent-teacher association is by invitation only. Do you know what I mean?"

"Absolutely," Bennis said. "I stay as far away from that stuff as I can."

"So do I. But that's still what drives me. And that, you see, is why I got so screwed up that I didn't realize I'd been making a mistake. That I had to have been making a mistake."

"Making a mistake about what?"

"About something I heard. If I'd really thought about it, with my mind instead of my gut—God, you have no idea how many column inches I've eaten up telling people that we all ought to think with our minds instead of our guts—I'd have realized I had to be wrong. I dream about it, do you know that? I dream about it just the way I heard it, and every time I wake up from one of those dreams there's something in my head telling me I haven't been paying attention. And I haven't been. I feel like such a damned idiot."

"I feel trapped in a car with a manic phase bipolar," Bennis said.

Liz pulled the car off the road and down the bumpy asphalted strip to an open place on the grass. They still hadn't paved this parking lot, she thought. The place was deserted. She cut the engine and handed the keys to Bennis. She got out of the car and looked around. The rain had become an off-again, on-again thing. Just this second, it was off again.

"I remember the year this was built," Liz said as Bennis came around to her from the other side of the car. "Everybody in town was so impressed. Our own park. Our own lake to swim in. No need to go hauling off to Rogers Park in Kennanburg. You ever been to the Caribbean?"

"Several times," Bennis said. "It's not my kind of thing. I'm a sit-in-tavernas-and-listen-to-strange-music-all-night person. I don't tolerate sunbathing."

"Jimmy's got this place in Montego Bay. Big Spanish-style house right on the water. We spent a couple of weeks there this past winter. Hot and cold running shrimp and great big avocados and great big drinks that came in glasses so cold that they have a sheet of ice coating them. You see, the thing is, I never questioned it. Never. Not even when Jimmy and Mark tried to tell me. And Geoff, too, God bless him. Even Geoff tried to tell me."

"Tell you what? That you had heard something wrong?"

"No, no. About Maris. You come up this way. Go through the gate and then halfway down to the beach but not all the way to the water."

Liz strode along ahead. Now that she was really here, she was having a hard time containing her agitation. She felt as if she had electrodes shooting all through her body. Every part of her wanted to twitch. She walked through the gates and halfway down to the beach and stopped. If the tall lifeguard's chair was new, it had been built to look just like the old one, made of gray weathered wood with broad flat arms on either side of the seat so that the lifeguard could put down his Coca-Cola and his tuna-fish sandwich without having to worry that they'd fall on somebody's head. The water looked as murky and cold as ever. The raft out near the center of it shuddered and shook on top of the water. Liz waited just long enough to make sure Bennis was keeping up. Then she took off again, up the little hill, into the trees.

It was dark when she got in among the pines, but it could have been pitch and she would still have known where she was going. She got on the path and continued upward without even glancing at the signs that told her which way the men's rooms were and which way the women's. The closer she got, the harder her heart pounded. It seemed to her that she had lived her life, her whole life, to a sound track of somebody else's music. She'd been starring in the wrong movie. She'd been trying to make the lyrics fit. It was like Jimmy said about the CDs she kept at home and in her car. She was always singing along to the competition. She thought she was going to be sick. She came out through a stand of trees and all of a sudden there it was, right in the clearing, the outhouses. They hadn't changed, either. This place had remained intact, untouched, for thirty years.

Bennis came chugging up the path, breathing heavily. "Is this it? Because I wasn't really ready for physical exercise. Oh—hot damn. Is this it?"

"This is it," Liz said.

"Are these the same ones? They can't be the same ones, can they? Wooden structures like these, loosely built. They'd have to be new ones by now."

"Would they? I have no idea. I suppose they must have replaced the door to the one I was nailed into. I wasn't actually conscious when they got me out, so I don't remember myself, but somebody told me later that they'd had to take the door off by the hinge. So there's that. It was raining that night the way it was raining here earlier today. It was totally insane. I can still remember the thunder rolling in. They were nailing the door shut at the same time and I was screaming and it was hard to tell what was what, but it was thunder. And in no time at all, it started to rain. And then I heard her screaming. And that, you see, is the problem. I thought I knew who it was."

"Who it was who nailed you in?"

"No, who it was later. Who it was who was screaming. I always knew who nailed me in. I always knew that Maris was a part of it, too. Jimmy thinks I kid myself about that, but I don't. It was just—Maris was always so much better than I was, at everything. So much prettier. So much smarter. I always thought that she was the real thing and I was a kind of fake and that someday the world would get wise to it and my whole career would collapse and she'd be on her way. And then, when that didn't happen, I felt guilty. So guilty. You have no idea."

"I know you're talking in the past tense," Bennis said. "I'm hoping that's significant."

Liz walked around the outhouses in a big circle. They were just outhouses. Satan did not live here. She got back around to the front where Bennis was. "After a while when the storm really got going, I started to hear somebody screaming. A girl. A woman. Whatever. She was screaming '*slit his throat slit his throat*' over and over again and it sounded like somebody having sex. Somebody having an orgasm. It was sick. It was nasty. It was depraved in a way we don't use that word anymore. Morally corrupt at the core. And then when they told me in the hospital that Michael Houseman was dead and I heard a few of the details, I thought I knew what had happened. I thought I knew whose voice I heard. I remember thinking that when they heard about this, Vassar would rescind my admission. I don't know why I thought that. It just felt as if it were my fault."

"How could it have been your fault? You were nailed into an outhouse."

"I know." Liz saw a movement in the grass and leaned over to look. Slithering along on the ground was a small black snake, not even three-quarters of a foot long. When she moved the grass above it, it seemed to freeze. She leaned down and picked it up, holding it by the middle, so that it twisted between her fingers.

"Look," she said, holding it out for Bennis to see. "The park is still full of them. You'd think they'd bring somebody in here to clean them up."

"I thought you were afraid of snakes," Bennis said warily.

"I was," Liz told her, and thought—that was in the past tense, too. Then she pulled back her arm and tossed the snake out into the trees in a great, graceful arc.

2

The call from the superintendent of schools came at exactly 3:46 P.M., and although Nancy Quayde had been expecting it, she found she wasn't ready.

The phone on her desk rang, and she jumped. She looked up and saw Lisa nodding at her from the desk outside. She picked up.

"Carol Shegelmeyer is on the phone," Lisa whispered, as if she suspected that Carol would be able to hear her if she talked loudly, even if she'd put Carol on hold. "She's clucking," Lisa said, "and if you ask me, this isn't good. Do you want me to tell her that you've already gone?"

"Yes," Nancy said, and then, "no. Wait. That's probably not a good idea. Did she say anything about what she wanted?"

"Just that she wanted to talk to you. I'd think it was obvious what the problem was. I mean, the police have been here today. She probably heard."

"Probably," Nancy agreed, thinking that if that were what Carol was worried about, there would be no problem. "Okay," she said. "Listen. Give it about a minute and then put her through, okay?"

"Okay. But are you sure? There's no reason why you shouldn't have left for the day."

"I almost never leave for the day before four, and Carol knows it. Give me a minute."

Nancy put the phone back in the cradle and closed her eyes and put her head down in her hands. It was important to breathe regularly and without gulping. It was important to be calm. It was important to remember that this was not a surprise. She'd known for hours that Carol was going to call sometime today. She'd known for hours what she needed to say and why. The trick was to stay in control.

The phone on her desk rang, and Nancy jumped. She took two long, steady breaths and picked up.

"Nancy?" Carol Stegelmeyer's voice said. "Is that you? This is Carol Stegelmeyer."

Well, of course it is, Nancy thought. Who else would it be? Did Carol think Lisa didn't bother to announce who was on the phone, or that Nancy took calls without knowing who they were from?

"Yes," Nancy said. "Yes. Carol. Hello. What can I do for you?"

"Well." Carol sounded stumped, as if this were a difficult question. She was *such* a stupid woman. "Well," Carol said again. "I've had a rather disturbing day. Do you know a Mr. Asch?"

Nancy stopped breathing. This was the worst-case scenario.

"Nancy?"

She'd been quiet too long. "Sorry," she said. "I've got a hot cup of coffee and I keep forgetting how hot. Yes. Yes, of course I know a Mr. Asch, if you mean David Asch. He's the father of one of our students here."

"Diane Asch," Carol said.

"Yes, exactly, Diane Asch."

"He said he talked to you today. Did he talk to you today?"

"He's talked to me on a number of occasions," Nancy said. "Diane has been having some problems. She's—well, you know what I mean. She's one of those teenagers who's going through a particularly awkward phase, and she's somewhat abrasive and obnoxious in her manner, so the other students—"

"Mr. Asch says they bully her. That they throw things at her and lock her in supply closets. I said that of course that wasn't possible, because if a student was ever to behave that way to any other student, then the student who committed the offense would be suspended at the very least. That's right, isn't it? That's our policy."

"Of course that's our policy."

"Mr. Asch says that on several occasions you sided with the student doing the bullying. I don't remember the names off the top of my head. Lynn somebody—"

"Lynn, DeeDee, and Sharon. Yes, I know who they are. Diane Asch is obsessed with them. And I do mean obsessed."

"Well, Nancy, if they really are bullying her, and physically attacking her—"

"Oh, for God's sake. Lynn is captain of the varsity cheerleaders this year. DeeDee is president of the student council. Sharon has been a prom princess three times and probably will be prom queen in a couple of weeks. It's the same old story. Diane is awkward and heavy and she's got a face like a pizza—"

"*Nancy.*"

"There's no point in sugar-coating it, is there? I've tried several times to get David Asch to listen to reason. I've offered to make sure Diane sees a good counselor and that the district pays for it. He just won't listen to reason."

"He feels," Carol said slowly, "that, under the circumstances, if Diane goes to therapy it will only ratify the charges of these three girls that she's, well, that there's something wrong with her."

"I see what you mean, but it's total hogwash. Lynn and DeeDee and Sharon aren't 'charging' Diane Asch with anything. Mostly, they're just leaving her alone. Oh, Carol, for God's sake. You know what these situations are like. She imagines insults where none exist. She follows them around until they explode at her, which maybe they shouldn't do, but it's perfectly human. She's a mess. She needs help. He won't let her get it."

There was a long silence on the other end of the line. Nancy began to twitch. Her throat was dry.

"He wasn't the only one who called," Carol said finally. "There was a man who said he was from the *New York Times*. He seems to be writing an article about Elizabeth Toliver, and he says—"

"What?"

"He says that there's a police record. A sealed police record. Showing that you were picked up on the night that boy died, whatever his name was, and that you'd been involved in an incident where you and some other girls nailed Elizabeth Toliver into an outhouse out at the park along with some snakes. I'm sorry I sound garbled. I really didn't understand the story."

"If the police record is sealed, how did a man from the *New York Times* get to see it?"

"He says he's got a copy."

"Which could be fake, or forged, or anything. A lot of people were in the park the night Michael Houseman died. Peggy was in the park the night Michael Houseman died. Chris Inglerod Barr was in the park the night Michael Houseman died. So what? What does it have to do with anything?"

"I don't think it's the death of that boy that's in contention," Carol said. "I think it's this story about the outhouse."

"I still don't understand what it has to do with anything," Nancy said. By now, she was being patient only by an act of will. "All that happened over thirty years ago. What does that have to do with Diane Asch?"

"What they're going to do, as an angle on the story, is to say that you were always, uh, the word he used was vicious, I'm afraid, I did protest, but—"

"Vicious," Nancy said. "He said I was vicious. Then what?"

"That you were always vicious to kids who were out of the social swim and not very popular, and you still are that way, only now you're principal, so that's why you don't do something about the girls who are persecuting Diane Asch. I did protest, Nancy, I did. I think the whole thing is absurd, but he just went on and on about it. And I must admit it's made me uneasy. Isn't there any way you can call these girls to account?"

"How can I call them to account if they haven't *done* anything?"

"Even if they haven't done anything, maybe you can call them in, you know, and have a meeting between them and Diane Asch and maybe her father, and call their parents in, too—"

"And their parents will quite rightly have a fit," Nancy pointed out. "They'll scream bloody murder. And they won't be any more sympathetic to Diane Asch than I am."

"I don't know," Carol said. "If this gets into the papers, and people start saying that you play favorites among the students, the district might be put into the position of ordering an investigation, and if we did that, we'd have to suspend you—"

"If you tried it, I'd sue your ass off."

"I'm sure you could institute a lawsuit if you wanted to, Nancy, but you wouldn't win it and I don't think the district would settle out of court. We couldn't afford to do that with a case we'd probably win. And we would probably win it because everybody these days is very concerned about the states of mind the loners are in, and the students who don't quite fit, and those people, because of all the school shootings. Not that I think Diane Asch is in any danger of becoming a school shooter—"

"She'd keel over from the kickback from a water pistol."

"—but you must see what I'm getting at. I wish you'd sit down and try to come up with some approach to this problem that didn't make all of us look bad. We really can't go to the press or the school board or the *Home News* saying that Diane Asch is some kind of paranoid psychotic, not unless you can prove she *is* a paranoid psychotic, which I don't think you can—"

"No," Nancy said. "She's not a paranoid psychotic. She's a fat, unattractive, whining, sniveling mass of insecurity complexes and it's no damned surprise to anybody who's paying attention that she has virtually no friends. We can't just cave in to this kind of thing. What are we supposed to do next? Cancel the prom? Abolish the cheerleaders? Chuck the whole student council? What Diane Asch needs is a good swift kick in the pants. What her father needs is some reality therapy."

"Yes," Carol said. "Well. I just thought I'd better warn you. He may be calling you later. The man from the *New York Times*. You might want to decide what you're going to say."

"Yes. All right. I will. Maybe I just won't take the call."

"I don't think that would be advisable. He'd put it in his story, that you refused to talk to him. That wouldn't look good."

"Fine, then. I'll talk to him."

"It's really too bad things like this have to get blown so out of proportion," Carol said. "Still, it's better to be safe. You must admit that. It's better to be safe."

"It's better to be safe," Nancy repeated—and then she hung up. She didn't say good-bye. She didn't wish Carol a good day. She didn't make any of the soothing noises that had come to be standard practice on ending a telephone call. She just hung up.

A second later, she realized she was frozen in her chair. Her muscles would not move. Her head felt screwed into her neck. All she could think about was the afternoon Emma and Belinda had held Betsy Toliver down on the floor of the girls' room in the junior high wing of the old building and put lipstick all over her face, on her cheeks, on her eyelids, on her ears. They'd done it because they couldn't stand the fact that Betsy never wore any of the stuff, but now that Nancy thought of it she could see how right it had been, how *just* it had been. None of the teachers then would have dreamed of interfering with what they were doing.

Crap, Nancy thought.

Then she got up and started throwing the things she needed for home into her attaché case.

3

Peggy Smith Kennedy had no idea why they had brought her to the hospital. It would have made more sense if they had sent her home to Stu. She was having a lot of difficulty holding on to time. She'd been sitting against the wall with that thing in her hand, and Emma had been spurting. Emma had been like a fountain of blood, spritzing thick red goo everywhere. The stain had spread along the front of her dress like the stain that spread across the front of the screen in that old Vincent Price movie.

The light changed in the room, and she shifted a little on her chair to get back into the center of it. She had been thinking that it would be nice to own a chair like this for her own living room. Stu always wrecked new furniture. She would like a new chair, and she would like flower boxes outside the windows at the front of the house, where she could plant pansies in the spring. When she was growing up and writing Stu's name all over her notebooks at school, she had had distinct fantasies about window boxes and pansies and big evergreen wreaths for the door at Christmas. It was odd. You never really thought about the important things. You never imagined paying the bills, or buying a car, or cleaning vomit up off the carpet in the bedroom hallway because Stu hadn't made it all the way to the bathroom before he'd started to throw up. You never thought about lying on your face on the linoleum in the kitchen with your right arm broken and your teeth aching where he had kicked them. You never thought about what it really meant to say you were in love.

The light in the room changed again, and Peggy shifted again, and then she realized that there was someone standing in the doorway.

The woman in the door seemed to lean forward. She was standing in shadow, and Peggy could not make out her features.

"Do you want something?" she called out to the form in the doorway. "Are you looking for somebody?"

"I'm sorry," Betsy Toliver said. "I didn't mean to disturb you. I was just wondering how you were."

It was not, Peggy thought, Betsy Toliver's voice as she remembered it. It was Betsy's voice from television, with its tinge of Britishness that probably came from living all those years in London. Peggy stabbed at her hair.

"You came all the way out here to see how I was doing?" she said.

Betsy came farther into the room. "Not all the way out to the hospital, no. I came out to the hospital to check on my mother. She's right down the hall."

"I'm on the geriatric ward?"

"I don't think so. I think it's more of a general ward, really. Are you all right? They told me you'd been found in the same room as Emma, all banged up. I haven't been able to see Emma. She's still unconscious."

"Is she on this floor, too?"

"No," Betsy said. "She's in some special care unit. I asked the nurse."

By now, Betsy was all the way into the room. Peggy could see her up close. Betsy was Betsy, but she wasn't Betsy at the same time. She still wore almost no makeup, and funny clothes, but even Peggy could see that these funny clothes were expensive, at least for Hollman. Maybe they were cheap for wherever it was Betsy lived now. Maybe Betsy hadn't really changed. Maybe.

"You look different," Peggy said.

"Well, I suppose I should. It's been over thirty years."

"I don't mean you look older. I mean you look different. I look older."

"I look older, too. Believe me. If I don't, it must be the light."

"You look different," Peggy said again. She didn't bother to explain. She shouldn't have to explain. It should be clear. And explaining was too much work. "If you'd looked like that in school, we'd probably have loved you. You'd have been the queen of everything. Except maybe Belinda. Belinda always hated you."

"Yes. Well. I rather thought that emotion was general."

Peggy flicked this away. "I have no idea what that means. I'm very tired."

"I'm sorry. I'll let you be. I only wanted—"

"They say Emma is going to be fine. You say she's in the intensive care unit—"

"No, I didn't say that. I said she's in a special care unit. Those were the words the nurse used when I talked to her."

"Whatever. They said downtown that she was going to be fine. Her fat saved her. That Mr. Demarkian said that. I heard him. Her fat saved her. It was so thick, the razor thing couldn't go all the way through her in one stroke, the way that it did with Chris. Do they all think you killed Chris?"

"No," Betsy said. "Not as far as I can tell."

"You'd think they would," Peggy said, "with the body in your yard and everything. But then, you were never somebody who got in trouble. I remember that. You weren't popular but you didn't get in trouble. Not like some people. Do you think it isn't fair, the way schools are? That some people get in trouble all the time and others don't for doing the same things and it's all a lot of personalities and luck?"

"I think it's more a matter of reputation," Betsy said. "People get reputations, and it's like those tags the characters had in Greek epics. Heraclitus the Wise. Andromachus the Malevolent. Once you have the tag, it never changes and it never disappears, and people think that's all you are."

"Some people deserve it, though, the treatment they get. Some people really do do things that are wrong and harmful and bad."

"Absolutely."

"Nancy always thought you deserved it," Peggy said. "She still does. Not that you deserve it now but that you deserved it then. She's a terrible person, really. She hates weakness of any kind, except half the things she calls weak aren't, they're just human. She hates Stu. She thinks she knows what it's like in my marriage. Do you hate Stu?"

"I don't know him. I never did know him, not even when we were all growing up. Maris told me you'd married him."

Peggy looked away. It was hard to look at Betsy. The clothes were nerve-wracking. Leather. Coach. Something expensive.

"Nobody knows what it's like in somebody else's marriage. Nobody can know. Everybody thinks Emma and George are all lovey-dovey and well suited to each other, but nobody knows. All kinds of things could be going on between them when they get themselves alone. He could be drinking up all the money they make. She could be having affairs on the side. I know you think it isn't possible because of her weight, but things like that have happened. The woman who ran the key booth at the mall had an affair with one of the janitors and she was married and he was black. Black. Do you remember when we used to call them Negroes? And nobody went to Kennanburg because there were too many of them there, and now there are twice as many and Hispanics, too, and everybody goes there anyway because you can't help it if you want to go to the hospital or get a copy of your birth certificate. I was always going to marry Stu. Everybody knew that. I knew that by the time I was five years old."

"Yes," Betsy said. "Well. I think they've pickled you in sedatives. You ought to get some rest."

"If you really love somebody," Peggy said, "if you really, really love them, you don't walk out on them because they've got a few imperfections. You love the imperfections. You cherish them. You *protect* them."

"Sometimes you can't protect them."

"You shouldn't have come back here," Peggy said. "Belinda's right about one thing. It isn't fair. What happened to you and what happened to us. It isn't fair. The world is supposed to make sense. It has an obligation to. You should have stayed in New York or Connecticut or wherever it is you live and left the rest of us alone."

"I'll leave you alone now. You should rest, and I need to get back to where I'm staying."

"You should have left us alone," Peggy said, but she was talking to air. Betsy was gone. Maybe Betsy had never been there. She felt very drowsy.

It was true, Peggy thought. You didn't just walk out on somebody you loved because they weren't as perfect as you wanted them to be. If you did, it wasn't love. It was convenience, or sex, or prestige, or position, or even habit. Love is stronger than that. Love accepts the bad with the good. Love learns to—

She was very tired. She couldn't keep her eyes open. Betsy had been right. They'd given her a lot of pills, a lot of sedatives. They'd been trying so hard to calm her down, and she hadn't been able to understand why. She hadn't been agitated. She hadn't even been restless. She was sitting so still, she could have been frozen into a stone. Besides, she didn't have anything to worry about.

Emma was all right. Emma would wake up, sooner or later, and tell everybody on earth who it was who had really attacked her.

FIVE

1

Gregor Demarkian decided to find out where the Radisson was because he couldn't find Bennis Hannaford, who was supposed to be there, but who wasn't answering the phone. If she was off on the floor where Jimmy Card and Elizabeth Toliver were hiding out, he was going to kill her. She hadn't given him that number—probably because she hadn't been authorized to—and she hadn't given him any other way to reach her. Gregor was beginning to realize just how much he had come to rely on cell phones.

He reached into the inside pocket of his jacket and pulled out the notebook he'd been using since before he'd first come out to Hollman. Kyle was driving as if everything would get out of his way when he needed it to, even trees. It was better not to watch the road while that kind of thing was going on.

"So," Kyle said. "What's that you've got there? The answer to all my problems?"

"It's a list." Gregor turned the notebook sideways so that Kyle could get a look at it. He didn't leave it up long, though, because he wanted Kyle concentrating on the roads. "In a way, it's a suspect list. It just wasn't supposed to be a suspect list for the death of Chris Inglerod Barr."

"What is it a suspect list for, then?"

"Oh, it's a suspect list for the death of Chris Inglerod Barr," Gregor said. "It's very efficient that way. It's just that, when I wrote it, Mrs. Barr was still alive and well and I only knew her as Chris Inglerod. I should say knew of her. We hadn't met. This is the list of names Jimmy Card gave me the afternoon he hired me. I've added a couple of names to it."

"Okay," Kyle said.

"I should have insisted on talking to Liz Toliver before I came up here." Gregor sighed. "As it is, I only met her after we both got to Hollman, and that was in the midst of the crisis about her mother's dog. And everything I knew about that night Michael Houseman died, I knew either from dry research or from Jimmy Card, and Jimmy Card doesn't give a flying damn about who killed Michael Houseman as long as it wasn't Elizabeth Toliver."

"It wasn't," Kyle said quickly.

"I know. But the thing is, since the beginning, my focus on this case has been what Jimmy Card set it up to be. But what struck him most forcefully, and what naturally strikes Elizabeth Toliver, isn't the murder but the outhouse. It makes much more sense for Elizabeth Toliver to be fixated on the outhouse and what happened to her in it than it does for her to worry about who killed Michael Houseman. She never even saw the body. And she never knew the boy very well."

"She'd have recognized him in the corridors in school. But they never hung out or were friends or anything of that kind."

"Exactly," Gregor said. "So Elizabeth Toliver thinks about the outhouse, not about the murder, when she thinks about that night. The only thing she ever says about the murder is that she heard somebody screaming—"

" 'Slit his throat,' " Kyle said quickly. "She told the police that at the time. She said she couldn't recognize the voice."

"She told Jimmy Card she couldn't recognize it as well," Gregor said. "But what that leaves me with, what it has left me with all along, is an investigative structure that hinges on the outhouse incident. And since the two incidents are connected in a very tenuous way—since they *overlap*, I should say—the suspect list is still useful. But it's not actually a suspect list for the murder of Michael Houseman, or for the murder of Chris Inglerod Barr, either."

"So who's on it?" Kyle said.

Gregor held the notebook up. "Maris Coleman. Belinda Hart. Emma Kenyon. Chris Inglerod. Nancy Quayde. Peggy Smith."

"Well, you can get rid of Chris Inglerod," Kyle said. "At least, as a suspect in her own murder. Do you think she killed Michael Houseman?"

"No."

"Well, you can't think she killed herself, can you?" Kyle said.

"I can't see Mrs. Barr doing it and managing to hide the weapon so well we couldn't find it," Gregor said. "No. I don't think she killed herself. And Emma Kenyon Bligh is eliminated because she was attacked this afternoon. Of course, there is a possibility that Mrs. Bligh inflicted that wound on herself. This time, we do have the weapon. And there's also the possibility that Mrs. Bligh was working with somebody else, possibly Peggy Smith Kennedy, and they had a falling out. But all in all, I'm inclined to think not. It's not a crime of that character. It has too much passion in it."

"Are you talking about what happened to Chris now, or what happened to Emma?"

"Both. Sorry. I've been thinking of them as one crime. The two women and the dog. And that sequence has a lot of passion in it, which is interesting, because from everything you've told me and everything everyone else has told me and everything I've read in the material you've given me, the murder of Michael Houseman was cold as hell."

"And you've got more suspects for that one," Kyle said. "There's me. And Stu Kennedy. You don't suspect either of us of murdering Chris Inglerod?"

"No. In fact, I know that neither of you did. Mr. Kennedy is not capable of pulling off something of this complexity, not unless he's also capable of getting himself sober and straight when he has to, which, from what you've told me, he isn't."

"Not from anything I've ever seen, no."

"I'd be willing to bet not, period," Gregor said. "And as for you, you couldn't have killed Chris Inglerod Barr because you didn't have time. You were with me most of the afternoon. Then I left to go out to the Toliver place. You would have had to make it out there before me, kill Mrs. Barr, and get away again, all before Luis pulled into the driveway with me in the backseat. And that ignores the obvious, which is that you'd have had to know that Mrs. Barr was going to be there in the first place. So no. I don't think you're a serious suspect in the murder of Chris Inglerod Barr, and you're no suspect at all in the attack on Emma Kenyon Bligh, because we were together the whole morning and I know where you were and what you did. Feeling relieved?"

"More than you know."

"It's not a bad suspect list for the murder of Chris Inglerod Barr," Gregor said, "if I remember to use it for that, instead of letting the list focus my mind on the outhouse. Because the thing about the outhouse is that it was almost beside the point. Almost. Not entirely. That's another mistake I made. First I took it too seriously, and then later for a while I didn't take it seriously enough. There's a big sign over there saying 'Radisson.' Shouldn't we do something about that?"

"I really hate that part of the detective novel where the detective tells his sidekick a third of everything he knows and then shuts up like a clam and acts like Buddha for fifty pages while the sidekick tears his hair trying to decipher all the Zen koans. You know what I mean?"

"I know what you mean. I'm waiting for one more piece of information, and then we'll do all the usual things that cops like to do and you can hold a press conference to announce the arrest. How's that?"

"Okay unless somebody else ends up dead in the meantime," Kyle said.

"I absolutely promise you not to hold a party to accuse each of the suspects in turn. Some of them would probably refuse to come. And I absolutely promise you that there won't be another death, unless it's the death of Emma Kenyon Bligh, and the last time we heard from the hospital, that was very unlikely."

"Right," Kyle said. He had pulled into a parking space against the building. It was a handicapped parking space, but he didn't seem to care. "Dozens of people have linoleum cutters. You can buy them in any hardware store."

"Of course, but why would she do that? Why not use something close to hand, like a kitchen knife?"

"Not sharp enough," Kyle said.

"You're giving her too much credit. She didn't think that far ahead. And I meant it. The forensics are hard. They take meticulous collection, and meticulous lab work. Even big-city, fully professionalized police departments screw them up. Investigation is easy. It's just a matter of thinking clearly, and remembering that somebody can be very logical without being in the least bit rational."

"We're back to Zen Buddhism again," Kyle said.

Gregor laughed. He popped his door open and got out. He waited for Kyle to get out and then went up the curving concrete walk to the front door.

"With any luck," he said, "there will be a fax waiting for me at the desk, and there will be Bennis waiting for me in the room. If we can get those two things, we can get this thing over with pretty quickly. And besides."

"Besides what?" Kyle said.

"Besides. You keep forgetting that Emma Kenyon Bligh is going to wake up."

2

Gregor was not sure what he was expecting when he checked in at the desk—the worst-case scenario was that Bennis had forgotten to tell anybody he might be coming, and he wouldn't be able to get up to the room, or even in touch with her—but as it turned out he was already on record as being one of the occupants of the suite, and there was already a sheaf of messages waiting for him in the mailbox. One of them was a fax from Russ Donahue. Gregor tried to remember if he'd told Bennis to have that faxed to the hotel or to the police department, and he was fairly sure he'd asked her to have it faxed to the police department. She might have asked for it to be faxed both places just to be safe. He folded that one in squares and put it in his right hip pocket. The other message was from Jimmy Card. It included a floor number and the words "password: goldfish."

"Whatever," Gregor said, frowning at the note. He put that away in his right hip pocket, too. "I think I'll go up to the suite and see if Bennis is around to talk to," he told Kyle Borden.

"Ms. Hannaford has gone out," the helpful young woman at the desk said cheerfully. "She left about two hours ago with—ah—with a friend."

The young woman arched her eyebrows. Gregor frowned. "A friend? How could she have left with a friend? She doesn't know anybody in this part of Pennsylvania that I've heard about."

"She left with a *woman* friend," the young woman said. Now it was her tone that was arched. Gregor was completely bewildered. "She said you'd know who it would be. Of course, under the circumstances, I couldn't mention the name in a place where we might be overheard."

Light dawned. It was an idiot light, but it dawned. "Ah," Gregor said. "All right then. Maybe I'll go upstairs and answer my mail."

"I hope you have a pleasant stay," the young woman said, cheerfully again.

Gregor got Kyle Borden in hand and headed for the elevators, but once inside the car he didn't press the button for the second floor, where his own suite was, but for the fourth. Kyle frowned.

"Didn't she say you were on the second floor?"

"Right."

"Why are we going to the fourth?"

"Because that's where Jimmy Card and Elizabeth Toliver are. They have the entire west wing of the fourth floor."

"And we can just walk on there anytime we want? They don't have any better security than that?"

The elevator car stopped on the fourth floor. Gregor and Kyle got out onto an open foyer-type arrangement. One set of signs pointed to the east wing. One set of signs pointed to the west. Gregor went toward the west wing doors and pulled them back. They were immediately blocked by a large man in a black suit. He looked like he should be doing a bit part on *The Sopranos*.

"I think you're lost, sir," he said, very politely, with no Brooklyn accent at all.

"Goldfish," Gregor said solemnly.

"Yes, sir," the man in black said, politely again, stepping back to let them through.

"What was that all about?" Kyle asked as they came out onto the fourth-floor west wing itself. "I feel like I'm in a James Bond movie."

"Security," Gregor said.

It wasn't much in the way of security. As soon as they were past the man in black, they could see Geoff DeAvecca running back and fourth between the rooms. Geoff saw them coming down the hall and veered in their direction. He came to a stop just in front of them and said, "Cool! Is that a real gun? Does it have bullets in it? Can I shoot it?"

Kyle put his hand protectively on his gun. "I always knew there was a reason why I felt stupid wearing a holster," he said.

"It's a real gun," Gregor said, "but you can't hold it and you can't shoot it. It would be far too dangerous. I can't believe your mother would approve of it."

"My mother doesn't approve of Donkey Kong," Geoff said majestically. "But she's a girl. Jimmy likes Donkey Kong."

Up toward the other end of the hall, a head poked out of a door. A moment later, Mark DeAvecca's entire body followed it, and Jimmy Card followed him. Jimmy was supposed to be the grown-up, but Mark was half a foot taller. Gregor always got the feeling that Mark was growing even taller as he watched.

"Mr. Demarkian! What's up? Have you seen Mom? She went out with your friend Bennis. What're you doing? Mom says you said she isn't a suspect anymore. Is that a real policeman?"

"Mark, for Christ's sake," Jimmy said.

"I'm just a little jumpy," Mark said. "I don't like the idea of her being out there on her own. She doesn't have a lot of sense."

Gregor cleared his throat. It was that or laugh. "We got your note at reception. We just didn't know what it meant. So we decided to come up here to see. Where did Liz and Bennis go, do you know?"

"No," Jimmy said. "We don't. Liz wouldn't tell me what was on her mind. She went downstairs to borrow Bennis's car, and then she called back up here to say that Bennis was going to go with her."

"I figure if she wanted somebody with her, she wasn't going to do anything stupid like commit suicide," Mark said. "And don't look at me like that. People do do that. They do it all the time. And she's been depressed."

"She hasn't been that kind of depressed," Jimmy said. Then he sighed. "I don't know what it was about. She's been acting peculiar practically since we got here. She keeps saying she thought she knew what she heard, but now she knows she's wrong. Does that mean anything to you?"

"No," Gregor said, although it did. He wondered why Jimmy hadn't thought of it, or Mark. Elizabeth Toliver had heard a voice in the woods on the night she was nailed into the outhouse and Michael Houseman died, a voice screaming "slit his throat." She'd always said she had no idea whose voice it was, but she might not have been telling the truth. Gregor had always suspected she wasn't. She hadn't been behaving like somebody who couldn't figure out who it was she had heard.

"I just hope she didn't get caught by reporters," Jimmy said. "That's just about all we'd need right now."

"She talks," Mark said. "You wouldn't believe it. She's on cable news all the time and she still doesn't get it. She just blurts it all out. But that's not what I'm worried about. I'm worried about the murderer. That's been the point of this exercise, hasn't it? Somebody's been trying to murder her? I've been trying to tell Jimmy that, but he won't listen."

"Nobody murders somebody just because they left town after high school and got famous," Jimmy said.

"Those two women who drove me home would be happy to see her dead," Mark said. "You didn't talk to them for an hour. I did."

"It took an hour to drive you home from the middle of Hollman?" Jimmy said.

"No," Mark said. "We talked some before we went. But you ask Mr. Demarkian. I'm right, aren't I? Somebody has been trying to kill her."

"No," Gregor said.

"This is new," Kyle said. "Why would you think somebody wanted to kill your mother?"

"What else could be going on?" Mark said.

"Nobody has been trying to kill Ms. Toliver," Gregor said firmly. "And nobody is going to be trying to kill Ms. Toliver in the foreseeable future, as far as I know. She may have enemies in New York or Connecticut that I'm unaware of, of course—"

"Senior citizens," Mark said solemnly. "These guys who are like sixty-five and seventy. They hate it that they've been sending their stories in for years and couldn't get published and there she is. They hate losing to a girl."

"I don't think that means they'd kill her," Jimmy said.

"Even if the killer didn't mean to murder her in the first place," Mark said, "couldn't he be meaning to do that now? There has to be some reason he killed Grandma's dog and left the body on her lawn. It's not like Grandma's house is convenient to anything."

"Maybe it is," Jimmy said. "There could be any number of things in the area."

"You have to drive to all of them," Mark said. "Ask Mr. Demarkian."

"Nobody is going to kill anybody for the rest of the day," Gregor said firmly, "at least, nobody involved in this case is. You don't have any idea at all where Ms. Toliver has gone? And Bennis?"

"I thought she might have gone to the hospital to visit Grandma," Mark said. "I mean, she's been agitating over Grandma all day. I don't know why. The woman's a complete bitch—"

"*Jesus*," Jimmy Card said. "She's going to blame me for your language. She always does."

"I'm being accurate," Mark said. "Grandma is a bitch. Especially to Mom. It's like she hates her or something. Except you wouldn't think a mother would hate her own daughter, but she does. I don't understand women. I mean, guys just do what they do, you know? Women get psychotic."

"Women are born psychotic," Jimmy Card said.

"Listen," Gregor said. "We just came up to make sure that everything was all right. We need to get back to the hospital and see if Emma Bligh is ready to be interviewed. If you give me the number, we'll call in when we get to the hospital. I really would like to know when you know that Bennis and Liz are all right."

3

Goldfish, Gregor thought as he and Kyle went down the elevator again, this time to the second floor.

"It's incredible, don't you think?" Kyle said. "A whole floor. What do you think that costs? What do you think Jimmy Card makes in a year?"

"I think this is our floor," Gregor said, although he had wondered the same thing.

The elevator let them off, and they headed for the east wing. 217E was the number on Gregor's room key, which was not a room key at all, but a little plastic square like a thick credit card. Gregor hated those.

At 217E, Gregor got the card out and pushed it horizontally into a slot opening in the middle of the door. He pulled the card out and tried the knob. It was still locked. He put the card into the slot again and pulled it out again. He tried the knob again. It was still locked. He put the card into the slot again.

"Here," Kyle Borden said. "If I let you do that, we'll be here all day."

Kyle pushed the card into the slot, pulled it out quickly, grabbed for the doorknob with his other hand, and turned. The knob did, indeed, turn. The door swung open.

"How did you do that?" Gregor said.

"You have to be fast."

"Obviously," Gregor said. He pushed through the door and looked around inside. The front room was pleasantly furnished with a good carpet and decent furniture and a very impressive television set, but it was also empty. He went through it to the inner room and found that much more like what he expected. The bed was covered with clothes, all Bennis's. There was a blue bathrobe hanging over the bathroom door that belonged to him, but it wasn't the one he had brought with him from Cavanaugh Street. It was the one he'd left home. Bennis must have brought it.

"I'm going to have to do something about getting hold of my clothes," Gregor said. "They're out at the Toliver place. I wish we knew where they'd gone."

"I thought you said there was nothing to worry about," Kyle said. "You told Jimmy Card and that kid—"

"Mark. I told them she was in no danger of getting murdered. She isn't. There are other things to worry about. The first is the reporters. I do think they're still around."

"I haven't noticed them. Maybe they've gone home."

"What do you think the chances of that are?"

"Nil," Kyle said. "This morning before you got to the station, they were asking me when I was going to hold a press conference. I've never held a press conference in my life. I wouldn't know how to start."

"When the time comes, I'll tell you how to set up a press conference. There's the possibility that Elizabeth Toliver has decided to act on what she knows, which is not a very good idea at all. It won't get her killed, but it might get her tangled up in something more than she needs to be. I don't think I've ever met a woman, especially not a famous woman, who is this—vulnerable—to the claims of other people. Most of them learn to put a wall up around themselves fairly early in the game. You should see Bennis when she's attacked by what she calls a psychofan."

"What's a psychofan?"

"Somebody who dresses up like Queen Amalia and tries to talk to Bennis in Zedalian."

"What?"

"It's a long story. Let's go back in the living room."

Kyle still looked bewildered, but he did as he was told. Gregor went out to the suite's living room and pulled out one of the chairs around its oval dining table. Then he reached into his pocket to get his folded-up version of Russ Donahue's fax. He spread it out against the table. The first page was one of those fax administrative pages and he pushed it away. The second page was full of Russ's lawyer's scrawl.

Gregor, it said. *I have no idea what you wanted this for, but here it is. There's not much of it. I checked a couple of sources and they all say the same thing. We weren't really collecting comprehensive crime records in this state back in 1969. What I was able to get were the big things that the municipal police forces thought were worthwhile to talk to Harrisburg about, but that doesn't give you much. Sorry I couldn't be of more help. Get in touch if you need anything else. Donna and Tommy say hi. Tibor says there's some Bible fanatic on rec.arts.mystery who claims that the King James Bible is a perfectly accurate translation of the Masoretic text, but he doesn't even know there are two Masoretic texts. I have no idea what that means, but he said you would. Take care. Russ.*

Gregor had no idea what the Masoretic text was, never mind that there were two of them. He put Russ's note away, thinking he would get back to it, and Tibor and rec.arts.mystery and the Masoretic text, when he had a little time. There were only two more pages left, and there wasn't much on them but bureaucratic verbiage about "felony crime reporting patterns" and "inadequacies in local law enforcement paradigms." He got out his notebook, flipped it to a fresh page, and got out his pen.

"So what's that," Kyle asked, "a list of all the crimes committed in Hollman in the last six days? What?"

"It's the only list available of the crimes committed in this county in July and August of 1969. It's nowhere near comprehensive, unfortunately."

Kyle came and stood behind Gregor's shoulder. "There doesn't look like there's much there but a lot of talk. Were there really practically no crimes here back then? I mean, even just in the last month, I could probably do you better than that in Hollman alone."

"In felony arrests?"

"Oh," Kyle said. "Well, no. We don't really get a lot of felony arrests."

Gregor looked through the first page and wrote a list that said:

July 5 Kennanburg arrest attempted murder weapon shotgun
July 7 Kennanburg arrest murder weapon blunt instrument
July 8 Kennanburg arrest attempted murder weapon pistol
July 16 Kennanburg murder weapon razor
July 17 Kennanburg arrest narcotics possession with intent to sell

July 18 Kennanburg attempted murder weapon shotgun
July 19 Kennanburg murder weapon razor
July 22 Kennanburg attempted murder weapon shotgun

He pushed that page out of the way and went through the next one. There was far less on this page. Russ was right to say they hadn't done much about collecting crime reports in 1969. Gregor wrote down:

August 2 Kennanburg arrest attempted murder shotgun
August 3 Kennanburg narcotics possession with intent to sell
August 12 Kennanburg arrest murder weapon pistol

Then he sat back and looked over what he had.

"Why do some of them say 'arrest' and others don't?" Kyle said.

"Because whenever the Kennanburg municipal police got in touch with the state police, some of the suspects were under arrest and some weren't. Which means sometimes they were asking for help with supporting evidence and sometimes they were asking for help finding the perpetrator."

"Why is it only Kennanburg?"

"Kennanburg is a denser population area. Denser population areas have more crime. They're also more likely to know who to talk to if they want help from the state. And, like I said, this is not a complete list. It's not anything like it. All kinds of mayhem could have been going on, and all kinds of mayhem could have been reported to the state police, without it actually showing up in this report. Even now, when we try to be careful about this sort of thing, we miss a lot."

Kyle came around to Gregor's side and leaned far over the table. "Look at that," he said. "Murder, weapon razor. Twice."

"That's right."

"Well, what about it? Did they arrest the guy who did it? Did they find the murder weapon? What? Because Michael Houseman could have been killed with a razor. We always thought it was a knife, but I never heard anything except that whatever it was had to be really sharp. And they never found the weapon."

"I think it would be a fair guess to say it was probably a linoleum cutter," Gregor said.

"Yeah?" Kyle brightened. "Jeez, you are good. I called a friend of mine up in Connecticut because I knew he'd met you up there and he said you were. Good, I mean. But, what are we talking about here? A serial killer? I thought you said that the murder of Chris Inglerod and the murder of Michael Houseman were connected."

"They are."

"So what have we got? A serial killer who just went out of business for thirty years until Betsy Toliver came back to town? Or maybe it's Betsy Toliver who's the serial killer? But that doesn't make any sense. I don't care about Hannibal Lecter. The guys who are serial killers are messes, most of them. They don't go running off to succeed on television. What about those murders? Did they find the perpetrators? Did they find the weapons?"

Gregor glanced back over the pages with actual report findings on them. "No and no," he said. "Not at the time the police filed the report, at any rate. They could have found both later, and we'd have no way of knowing from this. We'd have to check the files in Kennanburg itself."

"Well, then," Kyle said. "They could never have found either, right? And Michael Houseman would have been one of this guy's victims—but why come out here for that? I mean, why not just stay in Kennanburg? If you were this guy, would you come out to some small town? Except maybe he did, and maybe it's just not on the report. That's a possibility, isn't it?"

"It's a possibility, yes."

"You don't sound very happy," Kyle said. "I'd be ecstatic, if I were you."

Gregor put all the fax papers together and folded them up again and stuck them in his jacket pocket again. He was suddenly aware of the fact that it was raining outside again, slowly and steadily, without thunder. He felt as if he had conducted this entire case in Noah's flood.

He pushed back the chair and stood up. "So," he said to Kyle, "are you ready to come to the hospital with me and arrest Peggy Smith Kennedy for the murder of Chris Inglerod Barr?"

SIX

1

After two and a half hours of waiting, Maris Coleman was more than merely nervous, except that she wasn't, because she was anesthetized. "Anesthetized" was what they used to call it at Vassar, when they'd run off to Pizza Town right after their last final exam. She was in an odd floaty state that she couldn't quite keep hold of. It was like the state she got into when she "did something" about the bills, which usually meant turning the ringer off on the phone so that she didn't have to hear the people from the credit-care companies tell her that it was really important that she did something about her account as soon as possible. The credit-card companies. The telephone people. The mortgage people never bothered her, because Betsy had done something about that, Maris couldn't remember what. She did remember that she resented the fact that she had had to buy that apartment. It was a good location, but the apartment itself was so very small, and really only one room, when Betsy had that entire town house on the East Side and didn't even live in it. It was Jimmy Card who was messing things up and, of course, Debra, who had been scheming to get her out of the way since the day Betsy had hired her. Hired *me*, Maris thought, but now her head was starting to pound the way it did sometimes when she had too much to drink too fast or tried to get over a hangover more quickly than she had a right to. She should never have given up cocaine. She wanted to take an aspirin, but she was afraid to. It could be dangerous to mix alcohol with aspirin, or with anything. Karen Quinlan had ended up in a coma by taking acetaminophen with alcohol, and then her family had fought to take out her feeding tubes. In the year that that had been the big story, Maris had been working for a Wall Street law firm as a paralegal. That was the job that she had kept the longest, and for years she had believed—honestly believed—that she was indispensable. She should have gone to law school. She should have—she couldn't think of what she should have done. The universe seemed to her to be a huge conspiracy aimed directly against herself. The game had been fixed from the start. It wouldn't have mattered what she'd done. Even back when they were all in high school, there were forces working behind the scenes. She was flying high, but it was only a matter of time. She should have killed Betsy when she had the chance. She should have done something about Debra, too. She wanted to cry, and when she didn't want to cry she wanted to smash things. Would Betsy disappear without ever seeing her again? She'd left the house this morning without remembering that Maris had been there the night before, and was likely to be there still. Ever since she'd met Jimmy Card, she'd been more and more distracted, more and more distant. Maris knew the signs. She had known them every single time she'd been fired. She had seen them coming for months. She really did want to cry. It was like Belinda said. It wasn't *fair*.

When she heard the voices in the stairwell, she was drinking straight out of her Chanel No. 5 bottle. She capped it quickly and put it away in her bag, feeling guilty in the same way she had when she was a child and her mother almost caught her stealing cookies off the plate as they came out of the stove.

"I'm not sure she's in the apartment," Belinda said, sounding petulant and put out.

"I don't see why you think you can just waltz in here and treat the place like your own. I do have a life, you know. I'm very busy."

"I only need to talk to Maris for a moment if she's in," Betsy's voice said, perfectly calm, perfectly reasonable. "If she isn't, we'll go right back downstairs."

"What if she is? What then? Did you ever think that I might want to get some things done around the apartment? Did you ever think I might want a little private time?"

"It really will be just a minute," Betsy said.

"I don't even know who this person is," Belinda said. "You're bringing strangers into my house and you haven't even been invited."

I wonder who the stranger is, Maris thought. She had her feet stretched out on Belinda's coffee table, which would make Belinda livid, but right now it wouldn't matter. Belinda would never criticize her in front of Betsy Toliver. Belinda was sounding like a shrew. Maris suspected she often sounded like that, and that that had been one of the reasons her husband had left her. God, but that woman could *shriek*.

Behind her, the apartment's door opened. There was a shuffle in the doorway. Maris did not turn around.

"Don't think I'm going to offer you coffee," Belinda said. "I don't want you here any more than I wanted you at my lunch table in high school."

"I think that's Maris over there asleep on the couch," Betsy said. "I won't be but a moment. Keep your britches on, Belinda. You never were very good at self-control."

"Why, you little *bitch*," Belinda said.

"Oh, and by the way. The name is Liz, or Elizabeth, or Ms. Toliver. It has not been Betsy for many years, and you're being a damned fool to go on calling me that. Between CNN and *People* magazine, aborigines in the Australian outback know that people who are friendly with me call me Liz."

"Well, I call you Betsy," Belinda said. "I'm not friendly with you. You're nothing but a two-bit creepy little loser, and you'll never be anything else."

"My, my," a voice Maris didn't recognize said. It sounded a little like Katherine Hepburn's. "Are people around here always this rude?"

"Habitually," Betsy said. "They mistake it for a religion."

"God, you're such a little snot," Belinda said. "Just listen to you. 'Habitually.' Don't we know lots of great big words."

The voices were closer now. There were footsteps coming across the kitchen. Maris sat up a little straighter and turned around. Belinda looked insane. She must have been out in the rain. Her hair was frizzed up like the Bride of Frankenstein's. Betsy was wearing a T-shirt and a pair of those straight black linen pants she seemed to wear all summer and a blazer that looked old enough to have been worn in in every possible way. You could still tell it was expensive. Maris smiled at her slightly, because that was the kind of thing you did in situations like this. Maris had been in them before.

"Well," Betsy said.

"Who's this?" Maris asked, nodding toward the other woman, the small but perfect one with the black hair. "Have you started picking up women in bars?"

"This is Bennis Hannaford," Betsy said. "She's a friend of Gregor Demarkian's. You've met Mr. Demarkian."

"How do you do?" Bennis Hannaford said.

"Dennis?" Belinda said. "What kind of a name is that for a girl? Or is this one of your fancy schmantzy friends from college who went to one of those snob schools where all the girls have boys' names?"

"It's not Dennis with a D," Bennis Hannaford said. "It's Bennis. With a B. As in boy."

Betsy came around the back of the couch and took a seat on the very edge of the ottoman. She leaned forward and clasped her hands. "I promised Belinda I wouldn't be long, and I won't be. I don't want you coming back to the office after this trip. You're fired, effective now. You're owed a two-week severance check. I'll call Debra and make sure she cuts you one immediately. She'll pack up your desk and ship your things to you. Your mortgage account has enough money in it to cover your mortgage until the end of June. After that, it will be closed. If you give our office as a recommendation when you look for a new job, I will tell Debra to tell the truth about you as far as it is possible without sounding as if she's exaggerating."

"I could sue you for that," Maris said. "And you know how it would look. I'm not the one that would come off like trash."

"You know, all the way back to Vassar, I thought I knew what was going on," Betsy said. "I heard it, you know. That girl screaming. Slit his throat, she was saying. Slit his throat. And all that time, I thought it was you. When you started drinking like a crazy person in college, I thought that was what had caused it. I thought you'd gotten caught up in something and then in the heat of the moment one of you had killed poor Michael Houseman and now you were falling apart about it. I felt sorry for you."

"You felt sorry for me in college? I was a star in college. You were nobody at all."

"You were drinking every single night. I wasn't the only one who noticed it. You were completely out of control. And you were, of course, an utter bitch to me, relentlessly. But then you'd always been. And I thought I knew why you were behaving so oddly, and then, when we ran into each other in the city and you were so much of a mess—"

"I have never been a mess," Maris said. "Not ever."

"And you didn't have a job and you'd been fired all those times and it was obvious you were drinking. And then I didn't just feel sorry for you, I felt guilty, really, because I'd always thought of you as perfect. As golden. As destined for success in just the same way I was destined for failure. It's odd how ideas like that can lodge in your head and refuse to leave. And I thought that it was all just an accident. You'd been in the wrong place at the wrong time with all those mediocre people and the moment had overwhelmed you and your life was ruined. And it was just chance. It was just fate. Just like I thought it was just fate that I'd landed at CNN and Columbia, just a matter of being in the right place at the right time instead of the other way around. And it seemed so unfair."

Maris smiled. "Excuse me," she said, reaching down into her bag. She came up with the bottle of Chanel No. 5, uncapped it, and took a long swig. "We don't need to observe formalities, here, do we? It's not like you don't know what I keep in this thing. It was fate, you know. It was all chance and circumstance. There's nothing else on earth that could have gotten you where you are."

"On the night Michael Houseman died, I did hear a girl screaming 'slit his throat,' but it wasn't you. It couldn't have been you, and if I'd been thinking straight I would have realized it. You were with Belinda and Emma, right from the beginning. The three of you were hiding out in the stand of trees just up the fork from that outhouse because you wanted to see what I'd do when you got the door nailed shut. It wasn't you screaming 'slit his throat,' it was Peggy."

"Crap," Belinda said. "Why would Peggy Smith want to slit Michael Houseman's throat? She barely even knew him. He wasn't one of our crowd."

"So I started to think about it," Betsy said. "I started to wonder. If you weren't behaving the way you were behaving because you were traumatized by having taken part in the death of Michael Houseman without meaning to, then why *were* you behaving the way you were behaving? Do you want to know what conclusion I came to?"

"Do tell," Maris said.

"It seems to me that there's only one reason why you do what you do. Because you want to do it. You're not having a mental breakdown caused by post-traumatic stress syndrome or whatever I thought it was. You really are one of those mediocre people. You just happen to be one of them with decent grades, and that got you into a good college, and so for a year or two you looked more impressive than you really were. But you belong here, Maris. You're Hollman through and through. Small-minded, petty, envious, spiteful, and tenth rate—"

"Oh, dear. Let me tell a few strategic people all about that one. Won't that one look lovely in *People* magazine."

"What did you think she was going to do?" Betsy asked. "Did you expect her to murder me? What was the point of all this this past week?"

"I don't know what you're talking about," Maris said.

"She had the keys to your car," Betsy said. "To your bright yellow Volkswagen rental car. I saw her driving it on Grandview Avenue that day we had the big fight at the Sycamore, the day Chris Inglerod was killed."

"So maybe she stole the keys out of my purse."

"She wouldn't have been capable of it, and you know it. You may sell that line to the police, Maris, but you won't sell it to me. You gave her the keys to that car, and you told her when you thought I'd be home, and you were wrong both times, and that's where the trouble was. You must have known she was dangerous. My children were in that house, or they were supposed to be."

"I know you're having a wonderful time playing like you're the great detective," Maris said, "but I don't know anything of the sort. I don't think Peggy Smith did kill Michael Houseman, and I don't think she killed Chris Inglerod, either. I think you're just speculating to give yourself an excuse to trash me."

"An excuse?" Betsy said. "Do I need an excuse? After you've spent the last two years planting stories in the tabloids that make it sound as if I were the one who had killed Michael Houseman? And that even though you knew perfectly well that I could not possibly have done it? You nailed me into that damned outhouse yourself."

"Not all by herself, she didn't," Belinda said. "It wasn't just Maris. It was everybody who hated you."

Betsy didn't look as if she'd heard. Maris took a long swig on the Chanel No. 5 bottle. "If you do fire me," she said, "I might find it necessary to fight back a little. I might find it necessary to sell my story to the *National Enquirer*, for instance. How Elizabeth Toliver used me like a slave and then dismissed me like a servant and left me to starve. Or something along those lines. I think I did lay them out that day at the Sycamore, didn't I?"

"Well, yes," Betsy said, "you did. But at the time I saw no reason to respond. So let me respond now. If you try anything of the kind, I will make sure that Debra releases the detective files we have on you from the last two times we've kept you out of jail. The first time when you forged my signature on a check for two thousand dollars on September third last year. The second time when you forged Debra's signature on a check for five thousand on this past January seventeenth. Did you really think we hadn't noticed? Why do you imagine it suddenly got so hard for you to lay your hands on the checkbooks?"

"You had detectives follow me?" Maris said.

"Debra was worried you might be abusing drugs. It turns out you were only paying bills, and buying very expensive crystal at Steuben glass. I'm going to go now, Maris. Bennis probably wants to get back and Jimmy's probably frantic that I've been set upon by reporters, but I only care that I never lay eyes on you again. Don't come back. Don't even try to come back. And don't do anything stupid. If you try any more crap with the *National Enquirer*, I'll have you prosecuted."

Betsy stood up. Maris didn't move. She didn't think it was possible to move. Betsy didn't look anything at all like somebody who would be called "Betsy" now. And it was so cold. Maris had never been so cold. The woman Betsy had brought with her looked stunned. Liz, Maris thought. She'd have to remember to call that little creep Liz. It wasn't any fun to call her Betsy when calling her Betsy didn't bother her.

"Sorry to have taken up so much of your time," Liz said to Belinda.

Then she swept out of the apartment with Bennis Hannaford trailing behind her. Belinda slammed the door after them as they went.

"I can't believe that," Belinda said. "Betsy Wetsy. What a stuck-up little bitch. What a stupid little loser creep. Don't listen to a word she says. You can get her. You just go right ahead and do it."

Maris Coleman burst out laughing.

2

Emma Kenyon Bligh was awake when Kyle Borden came into her room with that man he'd been going around town with all day, but she didn't feel up to talking, and they didn't seem interested in asking questions, and finally they'd gone away. George was there, too, of course. As soon as he'd heard, he'd come running down from whatever real estate showing he'd had to see how she was. He was there watching her when she woke up, and he was there watching her still, except for going out for cigarettes every few minutes. George should quit smoking, he really should, but it was a lot like her resolves to quit eating. Somehow, there never seemed to be anything else to do with her time. When she tried to diet, she got hungry, but that wasn't what drove her back to food. Not eating caused a terrible void in the day.

Not eating meant looking down at her hands every half hour or so and thinking: *Is this it? Is this all? What exactly happened here?* The worst thing was that Emma thought she knew the answer. What had happened here was exactly what was supposed to have happened here. It was exactly what she had been trying to make happen for as long as she could remember. This was what it was like, the life she had wanted when she was seventeen. Some of it was good, like watching the children grow. Some of it was bad, like the times when the store hadn't been doing well and they'd been afraid of losing the building or having to declare bankruptcy. Mostly it was just dull, and repetitious, and strangely hopeless, as if in this life she had lived the future had ceased to exist. Except that it hadn't ceased to exist. She got fatter. She got older. The face in her mirror got paler, as if she'd been painted out of watercolors and somebody had left her out in the rain. She hadn't minded any of it until recently. Every part of her was floating. She remembered the sensation vaguely from when she and George used to smoke marijuana in his car up at Mountain Lookout the year after she graduated from high school. That was the year that it had begun to occur to her that she had made a mistake. Maris was coming back from Vassar on vacations. A few of the boys nobody had noticed were coming back, too, and really, suddenly, there was nothing to do in town, nobody to talk to, nothing to see. She'd thought she'd hated school, but she missed it, then. She wanted some kind of structure in her life. That was why she had decided to marry George as soon as she had. She already knew she loved him. They'd been going out forever. She already knew she liked sex with him. They'd started doing that on the night of her senior prom, which was what she had expected them to do. All the girls she knew lost their virginities at their senior prom parties, except for one or two, like Peggy, who couldn't wait, and did it the year before after the junior-senior semiformal. Peggy. Emma was finding it very hard to think about Peggy. Peggy had ruined everything. If it hadn't been for Peggy, Emma thought, she would never have started to feel as if there was no point in going on with life.

The Venetian blinds on the windows were pulled all the way up. There was light coming through the glass, but not much. Emma thought it might still be raining. She could see herself drifting out to sea with the waves bobbing her gently among the dolphins and nothing to think about, never again. She'd always been of the opinion that thinking was highly overrated. Now she didn't seem to be able to do anything but think, and it made her want to cry.

She fell asleep and came awake again and fell asleep again. She was aware of coming and going, and of George and the nurses and other people hovering right over her head. The nurses said soothing things. George promised that the girls would be coming in tonight to see her. The doctors wrote on the clipboard attached to the end of her bed. She wondered where Peggy was, if they had arrested her, if they even knew she was the one with that thing who was going around attacking people. How could that have happened? It wasn't normal people who did things like that. It was oddballs, misfits, outcasts. It was people like Betsy. That was why you had to be so careful about them. They were dangerous. People like Peggy, who had been a cheerleader and student council president, were people you could count on.

She fell asleep again, and woke up again, and fell asleep again. This time, when she opened her eyes, she saw a nurse sitting in the chair where George had been, looking through a magazine. Emma tried to turn on her side and found that it was almost impossible. Her whole front was taped up and she was far too weak to move her bulk, which for the first time seemed to her to be embarrassingly large.

She turned her head in the nurse's direction and said, "Are you there?"

The nurse looked up from what she was reading and frowned. She got out of her chair and walked over to the bed and looked down. "My God," she said, "you're up. I'll get the doctor."

"No," Emma said. "Not yet. The doctor was just in here a little while ago."

"Not in the last half hour."

"I'm sorry. I must have fallen asleep."

"There's nothing to be sorry for," the nurse said. "You should have fallen asleep. You're supposed to be getting some rest. Let me get the doctor."

"No," Emma said. "Not yet. Please. I want to—ask you things."

"What things?"

"About—about Peggy. First Peggy Smith. Do they know—"

"The woman who tried to kill you? They arrested her maybe an hour ago. They found her with you in the store, sitting off on the side with something or other in her hand. A razor, I think. They brought her here because she seemed to be in shock. I shouldn't be telling you any of this. I'm going to call the doctor."

"I don't want the doctor," Emma said.

The nurse picked up the call buzzer and depressed the button three long times. "Dr. Bardrieau will kill me if I upset you."

"Mark Bardrieau was in my class in high school."

"Was he?"

"He was a geek, though, I remember that. He was small and short and looked a lot younger than the other kids and he wore big black glasses that were really thick and George and his friends used to steal them the year George was a senior and Mark must have been a freshman. Do you think it's God? About the geeks, I mean. Do you think it's God who makes it so the geeks all get rich and successful after high school and the rest of us don't? Except some of us do, don't we? Meg Ryan was a prom princess. I read about it."

"You're making yourself out of breath."

A doctor came in, but only the resident, a young woman who looked raw. Emma lay still while she did what she was going to do—take her pulse, take her temperature, make a note on the chart. The resident was not anybody she knew. There was a time when Emma would have known almost everybody who worked at this hospital, but these days a lot of new people moved in all the time. They came from Pittsburgh and Philadelphia and Wilmington and even Rochester, New York. Everybody moved around restless. Nobody ever just stayed still. The resident came back to the head of the bed and said, "Do you want to sit up?"

"No," Emma told her.

"Do you want some juice?"

"No," Emma said again. Then she thought that she ought to have said "no, thank you."

"I'll have the nurse here get you some juice, just in case you want it later," the resident said. "She'll water it down a little. You ought to try to take fluids as soon as you can."

She bustled out the way she had bustled in, and Emma shook her head. "Did I nearly die? Is that why everybody is acting so strangely?"

"No," the nurse said. "You didn't come close to nearly dying. The razor or whatever it was didn't penetrate to anything really serious. You've got a fair amount of damage to your abdominal muscles, and you've lost a lot of blood, but that's about it. The doctor said it was the luckiest thing in your life that you were this heavy. If you hadn't been, she'd have sliced your intestines in half. Sorry."

"That's all right. I know what she was trying to do. She told me what she was trying to do. I guess I'm going to have to tell Kyle about it, one of these days."

"It would probably be a good idea."

"Maybe we should have told everybody what happened at the time. Did you know about that? That we all knew?

"We were just trying to protect Peggy. That wasn't wrong. We couldn't know she'd turn into a homicidal maniac. Or whatever she is. Do you know who Betsy Toliver is? Have you seen her since she came back to town?"

"A couple of times, yes," the nurse said. "She's brought her mother here once or twice."

"She calls herself Liz now. Maris told me. Belinda said she wouldn't change what she called her, no matter what. We called her Betsy Wetsy. I remember this day at Center School when we were all out on that playground, it was completely asphalted over except for the sand area and the sand area had that concrete ridge around it and in the middle there were swings and a slide. And this one day, she—Betsy—she was sitting in a swing by herself and Maris wanted to ride on it. And Maris took a stick, a big long tree branch that had fallen down in the wind or somehow, and started poking at her with it and calling her Betsy Wetsy, and then the rest of us got sticks, too, not big ones, there weren't a lot of big ones around. But we got them. And we all started . . . advancing on her . . . I guess that's what you'd call it. And Maris pushed her off the swing and then—and then I don't know what. I don't remember. I don't know if she cried or told the teachers or if we got away with it or got in trouble or what. I can only remember pushing at her and sort of chanting that name. Betsy Wetsy. Betsy Wetsy."

"I think you really are going to run out of air. Listen to yourself. You're gasping."

"I know." Emma closed her eyes. She did a lot of gasping. She gasped when she walked more than half a block without stopping. She gasped when she climbed stairs. It had been years since she had been able to take a full, deep breath without feeling as if she were being suffocated. All she had to do was wait, and the air came back to her. "The thing is," she said when she could talk again, "I was wondering. About her. About Betsy or Liz or whatever you want to call it. About what she was like. Did you know I met her son?"

"No," the nurse said.

"It's like they're all from a different planet. All those people. They don't think like normal people. They don't . . . I don't know. I don't get it. Why would anybody want to be that way? Why would anybody want to read books all the time and get into arguments and be . . . different . . . be . . . I don't know. It's like they like it. Being different. It doesn't make any sense."

"What would make sense is for you to get some more sleep," the nurse said. "I'm going to ask the doctor if he can't give you a little more of that painkiller."

"I was just thinking how odd it was," Emma said. She said it slowly. If she spoke slowly, it was easier to control her breathing. "There's this person who went to school with me, and now she's famous, and all I can remember about all the time we grew up together is us doing stuff to her. Me and Belinda and Maris and Chris and Peggy and Nancy and we all did things to her. Poked at her with sticks. Told her we wanted to meet her at the White Horse and then went somewhere else. Locked her in the supply cabinet in the gym. Nailed her into the outhouse. And I keep thinking that can't be right. That can't be all that happened. But I can't remember anything else. And Peggy said—Peggy said that she hated us. Do you think that's true?"

"No," the nurse said. "People don't keep grudges like that, for thirty years. You need to go to sleep now. It doesn't matter."

"It's all that matters," Emma said, but the words barely came out. She was beyond gasping. She was beyond thinking. She snapped her head from side to side, sucking in air, sucking in air. There wasn't air enough in the universe to fill her lungs. It was, she thought, really and truly all that mattered. It was all that had ever mattered. Her life was bound up in that small capsule of time, in brick buildings that had by now begun to crumble into dust, on playgrounds where nobody ever played anymore. For all the rest of eternity, she would be just fifteen years old and dressed in the frilled pastel blue chiffon ballerina-length dress she'd had for her first formal date with George. Her sleeves would be a pastel blue net and come halfway down her upper arm. Her shoes would have only one-and-a-half-inch heels, but the heels would be made in the same shape as the ones for three-inch-tall "classic pumps." Her purse would be dyed to match her dress. Her wrist-length gloves would be whiter than white. Her neckline would have an eyelet trim.

Maybe it was true that in some places the world had gone on, but it had never gone on for Emma Kenyon Bligh, and she had never wanted it to. Even at fifteen, she had known it was all going to be downhill from there. She could see the future looming up at her like a tidal wave. The trick was not to have a future at all—and she had managed that, but she hadn't realized, until now, that the strategy only worked if everybody around you was not having a future, too. Just let one of them step outside the circle and the game was up. The tidal wave had won. There was nothing left to look forward to. Except that that wasn't right, either. There had never been anything to look forward to. That was the point.

She turned her head back to look at the nurse, who was talking on the phone. It seemed there was a phone in the room that could actually be used, if she'd had the strength to use it, or any interest in calling anybody. She waited until the nurse put the receiver down and then said, "Please?"

"What is it?" the nurse asked her, coming close. "I've already told you. You've got to relax. You've got to sleep."

"Listen," Emma said, smiling a little, and closing her eyes. "I want to be dead."

3

In Bennis Hannaford's car, Liz Toliver's head seemed to be pounding out several beats at once, all from songs with titles that had the words "my life" in them somewhere. Bon Jovi. Billy Joel. Strong bass sessions. Lots of drums. It was true what she'd thought of back there during the day somewhere. This was the first generation in history in which every single person had a sound track for his life. They were all playing out their own particular screenplays to somebody else's music. For some reason, when she'd first said that, it had bothered her. Now it seemed entirely natural. It even seemed profound. She felt just a little drunk, and definitely giddy. She had never felt so free of Hollman in all her life.

She pulled the car around the last of the banking curves that led out to the manufactured flatland where the entrance to the Interstate was and the hotels were, too, all four of them. As soon as she did, she saw the cluster of cars standing in front of the reception door at the Radisson. There were so many of them—and they were so out of place—that if they'd had flashing lights she would have assumed there was a fire. Or a murder, she thought, although she didn't expect there to be another murder.

"Rats," she said. Then, when Bennis turned her head, she nodded toward the Radisson ahead. "They've found out where we are. Really, they've found out where Jimmy is. They don't care about me, unless I've just been charged in the murder of Chris Inglerod. Do you think that's likely to have happened?"

"No," Bennis said.

"I don't either. Let's just bull it out."

If cell phones worked out here, Liz would have used hers to call up to Jimmy and warn him she was coming. Since they didn't, she pulled the tangerine-orange Mercedes into the nearest parking space she could find and got out. She waited for Bennis and then tossed Bennis the keys. Bennis did something that made all the doors lock.

"You really think I could get my car painted a color I like better," Liz said. "I could just take it back to the dealership and have them do that."

"Probably. You could take it to a decent body shop, if you know one. They'd be faster and they'd be cheaper and they'd probably be just as good. What color do you want to paint your car?"

"Lemon-yellow." Liz looked up and through the big plate-glass windows that made up the wall that led to reception. "You ever done one of these before?"

"Not where they were interested in me," Bennis said. "And they're still not interested in me, so that ought to be all right."

"Unfortunately, they are interested in me and you're with me. Let me tell you what we do. We just walk in there, fast, looking straight ahead, and we don't say anything at all. Just keep moving. Get to the elevators. They won't usually follow you into the elevator because they're afraid of injunctions."

"Injunctions?"

"Yeah. The hotels get injunctions on them. Some of the real bastards have dozens in every city they go to, but nobody's going to have any here because I can almost guarantee that none of them have ever been in Hollman before. My God, what an awful place. Did I tell you that, that this is an awful place?"

"Several times, in the car."

"Well, it's true. And I don't just mean because it's small. Don't let them feed you all that crap about the wholesome goodness of small-town America. Some of small-town America may be wholesomely good, but some of it is Hollman. Petty, spiteful, envious, small-minded, provincial, stultifying—"

"I don't know that you should be in the middle of this lecture when we hit the lobby and there are a lot of microphones around," Bennis said.

"True," Liz said, and they were at the lobby right this minute. They were in front of the glass doors and then inside them, out of the cold and wet and into the carefully climate-controlled atmosphere of a place that was trying very hard to be a real hotel, even if it was far out into the rural wilderness. Liz could see the reporters massed around the desk. None of them was looking in their direction. She thought there might be just a chance to make the elevators before they realized she'd come in. Then one of them turned around and made a grunt and they were all turned around, some of them shouldering cams, some of them carrying notebooks, as if anybody ever really used a notebook anymore.

"Liz," one of them shouted.

Liz didn't turn around. She pushed her way to the reception desk and asked the shell-shocked young woman for her room key. The young woman handed it over as if it had been contaminated with the Ebola virus.

"Liz," somebody behind her shouted. "What do you think about the arrest? Does it upset you that one of your childhood friends has just been arrested for murder?"

"Ms. Toliver," somebody else shouted. "Can you give us your reaction to the arrest of Margaret Kennedy for the murder of Christine Barr?"

"Maiden names," Liz said to Bennis, under her breath, without moving her lips. She marched determinedly to the elevator, thinking about the old cliché, as if it were entirely new. *Do not pass go. Do not collect $200.* When she and Bennis got to the elevators, she stopped and pushed the call button. Of course, she didn't have the kind of luck that meant the elevator would already be right here at the proper floor.

People were still calling questions at her, and other people were photographing her. She could see the flashes as they went off behind her, reflected in the polished steel of the elevator doors. She ignored them all. There was no point in even saying "no comment." When the elevator doors opened in front of her, she stepped inside the car and pulled Bennis after her. She turned around and punched the button for the fourth floor. She smiled. The elevator doors closed.

"Sheesh," Bennis said. "Does that happen to you all the time? It would drive me crazy."

"It's not me, it's Jimmy. And it doesn't even happen to him all the time anymore. I think it does happen to people who are more current. Like Madonna."

"She can have it. This is all because of the murder?"

"The first time I got stuck in it, it was just after Jimmy and I started dating," Liz said. "And then it was mostly because they wanted to know who it was who had Jimmy on a string. It calmed down after we did the interview for *People* magazine."

"Right," Bennis said.

The elevator doors opened on four. Liz stepped out and looked around. Nobody had made it upstairs yet. She went to the door to the west wing and poked her head inside. "Anthony? It's me. Us. It's okay."

The door swung wide. Liz pulled Bennis onto the floor. Jimmy and Mark were way up at the other end of the hall. Geoff was closer, and saw her first. He came barreling down the corridor and threw himself at her.

"Mom! Mom! You're alive!"

"You didn't think I was going to be alive?" Liz said.

"Mark said—" Geoff turned to look.

"I did not," Mark said. "What do you take me for?"

"We'll discuss that later," Liz said. "What's been going on around here? Who got arrested?"

"Margaret Smith Kennedy," Jimmy said. "At least, that's what the news bulletin said. Gregor Demarkian called and said to tell you that if the name didn't ring a bell, I should tell you it was Peggy Smith. You know a Peggy Smith, right? She was on that list you gave me to give to Demarkian?"

"Yes, she was," Liz said. "But that's all? They arrested Peggy? They didn't arrest anybody else?"

"Not as far as I know," Jimmy said. "What did you expect, they'd arrest the whole lot of them? I'd be more than happy if they did, mind you, but I don't think anything you've got on them could be classified as a crime. You look odd. Are you sure you're all right?"

"I've been asking her that since we left here," Bennis said. "She's been behaving very oddly the whole time."

"That's just so odd, that they only arrested Peggy," Liz said, and then she let it go, because it was none of her business now. It had been none of her business for years. "Look," she said. "Does that proposal still stand? Do you still want me to marry you?"

"You mean have I changed my mind since I asked you again this morning?" Jimmy said. "No. I know I have a reputation for being easily distractable, but I usually am much better than that. Even about breakfast food. Never mind getting married."

"Fine," Liz said, ignoring all the rest of it. She ignored Mark and Geoff, too, who looked like they'd frozen in place. "Do me a favor. I want to get married three weeks from Sunday, in Paris. I want a suite for the four of us at the Georges V. It's the start of the high season. Is that possible?"

"It is if I spend enough money."

"Do you mind spending a lot of money?"

"Hell, Liz. I'd take grocery bags full of cash and throw the contents on the street if that's what it took. Are you serious?"

"I'm very serious. I want to have the reception at that place you took me to last year, the one with the mirrors—"

"Voltaire's."

"That's the one. Make your side of the guest list good. Make it very good. Do you think you could get Paul McCartney to come?"

"Yes."

"Excellent. I always wanted to meet a Beatle. And yes, I know I shouldn't say that to his face. I want that wedding on the cover of every tabloid from New York to Hong Kong and back around again. Can we manage that?"

"We can try," Jimmy said. "Liz, for God's sake, I'm delighted, but what's gotten into you? Are you all right?"

"Shut up," Mark said. "You go make reservations. I'll pack."

"Don't tell me to shut up," Jimmy said.

"You know what she's like," Mark said. "She'll change her mind. Make reservations. Go now."

"Does this mean Jimmy's going to be our stepdad for real now instead of for pretend?" Geoff said.

Liz thought she ought to pursue that one—how long had they been playing that Jimmy was their stepdad for pretend?—but she didn't have the heart, and she didn't mind anyway. She ran her hands through her hair. It was wet.

"I've got to call Debra," she said. "I just fired Maris in rather dramatic terms and she needs to know about it as soon as possible. Can we leave here now? If an arrest has been made, that means we're not under suspicion anymore, right? I want to pack up and get out as soon as possible. I don't care if it's the middle of the night. Can we do that, too?"

"Sure. We'll send one of the drivers to pack up at your mother's house," Jimmy said.

"You *fired* the ultimate bitch goddess?" Mark said.

Liz ignored him and started to hike down the hallway to her room, or the room with her suitcase in it, anyway. None of the rooms here had ever really been her room, any more than the bedroom at her mother's house had ever been her room. Brian Wilson sang about the joys of being in the safe haven of his room, but Liz's room at home had not been a safe haven. It had been a place where her mother could get to her, just as school had been a place where the girls could get to her, so that her entire childhood and adolescence had been one long resistance to a siege. Now she felt as if it had never happened—no, that wasn't right. It had happened, but it hadn't meant what she'd thought it meant at the time. It had never been of any importance, even while it was going on. If she had been able to understand that, it would not have been so terrible. Most of it might never have happened. It was one thing to live your life to somebody else's music. It was something else to live it by somebody else's screenplay, especially when it was such a terrible screenplay, so badly written, and so trite.

She sat down on the bed, picked up the phone, and dialed the number of the office in New York. It wasn't quite five. Debra would still be in. The phone rang and rang, and on impulse Liz got up and went over to her suitcase to rummage around in the bottom of it. There was one thing she always had with her. Even in the wake of Jay's dying, when there had been no money, when she had had no career, when they had had nothing at all, she had this, the way somebody else might have had a talisman. That was her problem in a nutshell. Other people carried lucky charms. She carried the evil totem for a voodoo curse.

She found it just as the receptionist picked up in New York, the Hollman High School *Wildcat* for 1969. She flipped open to the first page with its picture of the yearbook staff under the outsized numbers for 1969: Nancy Quayde, Chris Inglerod, Emma Kenyon, Maris Coleman, some boys she didn't recognize. She tore out the page and then tore the page itself into quarters. She flipped to the next page and the page after that and did the same thing, methodically, page after page.

"Kathy," she said, when she'd been bid a good afternoon in Kathy's best professional voice. "This is Liz. I need to talk to Debra for a second."

"Oh, my God," Kathy said. "Ms. Toliver. Are you all right? They said on the news that they'd arrested somebody we'd never heard of, so we thought—"

"I'm fine," Liz said, ripping out another page and tearing it, too, into quarters. She was going faster than she'd realized. There was a whole pile of page quarters on the floor now. Some of them had scraps of pictures on them with people she remembered.

"I'll get Debra on the phone right this minute," Kathy said.

Liz said "thanks" and found herself staring down at a photograph of herself. She was standing next to Belinda Hart, who looked so relentlessly vapid she might as well have been a cartoon. The shock was the picture of herself, which was not a picture of how she remembered herself, or even as she remembered seeing herself in this same picture all the other times she looked at it. This Elizabeth Toliver was not a Betsy Wetsy. She had high cheekbones and enormous eyes, and even the incredibly awful way she dressed did not stop her from being beautiful. She started to tear it and then hesitated. She wondered if this was one she ought to keep. Then Debra came on the line and she looked away.

"Debra? This is Liz. Get ready. I've just fired Maris Coleman in the most offensive possible way and agreed to marry Jimmy in three weeks in the same afternoon. I need to order a dress at Carolina Herrera and get hold of those checks Maris forged. Do you think that's too much for me to ask of you?"

"If you've really fired Maris Coleman," Debra said, "I will make myself your slave for life and peel every grape that even comes into the same room with you until the end of time."

Liz laughed, and as she did she looked down at her hands. She was still holding the same page with the same photograph on it. She still looked beautiful. Belinda still looked vapid. She tore it in quarters and then in eighths.

Sometimes you could keep a few things from the past and they wouldn't hurt you. Sometimes you couldn't. This was one of those times when you couldn't. Besides, she thought, she didn't care if she'd really been beautiful instead of ugly. She'd felt ugly. She'd lived in the conviction she was ugly. She'd been treated as if she were ugly, and stupid, and worthless besides.

She let the pieces of the page fall to the floor and then pulled out three pages at once, as much as she could get and still tear. She went on tearing all the while that she and Debra talked, until all the pages of the yearbook were nothing but scraps and confetti on the floor.

SEVEN

1

If he'd been somewhere else—back in Philadelphia, still with the FBI, on any case anywhere where the local law enforcement had experience in murder investigations that went beyond the religious viewing of *NYPD Blue*—Gregor could have gone back to Bennis until the police needed to take his statement, or written that statement up and gone straight back to Cavanaugh Street. He was tired and achy enough to do both. It had not been a good day. He'd never had time for a shower, and he felt it. Sweat was dripping off of him in odd places. His entire body felt sticky. He'd never really had a chance to take a breath and consider the situation they were all in in all its aspects. He really didn't like working on cases in a haphazard way. That was the FBI experience coming back to haunt him. City cops worked haphazardly all the time. They had to. There was too much crime and too much confusion to give them much time to think things through. The whole point of the FBI's Behavioral Sciences Unit—besides the practical one of providing a central database on serial killings that would make it possible for the police in one state to learn of a perpetrator's possible actions in another—was to have agents who had the luxury of thinking through all the aspects of a case, and the ramifications, and the future problems. Right now he felt half-finished. He could lay out for Kyle Borden and the state police what Peggy Smith Kennedy had done and why. He could even rely on the fact that Emma Kenyon Bligh was an eyewitness to her own attack to get them out of the worst of the problems a case like this would cause. What he could not do was to make the whole story gel in his mind, psychologically. It seemed to him that there was something fundamental they needed to know about Peggy Smith Kennedy that they didn't. Maybe it was just that he needed to know it. Cops and prosecutors were not famous for the deep way in which they understood the people they arrested and prosecuted. Cops were too busy making sure that they arrested the suspect without getting themselves or anybody else killed. District attorneys made their reputations on convictions. To get convictions, they needed only to be able to spin a coherent story for a jury and to keep that jury focused on the heinousness of a crime. The human aspects only got in the way. Gregor Demarkian was firmly convinced that the death penalty would cease to exist tomorrow if the majority of Americans were required to really know the men and women who were being put to death, instead of seeing them only when they were being painted as comic book monsters by the media. He was always profoundly shocked when an incident arose that seemed to indicate that he was wrong—like, for instance, the execution of Karla Faye Tucker. Millions and millions of people had watched her interview on *60 Minutes*. Millions and millions of people had heard her speak a dozen times in the days before her death. She was a quiet, ordinary, not very threatening woman. Her crime had been committed under the influence of drugs and—more telling to Gregor, although he'd never admit it to Bennis—of a man. She had even become religious in the way so many people said was so important to them. It didn't matter. They didn't care. They wanted her blood, anyway. It made Gregor wonder if there was any such thing as progress. We had trains and plains and automobiles. We had computers and microwaves and 1,500 television channels beamed in by satellite. We still reacted to our fellow human beings the way illiterate peasants had in the Middle Ages, when the old woman who had lived next door for forty years could suddenly grow horns and a tail and be in league with the devil. Any moment now, it would start here, the thing that happened in small towns in cases like this. This morning, Peggy Smith Kennedy was a woman they'd known forever, a local teacher in a bad marriage, someone most of them remembered as a popular girl in high school. Tomorrow morning, they would bring out every even slightly odd thing she had ever done. They would rewrite her life the way they rewrote their own, but in the opposite direction. They would find signs and portents in every word she ever spoke and every night she ever came in late from a date when she was a teenager, every drink she ever drank when she was underaged, every lie she ever told to get out of the fact that she'd forgotten to do her homework or had spent too long necking to make it in for her curfew. In the end, only one of the things about Peggy Smith Kennedy's life would matter, and they'd get that wrong. Gregor could see it coming. He'd nearly gotten it wrong himself. He'd almost forgotten what it meant for someone to be an obsessive.

Now he walked down the long expanse of open room behind the counter in the main room of the Hollman police station and poked his head into Kyle Borden's office. Kyle was sitting at his desk, surrounded by state police, a frown on his face. On the desk in front of him, he had a legal-sized sheet of paper covered with lines and arrows in black marker. Gregor had written it out for him to make sure he understood just what had happened when and that he could explain it. It wasn't clear that this had actually worked. Kyle looked worried. The state police looked confused.

They all looked up when Gregor stuck his head in the office door, and Kyle immediately relaxed.

"Mr. Demarkian," he said. "I'm glad you're here. I've been trying to explain this, but I think I keep getting bogged down in details. You want to tell them what you told me?"

"What I really want to do is call Bennis and have her come get me. She must be somewhere I can get in touch with her."

"I'll have Sharon call Ms. Hannaford. You sit down and explain things."

Kyle left the office, but Gregor didn't sit down. Peggy Smith Kennedy was downstairs, locked up in one of the town's only two jail cells, but Gregor didn't know how long that would last. Mrs. Kennedy was entitled to a lawyer. As soon as they got into court, she would get one, and that would almost assuredly mean bail. Gregor wondered what a judge would make of a prosecution move to deny bail on the grounds of wife battering—of Peggy Smith Kennedy *being* a battered wife. Because, assuredly, if that woman was allowed to go home, her husband would try as hard as he could to kill her long before the Commonwealth of Pennsylvania got a chance.

Kyle came back. "I found her. She wants to talk to you, too. She asked if it was okay for Elizabeth Toliver to leave town, and I said yes. It's okay, isn't it? You're not going to have us arrest her, too?"

"No," Gregor said. "You may need her to testify to something or the other about what went on at the Toliver house on the day the dog was found or the day that the body of Chris Inglerod Barr was found, but if you can manage to keep Mr. Kennedy away from Mrs. Kennedy, that may not be necessary."

"Why not?" one of the state police asked.

"Because," Gregor said, "I'm fairly sure she'll be more than happy to enter a plea as long as the sentence tops out at, say, twenty years. The issue, for her, is not going to be taking the biggest possible risk to see if she can get off without any penalty at all. It might be if she were willing to let an attorney wage a battered woman defense—"

"Wait," Kyle said. "I thought those were about women who kill the men who beat them, not about how they kill somebody else because their husbands beat them."

"Actually," Gregor said, "defense attorneys have taken both tacks. There was the Joel Steinberg case, with the child in New York who was battered to death, and the woman involved, Hedda Nussbaum, I think, her defense was that she took part in the abuse of her adopted daughter because she was suffering from post-traumatic stress disorder because her husband beat her. Except that I don't think he was her husband. I think they'd been living together a long time, but that they'd never made it legal."

"So, did the jury buy it?" the other state trooper said. "Did this Hedda what's-her-name get off because her husband beat her?"

"No," Gregor said. "But defense attorneys try the tack every once in a while. I was thinking about Karla Faye Tucker just a minute ago. Her case was like that. On drugs, battered and pathologically dependent on her boyfriend."

"It didn't help her, either," Kyle pointed out.

"No, it didn't," Gregor said. "And Mrs. Kennedy's case is different, because in all those other cases the man was present at the violence and took part in it. In a way it was a kind of sex. I've always wondered about those cases, if the man sees something in the woman so that some part of him knows all along that she's attracted to the blood and the pain and the violence, or if she's normal enough when she enters the relationship, and then—I don't know. Gets addicted to the man? Gets addicted to the sensation? You've got to wonder how it all starts, what she thinks the first time he goes violent, not against her but against somebody else. There's got to be some kind of psychological progression. I don't know if anybody understands what it is."

"But that isn't what happened in this case, is it?" Kyle asked. "Stu wasn't there when she killed Chris Inglerod. He wasn't there when she attacked Emma, either. She was on her own."

"Oh, yes," Gregor said. "The only time he was there was when Michael Houseman died, and then he was the one who committed the murder. She only stood by and watched. Or maybe that's too passive. From what Liz Toliver has told us about what she heard that night, it's possibly more apt to say that Peggy Smith Kennedy was a cheerleader off the field as well as on."

"Stu Kennedy murdered Michael Houseman," Kyle said. "This is insane. I thought you said that the same person who murdered Chris murdered Michael."

"No," Gregor said, "I said the two murders were connected. And they are connected. All of this is connected. None of this would have happened if Michael Houseman hadn't been, what did you call him, a Dudley Dooright?"

"Yeah," Kyle said. "He was a Dudley Dooright. Why did Stu Kennedy want to kill him?"

"Because Stu Kennedy was most certainly taking drugs that summer," Gregor said, "and he might have been selling them. Do you remember that crime record my friend in Philadelphia got for me? You were impressed with the other murders that might have been done by razor or knife around the same time."

"I remember that," Kyle said. "There were a couple of them."

"Yes, there were, but there was also one of possession with intent to sell narcotics. Everyone kept saying—you kept saying—that drugs were pretty much undergroud in Hollman in 1969. I didn't believe it. There were drugs everywhere in 1969. But I thought it was a good idea to see if there was any trace of evidence about the existence of drugs in the area at the time, and there was that. My guess is that there's a lot more if you look for it in the local records, maybe even in the local records here in Hollman. I wouldn't be surprised if your Mr. Kennedy hadn't been picked up once or twice for possession, or for intoxication, and just let go. That was before the drug war, when we treated casual users like casual users instead of the twenty-first-century personification of the Antichrist."

"Druggies are scum," one of the state troopers said virtuously.

Gregor rubbed his temples. "Anyway, that's what happened, that night in the park. I can't prove it. You're never going to try Stu Kennedy for murder, but I'd bet my life on it. Stu Kennedy was doing drugs and possibly selling them, and Michael Houseman threatened to turn him in. My guess is that they had a confrontation in that park, on that night. If Michael Houseman had known earlier, he probably would just have told. They had a confrontation, and Stu had the linoleum cutter—"

"But *why?*" Kyle said.

"If he'd started selling, for protection," Gregor said. "And my guess is that he had started selling. That was what all this was about. Somebody we interviewed—I'd have to go back and check on who—mentioned the fact that you could get stuff to get high with during your senior year in high school and the summer after. I think if we nailed that person down, we'd find that she'd gotten it from Stu—"

"Why she?" one of the state troopers said.

"Because everybody important to this case is she," Kyle Borden said. "It's been ladies' night all the way. So okay. Stu was selling a little dope in his free time, Michael Houseman caught him at it, Stu took what he had on him for protection and killed Michael Houseman. What was Peggy doing during all of this? What were the rest of them doing? Just standing there?"

"The rest of them weren't there when the murder took place," Gregor said. "They were all very protective of each other, but none of them would have cared a damn what happened to Stu Kennedy. If they'd all been together, not one of them would have been in danger of being charged as an accessory, because they could all back each other up about not being a party to what happened, about only being witnesses. Only Peggy was with Stu when Stu killed Michael Houseman, and the problem—for all of them—was that Peggy *was* an accessory. That's what they all heard that night in the rain. That's what Liz Toliver heard that she's dreamed about ever since, except that she's been misinterpreting it. As far as I know, she's misinterpreting it even now. But the rest of them never did misinterpret it. They knew exactly what they heard."

"And what did they all here?" Kyle asked.

"They heard Peggy Smith screaming, over and over again, '*slit his throat slit his throat slit his throat.*' I haven't talked to the rest of them yet about this, but you'll have to. Liz told me the voice sounded like a woman's in the midst of sex. Having an orgasm, she meant. And that's what it was. Sex and death. The erotic possibilities of murder. It's too bad that Liz Toliver didn't realize at the time whose voice she was listening to."

"She said she didn't know," Kyle said. "She said that at the time. She had no idea whose voice it was. They *all* said that at the time."

"I know," Gregor said. "But the rest of them knew—Belinda, Emma, Maris, Nancy, and Chris. They all knew who it was. And Liz Toliver was certain. She just lied."

"You just said she didn't know," Kyle said. "You make less and less sense every time I talk to you."

"I said she didn't realize who it was," Gregor said. "But that's not the same thing as saying she didn't think she knew. She thought she knew. She thought it was Maris Coleman's voice. And she didn't even consider the possibility of Stu having anything to do with it. What she thought was that Maris had committed the murder, gotten caught up in some kind of group hysteria, and done something she didn't intend to do that was threatening to ruin her whole life. Liz Toliver's relationship with Maris Coleman has always been as dysfunctional—to use a wholly inadequate word—as Peggy Smith's with Stu Kennedy."

"Even if we could verify all of this," Kyle said, "we couldn't use it. It might not even help us. I mean, juries don't tend to believe in lots of different murderers for one murder. If you know what I mean. They're going to think it was Stu who killed Chris Inglerod. And what I don't get is, why wasn't it? Why was it Peggy? Why didn't Stu just do it the way he had before, assuming he had done it before?"

"He had no reason to think he needed to," Gregor said. "Haven't you got the least bit of curiosity as to why this has all started up now that Liz Toliver has come home and not before now? After all, if Chris Inglerod was a danger to Stu Kennedy, he had thirty years of pretty decent access to her right here in Hollman."

2

Bennis Hannaford showed up wet. Outside, it had started to rain again, steadily and hard, and to thunder and lightning, too. Gregor found it significant that he hadn't noticed it. All day, he'd been thinking of nothing but how much rain there was. He'd been listening to drops pounding on roofs and in gutters. He'd been feeling the thunder roll through him every time it passed. Now he watched Bennis maneuver past the little clutch of reporters sitting in the police department's narrow waiting area and thought at first that she must have been drenched in somebody's lawn sprinkler. It was only after she'd said something to a much drier woman who did stringer service for the *Washington Post* that he'd realized the weather must have gone back again. When he went to the window to look out, he saw another steady fall of water and sharp snaking electrical lights in the sky.

"They want to know if they can leave," Bennis said, wedging herself into what room was left in Kyle Borden's office. There wasn't much. "You did say you were arresting someone else. You can hardly blame her."

"As far as I'm concerned, she can leave anytime she wants," Gregor said. "But I'm not the person in charge here. She wants to go back to Connecticut?"

"No, they want to go to Paris. It's all very romantic. They're finally getting married. And she's behaving very oddly. She said she wants to know if you're really going to arrest *only* Peggy Smith. And that's how she put it. *Only*. Is there any coffee in this place?"

"Not any that you'd want to drink," one of the state troopers said.

Kyle Borden looked frustrated. "She can go all the way to the moon as far as I'm concerned," he said. "According to your Mr. Demarkian here, we ought to be out arresting Stuart Kennedy, except not. Does he usually make this little sense when he talks?"

The state trooper who had warned Bennis off the coffee now handed her some in a tall foam cup. She took it, sipped it, and got up to put serious amounts of milk and sugar in it, except the milk was that nondairy creamer in little plastic tubs that you got at very low-rent diners, served up to you in heavy ceramic saucers that were never quite as white as they should have been. Bennis took another sip and made a face. She sat down again.

"So," she said. "What have you been telling these people to confuse them?"

Gregor sighed. He hated drinking coffee in foam cups. He thought it tasted funny. "There's nothing at all confusing about it," he said. "There *are* a few loose ends, but the point of a police investigation is to clean up the loose ends. To recap what I've told them already: you start with that night in 1969 when the girls nailed Liz Toliver into the outhouse and Michael Houseman was killed. None of the girls, including Peggy Smith, was intending to kill anybody, although what they did to Liz Toliver might have killed her. People don't take phobias seriously. They should. But they only went there to do that. They weren't intending to do anything else. So they nailed Liz Toliver into the outhouse, and then they retreated to the trees a little ways off to see what would happen."

"What did they expect to happen?" Bennis said. "I mean, the girl was scared to death of snakes and they nailed her in with over twenty of them. Did they think she was going to bond with them? What?"

"They thought she was going to scream," Gregor said calmly, "which is what she did. Now, Michael Houseman was in the park that night. So was Kyle Borden here. So was Stu Kennedy. But Stu Kennedy came to the park to do two things, to find Peggy, and to get high. He may have been meaning to sell some of whatever it was he had that night. He almost certainly was selling it, to his friends and to other people, at the high school. And Michael Houseman either knew about it, or suspected it, or caught him in the act on that night. It doesn't particularly matter which. What does matter is the one thing everybody says consistently about Michael Houseman."

"He was a Dudley Dooright," Kyle said gloomily. "He was, too. These days everybody goes to church all the time. Practically nobody did then. Michael did. He was an Eagle Scout. He handed in his homework on time. If he caught you smoking in the bathroom, he took your cigarette away or he turned you in. Some of us had times when we wanted to strangle him."

"Exactly," Gregor said. "He was a Dudley Dooright. So, faced with Stu Kennedy and a pile of drugs, whatever Kennedy was doing with it, Houseman would have been determined to hand Kennedy over to the authorities and Kennedy would have been faced with a problem that he could only solve by shutting Houseman up. So he took out the linoleum cutter—"

"Why a linoleum cutter?" Bennis said. "That never made any sense to me at all. I mean now, yeah, it might be what was around the house, but why would Stu Kennedy have a linoleum cutter on him in the park that night? Why not a knife? Or a straight-edged razor?"

"You think it would be more likely for him to have a straight-edged razor?" one of the state troopers said. "In 1969."

"It's one of those loose ends that needs to be cleaned up," Gregor said, "although not too strenuously, because it won't matter to the case against Peggy Smith Kennedy. The reason we know he had a linoleum cutter in the park that night is that Peggy Smith Kennedy used a linoleum cutter when she killed the dog and Chris Inglerod Barr. You know, you all sit around talking about how odd it was that he'd have a linoleum cutter in the park that night, but the fact is that it's even odder that Peggy Smith Kennedy has had one with her in the past few days. Several people have told us that Stu Kennedy used to be fairly handy before he went completely under with booze and dope. So maybe he brought it for protection. A linoleum cutter *is* a kind of straight-edged razor. Or maybe he'd been doing something around the house for his parents that day and had it in his pocket or on his belt. Whatever the reason, he had the thing, and when Michael Houseman confronted him, he used it. And that's where things started getting bizarre. Peggy was either with Stu by the time Stu committed the murder—remember, she didn't have to go far from where they all started out near the outhouse—or she got there in the middle of the act, but whichever it was, she responded with a kind of trance hysteria. She started screaming '*slit his throat slit his throat*' and the rest of them heard her. And they came. They—"

"That's not what they said to the police at the time," Kyle said. "I remember it. They said they were wandering around in the park sort of lost in the dark and they stumbled on the clearing and Michael Houseman was bleeding to death."

"You couldn't get lost in that park if you worked at it," Gregor said. "They followed Peggy's voice to the clearing and they found Peggy standing over Michael Houseman and Michael Houseman either bleeding to death or already dead. And the rain was coming down. And everybody got completely and utterly caught up in the moment."

Gregor said, "But the thing is, their first reaction was to protect Peggy from the consequences of anything Stu had done. And the only way they could do that was to keep their mouths shut and play dumb. And that's what they did. In other circumstances, it would have been a stupid move. The police could have found the murder weapon. The police could have pushed a little harder than they did and started Stu Kennedy talking. As it turned out, however, they didn't have anything to worry about. The case was never solved. It never came close to being solved. They went on living their lives. I wonder what they thought when Peggy married Stu Kennedy. Maybe they didn't think anything of it. Peggy and Stu had been a couple for so long. Maybe they thought it was only natural."

"Okay," one of the state troopers said, "but that was all thirty years ago. What about now? You said it wasn't him who did it this time, it was her, but I still don't get it. You said it yourself. If he'd wanted to kill the people he knew, he had thirty years to do it. Why now? And the same goes for her."

"It was her," Gregor said. "Emma Kenyon Bligh will confirm that as soon as we can talk to her. But you have to realize that it must have been her, if only because Stu Kennedy is no longer in any shape to successfully commit murder and hide it. He could commit murder. He could smash somebody up or cause a head-on collision or do a dozen stupid, violent things that would end up with somebody dead, but he's in no shape to murder somebody with a linoleum cutter and then get clean away so that he isn't noticed and hide the evidence well enough so that we weren't stumbling all over it as soon as the investigation started. Thirty years of substance abuse does tend to make someone less than competent at activities requiring mental agility and intellectual integration."

"But that still doesn't answer the question of why Peggy would want to kill Chris Inglerod Barr," Kyle said.

"She didn't," Gregor told him. "She wanted to kill Liz Toliver."

"But *why?*" Kyle said. "The woman's been away from town for thirty years. It's not like she was going to come back and get into everybody's life. I mean, Christ, would you do that if you were her? The whole thing is completely nuts."

"Think about it," Gregor said. "Every single person we talked to from that group of people, Nancy Quayde, Emma Kenyon Bligh, Belinda what's-her-name—"

"Hart," Kyle said, "or Grantling. Take your pick."

"Whoever. Each one of them told us the same thing, that Liz Toliver was writing a piece on the night she was locked into the outhouse."

"But that's not true, is it?" Bennis said. "I don't think she's writing a piece about anything at the moment. At least, she didn't mention any work. Why would they think she was writing something about being locked in the outhouse?"

"Guilty consciences," Kyle Borden said solemnly.

"I think that if you check with the remaining members of the group, you'll find that Maris Coleman told them that that's what Liz Toliver was doing. The information really couldn't have come from anywhere else. The tabloid press isn't big on reporting writing projects. And nobody else would have had the authority—I think I mean authoritativeness. You see what I'm getting at. Maris worked for Liz Toliver in New York. When Maris said that was what Liz Toliver was working on, the others naturally thought she knew what she was talking about."

"Wait a minute," Bennis said. "The car. Liz told Maris Coleman that she'd seen Peggy Smith Kennedy driving Maris's rented car. Rats. I can't remember how that went. We were in the middle of a terrific scene, and Liz was firing Maris and threatening to prosecute her over some checks and it was all because Liz had seen Peggy driving Maris's rental car."

"Thank you," Gregor said. "Kyle will have to check that out, too, but that solves the problem of the car. I knew she had to have had access to one, in spite of the fact that her husband won't allow her to drive, but I wasn't sure exactly where she was going to get it."

"Wait," Kyle said. "You mean that first Maris went around telling all the rest of them that Betsy—Liz—I don't know, that she was going to write some big article on the outhouse thing and, what? Tell who murdered Michael Houseman? Did she even know who murdered Michael Houseman?"

"She figured it out eventually, I think," Bennis said.

"The point isn't whether she knew," Gregor said, "but whether the rest of them thought she knew."

"And they did?" Kyle asked.

"I think Maris Coleman made sure they did," Gregor said.

"Okay," Kyle said. "So first Maris tells them Ms. Toliver is writing this thing on the outhouse incident and is, what, going to name names? Then she tells them that Ms. Toliver knows all about who killed Michael Houseman. Then she loans Peggy her car. What was she trying to do, get Ms. Toliver killed?"

"I don't think so," Gregor said. "I doubt if it ever occurred to her that anybody would resort to violence. She'd have known as well as anybody that Stu Kennedy was in no condition to cause that kind of trouble. And remember, Peggy Smith Kennedy didn't kill Michael Houseman. As far as Maris Coleman knew, Peggy had done nothing but be in the wrong place at the wrong time when Stu Kennedy got violent. No, Maris Coleman didn't want Liz Toliver dead—heaven forbid. Liz Toliver was her meal ticket. Maris Coleman wanted Liz Toliver embarrassed."

"Well," Kyle said, "Ms. Toliver certainly ended up embarrassed. Royally embarrassed. And Chris Inglerod ended up dead. And Emma Kenyon Bligh nearly ended up dead. And this still doesn't make any sense. If she really wanted to kill Ms. Toliver, what was Peggy doing attacking all these other people? What was the point here?"

"The point," Gregor said, "is what the point has always been for that woman, to protect her husband."

"Crap," Kyle said. "I mean, for God's sake—"

"Fucking *damn*," somebody said in the outer room. "You can't *tell* me I can't come the fuck in there if I the fuck want to, you fucking little cunt, I'll cut you up, I really will, and then I'll cut up the other fucking little cunt, you let me at her, you—"

All the police officers, state and local, were in Kyle Borden's office. There was nobody outside to hold the fort but Sharon, who was looking sullen and mulish. The men who were holding Stu Kennedy back were all reporters. Some of them were middle-aged. Most of them were out of shape. Stu Kennedy was dangerous mostly because he seemed to be hopped up on speed or coke or something else that revved all your motors and blew out all your corks. He looked awful. He had vomited down the front of his shirt some time ago. The vomit was crusted against the dingy blue material like the ridges on a three-dimensional topographical map. His face was filthy. His hands were cracked with dirt. If Gregor hadn't known who Stu Kennedy was, he'd have thought he was one of those crazy old drunks who lived on the streets in the worst back alleys in Philadelphia.

"Fucking *cunt*," Stu Kennedy said, over and over again.

The two state troopers moved in to tie him down.

3

There was no place to put Stu Kennedy in the Hollman town jail. The jail was only two cells in the basement of the police department, and at the moment Peggy Smith Kennedy was in one of them. The idea of Stu and Peggy in adjacent cells, while Stu screamed and Peggy did they didn't know what, gave pause even to the state troopers, whom Gregor had begun to think of as animatrons. They talked and moved so much like some bad movie's idea of what state troopers should be, he had a hard time accepting them as real. Kyle Borden was just stunned. It wasn't that he didn't know what Stu Kennedy was like. He was the one who had taken Gregor to Stu Kennedy's house only hours before, and he had sat through the barrage of bad language and hints of violence without looking in the least bit surprised. It was more that he hadn't expected everything to be so outfront and unambiguous. With little or no personal knowledge of real crime and real criminals—and especially with real murders and real murderers—Kyle Borden seemed to have expected subterfuge and puzzles, the kind of thing that went on in the novels of Robert B. Parker, or maybe on the *City Confidential* show that aired on Court TV. Actually, Gregor himself was highly addicted to Court TV. It was the only television he watched regularly. Still, one of the reasons he liked to watch it was that outside its broadcasts of actual trials it was a repository of law enforcement exceptions. Unsolved mysteries, convoluted clues, forensics nightmares: if you wanted to know what really went on in crime investigation, you watched those actual trials, where defendants tried to explain away the fact that they had been caught standing over the body with the smoking gun in their hands.

It was in the middle of the scuffle that Gregor suddenly realized there was something he wanted to do, something he did not get to do often, but that might be possible this time. He waited until Stu Kennedy was in handcuffs and the troopers were talking about what to do with him. Take him out to the state police car seemed to be their best suggestion, and then off somewhere else to be locked up. They had never been faced with just this situation before. They weren't sure what was legal for them to do. Stu bounced and struggled against the handcuffs. The state police debated among themselves: where to take him, what to charge him with, how to make sure he didn't do something stupid once he was released, which he would be, because he hadn't actually done anything except get rowdy. That meant that Kyle Borden could arrest him, but beyond that it didn't mean squat.

Gregor went up to Kyle and made him a proposition. Kyle seemed both surprised and unconcerned.

"I don't see why not," he said. "She only has to tell you to take a hike. I wonder if she can hear what's going on up here. I don't see why she wouldn't."

"I don't see why she wouldn't, either," Gregor said. "How do I get down there? Do I use the stairs out front?"

"Nah. That goes to the basement basement. We wouldn't put anybody underground like that. The jail is in the walkout. You take that door over there." Kyle pointed to a door in the wall on the opposite side from the one that led to his office. Gregor had seen it before, but always assumed it was a closet. "And you go right on down. You won't get lost. There's only the two cells. Christ. What does Stu think he's doing?"

Gregor thought that "think" was not high on Stu Kennedy's to-do list, but he didn't say that. He just walked across the big inner room to the door on the other side, opened up, and found that he had no need to switch on a light. There were already lights on in the stairwell, and lights on at the bottom of the stairs, too. He slipped through the door and closed it behind him. He went down the short flight of stairs and discovered what Kyle Borden had meant by "the walkout." This was not, technically, a basement. The police department building was built into the side of a hill, and this part of the lower level was entirely above grade. When he got to the bottom of the staircase, he found the two cells to his right, and a row of windows looking out at the side yard to his left. It was, he saw, raining yet again.

Peggy Smith Kennedy was in the second cell, the one farthest away from the stairs. Gregor thought she must have heard him come down, because it was possible to hear nearly everything down here. Gregor could even catch the murmur of voices from the floor above, although he couldn't distinguish words, and he wouldn't have trusted himself to distinguish persons. Stu Kennedy has been screaming, though. Gregor thought he would probably have been able to distinguish the who and what of that.

He walked down the corridor to the second of the cells. Peggy Smith

Kennedy was sitting on the lower of two bunk cots, doing nothing. Her feet were flat on the floor. Her hands were clasped loosely on her lap. Her eyes were on her shoes. She did not look up or greet him, even though Gregor knew she had to know he was there.

"Well," he said, after a while, clearing his throat as if that would somehow make a difference. "I came to see how you were."

She turned her head to him and blinked. "They won't be able to hold him," she said. "He hasn't done anything they can arrest him for. They treat him like an animal, but he always gets the best of them in the end."

Gregor cocked his head. It was hard to read her mood. "He did something he could get arrested for once," he said. "He committed a murder, back in 1969. And you saw it."

"Nobody ever understood him but me," she said. "None of them. Not even people like Maris and Belinda. Nobody saw the inside of him the way I did. Do you believe that there are people on this earth who are different from the rest of us?"

"There are a lot of people who are different," Gregor said, very careful. "Different in different ways. Every society has people who do not fit in."

"No." Peggy stood up abruptly, and turned to him. "Not that kind of different. Different in another way. In a *holy* way. Different because they're made of something the rest of us don't have. It's like the angels in that television program. They look like us, but they aren't us. They're angels. They're part of God."

"And you think your husband is part of God?"

"I never really thought of him as my husband. You can't really marry somebody like Stu. You can go through the ceremony, the way we did, but it doesn't mean what it usually means. You can't put someone like Stu into a harness and expect him to work his life away. You can't expect him to waste himself."

"What can you expect him to do?"

"I don't know." She turned away from him and started pacing. There was no place to pace. The cell was very small, maybe twice the size of Kyle Borden's office upstairs, and that office was claustrophobic. Peggy went to the interior wall and then turned around and came back toward the bars again. Gregor was struck by how old she looked—no, he thought, not old, but captured by that ugly lumpiness of unopposed middle age. If she hadn't been the center of a murder investigation, Gregor would have thought of her as one more of the supermarket women, the ones who pushed carts piled high with Pop-Tarts and Chee•tos through aisles crammed with carbonated sodas and frozen dinners, in dresses that neither fit nor didn't fit, with hair that stuck out at odd angles because it had been permed and bleached and teased over the years until it couldn't relax at all. She moved differently, though. There was no hint of defeat in her posture, and no suggestion that she would even consider the option of allowing her shoulders to slump.

"I knew from the very beginning that we'd never have what you would call a normal life," she said. "I knew that when we were both in kindergarten. It used to upset him even then, the world did. He'd get so angry, just at little things. Because a teacher shouted at him. Because one of the other boys won some game they'd been playing. Little, little things that the rest of us wouldn't see any importance in at all. But he saw the importance in them. He cared about them so deeply. And I knew, you see. I knew he'd never make an ordinary kind of life for anybody."

"I'd have worried that he needed psychiatric help," Gregor said. "What you're describing sounds to me very much like one of the borderline schizophrenic states. And schizophrenics can be very violent."

Peggy flicked this away. "You don't understand. None of them understand. He was the only member of our class that had true greatness in him. He's still the only one. I see it in him every day. He lets it out for me to look at it, even if he won't let it out to show to you."

"Well," Gregor said, "I'm not as close to him as you."

Peggy turned her back on him and went to the bunk again. She sat down and stretched her legs out in front of her. "They won't be able to do anything to him. I'm the one who killed Chris. And . . . and the dog. I didn't mean to kill the dog. I went out to the house to see if she was there. Maris said she was going to be there. And I thought I could talk to her. But I brought the cutter with me, anyway. Just in case."

"I know."

"I shouldn't have killed the dog. I just—wasn't thinking, that's what it was. I was thinking when I got there, and then nobody was home. And it was so quiet out there. There wasn't anyone around but the dog and it came up and bothered me. Poked me. With its snout, you know. Stu won't have dogs. They make too much mess, he says, and besides they bother him, too. I'm not used to dogs. It kept poking at me and poking at me and I got—I got angry. I don't get angry very often. But I got angry then. And then—then the blood went everywhere. Do you know what I mean? It spurted out. It got all over my clothes. I didn't realize there would be so much of it. And then I got scared, so I went back to the car, but when I got into the car there was blood everywhere, too. There was blood on the seat. I must have brought it with me, from the dog. I got blood on the steering wheel. And then, you know, I started thinking. Because it was so much like it had been the night Michael Houseman died, except there wasn't any rain. Do people always bleed so much, when they die?"

"It depends on what you cut on them," Gregor said.

Peggy shrugged. "When I went back the next day, I had on some of Emma's clothes. I took them out of her closet when she was busy in the store. It wasn't hard. But when I went out there, she wasn't there then, either. I walked around and around and then there was Chris. And then . . ." She frowned and shook her head. "There isn't really any then. She never understood him. Chris didn't. She never in her life understood him. And she started shouting at me about how I should have him arrested, or lock him up in an insane asylum, or something, and then—" Peggy shrugged. "And then there was blood all over everything again."

"You need a lawyer," Gregor said. "You do know that."

"Of course I know it. It won't matter, though. Emma will wake up and tell them. She'll tell them it was me, at any rate. She doesn't know all of it. Nobody knows all of it. Only I do. And Belinda is right. It isn't fair."

"What isn't?"

"What happened to Betsy Toliver," Peggy said. "She never understood anything, Betsy didn't. She never understood Stu, and she never understood us, and she always—she always—she'll probably write her article now, or her book or whatever it is. And we'll all look like stupid little hick town jerks. But Stu isn't stupid. If she accuses him of murder, he'll sue her. I'll help him sue her, too. I can do that even from jail, can't I?"

"I think you need a lawyer," Gregor said. "And I think, more than that, you need someone to talk to who can be of more help to you than I can. All I really know how to do is to follow the logic of criminal acts to their possible conclusions. I don't know much about anything else."

"I hear on the television sometimes, and in the in-service seminars we have, I hear about the people like Betsy and how put upon they all are. But that isn't true. It's people like Stu who are put upon. Really fine people. People that no one understands. You can't let someone like Betsy destroy someone like Stu. It isn't justice."

"I doubt if Elizabeth Toliver is very much interested in destroying Stuart Kennedy. I doubt if she's interested in destroying anybody."

Peggy turned her head around and smiled. It was the smile of a serial killer, and Gregor had seen dozens of them. It was the smile of someone who had cut her ties with the human race, permanently and irrevocably. Under the hard light of the fluorescents, her face almost seemed to glow, and her eyes did glow, like the pinpoints of a pair of flashlights through the holes in a black nylon curtain. It was, Gregor thought, the first time he had ever seen anybody he could truly describe as insane.

"He's got a piece of God in him," she said. "He's a piece of God himself. It doesn't matter what happens to the rest of us. It doesn't matter what happens to me. He won't want me back, now, but I don't care. I'll go on protecting him. He needs somebody to protect him. You're all trying to get rid of him. You've been trying since he was a child. I won't ever let it happen. They won't execute me. You know that as well as I do. They don't execute nice middle-class schoolteachers in Pennsylvania. They can't touch him if I tell them I committed all the murders by myself. They can't touch him no matter what Betsy Toliver says. He's a piece of God. He's immortal."

Up on the floor above, Stu Kennedy let out one more shouted stream of obscenities, and was wrestled out the door.

EPILOGUE

It's still rock and roll to me

—BILLY JOEL

1

Elizabeth Toliver and Jimmy Card were married in Paris on the fifteenth of July, and on the sixteenth, on a hot, muggy morning when the air was so full of water it felt like a casing of sweat, Bennis Hannaford bought a copy of the Philadelphia *Inquirer* so that she could read all about it. The story about Nancy Quayde and Diane Asch and the lawsuit in Hollman was in a bordered box on an inside page, so Bennis didn't even notice it at first. Actually, she wouldn't have noticed it even if it had been on the front page. She wouldn't have noticed an announcement of the second coming. It was barely after seven o'clock, and she was standing at the counter in Ohanian's Middle Eastern Food Store, buying not only the *Inquirer*, but everything else she could lay her hands on with Liz Toliver's picture. The stack next to the cash register included respectable entries like the *New York Times* and the *Washington Post*. The only reason Liz's picture was on the front pages of *those* was because she had friends on the staff, and Bennis had a suspicion she'd called in some favors to make sure the publicity was as insistent as it could possibly get. Unfortunately, the stack also included some less than respectable entries, including one called *Celebrity Sell*, which seemed to be nothing but photographs and headlines. In a way, that was the best one, because it was the one with the big wedding picture and the three oddly angled shots inside the reception. That one also had a picture of Peggy Smith Kennedy, placed behind a stylized set of black bars. Bennis scanned it casually—the only time she'd ever seen the woman had been at the Hollman Police Department, and then only for a second or two—and got her wallet out of her big leather and canvas Coach tote. Bennis didn't usually carry a tote, or anything else in the way of a pocketbook, but today she had to. Instead of her usual jeans, she was wearing a bright red linen "sundress," which basically meant a huge swath of material with armholes in it and no pockets. It was annoying what happened to you when the weather got hot. If it had been up to Bennis, she would have kept the temperature at forty-five degrees forever, and never taken off her jeans or her turtleneck sweaters. Except that lately, she wasn't even wearing turtleneck sweaters. The high collars bothered her. Maybe she was having a midlife crisis.

"So," Mary Ohanian said, ringing up the newspapers without seeming to notice which ones they were, and without cracking up, which was what was important to Bennis. "You got invited. If you're so interested, why didn't you go?"

"Gregor got invited," Bennis said. "I was sort of only along for the ride. And as to why we didn't go, that's a good question. Gregor said he'd had enough of them. The people from Hollman, I mean. Although why anybody would think Elizabeth Toliver had anything to do with Hollman, except accidentally, is beyond me."

"It's a kick, don't you think? Jimmy Card marrying somebody practically his own age. Usually they run off with women twenty-five years younger and talk about how they've finally found a soul mate."

"I used to think Jimmy's only criterion for choosing a wife was that she had to have been featured on the cover of the *Sports Illustrated Swimsuit Edition*. She came, by the way, Julie did. With Jimmy's daughter. And she brought her new husband. Number six."

"Jimmy Card's daughter has had six husbands?"

"No. Julie Haggerty has. Jimmy was the first. Since him, none of them have lasted more than a year or two. And she always has big weddings and hugely expensive bridal gowns. Of course, she does infomercials now. That's about as bad as it gets."

"You have to wonder what she thought about it," Mary Ohanian said. "Elizabeth Toliver, I mean. Having Jimmy's first wife at her wedding—"

"Second. Julie was Jimmy's second wife. The first one was somebody he knew from home. I don't remember. It was years ago. Anyway. I can't stand around here. I promised to meet Gregor at the Ararat, and Donna and Grace want me to do something. Grace is making harpsichord arrangements for some traditional Armenian folk music she got from the Very Old Ladies. Something like that. Don't you ever get out of here and go to a movie?"

"I do when my mother can take over at the counter. Listen, if you see Grace, tell her I've got some of that green loukoumia she likes in a box in the back of the store. There wasn't much of it in the latest batch, so I put it aside just for her, but I can't keep it forever. If she wants it, she's got to come get it in the next day or two."

"Okay. Green loukoumia. I didn't even know they had the stuff. Talk to you later."

Bennis gathered up her newspapers and headed out onto the street, up the block to where the Ararat was. She read a little as she was going along—the cover of *Celebrity Sells* was really quite informative—and then tucked the whole stack under her arm so that she could let herself in through the Ararat's plate-glass front door. The air-conditioning was turned up to full inside, which was a relief. Bennis marched over to the window booth with its low bench seats and dumped the stack of newspapers on the table. Tibor and Gregor both looked up at her and blinked. Donna Moradanyan and Grace Feinmann both took papers off the top of the stack.

"I think it's such a *shame* Gregor wouldn't go to this thing," Donna said. "You could have eaten pate in the shape of a gigantic pig, or whatever that is."

Gregor looked up and sighed. "I've been to celebrity weddings. I've even been to a wedding in the White House. No, thank you. Not again. Why on earth did you buy all those papers?"

"Just to see," Bennis said.

Linda Melajian came up, and Bennis asked for some coffee, "But iced coffee, Linda, as cold as you can get it. Four or five cubes of ice."

"I can shave the ice and pour the coffee over it," Linda offered. "That'll make it colder faster. But you know, maybe you ought to wait. It's pretty cold in here once you get used to it."

"Shaved ice," Bennis said. "Trust me."

Linda Melajian shrugged and moved away. Grace Feinmann picked up *Celebrity Sells* and turned to an interior page. "That's a Carolina Herrera wedding dress. She did Caroline Kennedy's wedding. God, I love that style. It's like a trademark or something. Who's the best man? I've never heard of him."

Gregor sighed. "That's Mark DeAvecca, Liz Toliver's son by her first husband, the one who died. And don't go getting ideas. He's fourteen."

"Is he really?" Grace said. "In this picture, he looks at least twenty-two. Cute."

"He's going to have to beat them off with a stick in a couple of years," Bennis said. "What have the two of you been doing this morning? When I came up the street, I saw you writing on napkins. You think it would be too hot to worry about anything on a day like this. I've got a mind to go back to my nice air-conditioned apartment and spend all day having a fight with KSSY on RAM."

Gregor frowned. "The Internet again," he said. "That newsgroup."

"Rec.arts.mystery," Tibor said. "I do not fight with KSSY on rec.arts.mystery. There would be no point. No, Bennis, Gregor was telling me. The key to the whole thing was who had something to lose *now*."

"Excuse me?" Bennis said.

Gregor pushed the napkin across the table to her. "It's all well and good to talk about how high feelings run even after thirty years, but the truth is that most people calm down at least a little over time. And there was the reality. Even if somebody did discover who had killed Michael Houseman, the chances are that it wouldn't matter. Nobody would ever be prosecuted for it. It would just be too hard to prove."

"But that isn't always the case, is it?" Bennis asked. "There was that case in Connecticut. The Skakels. And the murder of Martha Moxley. They prosecuted him after twenty-five years, and they didn't arrest anybody in that case at the time, either."

"No," Gregor said, "but they did have a good idea who they ought to arrest at the time. The reason they didn't was because Skakel was related to the Kennedys. Meaning the presidential Kennedys. I keep forgetting that the people in this case are named Kennedy, too. For some reason, I always think of her as Peggy Smith."

"Maybe everybody called her Peggy Smith," Bennis said. "It happens when you stay in the same town you grew up in. People you grew up with tend to think of you the way they always did, and not by your married name. If you know what I mean."

"Maybe. My point was that Stuart Kennedy, and by extension Peggy Smith Kennedy, were the only people who had anything to lose in the here and now by a revival of interest in the murder of Michael Houseman. And I mean a revival of real interest. Not a lot of scandal stories in the *National Enquirer*."

"I don't get it," Grace said. "Why did they have something to lose in the here and now any more than anybody else did? It was thirty-two years ago for them, too."

"Ah, yes," Gregor said, "but Stu Kennedy was still doing cocaine and half a dozen other illegal drugs on a regular basis. The danger was that somebody on the state police or with the Feds would take notice. Of course, everybody in town knew all about it, but they weren't going to bother him. They'd known him forever, and no matter what he'd turned into, they didn't want to see him locked away in maximum security for ten or twenty years. The state police weren't likely to feel that way. The DEA guys were definitely not going to feel that way. And they didn't. A week after we arrested Peggy Smith Kennedy, the DEA staged a raid on the Kennedy house and picked up enough contraband to stock a candy store."

"You'd think he'd have gotten rid of it and lain low for a week or two," Donna said. "I mean, he must have realized—"

"Stuart Kennedy isn't coherent enough to realize the time of day," Gregor said.

Bennis snorted. "He's coherent enough. Gregor is leaving a little something out. They found all this contraband, as he calls it, but there was never enough of any one thing to move the charge from possession to possession with the intent to sell. Which, by the way, makes an enormous difference in terms of jail time and that kind of thing. What's-his-name from Hollman called Gregor about it last week. He was livid."

"Kyle Borden," Gregor said. "Under other circumstances, the whole cache taken together might have gotten him a charge of possession with intent to sell, but he's so infamous as a drug addict, no prosecutor could expect it to stick. So he's going to accept a possession charge and get remanded to treatment. Kyle's livid because he thinks that gets Mr. Kennedy off. It won't."

"Why not?" Grace said. "That sounds pretty off to me. No jail time. And what's probation—making sure you don't get into trouble for a few months?"

"In Mr. Kennedy's case, it's going to be five years," Gregor said. "And that's my point. Stuart Kennedy will never stay clean for five years. He won't even be able to fake staying clean for five years. And if he drops off probation more than once, he's going to jail. My guess is that it'll take about a year to get him there."

"What about Peggy Smith Kennedy?" Donna asked. "What's going to happen to her? Are they, well, you know, are they going to ask for—"

"For the death penalty," Bennis said. "You can say 'death penalty' around me, Donna. I'm not some neurotic heroine in a Hitchcock movie who can't stand a single mention of her own past. I mean—"

Gregor cleared his throat. "Nobody is going to ask for the death penalty. Mrs. Kennedy is going to plead guilty to a reduced murder charge and receive life imprisonment. She'll be eligible for parole in about thirty years under the new standards, I think. Whether they will let her out then remains to be seen."

"Gregor thinks she ought to be locked up permanently in a hospital for the criminally insane," Bennis said. "Not that he thinks she's insane in the usual sense, mind you. He doesn't expect her to start seeing little green men from Mars delivering messages from Jesus—"

"She's a psychopath," Gregor said. "Whether she started out that way or got that way from the domestic abuse, I couldn't tell you. All I know is that at this moment, she's psychologically no different from a Ted Bundy or a Jeffrey Dahmer or a John Wayne Gacy. It's unusual that, to find it in a woman."

"What about that case in Florida?" Donna said. "Arlene or Aileen, I don't remember—"

"Exactly," Gregor said. "It's very unusual to find that in a woman. Although you do get it. Usually in connection with a man. Sometimes I think that sex in and of itself is a mind-altering drug."

"Well, it alters *something*," Grace Feinmann said innocently.

Linda Melajian came back with Bennis's iced coffee, served in a big ice cream soda glass filled to the top with shaved ice. It had a straw stuck in it, too, which was a good thing, since there wouldn't have been any other way to drink it. On the other side of the table, Gregor and Tibor went back to writing on their napkin, working out the intricacies of where the cars were and who had them when, how Peggy Smith had gotten around when she needed to, how other people had tried to cover up for her and thought they were really covering up for Stu.

Bennis drank iced coffee and listened to Grace tell Donna about how the harpsichord worked and why it was so difficult to compose for it, at least these days, when you wanted something other than the chamber music the instrument had been invented to perform. While she listened, she paged through the newspaper stories about the wedding. She liked the picture of

Geoff DeAvecca in his miniature tux, holding the rings on a white satin pillow. She liked the picture of Jimmy Card taking over at the piano during the reception. She liked the picture of Liz Toliver—who was going to keep her own last name, just as she had with her first marriage; the *Inquirer* mentioned it twice—throwing her veil into a fountain of something that might have been champagne.

We should have gone, she thought. And then she decided that she wouldn't have anything for breakfast. Even in the air-conditioning, it was just too hot to eat.

2

It wasn't until Bennis got back to her own apartment that she saw the boxed article about the lawsuit, and for a moment it didn't really register on her brain. Grace was home, too, upstairs on the fourth floor practicing something on her harpsichord—*one* of her harpsichords, Bennis amended to herself. Grace had three or four of them, all made by somebody named Peter Redmond in Virginia, which was apparently a very important thing, as Peter Redmond was a very important maker of harpsichords. Or something. Bennis spread the paper out on the bed that was never slept in anymore, since she always spent the night with Gregor these days and Gregor did not like to sleep in beds other than his own. Then she sat down at her computer and booted up. She had an article she had promised to send to *Good Housekeeping* about herself, which she'd promised the publicity department at her publisher that she'd write, because it was good exposure even if her ordinary reader wasn't much like the ordinary reader of *Good Housekeeping*. She had six fan letters to answer, snail mail, because they'd come snail mail and she didn't have e-mail addresses for them. She had begun to really hate having to put stamps on envelopes. In fact, she'd begun to hate having to use her printer at all. She used it for her books, because she couldn't send them e-mail without using something called a zip file, which she had no idea how to operate, and because she couldn't put them on disk. They were so long, they didn't fit on disk. Other than that, though, she usually got along without making hard copies, and she didn't really want to return to the process just to write a simple letter.

There was a lot of work she really ought to do, but what she did do was to sign onto the Internet and go to Amazon to see how her books were doing—Amazon listed every book's rank in sales just under the buying information on the book's page. *Zedalia Serenade* was at number 18. Not bad. Then she went to www.booksnbytes.com to see how Vicki had put up the new cover for display. The cover was up and looking fine. Bennis thought Vicki ought to establish Wish Lists the way Amazon did, so that people who wanted to buy a book for a friend's birthday or a cousin for Christmas would know which ones to get. She also thought that the picture of Jane Haddam didn't do her justice. Then she looked around for the picture of herself and decided that didn't do *her* justice, either, it was just something about pictures published on the Internet when they hadn't come from a digital camera. She got up and went to the kitchen to make herself some tea. She came back and typed in the Web address of the *Times* of London, read the front page, and went to the BBC. It was one of those days when nothing was really going on in the world. There was violence in the Middle East, but there was always violence in the Middle East. George W. Bush had done something that one-third of the country found smart, one-third of the country found stupid, and one-third of the country found outrageous. Senator Hillary Clinton had given an interview to *Vanity Fair* that had conservative pundits muttering about the totalitarianism of the nanny state. Attorney General John Ashcroft had given an interview to *Christianity Today* that had the liberal pundits muttering about the Taliban. Edith Lawton had a new essay up on her Web site, based on the (incorrect) premise that *Humanae Vitae* was an infallible document. CNN had pictures up of Elizabeth Toliver's wedding.

The kettle went off. Bennis got up to get it, got a huge cup down from the cabinet, and poured boiling water over one of the little round coffee bags Donna had turned her onto. She brought the cup of coffee back to the computer and was just starting to sign on to rec.arts.mystery—Tibor was involved in a really insane discussion about gun control—when she saw the boxed article with its two small pictures and its completely uninformative headline: *Another Year, Another Outcast.* She turned sideways in her chair. She used a big wicker chair to work at the computer. She hated those wheeled swivel things that were supposed to be so good for you. She picked up the paper. One of the small pictures was a formal head shot of the kind they took every year in public schools, the kind that eventually went into the yearbook in the section for seniors. That one was of a girl who, even posed and smiling, looked awkward and ill at ease. Discomfort seemed to flow out of every pore in her face. The other picture was a head and shoulders shot cropped from something larger. Bennis could see the arms and shoulders of other people at the edges of the frame. The woman who faced the camera was middle-aged, but very handsomely middle-aged. She had a good head of hair and a commanding bearing. Bennis looked at the caption and saw: *Nancy Quayde.* She looked at the picture of the uncomfortable girl and saw: *Diane Asch.* The pictures meant nothing to her, and the name Diane Asch meant less than nothing, but there was something about the name Nancy Quayde that nagged at her. She read through the article, but there wasn't much to it. Diane Asch's father was suing Hollman High School and Nancy Quayde as principal of Hollman High School for harassment, or failing to prevent harassment, or something along those lines. The piece was not exactly clear. It did mention a couple of incidents involving Diane Asch and "three senior students," who remained unnamed. The incidents were nasty in that casual way adolescent incidents of that kind always are: stealing

Diane's clothes while she was taking a shower after gym; hounding Diane out of a mixer in the school's auditorium; getting up en masse from a lunchroom table when Diane tried to sit down.

Bennis took a chance and punched "Hollman Home News" into the Yahoo! search engine. She got what looked like the right address three recommendations down. She clicked on the link and waited. She was rewarded with a front-page spread on exactly the story she was looking for, complete with pictures with serious captions, and continuing coverage "inside." The "three senior students" turned out to be three girls named DeeDee Craft, Lynne Mackay, and Sharon Peterson. The *Home News* had their cheerleading pictures, complete with uniforms and pompoms. Nancy Quayde turned out to be one of those women who gives professional a bad name. In a tailored skirt and blazer, she looked oddly like a dominatrix in a bad mood. Here was the virtue of weekly small-town newspapers. There wasn't much of anything else going on in Hollman to report, so instead of wasting its time fretting over the depredations of either George W. Bush or Hillary Clinton, the *Home News* reported on this. Bennis clicked a few more times to find the "inside" pages and came across a headline that said: *Lawsuit Ends Quayde Hopes for Superintendent's Job*. Out in the foyer, the apartment door opened and closed.

"Bennis?"

"I'm in the bedroom," Bennis said.

There were heavy steps in the hallway. Bennis leaned closer to the screen to read, but the article was not much more informative than the one in the *Inquirer* had been. The *bad* thing about weekly small-town newspapers was that their staffs assumed their readers to have a working knowledge of all the local scandals and tensions. Bennis didn't know anything about anything about Hollman, Pennsylvania, except that it was boring as hell and Liz Toliver had once lived there. Gregor came in and sat down on the bed.

Bennis said, "Why does the name Nancy Quayde ring a bell with me?"

"She was one of the women in that group of girls who were involved in that night in the park when Liz Toliver was nailed into the outhouse. She's principal of Hollman High School now."

"It says that here. Somebody's suing her. Did she want to be superintendent of schools?"

"I don't know," Gregor said. "She may have. She was a very professional woman."

"You talked to her?"

"When Kyle Borden and I were interviewing people after the murder of Chris Inglerod Barr. She was on my list to talk to from the beginning, though. The list Jimmy Card gave me. What's this all about?"

"Look." Bennis pulled away from the screen.

Gregor came forward and scanned the article. "That's not surprising, is it?" he said. "It's more or less what you'd expect of her. Considering the history, I mean."

"You mean considering what happened to Liz Toliver in high school?"

"Considering that, yes. People don't really change, you know. At least, they don't really change into something completely different from what they were. If you look at the pictures of Liz Toliver, going all the way back to kindergarten, you'd probably see that streak of charisma that's what's made it possible for her to be on television and make a success of it. Why would it be any different with Nancy Quayde?"

"Do you think that's what happens, that the principals and the teachers all harass the outcasts, too, or something? That's what this article seems to be saying. Diane Asch's father is suing because when these girls did awful things to Diane, Nancy Quayde told her it was all her own fault, and wanted Diane to go into therapy, and that kind of thing."

"I think I want to go somewhere and do something today. The Art Museum. Except not the Art Museum. I don't feel like being intellectual."

"We could go for a drive and have lunch out in the country somewhere."

"No, thank you. Not unless you hire a chauffeur. I don't feel like being dead, either."

"I got you back here from Hollman without any problem."

"You got me back here from Hollman. That's as good as it gets. Why don't we go shopping for that lamp you want? It sounds awful, but I suppose I might as well look at it."

"Thank you. I love the confidence you have in my taste."

"Come on," Gregor stood up. "Let's go find a cab. Let's go do something. I'll go insane if I have to hang around here doing nothing for the fourth day in a row. Maybe you want to see a movie?"

"I don't hate your movies. I hate your *films*. Come on, let's go. I want to see something with Mike Meyers in it."

He grabbed Bennis by the hand and pulled. Bennis barely had time to sign off before she found herself on her feet.

"Mike Meyers," she said. "You probably used to watch the Three Stooges when you were a kid."

"I watch them now," Gregor said solemnly. "But only when you're asleep."

3

Several thousand miles away, in Paris, Mark DeAvecca was having a very good day. His mother and his new stepfather were headed for the Bahamas, where they would probably have an excellent time doing things he had no intention of thinking about, and Geoff was safely back at the hotel with Debra, who had volunteered to baby-sit until they all got back to New York on Thursday afternoon. This had left Mark free to wander around on his own, which was something he had never been able to do before in Paris. He had on a pair of Dockers slacks and a black T-shirt and an almost-expensive sports coat. He would have had a much more expensive sports coat except that his mother refused to buy them for him until she was sure he had stopped growing, and he was already six inches taller than Jimmy Card. Whatever. He was sitting at a table on the sidewalk outside the front of the Café Deux Maggots. He had a small cup of the blackest, bitterest, and strongest coffee he had ever tasted. If all those old wives' tales about how coffee could stunt your growth were true, *his* growth would have stopped dead in its tracks with the first sip. He had the memory of Debra's brutal conversation with Maris this morning on the telephone, during which it had become clear, even to Geoff, that they would not have to put up with Maris Coleman ever again. And just to make everything perfect, two days of trying had left his face with a very nice coating of designer stubble.

What was really making Mark happy at the moment, however, was a girl. Her name was Genevieve, and she had both the eyes and the accent he had always hoped for in a really witchy French woman. At the moment, she was telling him, very sincerely, why it no longer made sense to read Jean-Paul Sartre and why he should read Luce Irigaray instead. She could have been talking about baseball, and it would have made no difference.

Mark was sure he had no idea how she'd gotten the impression that he was eighteen years old, and a sophomore at Brown.